FAR FROM HOME

Kate Munroe is only 16 years old when she is sent to live in Birmingham with her friend Susie. Alone and vulnerable, Kate is harbouring a dark secret – a deep passion for her cousin, Tim, back home in Ireland. Kate is shocked when her younger sister, Sally, arrives unannounced on her doorstep. What has her sister done to upset their formidable mother this time? Meanwhile, Kate has met David, an RAF pilot, but can she ever love him like Tim? When WWII breaks out and while the war wages all around them, Kate makes a discovery that questions everything she believes in.

FAR FROM HOME

FAR FROM HOME

by

Anne Bennett

Magna Large Print Books
Long Preston, North Yorkshire,
BD23 4ND, England.

British Library Cataloguing in Publication Data.

Bennett, Anne
    Far from home.

    A catalogue record of this book is
    available from the British Library

    ISBN   978-0-7505-3605-9

First published in Great Britain in 2012 by HarperCollins*Publishers*

Published in Large Print 2012 by arrangement with
HarperCollins Publishers

Magna Large Print is an imprint of Library Magna Books Ltd.

Printed and bound in Great Britain by
T.J. (International) Ltd., Cornwall, PL28 8RW

This book is dedicated to my lovely husband Denis in recognition for the way he battled lung cancer with such courage and determination and also for the way he kept up beat throughout.

ACKNOWLEDGEMENTS

Far From Home tells the story of Kate, an Irish girl who comes to work in Birmingham just a few years before the last war, encouraged by her mother because she was in love with a man she could never marry. Although she mourned for the man she had loved, she eventually faced the fact that he was lost to her and she began dating David Burton who she married just before war was declared and as soon as it was official he volunteered for the RAF. Shortly afterwards Kate, wanting to do her bit, became an ARP warden, helping in areas of the city through the Blitz, while David faces similar risks in the air. Then two and a half years into the war David is posted as missing and a few months later, Kate uncovers a secret that turns her world upside down.

I don't know where I got the idea for this story and I seldom do though it seems to be the one thing that most interests people when I give talks. Very occasionally I can pin point something that set off my train of thought, but more often characters and ideas just pop into my head.

I do a lot of research for all my books and this was no exemption and I used, *City at War – Birmingham 1939-1945* edited by Phillada Ballard, *Life on the Home Front* from *Reader's Digest*'s Journeys

Into The Past series, *Brum Undaunted* by Carl Chinn and People's War from the BBC website to help with detail. However, the most helpful site without doubt is the Birmingham History Forum. Whatever you ask there someone will have the answer. Stockland Green was not an area I knew well, though it had been Denis's stamping ground. But I needn't have worried, for people on that site not only told me about The Plaza Cinema but sent me photographs of it inside and out through the war years and one man sent me a photograph of his grandfather when he was a commissionaire standing on the steps by the entrance. They helped me too with personal memories that I was able to check, like the unexploded bomb that fell near Kate's house. Most amazing of all was from a lady now living in Vancouver who had been born in 1941 and lived in Stockland Green for some years who wrote a detailed account of life there just after the war, which I found immensely useful. So thanks and thanks again to all those helpful Brummies.

However, despite all the research and the blood, sweat and tears I spent writing it, the book wouldn't have been half as good if it had not been for the amazing Susan Opie who does such a marvellous job in editing it. Deep thanks too for my in house editor, the indomitable Kate Bradley who has taken over from Victoria. Thanks also to Amy Neilson who helped me publicize the book and my agent Judith Murdoch who is always so supportive. I am more especially grateful this year to all of you for your understanding and consideration when I hit personal problems.

Most of my regular readers know how much my family mean to me, my eldest daughter, Nikki and her husband, Steve, my son Simon and his wife Carol, my second daughter, Beth and my youngest, Tamsin and partner Mark who all play their part in encouraging me. My grandchildren, Briony, Kynon, Jake and Theo, on the other hand, keep me grounded lest I threaten to get above myself and no doubt little Catrin will be at it too soon enough. Thank you all for you for keeping me focused on what is important in life.

My friends also mean a great deal to me too and I appreciate them all, but a special thanks to Ginnie and Mike Mooney and Judith Kendall. Thank you all for just being you and for being there.

I wish there were more words to say thank you for I have used it so often and yet I truly mean it when I say that I owe the biggest debt of gratitude to you my loyal readers because without you there would be no point to anything I do. I love it when you write and tell me what you think of my books and some of you have already found me on Facebook. I am even just about getting to grips with Twitter too, as I am dragged kicking and screaming into the digital age of the 21st century. Immense and grateful thanks to each and everyone one of you and I hope you enjoy the book.

ONE

Kate Munroe's feet dragged as she reached the house. After a week's work in the radiator factory she was always tired by Friday and the cold and dank late October evening didn't help her mood. She was glad of the big, thick, navy coat, the light blue hat pulled on over her dark brown curls, and the matching gloves encasing her hands, which she had saved for weeks to buy.

She sighed with relief as she let herself into the entrance hall out of the biting wind, but it was very dark as she closed the door behind her because there was no light in the hall. 'I haven't bothered with the expense of having an electric light installed in here when the gas lamps were taken out,' the landlady had told her when she moved in. 'There's a streetlight just outside, so I thought it would probably be light enough.'

Kate thought that was all very well, but the door into the house was almost solid, so the only light came from a half-moon window right at the top. The house was converted into flats and so the postman would leave any letters there on the hall table for people to help themselves and sometimes in these dark, autumnal days, it was hard to read who the letters were for in such dim light. It was the same that night, and Kate was shifting through the pile of envelopes, scrutinizing them carefully, when suddenly there was a scraping

15

noise from the space under the stairwell and she called out a little nervously, 'Who's there?'

There was no answer and, gathering all her courage, Kate called out again, 'Come on. Come out and show yourself.'

Through the shadowy dimness, she saw a figure emerge and move towards her. She relaxed a little: it was obvious from the outline that the figure was female and slight, but it was not until she got up close that Kate gasped in recognition. Her dark brown eyes were looking straight into the anxious blue ones of her young sister.

'Sally,' she cried. 'What are you doing here?'

'I came to see you.'

'Don't be daft,' Kate said shortly, but suddenly her blood ran like ice in her body and she asked almost fearfully, 'Are you in some sort of trouble?'

Sally blushed, even in the half-light Kate saw her cheeks darken, but she answered decidedly enough: 'Not that kind of trouble. Not what you're thinking.'

In relief, Kate let out the breath she hadn't even been aware she was holding. 'Tell you the truth, Sally, I don't know what to think,' she said in exasperation. 'Let's get this straight. Is anything wrong at home?'

Sally hung her head and twisted her feet on the floor, as Kate knew she did when she was troubled about something, and mumbled, 'No, not really.'

'Well, how "not really"?' Kate said, feeling that she wanted to shake her younger sister. And then another thought struck her and she said, 'I suppose Mammy and Daddy know you're here?'

Sally lifted her head and Kate got her answer by

the stricken look in her sister's face, her eyes sparkling with unshed tears. 'Good God, they don't, do they?' she cried. 'They know nothing about this?'

Sally shook her head and Kate sighed as she snapped, 'Well, this can't be gone into in the entrance hall. You'd better come up to the flat. Have you anything with you?'

Sally nodded. 'The old brown case with the broken lock. It was all there was – I had to wrap a belt around it to keep it shut.'

'Well, fetch it,' Kate said. 'And I hope you are fit enough to carry it, because I have no intention of doing it for you. I live on the second floor.'

They made their way upstairs and Kate listened to her young sister labouring behind her with the large case. Her own mind was teeming with questions; there was no way Sally should be in Birmingham at all and she could see problems ahead. She had obviously left the family farmhouse in Donegal in Northern Ireland in a hurry, without the knowledge or permission of their parents, and Kate had the feeling that she was the one who would be left picking up the pieces of her reckless, young sister's decision.

She opened the door to her flat. Behind her she heard Sally sigh in relief. Kate ushered her inside and in the glare of the electric light saw her white and anxious face. 'Look, put your case down and take off your coat,' she said more kindly. 'There's a hook behind the door.' She crossed the room as she spoke and drew the curtains, cutting out the damp, chilly night. 'I'll put the kettle on and make a cup of tea and you can tell me all about it.'

Sally didn't answer, and when Kate came back into the room with two steaming mugs on a tray, she was standing in the same place. Though she had unbuttoned her coat, she hadn't taken it off, and as she looked at Kate she asked, 'Is this all there is?'

Instantly Kate bristled. 'Yes,' she said in clipped tones. 'What did you expect? The Ritz?'

'No,' Sally said sulkily. 'But you said...'

'I never told you or anyone else that this place was anything better than it is,' Kate said firmly. 'And if you thought it was, then that was in your imagination. I'm a working girl, Sally, and this is all I can afford.'

'So it's just the one room?' Sally said, still shocked by the bareness of the place her sister lived in.

'Basically,' Kate said. 'Behind the curtain in the far corner is my bed, and beside that is a chest of drawers for my things with a mirror on top so that it doubles as a dressing table. There are hooks on the wall for anything that needs to be hung up.' She led the way to two easy chairs in front of the gas fire and placed the tray on the small table between them. 'Take off your coat and come and sit down.'

Sally obeyed. As she sat down in the chair Kate had indicated, she asked, 'What about a kitchen?'

'British kitchens are nothing like cottage kitchens in Ireland,' Kate said. 'Here a wee cubbyhole of a place with a couple of gas rings and a few pots and pans and bits of crockery on some rickety shelves passes as a kitchen. But,' she added as she handed Sally one of the mugs, 'here I have run-

18

ning water and a proper sink, which is more than I had at home. We even have a bathroom on the next floor down and we can have a bath just by turning on the taps. It has a proper flush toilet that really startled me the first few times I used it.'

'I'm not surprised,' Sally said. 'People say they have them in the hotels in the town, but I've never had an occasion to go into the hotels, never mind use the toilets.'

'No, nor me before I came here,' Kate said. Then she added, 'This might not look much to you, but, let me tell you, it's a lap of luxury compared to the place we were reared in. So, now,' she added, fixing Sally with a steely look, 'are you going to drink this tea I've made and tell me what the hell you are doing here, or are you going to sit there all night criticizing the place I live in?'

Sally felt suddenly ashamed of herself; she swallowed the lump in her throat that threatened to choke her, obediently took a sip of the tea and said, 'I'm sorry, Kate. Don't be too cross with me because I'm already feeling that I've been really stupid.'

And then she shivered suddenly, and Kate saw tears drip down her cheeks. She said impatiently, 'Oh come on, Sally, cut out the waterworks. You know that won't help. You're cold and hungry too, I expect. You'll feel a bit better when I have the fire lit.'

'How will you do that?' Sally asked, looking at the ugly monstrosity sitting in the hearth.

'Like this,' Kate said, and she turned a tap to the side of the fire, lit a match and, with a pop, flames danced at the bottom of the grille. 'It's a gas fire,' she told her sister. 'And when I come home on a winter's evening, it has the room warmed in no time. It makes it look cheerier too. Now come on and tell me what this is all about. Did you have a row? Was that it?'

Sally shook her head. 'No. It was... Oh, I don't know. I suppose... I suppose I just got fed up.'

Kate stared at her. 'Sally, you can't run away from home because you're fed up,' she said. 'God Almighty, we all get fed up – you just have to get on with it. And what exactly were you fed up about?'

'You know,' Sally said. 'Being at the beck and call of Mammy really. It's "Sally do this" and "Sally do that" morning, noon and night. But nothing I do pleases her.'

Kate laughed. 'That's just Mammy's way,' she said. 'It's the lot of daughters to help their mothers. I had years of the same when I was at home, especially after young James was born. At the time, if I remember rightly, you weren't expected to do anything and were able to swan around the house like Lady Muck.'

'But you got away.'

'I was eighteen when I left home,' Kate said. 'And Susie had found me this flat, not far from her parents' house and a job of work. I didn't do as you did and up sticks and take off. You won't even be seventeen till the turn of the year.'

'Mammy's on to me all the time,' Sally complained. 'And I never have any money of my own. She buys all my clothes and doles out the collection for Mass, as if I was the same age as James.'

Kate knew Sally had a point – she'd never had

any money either. Just before leaving home her mother had taken her into town and bought her some new outfits and a nice smart case to put them in, and her father had pressed the princely sum of £10 into her hand. She had protested that it was too much, but he had insisted. 'Take it, darling girl,' he'd said. 'You will be a long way from the support of your family and may have need of this before too long.'

Sally had obviously been thinking along the same lines because she said somewhat resentfully, 'Mammy and Daddy couldn't do enough to help you leave home.'

'And I have told you why that was,' Kate said. 'I was older and wiser and doing it the right way, that's why.'

She knew it wasn't only that, though. She was sure her mother had guessed the feelings she had for her cousin, Tim Munroe. Tim's father, Padraic, and Kate's father, Jim, were brothers. On the death of their eldest brother, Michael, after the Great War, they'd split the farm between them, and so the families had seen a lot of each other. Tim was two years her senior, as familiar as any brother, and they had always got on well.

When she reached sixteen, though, she realized that she wasn't looking at Tim in a brotherly way any more, or even in a cousinly way. She knew she truly loved him as a woman. She knew Tim felt as she did – she had seen the love-light in his eyes – but he hadn't said anything about how he felt because it was forbidden for first cousins to enter into any sort of relationship, and marriage between them was totally banned.

Kate's mother, Philomena, had soon become aware of how the young people felt about each other, but she'd not said a word to either of them. She had been a little alarmed, but she had told herself they were both young and she thought and hoped it was a phase they would grow out of, *had* to grow out of: they knew the rules of the Church just as well as she did. She watched her daughter and Tim covertly for two years, but if anything their feelings seemed to deepen as they grew older. She didn't know what action to take for the best.

Then Susie Mason had come on her annual holiday to her grandparents' farm. She had always been a great friend of Kate's – Kate's parents liked her too, and always made her welcome, although Philomena often wished she wouldn't go on quite so much about the fine life she was having in Birmingham where she lived with her family. After she left school, she told them how she now had money of her own to spend and plenty to spend it on. Philomena would watch Kate's enthralled face as she listened. She was always worried that Susie's words might unsettle her – and indeed they did, because Susie brought the life and excitement of city life into that small farmhouse, and it contrasted sharply with Kate's more mundane existence.

Susie worked in a factory, but even that was not so bad, she declared. 'You think of the wages at the end of the week,' she said with a nod of her head and a twinkle in her eye. 'There's the clothes you can buy real cheap, especially when you go round the Bull Ring, and then you can wear those clothes when you visit the music hall or cinema.'

She went on to describe some of the acts she'd seen in the music halls that were peppered about the city, and described the cinema, proper moving pictures that she said she went to see once, maybe twice a week. 'Dancing is all the rage now,' she told them in the summer of 1935, and she seemed to almost squeeze herself with delight as she went on: 'Oh I just love dancing. I have started taking lessons to do it properly. You'd be great at it, Kate, because you have natural rhythm. Look how good you were at the Irish dancing, and there was me with two left feet.'

Kate, who would give a king's ransom to see even half the things Susie spoke about, looked at her with dull eyes. She always waited excitedly for Susie's annual visit and listened avidly to her news, but when she had gone it was as if someone had turned the light out. Kate would see the days stretching interminably out in front of her, each one the same as the one before. The only light in her life was her love for Tim, and she couldn't speak about that.

Susie was off again. ''Cos as well as the waltz and quickstep and that, they do the new dances coming in from America, music to the big bands, you know?'

No, Kate thought, *I don't know. I don't even know what she is talking about. How would I?*

Philomena watched Kate's face and suddenly felt sorry for her. She also saw that Susie might provide a way out of the situation as regards Kate and Tim. She hated the thought of her daughter leaving that small cottage and living a long way away, but she also knew that she and Tim had to be kept apart for their own good. And Kate had to be the one to go away because Tim couldn't be spared. He was his father's right-hand man and, as the eldest son, the one who would inherit the farm one day.

So to Susie's great surprise, Philomena said, 'Susie's right, Kate. You were always a fine one for the dancing. You'll have to go to Birmingham and see for yourself. Would you like that?'

Kate wasn't sure she'd heard right. She stared at her mother, and even Susie was silent and seemed to be almost holding her breath. 'Do ... do you really mean it, Mammy?' Kate said at last.

Philomena's heart felt as if it was breaking, because she knew that once gone, Kate would in all likelihood never come back to live at home again, but then thinking of the alternative said, 'Yes, of course I mean it.'

Kate had to get things straight. 'For a holiday, Mammy?' she asked. 'I'd love that. Oh indeed I would.'

'Well, just a wee holiday if you like,' Philomena said, and Kate heard the resignation in her mother's voice and the sigh she tried to suppress as she went on: 'Though if Susie here could get you set on some place, you could stay a year or two and see how you like city life.'

Both Kate and Susie looked at Philomena in amazement, and then Kate's eyes met her mother's and suddenly she knew why her mother was anxious that she should leave her home and family and travel to Birmingham. And she wasn't sure that she wanted to go, not for a year or two. Although she did hanker after more freedom, she knew that she would miss her family hugely. And she might never see Tim again, or at least for a good few years. On the other hand, she had to admit that it was torment seeing him so often and not even being able to speak of how she felt. At least she would be spared that.

'So,' Philomena said, 'what do you think?'

Susie was astounded at Philomena's apparent and sudden change of heart, but she decided she was going to do all she could to encourage such a venture because she thought Kate was wasted in Donegal. 'I could soon get you fixed up with a job and a flat and such,' she said reassuringly. 'Oh, it would be such fun if we were together.'

Kate smiled at her friend's enthusiasm, but she knew she was right. With Susie's company, a job of work and all the distractions that Birmingham could offer, she would surely be able to get the feelings she had for her cousin into some sort of perspective. And so she had nodded her head and had ended up following Susie Mason to Birmingham three years earlier in the autumn of 1935. She had confided everything to Susie once she had arrived in Birmingham; though Susie was sympathetic, she thought that Kate would soon get over her cousin. However, Kate had been incredibly homesick and was determined to stay true to Tim. 'If I can't have Tim then I'll have nobody,' she declared. 'I won't settle for second best.' She knew her attitude irritated Susie, but there was nothing she could do about that.

However, Kate knew that her young sister, Sally, had no idea of the real reason their mother had been so keen for her to leave home, and that was how Kate wanted it to stay, and so when Sally said, 'So why was it so different for you?', she put those memories to the back of her mind.

'I've told you why that was, and as for Mammy not giving you money, she doesn't think you need anything since she clothes you and feeds you. I never had any either, but if it bothers you that much, it would have been more sensible and more mature to tell them how you felt rather than rushing over here.'

And then a thought struck her and she said, 'But hang on a minute, if you had no money given to you, how did you pay your fare?'

'I took Mammy's egg money.'

'Sally!' Kate cried. Philomena had full care of the hens on the farm and she sold the excess eggs. That was her personal money and she guarded it jealously. Though they all knew the cupboard she kept it in, no one would dream of touching it – till now.

'That was stealing, Sally.'

'Well, I wouldn't have had to steal if I had been given a wage.'

Kate shook her head angrily. 'No, you can't get away with it like that, Sally. I bet you never even discussed getting any sort of wage for yourself, did you?'

'She wouldn't have agreed,' Sally said mulishly. 'You know what she's like.'

'You didn't even try,' Kate said. 'So, you can't be sure what Mammy would have done and Daddy might have supported you.'

'He always sides with Mammy.'

'No, he doesn't,' Kate said. 'He did when we

were small because he thought bringing up children was women's work, as it is, but he was better with me when I had grown a bit, so I'm sure he would be the same with you. He's very fair. Surely you should have tried to get them to see your point of view before you stole from your own parents?'

Sally was crying in earnest now but Kate had little sympathy for her. 'And just how did you manage to walk out anyway, especially carrying a thumping great suitcase. I mean,' she added sarcastically, 'weren't they the slightest bit curious?'

'They weren't there,' Sally said. 'Daddy and Uncle Padraic had been gone from early morning to Killybegs where they heard some farm equipment and animals were being sold after the death of the farmer.'

'And where was Mammy?'

'Helping at a birth. And James has been at school since September.'

'And when you got here, Sally, what did you expect to happen?' Kate asked.

'I thought I might stay with you,' Sally said.

'And so you could if this had been planned properly and Mammy and Daddy had agreed and I had known in advance,' Kate said. 'Then I would have welcomed you for a week or two, because I would have some holidays due to me from work and I could have taken you out and about a bit. But I can't do that at the drop of a hat. Like I said before, I'm a working girl.'

'But they wouldn't have let me come.'

'Don't talk nonsense.'

'They wouldn't,' Sally maintained. 'I heard Mammy say so last Sunday after Mass.'

'What are you talking about?'

'She was talking to old Biddy Morrisey after Mass and she asked how you were and Mammy said you were well as far as she knew. Then Biddy sort of nodded over to me and said that I would be the next one on the boat to England and Mammy said I would not. She said I wouldn't be let go, not even for a holiday, in case I didn't come back.' She looked up into her sister's eyes and said, 'And it wasn't just something to say, you know. She meant every word.

'And then yesterday she was yelling at me about something or other the whole time. I breathed a sigh of relief when she was sent for this morning, though she gave me a list of jobs to do before she left. All I could see was a lifetime of the same – living with Mammy and Daddy for ever, or if I should get married to one of those at home, all I would have to look forward to would be a lifetime of drudgery and a child every year. That has happened to lots of girls, as you well know, and I didn't want it happening to me. I want to see and do other things. I felt quite stifled at home.'

For the first time, Kate felt immense sympathy for her sister – she could understand how frantic she must have been. 'Stifled' described very well the way Kate had felt before she had left Donegal; it had only been the intense but forbidden love she'd had for Tim that had made life bearable.

'And whenever you write you always seem to be having such a fine time of it,' Sally went on. 'I just decided on the spur of the moment to come over and see for myself. It wasn't something I planned or anything, it was just that I knew I would never get such a chance again. It's seldom I have the farmhouse to myself.' Then she glanced up at Kate and said, 'I left them a note, tried to explain...'

'I doubt that will help much,' Kate said. 'And I do feel sorry for you, but I can't have you here, not like this. Really, this isn't the way to get more freedom. Your best bet is to write to Mammy and Daddy and say how sorry you are and make your way home again sharpish. Later, when the time is right, I will plead your case for you.'

'Oh, will you, Kate?' Sally cried. 'That will be grand. Mammy listens to you. But I can't write to her. She will be so cross with me.'

'Yes, and with reason, I'd say,' Kate snapped. 'Don't be so feeble. Go home and face the music.'

'I can't,' Sally cried in anguish. 'And anyway, I haven't any money left, or not enough for the whole fare anyway.'

'Oh, Sally,' Kate cried in exasperation. Keeping her temper with difficulty, she took a deep breath and said, 'I cannot have you here and that's final, so I suppose I shall have to loan you the money, but for now you write a letter to Mammy saying how sorry you are and promise that you will make it up to her. You know the kind of thing to say. And I would just like you to know that you have wrecked my evening good and proper, because I was going dancing with Susie Mason tonight, like we do every Friday, and now I will have to pop along to see her and cancel our plans. I shouldn't think she'll be best pleased either.'

'Sorry, Kate.'

Kate sighed. Sally was an irritating and quite selfish girl, but she couldn't keep telling her off. In

29

a few days she imagined she'd be on her way home and not her concern any more and, though her parents had always doted on her, or until James's birth anyway, she knew that her mother at any rate would roast her alive for this little adventure. So she looked at her sister's woebegone face and said, 'On the way home, for all you don't deserve it, I will buy us both a fish and chip supper.'

'Oh, will you, Kate?' Sally cried. 'I would be so grateful. I haven't eaten for hours.'

'That's why you're so tearful,' Kate said. 'A full stomach always makes a person feel more positive. I'll get going now and I'll not linger because I'm hungry myself. Write that letter and make sure you have the table laid and the kettle boiling by the time I get back.'

Susie was disappointed, but she could see Kate was too. 'And she just turned up like that?' she repeated, when Kate told her what Sally had done.

'That's right,' Kate said. 'She was waiting for me when I got in from work and admitted she'd sneaked out when both our parents were out of the house and James at school. Claimed she left a note explaining it.'

'Explaining what?' Susie said. 'Why did she do it?'

'Oh, that's the best yet,' Kate said. 'She said she was fed up. Like I said, we all get fed up. The trouble is she overheard Mammy telling someone after Mass that she would never let her come here, even for a little holiday. I suppose it was like the last straw for her – and then she got the opportunity with everyone out of the way, so here she is. She can be very headstrong.'

Susie nodded her head. 'She was always spoiled though, wasn't she?' she said. 'I saw that myself when I came to stay with my granny when my mother was in the sanatorium that time. Even as a small child she usually got all her own way.'

Kate remembered that time well. Susie Mason's mother, Mary, had been very ill when Susie was just ten and she had been sent to be looked after by her mother's granny in Ireland while the older boys, Derek and Martin, stayed at home with their father. In Copenny National School, just outside Donegal Town, where the Munroe children all went, Susie was put to sit beside Kate, who had been strangely drawn to the girl who seemed so lost and unhappy. She had once confided to Kate that she was scared she would never see her mother again and Kate thought that the saddest thing. And so did Philomena when she heard. From that moment, Susie was always made welcome in their house.

Susie's mother did recover, however, although Susie had been living in Ireland six or seven months before her father came to fetch her home. By then a strong bond had been forged between Kate and Susie. They wrote to each other regularly, and when Susie came back on her annual holiday, they would meet up whenever Kate could be spared.

'My mother said that you do a child no favours by giving in to them all the time,' Susie said to Kate.

'And she's right,' Kate said. 'But there's not much I can do about that. And now I'd better go and get those fish and chips before I fade away altogether. Can you hear my stomach growling?'

'Course I can,' Susie said. 'It sounds like a disgruntled teddy bear. But before you go, here's an idea: shall we show your sister round Birmingham tomorrow?'

'Oh, I don't know...'

'We may as well,' Susie said. 'I mean, you can't send her home till you hear from your mother, so what are you going to do with her otherwise? If we go late afternoon, we can stay on to see some of the entertainment in the Bull Ring – if it isn't too cold or raining.'

'All right then, yes,' Kate said. 'It will make up for not meeting up tonight. We'll come round about half two, then. Give me time to do the washing and clean up the flat a bit first.'

'All right,' Susie said. 'See you then.'

So that evening, as they ate the very welcome fish and chips, Kate said to Sally, 'How would you like to go into town tomorrow? We can show you round and then take you down the Bull Ring. You mind I've told you about it in my letters?'

'Yes, oh, I'd love to see Birmingham,' Sally said. 'And you said the Bull Ring was like a gigantic street market.'

Kate smiled. 'Yeah, like Donegal Town on a Fair Day, only bigger – but without the animals, of course,' Kate said.

'And yet it's called the Bull Ring?'

'I never thought of that,' Kate said with a shrug. 'I suppose they must have sold bulls there at one time. There's all sort of entertainment on offer there when the night draws in. I've told you about it in my letters.'

'Yeah. You said it was all lit up with gas flares so it was like fairyland,' Sally said. 'So what sort of entertainment? You never said much about that.'

Kate made a face. 'I wasn't sure Mammy would approve,' she said. 'It isn't wrong or anything, but sometimes Mammy takes a notion in her head to disapprove of something and that's that then, so I was always very careful what I wrote. Anyway, you'll see for yourself tomorrow, though I'm warning you now we're not hanging about too long if it's freezing cold or raining or both. There's no pleasure in that.'

'I still want to go,' Sally said. 'Ooh, I can't wait.'

Kate laughed. 'You'll have to,' she said. 'And first thing tomorrow we have to clean the flat and do the washing. It's the only day I have to do all this.'

'I'll help if you tell me what wants doing,' Sally said. 'It won't take so long with two of us at it.'

'No it won't,' Kate said, getting up and pulling her sister to her feet. 'Come on,' she said suddenly. 'You tidy up here and I'll nip out and post your letter and then we can hit the sack, because what with one thing and another, I'm whacked.'

A little later, as they were getting ready for bed, Kate said, 'Susie is coming with us tomorrow. We're meeting her at half past two.'

Sally made a face. She would hate Susie to be annoyed with her, because she had always admired her when she'd come to Ireland on holiday. Sally remembered her as having really dark wavy hair that she had worn down her back, tied away from her face with a ribbon like Kate's. It had been a shock to see that now Kate braided her hair into a French plait and fastened it just above the nape of her neck; she told her that Susie wore hers the same way.

'Ah, I liked her hair loose – and yours too,' Sally said regretfully.

'We would be too old to wear our hair like that now,' Kate told her as she loosened the grips and began to unravel the plait. 'Besides, in the factory, I have to wear an overall and cap that covers my hair, so wearing it down isn't an option for either of us any more. Anyway, it really suits Susie, because she always has little curls escaping and sort of framing her face. Most of the rest of us look pretty hideous.'

'She's pretty though, isn't she?' Sally said. 'I mean, her eyes are so dark and even her eyelashes and eyebrows are as well.'

'She takes after her mother,' Kate said. 'Her brothers look more like their dad. Pity about her snub nose, though.'

'Ah, Kate.'

'I'm not speaking behind her back, honestly,' Kate said as she began to brush her hair. 'She would be the first one to tell you herself. Anyway, her mouth makes up for it because it turns up by itself, as if she is constantly amused about something, so people smile at her all the time.'

'I know,' Sally said, 'I can remember – and her eyes sparkle as well. I used to love her coming on holiday because she used to liven everyone up. And her clothes always looked terribly smart, too. I really like her. I hope she won't be cross with me because I spoiled your plans for tonight?'

'No,' Kate said assuredly. 'Susie's not like that. Come on, let's get undressed. It will be funny sharing a bed with you again.'

'It will be nice,' Sally said as she pulled her dress over her head. 'Cuddling up in bed with you was one of the many things I missed when you left home.'

'I wouldn't have thought you missed anything about me that much.'

'Oh, I did,' Sally said sincerely. 'I was real miserable for ages.'

Kate saw, that Sally really did mean that, and she realized she had never given much thought to how lost Sally might have felt when her big sister just wasn't there any more. But she didn't want her feeling sad or to start crying again, and so she said with a smile as she climbed into bed, 'Come on then. Let's relive our childhood memories – only it might be squashed rather than cosy because you're bigger now than the strip of wind I left behind three years ago.'

'I think the bed was a lot bigger too,' Sally said, easing herself in beside her sister. 'Still nice though.'

And it was nice, Kate had to agree, to feel a warm body cuddled into hers on that cold and miserable night. She was soon asleep. Sally, though she was tired too, lay awake listening to Kate's even breathing and the city noises of the night. Slade Road, Kate had told her, was quite busy most of the time because it was the direct route to the city centre. And it was busy, and Sally didn't think she would sleep with all the unaccustomed noise from the steady drone of the traffic, overridden by the noise from the clanking trams and rumbling lorries. As she lay there listening to it, her eyelids kept fluttering closed all on their own, and eventually she gave a sigh, cuddled against Kate and, despite the noise, fell fast asleep.

TWO

The next morning, Sally woke with a jerk; she lay for a moment and listened to the city beginning the day. Then she climbed out of bed and walked across to the window. Though it was early enough to be still dusky, traffic had begun to fill the streets on both sides of the road, where horse wagons and carts vied for space with motor vehicles, and trams clattered along beside them. The clamorous noise rose in the air and filtered into the flat. The pavements too seemed filled with people and she watched some get off trams and others board them from the tram stop just up the road from Kate's flat, while others hurried past with their heads bent against the weather.

She sighed as she leant her head against the windowpane. There were so many people and so much noise that she didn't think she would ever get used to actually living here. She reflected on what it was like to awake in the farmhouse. The only sound after the rooster crowed was the cluck of the hens as she threw corn on to the cobbles in the yard, the occasional bleat of a ewe searching for her lamb, the odd bark of the dogs, or the lowing of the cows as they gathered in the fields for milking.

Birmingham seemed such an alien place, and yet Kate had seemed to settle into it so well. Now Sally was anxious to see the city centre; the previous evening she had been too distracted and it had been too dark to get more than just a vague impression.

In the cold light of day she wondered what on earth had possessed her to take flight. Why hadn't she at least tried to talk to her parents? Tell them how she felt? Maybe if she had explained it right they would have agreed to let her spend a wee holiday with Kate the following spring when she would be seventeen. Well, she thought ruefully, God alone knew when she would ever get the chance again. She imagined, after this little caper, her mother would fit her with a ball and chain.

In her heart of hearts she had known she had made a terrible mistake as soon as she had seen the grey hulk of the mail boat waiting for her as she alighted from the train in Dún Laoghaire. *Ulster Prince*, she'd read on the side, and she had almost turned back then, but the press of people behind her had almost propelled her up the gangplank and on to the deck, which seemed to be heaving with people.

She hadn't been on the deck long when there was a sudden blast from the funnels and black smoke escaped into the air as the engines began to pulsate and the deck rail to vibrate as the boat pulled away from the dock. Sally watched the shores of Ireland disappear into the misty, murky day, and wished she could have turned the clock back. She felt her insides gripped with a terrible apprehension, which wasn't helped by the sea-sickness that assailed her as the boat ploughed its way through the tempestuous Irish Sea. Cold, sleety rain had begun to fall too, making it difficult to stay outside. Inside, however, the smell of whisky and Guinness mingled with cigarette smoke, and the smell of damp clothes and the whiff of vomit that pervaded everywhere made her stomach churn alarmingly, while the noise, chatter, laughter, singing and the shrieking of children caused her head to throb with pain. Like many of the other passengers, she'd ended up standing in the rain, being sick over the side of the mail boat. By the time she'd disembarked and thankfully stood on dry land again, she had never felt so damp or so wretched in the whole of her life.

She tried to gather her courage as the train thundered along the tracks towards Birmingham. She told herself that – even if she was cross with her – Kate would look after her and make everything right, because she always had in the past. But she was so unnerved by her own fear and the teeming platform that she was almost too scared to leave the train at New Street Station – she had never seen so many people in one place before.

She'd never heard so much noise either. There was the clattering rumble of trains arriving at other platforms and the occasional screech and the din from the vast crowds laughing and talking together. Then there were porters with trolleys loaded with suitcases warning people to 'Mind their backs'. A newspaper vendor was obviously advertising his wares, though Sally couldn't understand a word he said, and over it all were equally indecipherable loudspeaker announcements.

She felt totally dispirited as she breathed in the sooty, stale air, but she knew that if she didn't soon alight, the train would carry her even further on, and so she clambered out on to the platform, dragging her case after her. She realized that the boldness that had enabled her to get this far had totally deserted her, and she had no idea where to go or what to do next. She looked around, feeling helpless and very afraid.

Most people were striding past her as if they were on some important errand; they seemed to know exactly where they were going, so she followed them and in minutes found herself in the street outside the station. If she had been unnerved inside the station, she was thoroughly alarmed by the scurrying crowds filling the pavements and traffic cramming the roads outside it. The noise too was incredible and she stood as if transfixed. There were horse-drawn carts, petrol-driven lorries, vans, cars and other large clattering monsters that she saw ran along rails – she remembered Kate had said they were called trams – all vying for space on the cobbled roads. And because of the gloominess of the day, many had their lights on, and they gleamed on to the damp pavements as she became aware of a sour and acrid smell that lodged at the back of her throat.

How thankful she had been to see taxis banked up waiting for passengers just a short way away. Not that she was that familiar with taxis, either; in fact she had never ridden in one before. It didn't help that the taxi driver couldn't understand her accent when she tried to tell him where her sister lived and she had to write it down.

Eventually, he had it, though, and Sally had gingerly slid across the seat, and then the taxi started up and moved into the road. She looked about her but could see little, despite the pools of brightness from the vehicles' headlights and the streetlamps and lights from the illuminated shop windows spilling on to the streets, because low, thick clouds had prematurely darkened the late afternoon.

And then when Sally had arrived at the address that Kate always put on her letters home, the door had been locked, so she'd lifted the heavy knocker and banged it on the brass plate. No one came, and no one answered the second knock either, but at the third the door was suddenly swung ajar and a scowling young woman peered around it. In the pool of light from the lamppost, Sally could plainly see the scowl. And she demanded brusquely, 'What d'you want and who are you anyway?'

'Kate,' Sally said, unnerved by the woman's tone. 'I want to see Kate Munroe. I am her sister from Ireland.'

The woman's voice softened a little as she said, 'Are you now? Kate never said owt about you coming.'

'She didn't know.'

'Nothing wrong I hope?'

Sally shook her head. 'I just wanted to give her a surprise.'

The other woman laughed. 'Surprise?' she repeated. 'Shock more likely. Any road, she ain't here, ducks. She lives upstairs but she won't be in yet. She's at work, see, and I think she comes home at six or thereabouts.'

'Oh.'

'You'd best wait for her here,' the woman said, ushering her into the entrance hall. 'I would take you into my place, but I'm off to work myself 'cos I work in a pub, see. I was getting ready, and that's why I was so mad at you nearly breaking the door down.'

'Sorry.'

'Well, it ain't your fault,' the girl conceded. 'But if I hadn't opened it I don't reckon you would have got in at all because I don't think anyone else is in from work yet.'

'So, can I wait for Kate here?'

'Oh yeah, no one will stop you doing that,' the woman said. 'And she'll be in shortly, I would say. Any road,' she said, 'I got to be off or I'll be getting my cards. Might see you around if you're staying a bit.'

It was very quiet when the woman had gone, and dark and quite scary, and Sally wished she hadn't had to leave. But she didn't want to take a chance on meeting any more of Kate's neighbours until she had met Kate herself and gauged her reaction, since she had a sneaky feeling that Kate wouldn't be as pleased to see her as she might have hoped. And so she had slunk under the stairwell and sank into a heap and, totally worn out, had fallen into a doze.

Sally had gauged Kate's reaction very well. She had been very angry, and remembering that now, Sally decided to get dressed and start to help in the hope she might put her sister in a better frame of mind. She wanted them both to enjoy their day in Birmingham. She sorted out clothes from the case on the floor, as Kate had said there was no point in unpacking it, but, quiet though she was, Kate heard her and turned over. 'You're an early bird.'

'Yeah, suppose it's living on a farm,' Sally said. 'Anyway, you said that there was a lot to do today before we can go and meet Susie.'

'And so there is,' Kate said, heaving herself up. 'And I suppose the sooner we start, the sooner we'll be finished. So we'll have some breakfast now and then we can really get cracking.'

Kate was impressed with the enthusiasm Sally seemed to have for cleaning and tidying the flat and coping with the laundry, an attribute she had never seen in her before. By the time they were scurrying up the road to meet Susie, everything was done.

'Don't you mind the noise of all the cars and stuff?' Sally suddenly asked Kate as they walked along.

'You know,' said Kate, 'I seldom hear it now.'

Sally looked at her in disbelief. 'You can't miss it.'

Kate nodded. 'I know. It's hard to believe but that's how it is now – though when I first came I didn't think I would ever be able to live with the noise. But now it sort of blends into everything else.'

'And what is that place over there on the other side of the street?' Sally said. Trees, bushes and green lawns could just be glimpsed beyond a set of high green railings bordering the pavement.

'Oh, that's the grounds of a hospital called Erdington House,' Kate said. 'I always think that it's nice it is set in grounds so that people can at least look out at green, which I shouldn't think happens often in a city. But then I found that it once used to be a work house and maybe the people in there had little time for looking out.'

'Maybe not,' Sally said. 'But it might have been nice anyway because I imagine any green space is precious here, I have never seen so many houses all packed together.'

'Remember, there are a lot of people living and working in Birmingham and they have to live somewhere,' Kate said. 'They have to shop somewhere too, and so while there are a few shops here on Slade Road, in a few minutes we will get to Stockland Green and you will see how many shops there are there – all kinds, too: grocer's, baker's, butcher's, greengrocer's, fishmonger's, newsagent's, general stores, post office; even a cinema.'

Sally was very impressed. 'A cinema!' she repeated in awe. 'I'd love to see a film.'

Kate remembered how impressed she had been when she arrived here, knowing a cinema was just up the road. 'You play your cards right and I just might take you tomorrow.'

Sally gasped. 'Oh, would you really, Kate?'

Kate nodded. 'And if there is nothing we fancy at the Plaza, we can always go to the Palace in Erdington Village – that's just a short walk down Reservoir Road and over the railway bridge.'

'Oh, anything will do me, Kate.'

'Yes, I know, it's just in case I've already seen it,' Kate said. 'Anyway, what do you think of Stockland Green? We're coming to it now,' and Sally was impressed to see that there really were all manner of shops virtually on the doorstep.

'Oh, that's a nice pub,' Sally exclaimed as they came to the top of Marsh Hill where the Masons lived.

'The Stockland,' Kate said. 'It does look nice, doesn't it? Not that I've gone inside it, but Susie said that though it was built not that many years ago, it was based on the design of a Cotswold manor house.' And then she gave a sudden wave because she saw Susie coming up the hill.

Susie had not seen Sally for three years because she had not been back to Ireland since Kate had joined her in Birmingham, but she was able to have a good look at her as she approached. The Sally she remembered had been little more than a child; she saw she was a child no longer, but a young lady. It was hard to believe that she was Kate's sister, for they were so different.

Kate had always claimed that Sally was the beauty of the family, and while Susie had to own that she was pretty enough with her blonde curls, big blue eyes and a mouth like a perfect rosebud, she didn't hold a candle to her sister. Kate didn't see it in herself, but she wasn't just pretty, she was beautiful. She also had a fabulous figure, while Sally was much plumper. Kate's hair was dark brown, with copper highlights that caught the light, and her dark eyes were ringed by the longest lashes Susie had ever seen. She might have looked quite aloof, because she had high cheekbones and a long, almost classic nose, but her mouth was wide and generous and her smile was warm and genuine and lit up her eyes.

However, there was another quality to Kate, and that was her ability to see good in most people.

She was a genuinely nice person, and it was her personality as well as the way she looked that drew people to her. The combination drew men as well, but Kate never took advantage of that – in fact quite the opposite, for she never encouraged them at all. At the dances she was lovely, polite and courteous, and danced with any man who asked her up, but it never went any further than that.

That had never bothered Susie much before, but three years had passed since Kate had come to live in Birmingham and Susie had met a man called Nick Kassel at the weekly dance. She thought he was one of the handsomest boys she had ever seen: his hair was jet black and so were his eyebrows, while his eyelashes ringed eyes of the darkest brown. He had a classic nose, beautiful, very kiss-able lips and an absolutely fabulous body, and it had seemed perfect when she realized that his mate, David Burton, was smitten with Kate.

However, Kate didn't feel the same way about David. They met them every week at the dance and, though when Susie pressed Kate she admit-ted that she liked David, that was all she would agree to. So when Nick eventually asked Susie out, she had shaken her head regretfully; al-though she had longed to accept, she felt that after urging Kate to come to Birmingham, she could hardly just swan off and leave her, as she knew that Kate relied on her. Nick hadn't really understood this and he had been quite grumpy when she'd tried to explain.

She had promised to redouble her efforts to try to get Kate and David together, but she knew that the time to talk about this was not on the tram on the way to town, especially with Sally there. So she pushed her concerns about David and Kate from her mind and there was a smile on her face as she greeted them both. 'We don't have to go into town to please Sally,' Kate told her. 'She is impressed enough by this place.'

'You haven't seen the cinema yet,' Kate said. 'The Plaza.'

'The Plaza,' Sally repeated, enthralled. 'Even the name sounds exotic,' she added, and was surprised when the two older girls laughed.

'It's all right for you two,' Sally said hotly. 'But I have never even seen inside a cinema. I can hardly believe that Kate is taking me in there to see a film tomorrow afternoon.' And she spun around with the excitement of it all and hugged herself with delight.

Susie laughed. 'Let's go and have a dekko on the boards outside now and see what's on.'

'What about the tram chugging up the hill at this very moment?' asked Kate.

'What about it?' Susie said. 'There'll be another one. Trams to town of a Saturday come every few minutes, you know that, and it won't take us long to have a look outside the flicks.'

Kate gave in, and when they passed the chip shop, which was opposite the cinema, Sally said to Kate, 'I can't believe either that you have hot food like this on your doorstep – and such delicious food as well. Is that the chip shop you used last night, Kate?'

'Yeah,' said Kate. 'There is one nearer down the Slade, but this one is better and gives bigger portions. And I was going to Susie's anyway, so it seemed sensible.'

Sally nodded, but then they crossed the road and the cinema took all her attention. Just to stand so close to that wonderful emporium while they studied the boards outside gave her butter-flies in her stomach.

'*The Lady Vanishes* is on at the moment then,' Kate said to Sally. 'That all right for you?'

'Are you kidding?' Sally said with a squeal of excitement. 'Going to the pictures is another thing I've never done in my life. I'd like to see anything.'

'It's just that it's a Hitchcock thriller and that means it might be a bit frightening for you, that's all.'

Sally shook her head. 'No, I promise, I won't be the least bit frightened.'

Kate smiled at the look of excitement on her sister's face and she linked her arm and said, 'Come on then, Sally. Birmingham, here we come.'

'Yes,' added Susie, taking hold of Sally's other arm. 'And if you think these shops are something special, girl, you ain't seen nothing yet.' And the three giggling girls hurried off to the tram stop. They had only to wait a few minutes before they spotted a tram at the bottom of the Streetly Road. As Sally watched it clatter up the hill, she said, 'I saw trams when I came out of the train station last night, and I don't mind admitting that I am really nervous of them.'

'I'm not surprised,' Kate said with a laugh. 'I was the same at first. Do you remember my telling you so in one of the letters I wrote when I first came to

Birmingham. I was terrified the trams were going to jump off the rails when they took a corner at speed or something, especially as Susie had told me that there had been some accidents in the early days.'

'Yeah, there were,' Susie said, as the tram drew to a clanking stop beside them. 'They are safer now, though,' she assured her as they boarded.

'We'll take your mind off the journey,' Kate promised. 'Let's go upstairs and it will be easier to point things out along the way.'

As the tram rattled and swayed down Slade Road towards the city centre, Kate and Susie told Sally all about the canals of Birmingham that ran behind the houses. 'A lot of them meet at a place called Salford Bridge,' Susie said. 'But you'll see this for yourself when we cross over the bridge in a minute.'

Once they were in sight of the canals, Sally admired the brightly painted boats she could see there, and was very surprised when Kate told her people lived in them. 'When my Dad was young my Nan said he was always messing about on the canals. He learnt to swim in there when his brother pushed him in,' Susie told them.

'Bit drastic.'

'Oh, I'll say,' Susie agreed. 'He was glad after, though, because in the summer a lot of the boys used to strip off and go skinny-dipping in there. Still do as well.'

'Oh, the boys do that in the rivers in Ireland too,' Sally said.

'I remember,' Kate said. 'And all the girls were forbidden to go near, never mind look.'

49

'And weren't you ever tempted to have a little peek?' Susie asked with a grin.

Kate exchanged a look with her sister and admitted, 'I was sometimes.'

'And me,' Sally said. 'But I never did. I mean, Mammy would go mad if she found out, but really it was because I would have had to confess it to the priest.'

'Oh, the priests in Ireland hold the morals of the young girls tight,' Susie said. 'And it annoys me sometimes that the boys have all the fun, but in this case – while I wouldn't mind plodging in the clear sparkling rivers in Ireland – you wouldn't get me near a mucky canal for love nor money.'

'Nor me,' Sally and Kate said together.

Sally turned her attention back to the sights. They were over the bridge now, leaving the canals to weave down behind the houses again. Kate said, 'Now we are coming to Nechell's, where you will see really squashed-up houses – I'd say not that much bigger than the canal barges.'

Sally agreed with her. 'They don't look real,' she said. 'And there are so many of them, all tightly squeezed together.'

'Oh, they're real all right,' Kate said grimly. 'They call them back-to-back houses. And you'll see plenty more when we go through Aston.'

'Yeah, Kate's right,' Susie said. 'And we're coming to Aston Railway Station now.'

Sally looked around her with interest. They passed a large brick building that Kate told her was a brewery and a big green clock that had four faces on it, standing in a little island all on its own; it was surrounded by all manner of shops,

50

very like those at Stockland Green. Susie told her, 'There are factories too. Small ones tucked in beside the houses.'

Sally shook her head. 'It's all so different from Ireland,' she said. 'You must have found it all strange at first, Kate.'

'Oh, I did,' Kate admitted. 'And for a time I was really homesick, but it was something I knew I had to get over. But now I've made my life here and I wouldn't ever want to go back to Ireland to live. And look, we're passing the fire station now and soon we'll turn into Steelhouse Lane and reach the terminus.'

'Steelhouse Lane is a funny name for a street.'

'Not if the police station is on the Street too,' Kate answered. 'And opposite is the General Hospital and that's another hospital that used to be a workhouse.'

'Yes, and people have got long memories,' Susie said. 'Mom says there are old people today who still refuse to go in that hospital.'

And Sally could understand a little of the trepidation people felt when she alighted from the tram and stood before the solid brick building of the General Hospital. It had a great many floors and she imagined all the poor inmates housed in there when it had been in use as a workhouse. 'Come on,' Kate said to her sister, catching hold of her arm, 'there are much more interesting places to look at.'

Sally tore her eyes away from the hospital and allowed herself to be led up the wide, tree-lined street with tram tracks running up the middle of it that Susie told her was called Colmore Row.

They passed an imposing building with arched windows to the front and supported by ornate pillars. 'Another station,' Susie said to Sally. 'That one's called Snow Hill.'

'And if you look across the road you will see St Philip's Cathedral,' Kate said, and Sally looked across and saw the church set in a little oasis of green interspersed with walkways and benches set here and there. 'It isn't the Catholic one,' Kate went on. 'And I don't think it's very big to be a cathedral. I thought it would be much bigger than it is.'

'I would have thought so too,' Sally said. 'It's pretty, though. I bet when the light shines through those stained-glass windows it's lovely inside.'

Susie nodded in agreement. 'We're going to cross over the churchyard now because we want to show you the shops.'

The pavements on New Street were crammed with busy shoppers and the road full of traffic, and because the cloud was so low and dense, like on the previous day, many had their headlights on, glimmering through the slight mist. But the shops were magnificent, many of them with more than one floor and so fine and grand that Sally said she was a little nervous. Her anxiety wasn't helped by the frightening-looking man in uniform standing outside the first shop they came to. 'What's he doing?' she said quietly as they drew nearer.

Susie and Kate laughed. 'He's a commission-aire,' Susie told Sally. 'He stands there to keep the riffraff out.'

'Like us you mean?' Sally said with a laugh.

'No, not like us at all,' Susie said in mock indignation, and with a broad grin she pushed open the door with a confident air. Sally, her arm linked in her sister's, followed her more cautiously, blinking in the shimmering lights that seemed very bright after the dull of the day. Kate smiled at the rapt attention on her sister's face as they wandered around the store, remembering how she had been similarly awed in her initial forays into the city centre.

The models were draped in all sorts of creations, fashionable clothes the like of which Sally had never seen, and in materials so sheer or so luxurious that the spectacle rendered her speechless for a moment. She loved the vast array of colours used. She remembered the dullness of the shops in her home town, where material for their clothes was purchased at the draper's and run up by a dressmaker. 'Nice, aren't they?' Kate said as she saw Sally gently touching a velvet rose-red ball gown.

'Oh, far more than just nice,' Sally said. 'And the colours, Kate. Do you remember the way it was done at home: straight up-and-down clothes with no style to them at all?'

'I remember it well,' Kate said with a grimace. 'And the colours on offer were invariably black, grey, navy blue or brown. But to be truthful, though we thought it would be fun to show you the store, most of what they sell is too dear for my purse. Susie has a bit more left over at the end of the week than me, don't you?' she asked her friend.

'Yeah, because I still live at home,' Susie said. 'But I still have an eye for a bargain. I don't want to throw money away.'

'And the bargains are to be had in the Bull Ring, which is where we are going later,' Kate said. 'But for now come and look at the hats,' and she led the way up a short flight of stairs.

There were hats galore, of all colours, shapes and sizes, displayed on head stands or on glass shelves. Most were breathtakingly beautiful, decorated with ribbons and bows or the occasional feather and veil. Others were frankly bizarre: artistic constructions that looked ridiculous and even comical.

Sally smiled at the thought of the stir it would cause if she was to wear any one of those to Mass at home. But still she said to the others, 'Wouldn't you love to try some of these on?' And she spoke in a whisper because it was the kind of place where to whisper seemed appropriate.

'Shouldn't, if I were you,' Susie warned. 'Not with hatchet face looking on.' Sally followed Susie's gaze and saw a very haughty woman behind a nearby counter who seemed to be keeping a weather eye on them, and so they wandered back to the main floor. No one paid them any attention there because it was very busy and Sally watched the smart shop assistants standing behind gleaming counters, confidently punching numbers into gigantic silver tills. Sally had seen tills before, but never any so large or magnificent.

They visited other stores, too: Sally found the most entertaining were those that had no tills at all. There the assistant would write out the bill and put it with the money into a canister. This would be carried on wires crisscrossing the shop until it reached the cashier who would sit in a high glass-sided office. She would issue a receipt and this, together with any change, would be put into the canister and the process reversed.

After Sally had watched this a number of times, Kate said, 'If I'd known that this would entertain you so much, I wouldn't have bothered to take you to town at all. I could have just taken you to the Co-op by the Plaza and you could have watched it all afternoon – they use the same system.'

'Do they?' Sally said. 'I think it's a great way of going on.'

'Maybe it is,' Kate said with a smile. 'But I want to pop into C and A's as we pass Corporation Street on our way to the Bull Ring. Let's see what you think of an escalator.'

'What's an escalator?'

'You'll soon find out,' Kate said, taking her sister's arm in a firm grip and leading her into the street.

'They move,' Sally exclaimed a little later. 'They're like stairs but they move up on their own.'

'And down,' Susie said. 'Round the other side they go down as well. D'you want a go?'

Sally shook her head. 'I'd be scared.'

'Nothing to it,' Kate said airily.

'Oh, just hark at her,' Susie said with a hoot of laughter. 'Let me tell you, Sally, your sister was shaking like a leaf when she went on the escalator first.'

'I was not!'

'Yes, you were,' Susie said. 'I well remember it. Come on, Sally,' she said, offering her arm for

Sally to link, which she took gratefully. 'Don't let Kate get one over on you. Show her how brave you are.'

'Right, I will then,' Sally said, and stepped forward, boldly holding Susie's arm.

After the initial tingles of nervousness, Sally enjoyed the escalator, and went up and down quite a few times and on her own too before Kate and Susie could get her off it. 'I've had such a lovely time already,' she said as they hurried along. 'And now I have the Bull Ring to look forward to.'

THREE

By the time the three girls reached High Street and the top of the incline leading down to the Bull Ring, dusk had fallen. Sally gasped as she surveyed the market below them. 'Oh,' she exclaimed, 'it's just like you said, Kate. Fairyland.'

And it was, because every barrow in that large vibrant market was lit by gas flares, just as Kate had told her it would be. She smiled at her younger sister's enthusiasm, and Susie led the way down the incline. And when they reached the cobbled streets of the Bull Ring itself, Sally looked around in some amazement at the swelling throngs of people all around her. The chatter, laughter and general buzz of the whole place rose in the air, punctuated here and there by the banter of vendors still plying their trade.

'The traders do good business on Saturday night,' Kate said. 'You won't see the flower girls, though. They usually stand round Nelson's statue there,' she said pointing. 'If there's lots, though, the others cluster around St Martin's, the church over there.'

'And that's the Market Hall,' Susie told her, pointing to the other side of the road where Sally saw stone steps leading up to an impressive-looking building, with arched windows to either side of the steps and supported with huge and ornate stone pillars. And if it's all the same to you, we'll make for there first, because I'm gasping for a cup of tea.'

'Me too,' Kate said.

'But won't they all have shut by now?' Sally asked.

'Not the ones in the Market Hall,' Kate said. 'Come on. By the time we have the tea drunk, all the entertainers will have started arriving.'

Everyone was in agreement with that, and so they made their way through the market. Sally saw that the traders were selling all manner of things and all their barrows were mixed together, so one might be selling various cheeses, another fruit and vegetables, and they might be next to one selling bedding or towels. There were crockery and saucepans in baskets on the ground and various smells rose in the air. Sally was quite surprised at what Kate called banter between the traders and the customers. 'Come on, darling,' she heard one say as they passed a barrow selling greengrocery. 'Christ, I'm giving the stuff away. Only a tanner for this big bag of tomatoes. Don't tell your old man, but I'm only letting you have them at this price 'cos I fancy you.'

Kate and Susie turned away smiling, but Sally was rather shocked. Market traders didn't do that in Donegal Town. 'He don't mean it,' Susie said, seeing the look on the young girl's face. 'He goes on like that to sell more of his stuff.'

'And it works,' Kate said. 'And you have got to watch him because the best tomatoes might be on the top but the rest of the bag could be filled with bruised, squashed ones. We were taken in by that once or twice.'

58

'We were,' agreed Susie. 'But we're quick learners.'

'Not half,' Kate said as she mounted the steps to the Market Hall and opened the carved wooden doors.

Sally stood on the threshold and looked about her. The Market Hall stalls had the same gas flares as those outside, and in the sputtering pools of light it looked a cavernous place with huge high ceilings. They were crisscrossed with beams, and long metal poles led down from the beams to help support the roof. High arched windows lined the walls. At a quick glance she saw that the goods for sale inside were similar to those sold in the open-air market; the smell was indescribable and so was the noise reverberating off the walls and ceiling.

And then a little tinkling sound was heard and the noise in the Market Hall abated a little. 'They're waiting for the clock to strike,' Kate said in explanation, pointing to the wall. Till then Sally hadn't even noticed the clock, but now she saw that it was a magnificent structure made of wood. First a lady emerged and then three other figures that Kate told her were knights as the tune heralding the hour came to an end. Amid a breathless hush, the knights struck the bell six times. 'Six o'clock,' Susie said when it was over. 'No wonder I'm hungry.'

'I'm hungry too,' Kate said. 'What do you say to tea and teacakes all round?'

No one argued with that, and they made short work of them. 'Those were delicious,' Sally said, licking at her sticky fingers. 'I didn't realize how hungry I was.'

'That's often the way until you start eating,' Kate said. 'And you'll feel warmer with food inside you, anyway. It will be cold enough out there now that it's fully dark.'

'There's other stuff to eat as well if you feel peckish,' Susie said with an impish grin.

'What sort of food?' Sally asked.

'Oh, lovely stuff,' Susie said, 'like jellied eels and whelks and that, but me and Kate never fancied anything like that.'

'I don't even know what they are.'

'Seafood,' Kate said. 'Like that song, "Molly Malone". You must know that one – she sold cockles and mussels and that sort of stuff.'

'Yeah, I know the song all right,' Sally said. 'Have even sung it a few times, but I never knew what any of the things she sang about were, or looked like.'

'You can have a peep tonight,' Kate promised. 'But if you don't fancy those, there's a man who bakes potatoes in a little oven and they are lovely with a bit of salt. If we are still hungry we can get one of those – honestly, they smell so delicious that you always feel hungry when you get the whiff in the air.'

'That's true,' Susie said, jumping to her feet. 'But right now we're wasting time. Come on, it's probably all happening in the streets.'

The first sight that greeted Sally as they went out of the door and down the steps were the men walking around – seemingly effortlessly – on high stilts that their long, long trousers hid from view. 'How do they do that?' she asked in awe. 'Specially on these uneven cobbles.'

Kate shrugged. 'Search me,' she said. 'And I've never seen any of them fall off.' She linked her arm around Sally and said, 'Come on, let's show you the boxing ring set up.'

At the boxing ring, a small man in a black top hat and red jacket was encouraging men standing in the crowd to try their luck at beating the champ for a prize of five pounds. The champ, a huge and glowering man, was broad and hefty-looking with arms like tree trunks and fists like giant hams. These could be seen plainly because he was naked to the waist, with tight trousers fastened around massive beefy legs, and he had a slight sneer on his face as he regarded them all. 'Step this way, gentlemen,' wheedled the little man in the jacket. 'Impress the ladies – after all, five pounds is five pounds.'

But though some of the men shifted uncomfortably on their feet, none stepped forward and Sally couldn't blame them one little bit. She found the man unnerving. 'Has anyone beaten him?' she whispered as they walked away.

Susie and Kate both shook their heads. 'Seen some nearly killed having a go though,' Kate added.

'Well, no one seemed that keen on trying their luck this evening, anyway,' Sally said with slight satisfaction.

'Too early, that's why,' Susie said sagely. 'Give them a few hours in the Bell pub over there and many will think themselves the strongest men in Christendom and then they will take on the champ.'

'Ugh,' Sally said. 'Well, I think it's horrid and I don't see why anyone thinks it might impress us.'

'Nor me,' said Kate. 'Tell you the truth, I would have severe doubts about any man who was willing to allow himself to be punched into the middle of next week for five pounds.'

'Me too,' Susie said. 'Funny ideas about women some of these men have. Now, do you want to see the man tied up in chains or the one lying on a bed of nails first?'

Sally laughed. 'As I have never come near seeing anything like either of those, it's all one and the same to me.'

'Right then,' Susie said decisively. 'Let's see Birmingham's answer to Houdini first.'

Sally hadn't been sure who Houdini was, but she was soon enlightened when she saw the man standing with coils of chains all around him: he was urging the audience gathering around him to test their strength. Kate and Susie dropped coins in the hat that was lying on the floor watched over by an assistant, and Kate whispered to her sister, 'He will do nothing until there is a pound in the hat.'

'Then what does he do?'

'Well, his assistant ties him up with chains, pulls a curtain around him and he frees himself.'

'How?'

'I don't know,' Kate admitted. 'And you can test those chains. Anyone can. Me and Susie have done and neither of us can see how it can be a swizz. He does the same thing every week.'

However, the money in the bucket rose only slowly and it was cold to stand in one place for long, so after a while the girls wandered away. The stilt walkers were still parading around, bowing to people and proffering their raised hats, and Sally heard the chink of coins as people showed their appreciation of such skill.

When she got her first glimpse of the seafood being sold from a van, she thought that she had never seen anything so disgusting in her life. It didn't seem to her like any food a person should eat and the jellied eels looked positively slimy. 'Fancy some?' Susie said, seeing the distaste on her face.

'Not likely,' Sally said. 'I'd say that I would have to be well hungry before I ate anything like that – near starving, in fact.'

'I feel exactly the same,' Susie admitted as they wandered back to the man now being encircled by the chains. Sally watched with awe. The man was trussed up like a chicken and she didn't see how he was ever going to escape. The curtain was pulled and the assistant began a drum roll. The curtain billowed out in places as the man struggled inside it.

People watched, some as anxiously as Sally, but she was also enthralled by the excitement of it all. And then the drum roll reached a crescendo, there was one last billow of the curtain, and then the man was standing before them, unharmed and unfettered, as he rolled up the curtain and tossed it to his assistant while he took a bow.

Sally clapped as energetically as anyone and was still talking about it as they walked away. Kate remembered Susie taking her around the Bull Ring one Saturday night not long after she'd arrived in Birmingham and how amazed she had been by everything, so she knew just how Sally was feeling. 'Another treat in store for you,' she said.

This time it was a man lying on a bed of nails. All he had on was a white sort of nappy and another white cloth on his head that Susie told her was called a turban. In the light from the spluttering gas flares, Sally saw his brown body gleaming, as if he had oiled it. 'Wouldn't you think that he'd be cold?' she said in a quiet voice to Kate.

'Probably doesn't feel it,' Kate said. 'I mean, let's face it, a man who can lie on a bed of nails as if it was a feather mattress is probably not concerned about little things like being a bit chilly.'

'No, probably not,' Sally agreed. 'Is that all he does, just lie there?'

'No. Watch.'

A fair crowd had collected around the Indian lying on the nails and amongst them a group of about six girls. Those were the ones the assistant targeted. Eventually, coerced by the man, and urged on equally strongly by her friends, one of them stepped forward. 'Up you go, darling,' the assistant said. 'He promises not to look up your skirt. Ain't that right, Abdul?'

'That's right,' said Abdul, though he still had a great grin on his face.

The girl removed her shoes and then, holding the assistant's hand for balance, stepped cautiously on to the man's stomach. A sympathetic 'Ooh' ran through many of the women watching because the nails could clearly be seen pressing into the Indian's skin, but he made no sign that he could feel it and even the expression on his face didn't change. To Sally it was almost unbelievable, and she watched avidly until the girl had got off Abdul and he had risen to his feet to take a bow. Then she gave a great sigh of relief. 'Gosh, I thought when he stood up he would be all over holes,' she said to Susie and Kate as they began to walk away, 'but he wasn't.'

'I know,' Kate said. 'We've seen him many times.'

'But how does he do it?'

'I haven't a clue.'

'Come on,' Susie urged. 'Stop worrying about him. It's time for a bit of jollification now because the fiddlers and accordion players are setting up in the corner there, see?'

'Oh yes,' Sally said, following the direction of Susie's pointing finger. As they approached them, Susie said, 'They will play songs and tunes from your homeland first. It used to make Kate feel really homesick sometimes, didn't it?'

'It did. I'll not deny that,' Kate said. 'But it was the people I missed rather than the place and now I think it's nice to hear the tunes I grew up with.'

Sally agreed with that, and even more as the music began and it made her feet tap. 'A lot of this is really music to dance to,' she said.

'I know,' said Kate. 'But if you tried that here you might end up being locked up. They'd prob-ably think you'd gone doolally tap.'

'Yes, they might,' Sally said with a smile. 'Don't worry, I won't do anything. I just wish I could.'

Seeing the two of them so engrossed in the music, Susie stole away to where she had seen the baked-potato man park up. She could smell the delicious aroma of the potatoes cooking as she approached, and a little later, Kate and Sally were delighted to be given one each, served in a poke of paper folded over into a triangle to protect their hands. 'Aw, that was really nice of you. Thanks,' Sally said, tucking into the potato with relish.

'That's all right,' Susie said. 'Like Kate said, as soon as the smell wafted down, I felt hungry.'

'Well, we did only have teacakes earlier,' Kate said. 'They don't fill you up over much.'

'Yeah, and I thought you needed your strength built up for the singing,' Susie said.

'What singing's that then?'

'Songs from the music hall,' Susie said. 'That's quite popular in Birmingham. You probably won't know any of the songs, but they're easy to pick up. It's mainly funny stuff, you know?'

And Sally found that it was just as Susie said – she was able to pick up the choruses when she'd heard them a couple of times. They started with 'Hello, Hello, Who's Your Lady Friend?', and then went on with 'If You Were the Only Girl in the World'. 'I'm Henery the Eighth I Am' made Sally laugh, and so did 'Oh Mister Porter', and she loved 'Tar-ar-ar Boom-de-aye', and the fact that it was repeated eight times, which meant that she could belt it out with as much gusto as the rest. 'Daisy Daisy' got everyone swaying, and when they announced 'Roll Out the Barrel' was the last one, the noise was incredible.

It was as the strains of the music faded away that Sally heard the sound of more music in the air. 'Yeah, that's the Sally Army playing "Jerusalem",' Susie said.

'Sally Army?'

'Susie means Salvation Army,' Kate said, seeing her sister's confusion. Just then the band turned into the Bull Ring filling the air with the sound of their trumpets and trombones and the big bass drum at the front, keeping the beat of their marching feet. Those not playing a proper instrument were shaking or banging a tambourine and everyone was singing with all their might.

'I'm ready to call it a day, if you are,' Susie said to Kate and Sally as the Salvation Army launched into 'The Old Rugged Cross'.

It was as they were threading their way between the stalls that Sally caught sight of a few women standing behind them. Most had shawls about their shoulders and they all had children with them. Kate followed her gaze. 'They are the city's poor,' she said, putting her arm through her sister's and leading her away. 'The stalls will be closing up soon, see, and they wait there for anything the butchers and greengrocers might be giving away. There used to be a fair army of them some nights. There are fewer now.'

'Yeah,' Susie said. 'Dad said that's because we're going to have a war.'

Kate looked at Susie in amazement. In the light of the gas flares, she saw her face seemed very white as she said, 'Don't be daft, Susie. Chamberlain only came back from Munich a few weeks ago and said that it would be peace for our time.'

'Yeah, I know,' Susie said. 'Dad reckons that's a ploy to give us time to get ready and that.'

'I think that's a daft notion,' Kate declared.

'And even if it was, what's that got to do with the poor?'

'Well, Dad said that there're more jobs about,' Susie said. 'Like the BSA going over to making guns. Military guns for the army and that.'

'How does he know that?' Kate asked. 'The BSA is miles away.'

'I know, but my Uncle Robbie lives that way and has just got a job there,' Susie said. 'He's been out of work for three years and he told us that they are setting up new lines all over the factory. And then, the other day, some bloke was telling him that he heard tell that Longbridge and maybe other car factories were building shadow factories beside the real one to make jeeps and other army trucks and that.'

'Still, don't mean we're going to war though, does it?'

'Well, no,' Susie had to admit. 'But it does mean that we might be getting ready in case we do and that means there are more jobs about and so all them that were unemployed will have more chance of getting one.'

'Yeah,' Kate said with a grin. 'As my Dad would say: every cloud has a silver lining.' She was annoyed with Susie though. 'Trust you to spoil a really nice night,' she said sharply.

'She hasn't,' Sally said. 'Not really. I think Birmingham must be one of the most exciting cities in the world because I have never had such an interesting time in the whole of my life.'

Susie's words about war bothered Kate more than she realized – she had lurid dreams all night and even the next day she was preoccupied. Sally was aware that Kate was thinking hard about something, but didn't know what it was, and eventually, as the two of them walked the damp wet streets to Mass at St Mary's and St John's under the partial shelter of an umbrella, Sally said, 'Penny for them.'

'What?' Kate said with a start. Then, seeing Sally's eyes on her, said, 'Oh, they're not worth a penny, Sally, really, but I can't get what Susie said out of my head.'

'About preparing for war and that?'

Kate nodded her head. 'And it's stupid because no person in their right mind wants another war. I mean, you didn't see them last night, but in the day those steps to the Market Hall are lined with old lags. Some wander around the market as well.'

'What do you mean, old lags?'

'Susie's dad calls them flotsam from the Great War,' Kate said. 'Most of them are injured in some way and can't get a proper job, so a fair few of them have trays around their necks selling boot-laces and razor blades and stuff like that. I have bought loads of stuff I haven't needed because I feel sorry for them. It can be quite upsetting to see them too, because some of them have missing limbs, or are shell-shocked or even blind.'

'Ooh, that's horrible.'

'It is, I couldn't agree more,' Kate said. 'Susie's dad gets really mad about it. He says they laid their life on the line for Britain and now the government should look after them better. But they don't. They are like thrown on the scrapheap and surely no one wants to risk that sort of thing happening again.'

'I'd say not,' Sally said. 'But Susie was just talking about getting ready, wasn't she? Maybe it was sort of in case.'

'Um,' Kate said pensively. 'I'd like to believe you are right. What's more, I know that even if I talk and worry about this from now till doomsday I will not change the outcome one iota.' She gave a sudden shiver and said, 'Let's hurry, this is a foul day. Good job this sleety rain wasn't falling last night. Anyway, looks like it's set in for the day so it's a good job we have that film at the cinema to see.'

'Ooh, yes,' said Sally. And then she added, 'Thanks ever such a lot for taking me out yesterday. I really did enjoy myself, but I was so overawed I don't know if I ever said thank you.'

'That's all right,' Kate said good-naturedly. 'I always like going down the Bull Ring, and I know how much it was appreciated because your face was a picture.'

'Yes,' Sally said with a sigh. 'Donegal will seem dreadfully dull after this.'

They walked in silence for a minute or two and then Sally said, 'I understand the reason you came to Birmingham now I've seen it myself, though I couldn't see the attraction at the time.'

'I could take you to see more of it if the weather is kinder to us,' Kate said.

'Ooh, yes,' Sally said, 'I'd like that.' And then she added: 'Is Susie coming with us tomorrow?'

'No,' Kate said. 'She would like to, especially as she hasn't seen *The Lady Vanishes* yet either, but

70

she has to go with her mother and sister to visit her father's mother. She isn't that keen on the old lady, but she has just come out of hospital and her mother has insisted that they all go and see her.'

'Shame,' Sally said. 'I really like Susie. But I suppose we'll meet her at Mass.'

Kate shook her head. 'I'm afraid not,' she said. 'The Masons all go to St Margaret Mary's on Perry Common Road – it's much nearer to them.'

'Gosh, there seem to be plenty of churches,' Sally remarked.

'Well, there are plenty of people.' Kate smiled.

Sally gave a sudden shiver and Kate said, 'Not much further now.'

'I'm not really shivering because I'm cold,' Sally said. 'It's just... Oh, what I'd do to be able to put the clock back.'

Kate knew exactly what her sister meant. 'There's not many of us that haven't wished that a time or two,' she said.

'Oh, I know,' Sally said disconsolately. Kate didn't blame her: she knew she wouldn't be in her sister's shoes for all the tea in China. It was no good saying that, though. She gave her sister's arm a squeeze as she said, 'If I were you I would pray as you have never prayed before – and maybe light a candle for good measure, too, and I will do the same.'

The only thing that spoiled that magical afternoon was the weather: a buffeting wind that attempted to wrest the hats from both their heads and had their coats billowing out around them, and a lashing rain attacking them, despite the umbrella, as they scurried arm in arm up the road.

Sally was astounded by the queues forming all down the side of the cinema when they arrived, and by the sight of the commissionaire standing on the steps. He was the smartest one she had ever seen, even counting the ones she had seen in Birmingham the previous day. His dark blue coat reached his knees and was piped in gold and so were the epaulettes on his shoulders. It was fastened with shiny brass buttons and the belt had a brass buckle; he had a row of medals pinned to his chest, which Kate whispered were from his time spent fighting in the Great War. He also had a shiny peaked military-style cap on his head with an emblem on it, smart black trousers with a razor-like crease and highly polished black shoes.

'Golly, isn't he smart?' Sally said quietly to Kate as they joined the queue.

Kate nodded. 'He's all right, though. I mean, he's always been nice enough to me, and at least if he's there you know that no one will try pushing in. That would be really annoying if you had queued for hours.'

'Oh, I'd say it would,' Sally said. 'And I hope we haven't got to wait too long here, 'cos it's freezing.'

'I hope not either,' Kate said. 'But I know from experience he won't let anyone in before he gets the signal from inside that they are ready for us.'

It wasn't very long before the doors opened and the crowds began shuffling forward. And when they pushed their way through the doors, Sally felt as if she had been transported to another world, for the foyer was bathed in diamond-bright light from the sparkling chandeliers hanging from the ceiling. Kate was shaking her umbrella outside under the cover of the canopy to get the excess rain off, so Sally could stand and stare for a few minutes. She was almost embarrassed to walk with her wet, slightly muddy shoes, on that gleaming floor with patterns set into it, and so she waited for Kate and then followed her to the glass building that Kate said was the box office where they had to buy the tickets.

Either side of the box office were wide stairs; these were carpeted and even the brass stair rods shimmered in the light. Sally mounted the stairs behind her sister and felt her feet sink into the carpet. The walls were decorated with elaborate patterns and it all seemed very grand; she could scarcely believe that soon she would be watching moving pictures.

Then Kate opened the double doors. Sally stepped into the auditorium and it fair took her breath away. It was so vast, with walls decorated to either side and filled with dark red velvet-type seats. A man was playing an instrument like a piano in front of a thick velvet curtain, all ruched up in folds. A very smart lady in a blue uniform with silver embroidery on the front and shoulders of the jacket, which also had silver buttons and a silver torch fastened to her belt, took the tickets Kate had just bought, ripped them in half and directed them to their seats.

It was when she turned slightly to go into the row that Sally noticed the gallery above them also filling up with people behind an elegant and ornate balustrade; she was so astonished her mouth actually dropped open. 'That's the circle, where the better-off people go,' Kate said quietly.

'I don't care,' Sally said. 'I prefer to be down here. I think I would be feared to be up there.'

'Well, we'd better take our seats wherever they are,' Kate said. 'We're causing a blockage here.'

Sally obediently shuffled down the row and thought the seats very high and uncomfortable until Kate showed her that they folded down. 'They're flip-up seats,' she said. 'Then if people want to get past you for some reason you can stand up and the seats flip up behind you and there's more room for them to get through, see.'

'Oh, yes,' Sally said. 'What a good idea... And who's the lady who ripped your ticket up?'

'She's an usherette,' Kate said. 'She shows people to their seats. It's all right when the lights are on, but if people come in when the film has started and the whole place is in darkness, then she has to use that silver torch she has fastened to her belt. It's for winkling out troublemakers too,' Kate added. 'If people keep talking through the film, or are making a nuisance of themselves in other ways, then the usherette comes down and shines the light on them and tells them off – or in some cases chucks them out.'

'Better behave myself then.'

'Yes, you better had, or I'll throw you out myself,' Kate said with a grin. Then, with a glance at her watch, she said, 'It's all going to start in a minute. That organ will fold away down below, the lights will go down, the curtain will open and...'

'*The Lady Vanishes* will start,' Sally finished for her.

'No, it won't,' Kate corrected. 'Or not straight-away anyway. They have a B-film first and then Pathé News and advertisements for what's coming next week before the main film.'

'I can hardly wait.'

'You won't have to. Look.'

The tune on the organ came to an end and then the whole thing, man as well as instrument, slowly vanished. The lights began to dim and the excitement began in Sally's toes and spread to fill her entire body. There was a whirring sound behind them and Sally saw the beam of light directed on to the screen. She sighed with happiness.

She enjoyed the film that Kate had disparagingly referred to as a B-film, and she loved the cockerel heralding Pathé News, and even the way the news was presented in a slightly comical way. But when it eventually drew to a close, the lights came on again and the usherettes appeared down each aisle, this time carrying trays around their necks.

'What sort of ice cream do you want?'

'Oh,' Sally said, her face aglow. 'I can't remember ever having an ice cream before.'

'No,' Kate agreed. 'I hadn't till I came here, but now a visit to the cinema is not the same without an ice cream. You can have a cornet, a tub, or my favourite, a choc ice.'

'Is that what you're having today?'

'Think so.'

'Then I'll have the same,' Sally said. 'And thanks very much.'

Afterwards, she thought she had never tasted anything as delicious as that first choc ice. The crisp chocolate split as she bit into it and her mouth filled with cold and creamy ice cream. She said not a word until it was all finished and then she licked her fingers and said, 'I have never tasted anything like that before in my life. It was wonderful.'

Kate laughed. 'You're easy to please,' she said. 'Now settle down in your seat because the main film is about to start.'

And what a film it was: Sally was captivated from the start. It was just as if she was actually in it. Kate was as entertained by Sally's reaction as she was by the film itself and they talked about it nearly all the way home.

'Do you go to the cinema a lot?' Sally asked.

Kate nodded. 'A fair bit,' she said. 'But sometimes we have to wait for the big films. They tend to go to London first and then the other big cities.'

'I wouldn't mind how long I waited,' Sally said. 'I think it's great to have all this so handy.'

'It is, I know,' Kate agreed. Then she asked, 'And what are you going to do with yourself while I'm at work tomorrow?'

'Oh, I'll have a mooch round the shops and that and I'll do any shopping you need as well.'

Kate nodded. 'That's good,' she said. 'I will be grateful for that. I'll give you a key; I have a spare. Just don't get lost.'

'I won't.'

'And if you get fed up looking at the shops and all at Stockland Green, you could always go down to Erdington Village,' Kate said. 'It's only up Reservoir Road and it's well worth a look around there too.'

FOUR

The following morning, as Susie settled herself in the tram beside Kate on their way to work, she said, 'Nick came round yesterday.'

'Nick?'

'Nick Kassel,' Susie said. 'You know, David Burton's friend?'

'Yeah, I know who he is,' Kate said. 'What did he want?'

'To see if we were all right, because we weren't at the dance on Friday.'

'It isn't compulsory.'

'I know,' Susie said. 'But I thought it nice. He thought we might have been poorly, that's all. He only just caught us because we had just got in from seeing my nan.'

'It was tipping it down yesterday.'

Susie nodded. 'Don't I know it?' she said. 'We were a bit damp, but Nick was saturated. Mom had his coat steaming over the fire before you could say Jack Robinson. And she insisted he stayed for tea. Said he had to, or his coat wouldn't be dry, and she would not like to be held responsible for him catching pneumonia.'

'And so at last your parents have met the illustrious Nick, who you dance most of the night with, every Friday.'

'Yeah, and they liked him, and to be honest I'm glad because I would like to do more than just dance with him.'

Kate turned to her friend and saw the light shining in her eyes as she asked gently, 'And how does he feel?'

'To be absolutely straight with you, Kate,' Susie said, 'Nick feels the same way. He has asked me out but I have refused.'

'Why?'

'Because I don't want to leave you on your own.'

Kate felt suddenly cold. She knew Susie loved her, they were best friends, and she also knew she wanted her to leave the past behind her, where it belonged, and begin to look forward. And this was compounded when Susie said, 'What do you really feel about David Burton?'

Kate shrugged. 'I don't know.'

'He's nice,' Susie said. 'And you did admit that you liked him.'

Kate nodded. 'I know.'

'D'you think you could ever feel more than just liking?'

Kate shook her head. 'To promise him anything more wouldn't be fair to him,' she said. 'Most of my heart was left in Donegal with Tim Munroe.'

'I think David would take anything you had left,' Susie said. 'He really has got it bad. Nick said he's dotty about you.'

'That's why it wouldn't be right for me to encourage him,' Kate said.

She wished she could, really she did, because she knew that it would please Susie and she really wanted to please her, but – even though she did like him better than any other man she had met since leaving Ireland – all she felt for him was a warm friendship. She looked at Susie and shook her head slowly. 'I'm sorry, Susie. I'm not ready to love anyone else yet.'

'I'm sorry, too,' Susie said, adding angrily, 'and it is you that I am sorry for – because you might never be ready. You have been here three years now, and unless you get out of this mindset you'll never find anyone to match up to your precious Tim, and you'll look back when it's too late and see the wasted life you've had.'

Kate was sorry that she had annoyed Susie and very glad that they had to leave the tram then. As soon as they alighted they were joined by a gaggle of girls all making their way to the factory, but the words Susie had flung at her stayed in her mind all day as she worked on her machine.

Sally had found her way to Erdington and walked down until she came to the village green and a public library that opened on to it. She entered cautiously, glad to be out of the blustery wind, and inside she saw a room spread out with newspapers and magazines and people just sitting reading them. A rather stern-looking young woman was behind the high polished wood counter, dressed in a pale blue blouse that buttoned to the neck and was decorated with a cameo brooch. 'Can anyone do that?' Sally asked tentatively.

The woman smiled, which made her look much more human, as she asked, 'Do what?'

'Sit in there,' Sally said, pointing to the room. 'And read the papers?'

'Certainly, they can,' the librarian told her.

'That's what it's for. It's our reading room.'

Sally couldn't remember a time when she had been able to sit and read unmolested. Even when she had been at school, homework was one thing, but when that was done, just reading was not a thing her mother had much time for – she would always find a job for Sally if she dared pick up a book. So to sit down in a warm room, ensconced in one of the leather chairs, spread out a paper or magazine on the shiny wooden table in front of her and start to read was a treat for her.

She left when her stomach told her that it was near dinner-time and retraced her steps back to the flat and made tea and toast for herself as Kate had instructed her to do that morning before she'd left. Then she tidied everything up, picked up the shopping list and basket, bought the things for tea and had a meal waiting for Kate when she came in.

Kate was grateful, and said so, and then as they sat together at the table, Sally told her about the reading room in Erdington Village Library where she had spent the morning. 'You can take books out as well,' Kate told her. 'And keep two books for a fortnight. It is nice to have a book to read in the evening sometimes. In fact, I have two to return this Saturday.'

'I will probably be on my way home by then.'

Kate nodded. 'More than likely,' she said. 'Though if Mammy got the letter this morning, the earliest we could get a reply would be Wednesday.'

'Unless she sent a telegram?'

'No,' Kate said with a definite shake of her head.

'Mammy wouldn't use a telegram. I imagine she has a heap of things to say to you and she could hardly do that on a telegram. Rest assured, Mammy will send a letter.'

However, Wednesday came and went, but on Thursday, just as soon as Sally went back into the house, after spending another morning at the reading room in Erdington Library, she saw the envelope lying on the hall table. Her stomach flipped over in nervousness and she carried it up to the flat as if it was hot and might burn her. It was addressed to Kate. How much Sally wanted to steam it open and read what her mother had to say, but she didn't dare, and, though she kept herself busy, the hours seemed to drag till she heard Kate's key in the lock.

And then perversely she didn't want Kate to open the letter and read the dreadful things she knew her mother would say about her. Kate saw her agitation and guessed the reason for it and she said gently, 'We have to know, Sally. Tell you what, let's leave the meal for now. Just make a cup of tea and we'll eat when we know what's in the letter.'

However, Kate was as surprised as Sally at her mother's words. She first spoke of her shock and outrage at what Sally had done, which Kate had expected.

Though I soon knew where she had gone for though her scribbled note told me nothing, Dinny Malone, you know him from the rail bus booking office, saw your father passing through town that same day and told him of yon lass booking her passage to Strabane and telling him she was going to England to see her sister. He thought your father knew all about it though I know he would find it strange that there had been no word of it before. Of course your father knew nothing and was so taken by shock and surprise he had Dinny repeat the tale again before he could bring himself to believe it.

I was as stunned as he was. When I arrived home and saw no sign of her, if your father hadn't met up with Dinny I would have had the Guards out and the whole county alerted for I hadn't seen the note at first.

As it was I began wondering what she had used for money to pay her way. I knew that though she'd run to you, you would be ignorant of what she intended to do, and would never have sent her money to carry out such a thing, you are far too sensible. The only money in the house is the money for the eggs and I checked it, though I felt sick at the thought that one of my children would steal and from their own parents.

But that is exactly what Sally did. She took every penny and for that reason she is no longer my daughter and she has no home here for we could never trust her again. She now must make her own way in the world.

Kate read over the letter again because she could hardly believe it. She would never turn Sally away to fend for herself, and her mother knew that. She was handing over her younger sister's welfare and care to her and Kate didn't really want that responsibility. It wasn't fair to ask that of her.

'Is it really bad?' Sally asked, alarmed by the look on Kate's face.

And because the news was as bad as it could be, and there was no way of shielding her, Kate nodded her head and said, 'Mammy said she has disowned you and doesn't want you to go back at all. In fact, she says the farm is no longer your home.'

'Disowned me?' Sally repeated disbelievingly, for she didn't think either of her parents would ever do that.

'That's what she said,' Kate said. 'It's because you stole the egg money. She says neither she nor Daddy will ever be able to trust you again.'

'Oh, Kate, what am I to do?'

'Well, I know what I'm going to do, and that is write to Mammy and beg her to reconsider and say you are desperately sorry and that you will promise to never ever do anything like this again – and see if that does any good. I advise you to do the same; if we get them sent off this evening she will get them by Saturday at the latest.'

The two girls set to work right away and Kate poured her heart out to her mother, telling her how contrite Sally was and how even as the boat sailed across the Irish Sea she'd known she'd made a grave mistake, but that it had been too late to put it right. She begged her mother to give her one more chance. Sally's letter was similar, though some of the words were smeared from the tears that had fallen as she wrote. She went out to the postbox right away to post them.

'D'you think she'll come round?' Susie said at work the next day when Kate told her about the letter. 'Like, you know, it was done in the heat of the moment?'

'It can't really be done in the heat of the moment when you are writing a letter,' Kate said. 'It's not like saying something and then regretting it. Mammy wouldn't have said she was disowning Sally without talking it over with Daddy. And then Mammy has always been rigid. Once she has made up her mind, then that is usually that.'

'So, you haven't much faith in the letters you sent?'

'To tell you the truth, Susie, no, I haven't,' Kate said. 'But if Sally can't go home, I am landed with her. I can hardly put her out on the streets.'

'No, course you can't. Hope you are wrong about those letters making a difference then. Is she very upset?'

'What do you think?' Kate said. 'She is still only sixteen. Anyway, after leaving her on her own all day, I can hardly do the same half the night as well, and so I won't be at the dance tonight either.'

'All right,' Susie said. 'I do understand that, but I might go anyway.'

'On your own?'

'No,' Susie said. 'Nick asked to take me when he came round last Sunday. We were going to call for you too.'

Kate felt strangely hurt and yet she knew that was an unreasonable way to feel. 'Well, now you don't have to,' she said briskly to hide her pique. 'And I hope it stays fine for you.'

Susie shrugged. She was sorry to upset Kate, but it couldn't be helped, and she went to the dance that night and tried to help David get over his disappointment that Kate hadn't been able to make it again.

Kate and Sally's energies and thoughts all over the weekend were totally centred on the reply their mother would make to their impassioned plea, but it didn't come until Tuesday, and in it she said that she had talked it over again with their father and he was in agreement that they stand firm. Sally was no longer their daughter and would not be welcomed at the farm, which she could never again consider her home.

'That's it then,' Kate said that night when she had read the letter. She handed it to Sally as she said, 'You are stuck with me in Birmingham, whether you want to be or not and things are going to be a bit different now.' She sighed and said, 'You will have to get a job for a start because my wages won't run to keeping the two of us. I'll start bringing in the *Mail* and *Despatch* at night and see what's going. After Christmas, we will have to look at finding a larger flat, because this will probably be a bit cramped with the two of us living in it on a permanent basis. We certainly need a bigger bed at least – I nearly landed on the floor again last night.'

'Sorry,' Sally said. 'I am causing you an awful lot of trouble, aren't I?'

'Yes,' Kate said candidly, 'you are, but I suppose this is what big sisters are for.'

In the end, it wasn't hard to find Sally a job. On the following Saturday morning, Sally had been buying food at the shops at Stockland Green for the evening meal. She'd crossed to the Co-op to buy the bread Kate had specifically asked for, when she saw an advert in the front of the Plaza cinema for a trainee usherette. It was exactly the type of place she would love to work in, and she turned to the commissionaire who was outside having a smoke. She wasn't surprised that he smiled at her – most men smiled at Sally – and so encouraged, she said, 'Do you know if they are still looking for an usherette?'

The man nodded. 'Oh yeah, they're still looking,' he said. 'Freda only left yesterday; she couldn't give proper notice see, because she had just had word that her mother had been knocked down by a car and was in a bad way. She just had to go quick like.'

'Oh I see.'

'If I were you, I would go in now and see the manager,' the man advised. 'Could you start straight away like?'

'Oh yes,' Sally said. 'I'm looking for a job and I'd love to work in the cinema.'

'Well, you have a good chance of being able to,' the man said. 'The boss has a soft spot for Irish girls and that's a lovely brogue you have. I'd go and see him if I were you. Name of Winters and he won't bite.'

And Sally found that he didn't bite and she was able to face Kate across the room a little later and tell her in a breathless voice that she had a full-time job as an usherette in the Plaza cinema. Kate couldn't have been more pleased because she knew it would be a job that Sally would enjoy and therefore would stick at. And however little the pay was, it was better than nothing at all. 'When do you start?' Kate asked her sister.

'Oh,' Sally said. 'That's the even better bit. See,

the girl I'm replacing left them in a bit of a fix, because her mother was knocked down and was in a bad way, the commissionaire said, and so she didn't work her notice or anything, and so the manager wants me to work as soon as possible – tonight if I can.'

'Oh,' Kate said. 'That is short notice. Still, I suppose you weren't doing anything else pressing and I assume they supply the uniform.'

'Yes, except for the white blouse,' Sally said. 'I'm supposed to buy that.'

'You'll need more than one white blouse if you are to be working there full time,' Kate said. 'And that will cost a pretty penny.'

'I've got some money, Kate,' Sally said. 'It was left over after I paid the fare to come here, but I never spent it because I was going to give it to you so you wouldn't have to pay the whole cost of me going back home. The only thing is, I haven't really got time to look for blouses now because he wants me to start at two o'clock and it's after eleven now.'

'I can loan you one for now,' Kate said. 'When are you working next?'

'Monday, and I start again at two o'clock. Every day I will start then and finish at eleven o'clock. I will get another two days off in the week, but that's worked out on a rota.'

'Oh, well that's all right,' Kate said. 'First thing Monday morning you go and get yourself a couple of white blouses, but if you have to start at two and won't get home until after eleven, then you'd better have something to eat now. I'll make up some sandwiches to take with you. Can't have you fainting through hunger on your first day.'

Sally took to the work at the cinema like a duck to water. She loved everything about being an usherette. She loved the smart uniform and spent ages in front of the mirror in the cloakroom where they changed getting it just so, and she especially liked the jaunty little cap that she set to the side of her head and secured with kirby grips. She didn't even mind serving out the ice creams and drinks where her good humour and ready smile endeared her to many, and sometimes she collected a good few tips. Each week the tips were counted out and spread out amongst them all, and that did mean that there were usually a couple of shillings extra to add to the twelve and six she got as a trainee to take home to Kate, but Kate allowed her to keep the extra and gave her another two shillings to add to it, and Sally was pleased enough with that.

As Sally was working most evenings, Susie and Kate started back on their old routine of going to the pictures at least once a week, sometimes to the Plaza where they would see Sally, and sometimes further afield, and also going back to the dances because Sally was usually working on a Friday anyway.

Kate was soon aware that things had changed while she'd been out of the scene for a bit. Nick and Susie were being seen as a couple, and she was soon aware of Nick's resentment towards her. Susie had told him that Kate's sister had moved in and was staying with her, and he had thought that might lessen Kate's dependence on

Susie. Susie said it wasn't like that, but to appease him she did promise that something would be decided by the New Year.

Christmas was only around the corner, and one day as the girls settled themselves in the tram on their way to work, Susie asked Kate if Sally still liked her job. 'Loves it,' Kate said. 'I imagine she thinks she has died and gone to heaven.'

'She certainly has a smile that near splits her face in two whenever we go there to see a film,' Susie said. 'But doesn't she mind seeing the same film over and over? I think that would really get on my wick after a while.'

'Are you kidding?' Kate said. 'She can't seem to get enough of the silver screen. I know what you mean – I would get bored too after a while – but it suits Sally well enough. She gets on well with the other usherettes too. She says a fair few of them are young like she is and they have great fun together sometimes. This is what she missed in Ireland, you see: friends her own age. She's told me she used to get very lonely.'

'Yeah, I see that,' Susie said. 'That would get anyone down after a while, I would imagine. And talking of Ireland, has there still been no movement from your mother?'

Kate shook her head. 'Every week she writes to me and never even asks about Sally and if I tell her anything she ignores it. She never even acknowledges the postal orders I send her.'

'Postal orders?'

'Yes,' Kate said. 'Every week I send her a two-shilling postal order. It's not my money, it's Sally's. She's paying back the money she took, but she is afraid to send it direct to Mammy in case she burns her letters or something without opening them.'

'Would she do that?'

'Oh, easily, I would say, if she was mad enough,' Kate said. 'She never replies to anything Sally sends anyway. When she started her job she wrote and told Mammy all about it, but she never got as much as a line back. She wrote again the next week and the next, but she has given up now.'

'Well, I should imagine that it's hard to keep writing and getting no reply.'

'Yeah, I'd say so.'

'Maybe when she pays back all the money, your mother will relent?'

Kate sighed. 'Maybe,' she said, but she said it doubtfully, and Susie asked, 'Does Sally still get upset about it?'

'Not now so much,' Kate said. 'But she used to, as you know, and that's possibly leading to another problem.'

'How's that?'

'Well, she was crying one day at work and the trainee projectionist, a young man she said is called Phil Reynard heard her, and in her words was "very kind" to her. Next thing they are walking out together.'

'Gosh, she's a quick worker.'

'I'll say.'

'Well, what's wrong with that?' Susie said, laughing at the look on Kate's face.

'Well, it's just that she's only … she's just…'

'She's nearly seventeen,' Susie said. 'And a very pretty girl. Oh, come on, Kate,' she burst out. 'You might think there is only one man on the planet, but you can't expect Sally to feel the same. I should imagine she was taught right from wrong, as we all were, so what are you worried about?'

'I don't want to have to police my sister,' Kate said. 'That should be my mother's job.'

'Well, she's not going to do that, is she? She's made that clear.'

'I know,' Kate agreed with a sigh. 'And the point is, if she did relent now, I think Sally would refuse to go home anyway. Even before this Phil Reynard, she was enjoying Birmingham a great deal. He is just another thing to keep her here, and so after Christmas we really must look for a larger place.'

'I can see that,' Susie said. 'I'll help you look, if you like.'

'Thanks,' Kate said, getting to her feet as the bus pulled into their stop. 'I just might hold you to it.'

FIVE

Kate knew that if this antagonism her mother had for Sally was to abate, even slightly, then surely Christmas was the time to build bridges and heal wounds. Though she doubted that Sally would want to return to Ireland to live, she knew she hated being on such bad terms with their parents. And so Kate wrote her mother a long letter and mentioned Sally a lot and said how helpful she was and how mature she was becoming and told her that she was enjoying her work as an usherette at the cinema and hoped it would help thaw her mother's anger a little.

Sally thought the same way as Kate did, and was more than glad of the tips she was getting, which had increased slightly as Christmas drew nearer, because the extra money meant she was able to buy her mother the softest cardigan in pale blue and a rugged navy blue jumper for her father and a spinning top for James. She packed them up with a card in plenty of time, but she never had any acknowledgement that they had even been received.

Philomena did write to Kate, though, and thanked her for the presents she had sent: a pair of warm slippers for both parents and a small toy horse and cart for her brother. Other news in the letter sent consternation running through Kate, though, and she couldn't wait to get to the tram stop that morning and discuss it with Susie.

It was the day before Christmas Eve and the first thing Susie said as they got on the tram was, 'Has Sally heard anything from your mother?'

Kate shook her head. 'I did hope that Mammy would relent with Christmas approaching,' she said. 'After all, Sally has paid back nearly all the money she took and she has said how truly sorry she was, still is, and she also sent them lovely presents.'

'There's always tomorrow,' Susie reminded her friend.

Kate shook her head. 'I think that she would have heard before this. Mammy sent me a long letter inside the Christmas card telling me all the news and when I had read that for a moment or two I wished I hadn't.'

'Why?' Susie cried. 'What on earth did she say to you?'

'She told me that Tim is walking out with a girl called Maggie Mulligan,' Kate said miserably, and added, 'Maybe you might remember Maggie? She was about our age.'

Susie thought for a minute and said, 'Wasn't she the girl whose plaits were always coming unravelled?'

'That's the one,' Kate said with a rueful smile. 'The schoolmaster used to say that by the time the bell rang at the end of the day she looked as if she'd been pulled through a hedge backwards. Anyway, I would imagine she has full control of her hair now.'

'And you say her and Tim are walking out together?' Susie asked, but she spoke gently because she knew how Kate still felt about her cousin.

Kate nodded dumbly and then said, 'I could almost feel Mammy's relief because that's it, really, isn't it? When you walk out with someone in Ireland you are almost committed. Maybe you remember that?'

'A little bit, I do,' Susie said, with a brief nod. 'But really–'

'And added to that,' Kate said a little bitterly, 'Maggie is a farmer's daughter, like me, but her father has no sons and Maggie is the eldest and so, once married, Tim will eventually have control of the Mulligan farm as well as his own. That will be the reason he has behaved like this.'

'Like what?' Susie said. 'In all fairness, he has done nothing wrong.' And then as Kate made no response, she went on, 'Ah, come on, Kate, you accepted that you had no future together when you came to join me in Birmingham. And I can quite understand your mother's relief, can't you?'

Kate sighed and nodded. 'Yes,' she said. 'Course I can, because it is so final now. Mammy said that Aunt Bridget is very relieved too, because he had shown no interest in any of the girls around until now. But he did say to me once that he wanted to get married one day and have children, ideally a son to take over the farm after his day.'

'Oh, farmers set great store by that,' Susie said. 'You wrote and told me how cock-a-hoop your father was when James was born, and I saw that for myself when I went on holiday that year. He was only a few months old and you would think him the greatest child that had ever been born.'

'Oh, yes, our parents were very like that at first,'

Kate agreed. 'And I understand that Tim might have designs that way too, but do you think he has forgotten already the passion I know we shared.'

Susie had never really known Tim well, and she only had Kate's version of the forbidden love that they had never even spoken of. So she didn't really know whether with Tim it was 'out of sight out of mind', or that he still had a lingering love for her best friend, but she knew what she wanted to hear. So she said, 'I doubt either of you will ever forget that, because for both of you it was a heady first love, but you could do nothing about it. Tim has accepted that and moved on.'

'As I must do,' Kate said. 'That's what you're saying, isn't it?'

'What I am saying, Kate,' Susie said firmly, 'is I want you to take life in both hands and learn to live it to the full, or else you will exist in some sort of half-life, wishing things had been different.'

Kate had no time to answer because the tram had pulled up at their stop and they were soon surrounded by workmates. It was as they made their way home that she had any free time alone with Susie again and, as if there was some sort of tacit agreement between them, Susie kept off the subject of Tim Munroe and asked Kate instead about her sister and Phil, the trainee projectionist.

'Did you mention this "Great Romance" to your mother?'

'I did not,' Kate retorted. 'I said not a word about it because that would have blotted Sally's copybook right and proper. I'm sure Mammy thinks that she is about seven years old, certainly not old enough to have an eye for the boys.'

'Be fair,' Susie said. 'It is only the one boy she has the eye for.'

'I know,' Kate said. 'And maybe I am worrying unnecessarily, but it is very intense at the moment, I think.'

'But they are working nearly every night,' Susie protested.

'Ah, but you see they have two days off in the week, don't forget, and they do their level best to try and wangle to have the same days off,' Kate said. 'And another thing, one of the girls upstairs said she was sent home from work bad last week, and as she was going up the stairs a young man passed her. I mean, we know everyone in the flats, and knowing that Sally was probably on her own, she watched where he was going. And he knocked on our door and she said Sally was obviously expecting him because the door opened very quickly and she said Sally greeted him very affectionately.'

Susie smiled. 'I suppose you asked her about it?'

'I surely did,' Kate said. 'And she freely admitted that Phil called for her most mornings. She had not a whit of shame or embarrassment about it at all, and said that she hadn't bothered to mention it to me because she didn't think it was important, and then went on to say that in case I had any other spies in the streets that this Phil walks her home at night too. In fact, she said he will not allow her to walk home alone.'

'He has a point,' Susie said. 'It could be dangerous for her because it's late when she finishes and you get all types on the streets these days.'

'Yeah,' Kate said. 'I agree that could be dangerous, but being alone with a young man in the dark of the night is just as worrying, in my opinion.'

'She is a young woman with needs of her own,' Susie said. 'And it isn't bad to want someone special in your life. It's what everyone wants deep down, isn't it?'

Kate didn't answer and Susie went on: 'Don't you want a home of your own, a family of your own one day?'

'I suppose.'

'Well, why don't you get to know other men? Give them a bit of encouragement. You might be pleasantly surprised.'

'You're talking about David Burton, aren't you?'

'Not particularly,' Susie said. 'But at least you like him a bit, don't you?'

'Course I like him, but liking isn't loving, is it?'

'Maybe not, but it's a good starting point,' Susie said. 'And I dare say with a bit of effort on your part you could grow to love David Burton.'

'I thought we were discussing Sally,' Kate said.

'Well, if you ask me, Sally is doing all right,' Susie said. 'She has certainly grown up a lot in the short time she has been here and she is having fun and enjoying herself and where's the harm in that?'

'I know but–'

'But nothing, Kate,' Susie said. 'Look, we are only young the once and you are letting your life float past.'

'I'm not,' Kate protested. 'We're out tonight, aren't we? And it's a Christmas dance, with spot prizes and everything. So how can you say I am letting my life float past? And I never seem to be short of partners at the dances – you have to agree with that.'

She was right too, but Susie said, 'I know, Kate, but sometimes it is nice to have someone special.'

'I don't feel the need for anyone special just now,' Kate said dogmatically. 'But if David Burton asks me up, then I will dance with him.'

'He'll ask you all right,' Susie said assuredly. 'But you won't dance with him exclusively, will you?'

'I doubt it,' Kate said.

'If he asked you to just dance with him, or to dance with him most of the time, then would you?'

'Give over, Susie.'

'What's the matter with you anyway?' Susie demanded. 'The way you are going on you'll end up a crabbed old maid.'

That made Kate smile, and, as the tram pulled up at their stop, she said, 'All right then, I'll think about it, now stop nagging me. Anyway, how about going down the Bull Ring tomorrow?'

Susie knew that Kate was trying to change the subject. She was a dab hand at doing that, and she could be aggravatingly stubborn at times. 'Well, do you or not?' Kate demanded. 'Surely you're not sulking because I can't be filled with lustful passion at the mere mention of David Burton's name?'

Even Susie had to smile at that, and Christmas Eve in the Bull Ring was not to be missed, especially if it fell on a Saturday as this did, and so she said, 'All right then.'

'You can help me choose some little thing for Sally for Christmas,' Kate said. 'Whatever she says, she is bound to feel it, the first Christmas away from home. I know we have been invited to your house for dinner again this year, but I'd like her to have something to open when she comes home from Mass.'

'Oh, you're on,' Susie said as they alighted from the tram. 'I love choosing presents for people. Anyway, see you later.'

'Yeah, I'll be up about half seven,' Kate said, and with a wave they went their different ways.

Kate had planned what she was going to wear that night, having bought a dress from the Rag Market the previous week. She'd tried it on at home so that Sally could see it. She valued her sister's opinion because she knew all about fashion from watching all the stars on the screen. Sally was really enthusiastic about the full-length silk dress in the softest pink. Apart from the ruffles at the neck, the dress was plain and sleeveless; it fell in shimmering folds to the floor.

'Oh, Kate, that's so gorgeous,' Sally enthused.

'Do you really think so?'

'I know so.'

'Susie thought I should have something with a fuller skirt to accentuate my waist. She had one like that with little grey and black flowers all over it, with big butterfly sleeves. It's ever so pretty.'

'So is that,' Sally said. 'You look like a Grecian goddess – only someone as slim as you could wear a dress like that.'

'That's what the woman on the stall said,' Kate said to Sally. 'She said she thought she might have had it left on her hands.'

'I'm not surprised,' Sally said. 'It would look awful on someone my shape, and I don't think even Susie could carry it off.'

'If you're sure then?'

'I am,' Sally said. 'The only thing is – unless you are dancing every minute – your arms might get very cold.'

'Oh, no, I've got this to wear after I've taken my coat off,' Kate said, and withdrew a silver fur stole from another bag. 'It's artificial,' she said. 'But in a way I prefer that.'

'Yeah, I know what you mean,' Sally said. 'But that settles it really. Kate, you will be the belle of the ball.'

'Don't be so silly,' Kate said, colouring at the unaccustomed praise. But it did mean that that night she could dress with confidence, knowing that she looked good, and she did cause a bit of a stir when she went into the dance and she saw David's eyes widen in appreciation. She smiled at him as he approached and put two hands on her shoulders as he said, 'Kate, you look beautiful, absolutely stunning.'

She couldn't be anything else but pleased, any woman would feel the same, but the gesture did not go unnoticed. It was like a stamp of ownership – many of the other men were aware of this and so gave Kate a wide berth. She noticed, but she liked David too much to want to upset him, and he had made no secret of how he felt about her. So David got his heart's desire as Katie

100

danced almost exclusively with him. He knew she would rather dance with him than not dance at all, and especially as the band were playing much of the swing music seeping over from America, performed by people like Duke Ellington, Tommy Dorsey and, of course, Glenn Miller.

And David was a superb dancer and a proper gentleman and very attentive, and it was as they were taking a well-earned breather that he said, 'Nick and Susie seem to be getting on all right.'

'Yes, yes, they do.'

'We could do the same.'

'What?'

'You know, get on better,' David said, and Kate heard the tentative eagerness in his voice.

'I don't think we could get on better,' Kate said, looking into David's deep brown eyes. 'We get on very well now, but that isn't the same as loving someone.'

'I know that,' David said. 'But I have enough love for both of us.'

Kate smiled a grim smile and shook her head. 'I don't think it works like that.'

'Look,' David said, deciding to lay his cards on the table. 'Tomorrow night, Nick is taking Susie with him to see the pantomime of *Sleeping Beauty* at the Hippodrome in the town.'

'Oh,' Kate said – she loved pantomimes. They were such fun and very Christmassy. Susie had taken Kate to see *Cinderella* the first Christmas she had been in England, and she had been amazed because she had never seen anything like it. Plays of any sort were sparse in Donegal, but plays where the Prince Charming that Cinderella falls in love with is actually a girl and the old stepmother really a man was out of her understanding. When she found that the audiences were encouraged to boo the baddies and cheer the goodies, she had been astounded. She had soon got into the spirit of it, however, and had been as vocal as everybody else. She had a sudden longing to do it again.

'Point is,' David continued, 'I will be at a loose end and so will you, and it is Christmas Eve, so I was wondering if you wanted to see the pantomime as well. As friends,' he said, holding up his hand. 'Scout's honour.'

A smile dimpled Kate's cheek and David felt as if his heart had stopped beating. 'You are a fool, David, and I'd love to go with you, but I'd better say no,' she said, but had to bend her head so that she couldn't see the disappointment that flooded his face.

'Kate,' David said, 'I've never asked you this before, but is there someone else?'

Kate thought of Tim, the man she had given her heart to but who would soon belong to Maggie Mulligan, and she shook her head. 'No,' she said quietly.

'Then, why not come out with me?'

Why not indeed? said the little inner voice inside her head. *I'm not agreeing to marry him just because we watch a pantomime together.* 'All right then,' she said. She saw relief light up his eyes as she added, 'Though I doubt we'll get tickets for tomorrow night's performance at this late stage.'

'No,' David said. 'So it's a good job that Nick and I bought the tickets a fortnight ago.'

Kate stared at him in shocked surprise. 'You were very sure of yourself,' she remarked.

'Oh, no,' David said with a heartfelt sigh. 'I wasn't sure at all. I just hoped you'd agree.'

'What if I'd refused?'

'Then I would have given them away,' David said. 'I mean, I could hardly go and sit beside Nick and Susie on my own. I'd have felt right awkward.'

Kate knew he would and she thought she had made the right decision. She was even more certain of this when David took her hand and led her on to the floor for the Last Waltz. She went willingly and felt they fitted beautifully together, but when David held her close and she felt his heart banging in his chest, she felt quite protective towards him and didn't fully understand why.

It was when she went to retrieve her coat at the end of the night that she saw Susie again, and then she took in her friend's slightly dishevelled appearance and she knew what she had been doing with Nick. Susie, however, was more interested to learn that Kate had eventually agreed to go out with David. 'At last you realize that the man hasn't got three heads.'

Kate laughed. 'I never thought he had,' she said.

'And maybe when you go out with David you will find yourself bowled off your feet,' Susie continued.

'And maybe I won't.'

'Well, you do as you please,' Susie said, 'for I intend to enjoy myself; and, so far, this Christmas is shaping up to be one of the best I have ever had.'

Kate had never actually been on a date before and she dressed with care. She seldom bought much for herself, but she had seen another snip of a bargain in the Rag Market earlier that day when she had gone in with Susie, who urged her to buy it. And so she was wearing a calf-length dress in muted shades of blue when she opened the door. The dipped neckline was edged in lace, the skirt was full from the nipped-in waist and the butterfly sleeves were the height of fashion; again David thought she looked stunning and knew he would be proud to be seen walking out with her.

He had also made an effort, and he too looked incredibly smart. Kate noticed the cuffs of the pure white shirt peeping from the sleeves of his tailored overcoat and the smart tie at his neck. She also saw his light brown and rather unruly hair had been tamed and darkened with Brylcreem. His smile was so wide it lit up his whole face and made his eyes sparkle for he was hardly able to believe that Kate had at last agreed to go out with him and he held out the flowers with hands that shook slightly.

Kate blushed as she took the flowers from him and that just made her ever prettier. 'Oh, David,' she said, 'what a lovely surprise!' and she asked him in while she found water. When she disappeared into the little kitchenette, he took the opportunity to look around the room. 'You have it nice,' he said when she returned with the flowers in a vase.

Kate wrinkled her nose. 'Bit small now,' she said. 'Though it was all right for one, it's cramped now my sister lives here too.'

'She must be company for you, though.'

'Not really,' Kate said. 'She's seldom here in the evenings because she works as an usherette in the Plaza. And to be honest, I never envisaged her living here at all.'

'Oh?' David said, his eyebrows arched in enquiry.

'Oh, I'll tell you the whole tale as we go,' Kate said. 'We're meeting Susie and Nick at Stockland Green and we had best be off now or we'll be late.'

So, as they walked together that cold, frosty night, Kate didn't object when David linked her arm and pulled her tight against him as she told him of Sally's flight from their farmhouse in Donegal. 'And she had told you nothing about what she intended?' David asked.

'No, not a hint of it,' Kate said. 'She was waiting for me when I came home from work. I thought our parents would have her back because she wrote and said how sorry she was, but they won't.'

'So you're stuck with her?'

'That's about the strength of it,' Kate said.

'You must get on all right,' David said. 'I do nothing but fight with my brother, Lawrence. There would often be wigs on the green if we shared a place.'

'We don't argue much,' Kate said. 'But then with different work patterns we don't see that much of each other.'

'And does she like Birmingham?'

Kate nodded. 'She loves it,' she said. 'She loves her job and the fact she has money in her pocket, which in itself is quite a novel experience, and she can't get over all the entertainment there is for her to enjoy when she does have time off. But I think, most important of all, she's become very friendly with the trainee projectionist at the cinema, and I definitely don't think she would like leaving him.'

'Isn't she rather young for that?'

'Probably,' Kate said. 'But what can I do about that?'

'Not a lot,' David agreed. 'What about her elder sister?'

'What do you mean?' Kate said, though she knew full well what David was getting at. And then, with relief, she saw Susie and Nick waiting at the tram stop and she said, 'Come on, let's hurry. It's too cold to stand for long in this weather,' and the opportunity to talk further was lost.

In the interval, Susie and Kate headed off to the Ladies', and Susie barely waited till the door shut behind them before saying, 'Well?'

'Well what?'

'Come on, Kate. I've been dying to ask you.'

'Ask me what?'

'Don't be stupid,' Susie snapped. 'You and David, of course.'

'What about me and David?'

'You know,' Susie said. 'You looked ever so lovey-dovey to me when you arrived at the tram station earlier.'

'It seemed sensible. It was cold, that was all.'

'And was it sensible of him to buy you a whole box of chocolates?'

'No,' Kate said. 'That was far from sensible. I didn't expect him to do that and he is very generous, but I know what it is to truly love someone.'

'D'you know?' said Susie. 'I'm not sure that you do. It might not be love that you feel for Tim Munroe at all, but infatuation, probably made all the sweeter because you knew from the start he was unobtainable.'

Kate stared at Susie and Susie knew she had hit home. For the first time she saw doubt flit across Kate's face as she digested Susie's words and wondered if there was an element of truth in them.

'I mean, you have never been courted by Tim – walked out together or anything, have you?' Susie asked, knowing they hadn't. 'The most you two have done is gaze at each other. You don't know anything about him really.'

'Don't be daft, we nearly grew up together.'

'I know that. So you know Tim the child, the boy, but nothing at all about Tim the man. I bet when you got to a certain age, your mother at least made quite sure you were never left alone together.'

Kate nodded, because that had been true.

'Well, here there's a man that you have admitted you like and who more than likes you. I mean, you've really enjoyed yourself tonight, haven't you?'

'Oh, yes,' Kate said. 'And the pantomime is great, but we should really be getting back because the first bell has just gone.'

'I know,' Susie said. 'We'll go now, but you will think about what I said?'

Kate nodded. 'I will,' she promised, and she would because – quite apart from anything else –

she felt she owed her friend a favour, and knew it would make life easier for the budding relationship between Susie and Nick if she agreed to go out with David.

SIX

The next morning, Kate got up in a really good mood, remembering how much she had enjoyed the previous evening. The day before, as well as getting the dress for herself, she had bought Sally a lovely Fair Isle-patterned hat, gloves and scarf set for Christmas. They had never got much in the way of presents in Donegal, and any they did have they left until after Mass to open, but the weather was so raw that morning that Kate decided to give Sally her presents before they left for church because she knew it would keep her a lot warmer, especially as they couldn't have a warming cup of tea or a bite to eat as they were both taking communion.

Sally had really sad eyes that morning and Kate thought she was probably thinking of their home. She knew that her younger sister had really hoped that her mother would write to say she had forgiven her, especially as she had paid back nearly all the money she had taken, but she had received nothing. When Kate gave her the present, Sally was so overwhelmed with sudden love and gratitude for her sister that tears stood out in her eyes. Kate was so moved by Sally's response that she said, 'You might as well have the other things as well,' and gave her the set of lace hankies and a little bottle of California Poppy perfume.

'Oh, Kate, you are so lovely,' Sally said, dabbing

the perfume behind her ears immediately. 'I have things for you too.'

'You shouldn't have spent money on me,' Kate said. 'I told you not to. You don't earn that much.'

'I know I don't,' Sally said. 'But I owe you so much that I would buy for you if I couldn't afford even a card for anyone else. And ooh, I can't really wait until after Mass to give them to you either, so you must have them now.'

Kate was thrilled because the silk stockings were of the best quality and the slippers were fur lined, and she exclaimed in delight, 'My feet will be as warm as toast in these.'

'Yeah, well, I saw your others were thin and very raggedy looking.'

'It was one of the first things I bought when I came to Birmingham three years ago,' Kate said. 'Because my feet used to ache so much after standing all day on the factory floor and I have never thought to replace them. In fact, I like these new ones so much I will take them with me to Susie's house and wear them all afternoon.'

'Good,' Sally said with a large grin on her face. 'But hadn't we better be making our way to Mass now, or we'll be late.'

'Oh, yes,' Kate said. 'You're right, and it might be hard to hurry because I think it's quite icy out there.'

It was. The cold was the sort that almost burnt the back of the throat and the frost sparkled and crunched underfoot, and they linked arms for greater warmth. The streets were quiet and the only ones out were people like themselves making their way to a church of some kind. Many of them greeted the two girls as they walked past.

When they had gone a little way, Sally, her voice slightly muffled because of the scarf wrapped around her mouth, said to Kate, 'So, who were the flowers from?'

'Tell you later; too cold now,' Kate said, puffs of white spilling from her mouth as she spoke.

'That's not fair,' Sally protested. 'When I got in last night, they were sitting there in the vase and there was no sign of you. And when you did come in you said you were too tired to discuss it. Then this morning when I asked again you said we haven't time. So, what's the big mystery?'

Kate looked down at her younger sister and decided she might as well know. It wasn't as if she was doing anything wrong. 'They were from a friend,' she said.

'I guessed that much,' Sally said with a grin. 'Not many enemies would give you a bunch of flowers.' And then she put her head on one side and asked in mock innocence, 'Was he male, this friend?' Then she exclaimed, 'Oh, Kate, he must have been because you've gone all red.'

'No. 1 haven't,' Kate protested. 'That's just the cold reddening my cheeks, and, yes, Sally, a male friend gave me the flowers. His name is David Burton, and last night he took me to the pantomime.'

'Thank heaven for that,' Sally said. 'I thought you were turning into a right old maid.'

'Whatever gave you that idea?'

'Well,' said Sally, 'in your letters home you told us of all the things you and Susie got up to and all the places you went to. Never once did you mention any men you might have met, never mind go out with. And since I have been here it's been the same.'

'Maybe I'm choosy,' Kate said. 'And don't go out with the first man who asks me.'

'Is that a jibe at me and Phil?'

'Not especially, no.'

'Because I do like him, you know,' Sally said. 'I didn't just go out with him because he asked me. Anyway, what's this David like?'

Kate shrugged, 'He's just ordinary, I suppose.'

'Oh, Kate,' Sally cried in exasperation. 'Talking to you is like pulling teeth. Is he short or tall? Fat or thin? And what colour are his eyes, his hair? Go on,' she demanded. 'Describe him to me.'

'Don't see why I should,' Kate said with a smile, 'or why you are so interested; but I suppose he is quite tall, certainly a head taller than me and on the lean side. His hair is sort of, almost light brown, though he said that it was pure blond when he was a boy and it has darkened since he grew up.'

'And his eyes?'

'Oh, they are really deep brown.'

'And is he a good kisser?' Sally asked. 'What are his lips like?'

'Sally, what a question to ask!' Kate said, clearly shocked.

'Why?' Sally asked. 'You did kiss him I suppose?'

Kate wondered if the chaste peck on the cheek that she allowed David counted and thought not, and so her answer to Sally was, 'That is none of your business and something we shouldn't be

112

talking about on our way to Mass on Christmas morning.'

Sally smiled to herself, but said nothing more. She didn't want to risk Kate being in a bad mood, because after they'd eaten dinner with Susie and her family she had agreed to meet Phil. And then, after spending the afternoon together, she was having tea at his mother's house. She wasn't at all sure how Kate would react to the news.

Kate wasn't at all impressed with Sally's plans and told her so as they walked to Susie's later. 'I don't see what's the matter with it.' Sally said, genuinely puzzled. 'Or why you should be in such a tizzy.'

'I think it is most incredibly rude and I don't understand why you can't see that for yourself.'

'Well, I can't,' Sally said. 'And I don't think Susie will. Or her parents, if they are anything like her. It's all right for you and Susie. You will have two more days to spend with your boy-friends if you want to. Both Phillip and I are back at work tomorrow.'

Kate knew that Sally had a point. Because Christmas Eve and Christmas Day had fallen on a Saturday and Sunday, and as they were days they wouldn't have been at work anyway, they had Monday and Tuesday off in lieu. However, the cinemas were opening again the following day, so Sally was only off work on Christmas Day itself. Ignoring the reference to David being her boyfriend, Kate said, 'All right, I see that you have a point there. But do you think it sensible to go to Phillip's for tea and meet his parents and everything? I mean, you don't know him that well and isn't it quite a formal thing to do, as if you had some sort of understanding.'

'Phillip wants me to meet his mother,' Sally said. 'They only live in Bleak Hill and that leads off Marsh Hill, so it's no distance from the Masons'.'

'What about Phil's father?' Kate snapped. 'Doesn't he want to meet you too?'

'Well, he might,' Sally said with a slight shrug, 'but that would be difficult because he died when Phillip was only small. Apparently, he had two brothers and a sister and they all died of TB as children – and then his father died of the same thing. It was only Phil, the baby, who survived.'

'Sorry, Sally,' Kate said. 'Phil's mother must have suffered greatly.'

'I'm sure she did,' Sally said. 'And Phil is very protective of her because it has been just the two of them for years and he doesn't want to leave his mother alone all Christmas Day. He has told her all about me and she says she'd like to meet me, so he thought Christmas afternoon might be a good time.'

'Yes, I see all that,' Kate said. 'And it is a nice thought, but in a way it does put things on a more formal footing. Surely you can see that? You are really too young for that kind of commitment.'

Sally shook her head. 'I don't think either of them sees any more significance in it than me just going for tea on Christmas Day,' she said. 'Maybe it's different in Birmingham. I mean, Dulcie, who is only a year older than me, is dating a boy from the next street, and the families have known each other for ever. She was in and out of the house all the time anyway as she was best friends with the daughter long before she was of an age to date her older brother.'

'Yes, but it isn't the same for you, is it?' Kate said. 'And his mother could well be possessive with Phillip being her only son and that.'

Sally nodded. 'I worked that out too and in a way it's understandable,' she said. 'And it will still be nice to meet her because Phillip talks about her a lot. Anyway, I've told Phil I would go and so I am going, Kate, whether you approve or not, and regardless too of how Susie feels about it.' She hesitated for a moment and then added, 'I bet she won't mind, though, but to tell you the truth I am a bit nervous of having dinner with the Masons because I don't know any of them except Susie. I know she has two brothers, but I've never seen them – not that I know of, anyway.'

'Yes, she has,' Kate said. 'They're called Derek and Martin and they came to Ireland when they were young, but you'd not remember that. I only have vague recollections of them then. In fact, I only took more notice of Susie when she came home to live, the time her mother was so sick.'

'So what are they like?'

Kate smiled, 'Oh, all right, you know. They tease a bit, like most lads seem to. There'll probably leave you alone, but I am considered fair game now they know me so well. And Susie's parents, Frank and Mary, are just great – so kind and generous and just ... well, just lovely. Tell you, Sally, it would have been far harder for me to settle down in Birmingham if I hadn't had the

Masons to rely on.'

'Do you call them Frank and Mary?'

Kate nodded her head. 'They insisted on it,' she said. 'Wouldn't have any truck with Mr and Mrs Mason. Anyway, we're nearly here now, so you will see the set-up for yourself.'

Kate turned into a drive from the tree-lined road as she spoke and Sally looked at the semi-detached house with bay windows set behind a neat hedge. Susie was in the doorway waiting to welcome them.

The whole family made much of Sally, particularly Mary and Frank, and Kate guessed that Susie had told them about the circumstances that had led to Sally arriving in Birmingham in the first place, and their mother's reaction to it. This was their way of making Christmas slightly better for her, and Kate warmed to them even more as she saw Sally relax.

As usual, the dinner at the Masons' house was sumptuous, and the talk and banter around the table as much fun and as riotous as ever. As they were tucking into the plum pudding and brandy sauce, Sally told the Mason family of her plans for that afternoon. No one seemed to mind.

'Christmas afternoon is getting more flexible as we all get older,' Susie said later as she and Kate washed the dishes in the kitchen. 'My brothers are doing their own thing too, and, as my mother said, she would never like it said that she got in the way of true love.'

'It's hardly that at Sally's age,' Kate said.

'Can't tell with matters of the heart,' Susie said.

'Just how old were you when you found that you loved Tim Munroe?'

'That was totally different,' Kate protested. 'I had known Tim all my life.'

'I don't see that that has got anything to do with it,' Susie said. 'All I know is that, whether it was the real thing or imagined, that love was strong enough to stop you looking for anyone else. Look how you were with David Burton.'

'What do you mean?' Kate demanded. 'I was very nice to him.'

'Not nice enough to agree to go to the New Year's Eve Ball with him, though?'

'Well, no.'

'Yeah, well, that has put me in a very delicate position,' Susie said.

Kate raised her eyebrows. 'I can't see how it could have done.'

'Well, because I thought you would agree. I mean, you seemed to be getting on very well at the pantomime,' Susie said. 'Anyway, when Nick asked me to go with him, I said yes.'

A cold feeling of loneliness stole over Kate suddenly. 'Is it serious between you?' she asked in a bleak-sounding tone.

Susie shrugged. 'Serious enough, I suppose. We are meeting up tomorrow as a matter of fact.' And then she caught sight of Kate's face and said quite sharply, 'It isn't a crime, Kate, and I do like him well enough. Anyway, I was just telling you about the ball because we have always gone together. I mean, there's nothing to stop you walking up with us, but you'll have to be sort of prepared that we might not be coming back the same time.'

Kate looked at her friend's shining face and saw that, though she was a little embarrassed telling Kate this, she was as determined as Sally had been. She faced the prospect that someone was becoming more important in Susie's life than her; there was someone she would rather spend time with. It was Nick now, but if not him it would be someone else. Kate found that it was with little enthusiasm that she looked forward to 1939.

The next day, after Sally had left for work, sporting the beautiful brooch Phillip had bought her for Christmas, Kate found that she was at a loose end. Normally, she would have wandered up to the Masons', but she couldn't do that when Susie had told her that she was meeting Nick.

She busied herself at first, tidying and cleaning a flat that wasn't really dirty, and eventually sat down with a cup of tea and one of the mince pies Mary had insisted she take home. Alone with her thoughts, she surveyed her future and didn't really like what she saw.

She suddenly felt more achingly lonely than she thought it was possible to be. She knew that she could no longer continue to count on the Mason family and Susie in the way she had been doing since she had moved to Birmingham. She knew she would always be immensely fond of all of them, and between her and Susie there was a special bond, but it had become almost too easy to rely on them.

Then she thought about David Burton, whom she did like immensely. She didn't feel for him the way she still felt about Tim, but Susie was right: it was time for her to grow up and face facts. She decided she would tell Susie the very next day and make arrangements to go with David to the New Year's Eve Ball after all.

Susie was very pleased to see her friend standing on the doorstep the following day and she pulled her inside quickly out of the cold as she said, 'Oh, Kate, I am so glad to see you. I have lots to tell you, but the first thing is that Nick took me to meet his family yesterday.'

'Oh,' Kate said, genuinely shocked. 'I had no idea that things were as serious as that.'

'They're not,' Susie said. 'Well, I mean, the more I see of Nick, the more I like him and that, but these days just because you meet a chap's parents doesn't mean you will be getting engaged the next minute or anything.'

Kate remembered her younger sister had said something similar about how things were arranged in Birmingham, but she still said, 'It signifies far more than that in Ireland.'

'Maybe it does here in some rural backwaters,' Susie conceded. 'But such ideas are very outdated in today's world. Anyway, his family were very nice and welcoming, his mother in particular. She said she had thought that Nick would never settle down and nothing would please her more than to see me and Nick together.'

'Sally seemed to really get on with Phil's mother as well,' Kate said. 'Seems like everyone is getting fixed up.'

'And how about you, Kate?' Susie said gently. 'Did you think any more about what I said on

Christmas Day?'

Kate nodded her head. 'I did a lot of mind-searching yesterday and let's just say I have come to my senses at last,' she said. 'You were right. Tim is part of my past and I must leave him there and move on.'

'So, you will go out with David?'

Kate nodded. 'If he still wants to, I will.'

Susie shook her head. 'I think I can guarantee that he will,' she said. 'Tell you something else. I didn't think I loved Nick, not at first anyway, but it has sort of grown on me. I was asking my mother about this love business the other day and she said that liking someone was just as important as loving them. She said that you can love a person to distraction but if you don't like them as well you are setting yourself up for a life of misery.'

'So I suppose if we like them in the first place we are in for a life of happiness?' Kate said with a grin.

'Something like that,' Susie said. 'And how about putting this to the test straight away? Nick wants to take me to the pictures tonight.'

'Well, *Having a Wonderful Time* is on at the Plaza,' Kate said. 'Sally says it's just great.'

'She says that about everything.'

Kate gave a short laugh for she had to agree with Susie. 'I suppose she does,' she said. 'I wouldn't exactly call her the discerning type, but it has got Ginger Rogers in it.'

'Yes, and Douglas Fairbanks,' Susie said with a sigh.

'Ooh, yes – isn't he just so handsome?'

'I'll say,' Susie said. 'So, are you up for it then?

120

Will you go out with David tonight?'

Kate hesitated, but only for a moment or two before she said, 'Yes, I will.'

'Oh, good for you,' Susie cried, throwing her arms around her friend. 'I am so happy for you and I know David will be too.'

David was so happy that Kate felt humbled and she did have a truly wonderful time. Sally was right for once – the film was well worth seeing – and they came out on a high. When David saw Kate home and she asked him in for a drink before he went on his way, he didn't hesitate.

'I've nothing stronger than tea, I'm afraid.'

'Tea will do me fine,' David said.

'And you can help me share that second box of chocolates you bought me,' Kate said. 'You must stop spoiling me like this. If I was to eat all the chocolates you bought I would soon be the size of a house.'

'Ah, but you don't know how long I've wanted to spoil you,' David said, and Kate was surprised at the lump that lodged in her throat at the sincerity in David's voice.

They were still sitting talking, mainly discussing the film, when Sally came home. Phillip Reynard took her as far as the door of the flat. Hearing them bid each other goodnight, Kate suddenly realized that she should at least meet the young man her younger sister was so fond of, so she invited him in. She could see how pleased her sister was by the big beam plastered across her face as she took Phillip's hand and drew him into the room.

Kate told Susie all about it on her way to work

the following morning. She also admitted that she had seldom had such a good time as she'd had with David at the cinema.

'And did you ask David in this time?' Susie wanted to know.

'I did,' Kate said. 'In fact, I went further than that, because when Phillip brought Sally home a little later I asked him in as well.'

'Golly,' Susie said. 'That is a turn-up for the book. I thought you didn't really approve.'

Kate shrugged. 'I haven't any right to try and control Sally's life. On the whole I think she has turned out far better than I thought she would when she first arrived, and really they are doing no harm. As he is her choice, I thought I ought to get to know him better.'

'And?'

'He is a very kindly young man,' Kate said. 'And one who is extremely caring towards his mother. Apart from that, he had an open face. You know the sort of thing I mean?'

'Yeah,' Susie said. 'So, he looks quite honest and genuine?'

'Yeah,' Kate said. 'And he's got dark blond hair, these lovely dark brown eyes and full lips.' And here she smiled and said, 'Sally would probably describe them as kissable.'

'Really?'

'Well, she asked me if David had kissable lips the first time I went out with him.'

'Oh, did she?' Susie said and asked coyly. 'And what was your answer?'

'I told her that it was none of her business and I'm telling you the same. We are discussing Phil

Reynard, not me and David. All I can say is that he is a personable young man and quite handsome without being cocky and I can quite see the attraction.'

'And, how is he with Sally?'

'He appears to love her to distraction,' Kate said ruefully.

'So, has that laid some of your worries to rest?'

'In a way, because it pleases me that she has chosen a decent man for herself,' Kate said. 'David got on with him very well too, because he was asking him all about his job and it was interesting. I just made more tea and we sat on until the early hours. I tell you, I didn't want to get up this morning. Lucky Sally, who can have a lie-in.'

'Doesn't hurt to go to bed late once in a while.'

'Suppose not,' Kate said. 'Tell you what surprised me about David, though. When Sally and I went to wash out the cups and make more tea, he got talking with Phil about what he would do in the event of a war. I ask you. I mean, what war? Anyway, David told Phil that he and Nick will be going for the Air Force.'

'God,' Susie said with a slight shiver. 'You would never get me up in one of those planes.'

'Nor me,' Kate said in agreement. 'My mother used to say that if God had wanted us to fly he would have fitted us with wings.'

'She might have a point, but anyway, I don't cross bridges before I come to them,' Susie said. 'Let's talk about more important things, like you and David and how much you enjoyed the evening.'

'I had a truly terrific time,' Kate said. 'David

was really good company and later I was pleased that he got on so well with Sally and Phil.'

'Oh, David would get on with anyone – he's so accommodating,' Susie said.

Kate nodded. 'He is that,' she said. 'He's a lovely person.' Susie heard the gentle tone in Kate's voice and she smiled as she said, 'Did you reward this lovely person and give him a proper kiss goodnight?'

'That's none of your business,' Kate said, and she was very glad the next stop was theirs as she was able to hide the telltale flush that flooded her cheeks at the memory of those kisses that had taken her a little by surprise. She knew that if Sally was to ask her now the same question she had asked her on Christmas Day, she would be able to tell her that David's lips were very kissable, very sweet altogether. But that news was not for sharing.

There was a lot of chatter that morning in the cloakroom as the girls discussed what sort of Christmas they had all had and the forthcoming New Year's Eve celebrations. It seemed that everyone had something planned, and Kate was suddenly very glad that she was going to the Ball with David and could share that news around. 'You dark horse,' remarked the girl who worked at the machine behind hers. 'Didn't think anyone would match your high standards.'

'I don't have high standards.'

'Well, you must have summat,' another put in. ''Cos I've seen the boys near turning cartwheels on the dance floor to get your attention.'

'Nonsense,' Kate said, but she was laughing at the image that conjured up.

'It ain't nonsense,' said the first girl. 'You must have noticed it too, Susie.'

Susie shrugged. 'That's just Kate,' she said. 'But she has got David now and he is really lovely.'

'Will you lot stop talking about me as if I wasn't here,' Kate complained. 'I'm just glad that New Year's Eve falls on Saturday this year,' and there was a chorus of agreement to that.

'It means that I can have my hair done that day and I intend going down the Bull Ring to see if something festive catches my eye,' Susie said. 'Fancy coming with me, Kate?'

'You bet,' Kate said. 'In fact, you try and stop me.'

'What would we all do without the Rag Market?' one girl remarked, and another said, 'I don't know. C and A does some nice stuff and it's reasonable enough.'

'Yeah, they are all right for daytime use,' the first girl said. 'But you need more glamour for night-time.'

'Oh, no,' Susie said in disagreement. 'I've got some lovely things at C and A, and for this New Year's Ball, that's where I am going to go first.'

'Yeah, I think I will too,' Kate said. 'Can't hurt to have a look, anyway.'

'Come on, Kate,' shouted another girl, 'you'd look good in a sack.'

'Oh, do shut up,' Kate said, but she said it good-naturedly because she was used to teasing like this. 'D'you know what? I think the lot of you

125

should go and get your eyes tested. They're obviously faulty.'

There was a burst of laughter at this but one girl said, 'Well, whatever we look like we have to make the most of what we have, and I for one can't wait. I want to buy something a bit festive as well. I always think the New Year is a special time somehow.'

'Well, it's like a new start, isn't it?' said another.

'Yeah. I mean, I wonder what 1939 will bring.'

'Well, I can't answer that,' Susie said. 'But I can say without any shadow of a doubt that we will all have our wages docked if we don't get going. It might have escaped your notice, but the supervisor is glaring at us through the glass and if we don't start work soon we might find that our wages are light this week.'

There was a collective groan, but all the girls knew that what Kate had said was right. They trooped out to the factory floor, where any chatter was halted, because nothing could be heard above the noise of the machines.

SEVEN

Kate and Sally went to town first thing the next morning where as agreed they went first to the C&A store where they bought glamorous ball gowns for the dance that night. 'Golly,' Kate said as they settled in the tram to go home, 'I feel like a real spendthrift – I can never remember buying so many clothes before, and certainly not all in one go.'

'You've never had a boyfriend before,' Sally reminded her.

'No,' Kate admitted. 'And I do like looking nice for him. He does notice, and he is always so smart too. He even used to come well turned out to the weekly dance, if you remember.'

'Yeah, him and Nick both,' Susie said; and then she gave a sigh and said, 'Pity your Sally is working every evening. She is really missing out. She could have brought her Phil to the New Year's bash and we could have given him the once-over.'

'Huh, and frightened the lad off altogether,' Kate said with a grin. 'Anyway, Sally and Phil will be having some sort of celebration of their own because the cinema manager has invited them all to a party at his house as soon as the cinema closes. I was really glad that something had been arranged for them. Sally said she might not be back till the early hours, so it's a good job that she won't be working tomorrow.'

'It doesn't worry you that she will be out so late?' Susie said, knowing that at one time Kate would have fretted about something like that.

Kate shrugged. 'It is New Year's Eve,' she said, 'and as you are always saying, Sally is a sensible girl and Phil of course will see that she gets home safely. Anyway, I don't suppose we'll be back till the early hours either.'

'So, it's probably a good thing we don't work on Sunday too.'

'S'pose. Though we still have to get up for Mass,' Kate said. 'Bet Sally will be hard to rouse for that, but generally speaking she isn't really any bother now. She has turned out much better than I thought she would.'

'That might be partly Phil's influence,' Susie said. 'See, there can be advantages having a man at your side.'

'I never said there wasn't, Little Miss "I told you so",' Kate said with a laugh. 'She will likely already have gone by the time I get home, but I would value her opinion on the dress.'

'The dress is fine.'

'Yeah, I know you said that, but I'm not totally sure.'

'The trouble with you, Kate, is that you have no self-confidence,' Susie told her.

'I'm not used to buying clothes,' Kate said. 'Not clothes like these, anyway.'

'Even the shop assistant said how lovely you looked.'

'Ah, but they are trying to sell the clothes and so they will say anything,' Kate said.

'She wasn't half as complimentary about my ball

gown, though,' Susie complained. 'Even though the geometrical shapes decorating it are all the rage at the moment. Come on,' she said, suddenly leaping to her feet, 'this is our stop.'

'You looked beautiful,' Kate said to Susie as they stood on the pavement. 'And that dress really suited you.'

'Don't see why I should believe you when you never believe a word I say,' Susie said, with a wry smile, and then gave Kate a dig in the ribs as her face dropped. 'I'm joking, you dope. I'll see you tonight, and if you don't look a million dollars I will eat my hat.'

'You haven't got a hat.'

'That can soon be remedied,' Susie said, giving Kate a wave as she turned for home.

Kate smiled, and, despite the bleak coldness of the day, she felt warmed from the inside both because of the friendship she shared with Susie and the prospect of seeing David again in just a few hours' time. Life, she decided, was very good.

When she reached the flat, Sally hadn't left for work, and nor was she scurrying about getting ready to go. 'Mr Winter owes me some hours for the extra shifts I took on over Christmas,' she told Kate in explanation. 'So I'm not on until six tonight. Where did you go?'

'Just into town.'

'Well, I can see by your bags you bought something new again.'

'I did, yes,' Kate said. 'I bought another new dress.'

'Good for you,' Sally said in approval. 'Go and try it on then.'

All of a sudden, Kate was strangely reluctant. 'Oh, no, I won't bother.'

'Oh, yes,' Sally contradicted. 'I want to see it before I go.'

Kate gave a sigh but disappeared behind the curtained area with her bags. The dress fell to her feet like the dress she had worn to the Christmas dance and rustled deliciously as she walked.

'It's gorgeous, Kate,' Sally said, as Kate appeared before her a little self-consciously. 'I love that soft lilac colour, and all the swirls on it are really pretty.' She felt the material between her fingers before saying, 'Isn't that the fine wool crêpe that's all the rage at the moment?'

'Yes, the sales woman recommended it.'

'I'm not surprised,' Sally said. 'Spin round slowly.'

Kate did as Sally bade her and felt the skirt fall around her legs in soft folds. 'I love the embroidery of darker lilac around the scooped neckline,' Sally said. 'And those flowing sleeves just make it.'

'You don't feel the neckline is too scooped, though?' Kate said anxiously. 'I would hate David to think me fast.'

Sally fairly pealed with laughter. 'Kate, no one would think you fast in a million years, and your neckline is fine. No use in having bosoms if you don't highlight them now and again. I have just the thing.' She ran into the bedroom alcove and came out with a pendant in her hand. 'It has a purple stone in it to match the embroidery,' she said. 'And it will set the dress off lovely.'

'Oh, it does,' Kate said, turning around in front of the mirror so that the stone caught the light.

'Wait till David sees you in that dress,' Sally said. 'I just wish I was here to see his face.'

Sally left for work eventually and Kate got herself ready, but she wasn't quite finished when David knocked on the door. When she opened it, his mouth dropped agape. He recovered himself and said, 'Oh, Kate, you look so beautiful this evening that you have fair taken my breath away.'

'Nonsense!' Kate said, feeling the heat on her cheeks.

'No, it's not nonsense at all. I'm telling the truth,' David said. 'And I must say you look even more beautiful when you blush.'

'David, you are totally embarrassing me,' Kate said. 'But thank you anyway. And you look very handsome yourself in that smart brown overcoat, but I would take it off now or you will not feel the benefit when you go out. I'm not quite ready.'

David obediently removed his coat, remarking with a smile as he did so, 'Is a woman ever completely ready?'

Kate was pleasantly surprised by David's appearance for beneath his coat he was wearing a dark grey pinstriped suit she had never seen before. The trousers had razor-sharp creases running all down them, and turn-ups that rested just above his highly polished black shoes. The jacket was beautifully cut and the hanky in his top pocket matched the expertly knotted tie at the neck of his snow-white shirt; gold cufflinks sparkled in the light. 'Well,' said Kate in admiration, 'you certainly look the business too.'

'Well, it is New Year's Eve.'

'It is indeed, and I intend to enjoy myself.'

After that there was only one word to describe the New Year's Eve Ball, and that was 'magical'. Kate was on her feet dancing all night as the band played a variety of songs to please all, but the last one was the Anniversary Waltz and, as David held her in his arms, she felt a stirring of the heart she had thought had been left behind in Donegal. They had danced the Anniversary Waltz before, but Kate had not been his girl then and she had danced with a slight restraint between them. This time, David felt her totally relaxing against him for the first time and he sighed in contentment.

The next morning, Kate hugged herself in delight as she lay in bed and relived that wonderful night over and over, acknowledging how good and right it had felt to be held in David's arms. The invisible barrier she had used to prevent her getting close to anyone had come tumbling down, and she knew that it would stay that way, because what she now felt for David Burton was far more than mere liking. She didn't know if it was love, but just to think of meeting him again that day, after she had been to Mass, sent little frissons of excitement shooting through her body. That was enough, she thought, to be going on with.

Sally was sluggish and hard to wake that morning and Kate knew she must have been very late coming in. 'What time was it?' she asked her as Sally eventually climbed out of bed and began to dress half-heartedly.

'About half past two,' Sally said. 'But it's only fair, really, because we didn't start arriving at the

Winters' house until after eleven, so our party only really started after twelve. I bet yours started about eight o'clock.'

'Yeah it did,' Kate said. 'And finished at about half twelve. I was far away in the land of nod when you came in.'

Sally smiled. 'I know,' she said. 'And snoring like a good un. And,' she added, 'I'll tell you something else: you had a dirty great grin plastered across your face like you'd had a really nice time.'

'I did,' Kate admitted. 'Best night ever, and Susie and Nick seemed to enjoy it as much as I did.'

'What about David?'

'Yeah, he enjoyed it too.'

'I don't mean that,' Sally said. 'I mean about you and David.'

'Sally, if you don't get a move on, we'll miss Mass.'

'No, we won't, and you're changing the subject,' Sally said. 'And you've gone as red as a beetroot.'

'Sally!'

'All right,' Sally said. 'Keep your hair on. I'll get ready in double-quick time and you can fill me in on the gossip on the way to Mass.'

In actual fact, Kate didn't tell Sally much more, though she did say that she had agreed to see David again and that she was meeting him that day for a walk around Witton Lakes. Then she asked Sally about her night, and, as Sally liked to recount everything she did in the minutest detail, the church had come into view before she was finished.

133

Despite the intense cold, Kate thoroughly enjoyed her walk around the lakes and it was more than pleasant snuggled against David. But eventually the cold had begun to seep into her and she shivered as she said, 'Shall we head home now and warm up a bit? We'll have the place to ourselves because Sally is going to Phil's house. She told me this morning.'

David approved of Kate's suggestion and very soon the two were in front of the fire in Kate's place with a mug of cocoa each and a plate of mince pies. 'I really did enjoy last night,' Kate said after a minute or two. 'I know that I have said that already, but I haven't really thanked you for taking me.'

'You don't really have to thank someone when they have enjoyed it just as much,' David said. 'I was very disappointed when you refused me at first.'

'I know, and it was silly of me and rather unkind,' Kate said.

David shook his head. 'You are never unkind, Kate, and I'm sure you had your reasons for saying no initially.'

'I had,' Kate said. 'But to be honest, they weren't terribly good ones.' She hesitated and then went on: 'You asked me once if I had someone else and I said no.'

David's face looked suddenly stricken. 'And you have?' he said softly.

'No,' Kate said. 'It just wasn't the whole truth... It's time you knew about my cousin, Tim Munroe, who I left behind in Donegal.' She told him how she had always loved him, and how her cousinly love had turned into something else as she matured, but that she couldn't speak of it, never mind act on it, because they were too closely related.

'So, where does Susie come in then?' David asked. 'She told Nick you had been friends for years, yet you grew up in Ireland and she grew up here?'

'Oh,' said Kate, 'that came about because Susie's mother became ill, and Susie was sent to her grandmother in Ireland and she came to school with me. We were both ten years old then and we were soon fast friends, even when she went back home again after six months because she came back every year on holiday. When she left school and was earning wages and seemed to have plenty to spend her money on, I was envious, and at first Mammy hated her going on about the delights of Birmingham, until she realized how Tim and I felt about one another. That was over three years ago, and from then on she encouraged Susie in her tales of Birmingham. When Susie said she could find me a job and a place to stay, Mammy persuaded me to come here and stay for a year or two. I knew that she wanted me out of the way. Susie knew nothing then, though. When I told her about Tim, she was sympathetic, but said that I should put it behind me and get on with my life.'

'And you couldn't?'

'Not really,' Kate said. 'Susie says it's my fault, that I won't allow myself to get over it.'

'Is she right?'

Kate shrugged. 'She could be, because even

though I liked you a lot I wouldn't let myself go any further. I thought – and still think – that it's unfair to go out with someone if you are thinking of them as second best. I would hate to be treated that way myself, so there is no reason why I should treat a man like that.'

David smiled the slow smile that crinkled his eyes, and Kate felt her heart do a flip as he said, 'I would put up with being second best to this Tim, if that is how it must be, and I would do it because I love you.'

David's words, said so sincerely, sent a shiver down Kate's spine, and she felt for a moment as if her heart had stopped beating. She just stared at him. 'You ... you love me?' she stammered incredulously.

'Heart, body and soul,' David said. 'I think that I loved you from the first moment that I saw you. You made me the happiest man on earth when you agreed to come out with me, and I love you more every time I see you, if that's at all possible.'

Kate was speechless for a moment, feeling a lump in her throat, but eventually she said, 'David, I–'

'Hush,' said David, putting his fingers gently over Kate's lips. 'I meant what I said. I will take what you can offer me.'

'My mother wrote to say that Tim was walking out with a girl called Maggie Mulligan,' Kate told him. 'I was at school with her. I know it might be different here, but over there, if you walk out with a girl, you are committed to her, so some day they will marry. So you needn't fret. The road back to Tim is closed to me, even if I had wanted

– or been able – to travel down it, and now I have no desire to do that.'

She felt rather than heard the relief flood through David's body as he said, 'You mean that?'

'Every word,' Kate said. 'I said that I liked you, and I still do, but there is a part of me that more than likes you. I think Susie was right when she said that liking a person at first was more important than loving them.'

'Love can grow out of liking.'

'I know,' Kate said, in a voice little more than a whisper. 'I think maybe that's what's happening to me.'

'Oh, Kate,' David said, his heart swelling with love. He knelt down by Kate's chair and took her hands in his and stroked her fingers gently. She had opened her heart to him; he was touched that Kate had told him so honestly all about her cousin. And yet, though he hid it well, he was suddenly almost consumed with jealousy. It was far from reasonable, but he was resentful that this Tim probably knew more about Kate than he ever would.

This all-consuming love he had for Kate had come unbidden into his life; he had felt as if he'd been hit by a sledgehammer the first time he had seen her at the Friday-night dance. He and Nick had been going along fairly happily in their bachelor lives, and he had dated a fair few girls who had been nice enough. But no one had stirred him like Kate. 'You only want her because she is so remote and unobtainable,' Nick had said when he'd confided in him. 'It's the thrill of the chase. If you were ever to get her, you'd very likely not want her. Anyway, I haven't time to waste on people like that. I much prefer her friend, Susie. That's who I am going to pursue.'

And he had, of course. Now he and Kate were closer than they had ever been and so he tried to push the jealous thoughts away. He had to build on what he had, but slowly, for Kate's feelings for him were tenuous as yet. But the nub of resentment against this man, Tim Munroe, persisted, and he had the sudden desire to crush Kate to him and stake his claim somehow; show her how much he loved and wanted her. He controlled himself with difficulty and, instead, lifted her fingers and kissed them one by one. Then, getting to his feet and drawing Kate into his arms, he felt her melt against him as their lips met.

'Ooh, you and David, I can hardly believe it,' Susie said the next morning as she settled herself in the tram as they made their way to work. 'And, he actually said he loves you?'

Kate's smile was broad and her eyes sparkling as she nodded her head vigorously. 'He did. Isn't that wonderful?'

'I'll say,' Susie said. 'And what was your reply?'

'Tell you the truth, I didn't know what to say,' Kate said. 'I was completely stunned. I mean, it is special to say you love someone, isn't it? I mean, it isn't something you say to everyone?'

Susie smiled. 'Some boys do,' she said. 'But David isn't like that. So, you didn't say you loved him back or anything?'

Kate shook her head. 'Not exactly, and there was little time to say any more because Sally and

Phil came in. They disturbed us in a clinch as it was.'

'What bad timing.'

'Yes, it was,' Kate agreed. 'They brought the cold of the night in with them and were glad of the fire. We sat around it talking for a bit and then, despite the fact that Phil and Sally had had Sunday tea at Phil's mother's, everyone was suddenly starving hungry, and so I ended up cooking bacon and eggs for everyone and then we played cards together. It was a good night, but it gave us no private time together.'

'So, when are you seeing him again?'

'Tomorrow,' Kate said. 'Gracie Fields is on at the Aston Hippodrome and David asked me if I wanted to go. Of course I said yes.'

'Oh, yes,' Susie said. 'Nick mentioned it. It's a good line-up too because Tommy Trinder is on as well – and Max Miller.'

'He is funny, that Max Miller,' Kate said. 'And I love the funny walks he does, but some of his jokes embarrass me a bit.'

'You're easily embarrassed, that's all I can say,' Susie said unsympathetically.

'I can't help that,' Kate protested. 'And I am still going and looking forward to it.'

'Not surprised,' Susie said. 'I fancy going there as well. I'll mention it to Nick and see what he says.'

'Oh, yes,' Kate said, knowing she would feel much more relaxed if the solid presence of her friend was in the next seat. 'And,' she added, 'David has asked me up to meet his family next weekend.'

'Oh,' said Susie. She was well aware that Kate thought that going to see one's family was tantamount to becoming engaged, and so she went on: 'Will you go?'

'I suppose so,' Kate said. 'I did hesitate, but you are always telling me that meeting the parents means very little these days. Anyway, it will please David.'

'And that's important, is it?'

'Of course it's important,' Kate said. 'I owe him something. No one has ever said that they loved me before.'

EIGHT

Kate was interested in where David's family lived. He had told her they lived in Chudleigh Street, which was just off Reservoir Road, in an end-of-terrace house. As they walked up the road, she saw that the houses were smallish, but not as small or as squashed up as some she had seen. When they came to David's house, instead of going to the front door, which opened almost directly on to the street, he took her down a small entry by the side of the house. 'This is the back way,' he said. 'It's the door we usually use.' The entry led to a scrubby garden at the back, where Kate had a glimpse of an outside toilet and a coal shed, and then David was opening the door into the kitchen.

His mother was lifting something out of the oven, and she straightened up and turned when she heard them come in. 'Hallo, Ma,' David said, and the smile on Kate's face died as the woman's small dark eyes, which had settled like currants into her podgy red face, looked her up and down almost in a disparaging way. Her mouth seemed like a discontented slash across her face, and Kate felt her head lift slightly as she stared back. David's mother was very plump, her round, red face surrounded with a frizz of hair, which had once been brown but was now liberally streaked with grey. She had an apron tied around her

141

ample waist and her sleeves rolled up to reveal bulging, slightly pink forearms that reminded Kate of a couple of large hams. She pushed that image quickly from her mind.

David seemed unaware of the chilled atmosphere and, because the woman was David's mother, Kate resolutely fastened another smile on her face as the woman eventually said, 'Hallo, it's Kate isn't it? Our David's young lady?'

It was a lacklustre welcome, and Kate had the distinct impression that the woman David had introduced as his mother, Dora, wasn't a bit impressed that she was David's young lady. 'Yes,' she said as she shook the woman's hand. 'My name is Kate Munroe, Mrs Burton. I'm very pleased to meet you.'

'Where is everyone, Ma?' David said as he removed his coat and helped Kate with hers.

'Your father and Lawrence went for a drink after dinner,' Dora said.

'Why did they slope off to the pub? I told them I was bringing Kate to tea.'

Dora sighed. 'You know they go for a drink every Sunday. I'm sure your young lady understands that.'

Before Kate was able to say anything, David said truculently, 'It's not the point whether Kate minds or not. Surely to stop in one week wouldn't hurt them?'

'I suppose they didn't think you'd be here so early,' Dora said. 'I certainly didn't. You said you were going for a walk.'

'We did, didn't we, Kate?' David said, putting an arm around her as he did so. 'But it was far too cold to be out long.'

'I should think so,' Dora said, moving to the fire and giving it a poke. 'Cold enough to freeze a penguin's chuff, as your father is fond of saying. Come up to the fire and I'll make us all a cup of tea. Kate can tell us all about herself ... because he,' she said to Kate, jerking her head in David's direction, 'never tells us a thing.'

'That's because you've never shown the slightest bit of interest,' David said rather bitterly; though he was gentle enough with Kate as he led her to the settee in front of the fire and sat beside her. Kate was glad of his presence, though a little concerned about the undercurrent in the house. Dora, her lips pursed even tighter, had gone off into the kitchen, but she saw that lines of strain still furrowed David's brow. If he had asked her, she would have said she was glad that she only had his mother to contend with, and that she didn't care a jot that his truant father and brother were at the pub. However, he didn't ask her; he didn't say anything at all and neither did she as they sat side by side, the only sound in the room the crackling fire and the ticking clock.

She was relieved when Dora came through from the kitchen carrying a tray and saying as she did so, 'A cup of tea will see us all right. I always think it puts new heart in a body.'

She placed the tray on the small table to the right of the settee and when the tea was poured and the biscuits offered, she said to Kate, 'Now, Kate, where do you come from? I can tell by your accent that you're not from round these parts originally.'

'No,' Kate said. And she went on to tell David's mother about living on the farm in the north of Ireland and then how she had become such close friends with Susie Mason, who had helped find her a place to live and a job when she decided to travel to pastures new.

'A smoky industrial city must have been a shock after living on a remote farm,' Dora said.

'Oh, it was – even our nearest town in Ireland is very much a country one. I was very homesick at first and very glad to have the friendship of Susie and her family. Without them I would have been lost.'

'And yet you stayed?'

'Oh, yes,' Kate said, 'because I began to enjoy having so much to see and do. My home and the county I was born and brought up in is a very beautiful one, but there's little in the way of entertainment. I had never seen a cinema or music hall before I came here, and the only dances I had attended were church socials. Another spur to my leaving was the fact that I never got any sort of wage when I worked on the farm and it is nice to have my own money in my pocket, however little it is.'

'In fact, she described Birmingham in such a favourable light that her younger sister came to join her,' David said.

Kate was glad that David went no further than that, since she didn't want to explain her sister's flight. So she just said, 'That's right. I have Sally living with me now – she'd only been in Birmingham a few days when she got a job in the cinema.'

'You seem to get on very well with your sister.'

'I suppose I do,' Kate said. 'It works better than I thought it might. Course, I am that much older than her, so I am used to looking after her.'

'Maybe you could take a leaf out of Kate's book there,' Dora said with a wry glance at her son.

David glowered back at her as he snapped, 'Kate said she looked after her sister, not bullied her. Therein lies the difference.'

Kate remembered David telling her that when he had been a boy he had never hit it off with Lawrence. Maybe the actual fights had stopped, but it seemed clear from David's reaction that relations between them were still a bit sticky. She longed to ask him why, but she couldn't really say much in front of his mother, and anyway she didn't want to do anything to make an obviously fraught situation worse, so she said, 'Oh, I'm no saint, Mrs Burton, and neither is my sister. She could be a right little madam when we were growing up. She was the spoilt baby for some years before our little brother James came along. He is only five now, and of course the only boy, so he was made much of and Sally had her nose pushed right out of joint.'

'I can see that,' Dora said. 'David was our youngest, of course.'

The implication that he too had been spoiled hung in the air, especially when Dora went on to say, 'One of the reasons maybe that he and Lawrence never seemed to see eye to eye.'

'You don't have to be the youngest to be ruined by your parents,' David said angrily.

Kate, slightly embarrassed, decided to change

the subject entirely, and so she said: 'David was telling me the line of work he is in, an electrician. Must be very interesting.'

'Don't know how interesting it is,' Dora said. 'I just know that there's plenty of work about. So many people are changing over to having electricity in their houses now. Course those gas mantles were so fragile. Electric light is much better – and safer too, I think.'

'Yes, but he doesn't do many lights now though, does he?' Kate said. 'He was telling me he is now mainly building wirelesses. That's why I said it must be interesting.'

'I never knew that,' Dora remarked. 'You never said.'

'I did, Mom,' David said. 'You just didn't hear. Anyway, now you know. People who once had their wirelesses run by accumulators, because they had no electricity in their houses, now want wirelesses run on the mains. In fact, there's a great run on wirelesses altogether. And,' he added, 'before too long people are going to be wanting televisions.'

'And what's that when it's at home?'

'That, Mom, is moving pictures in your own home – you can plug it in just like a wireless, but even better.'

'Never! Moving pictures in our own home,' Dora said in awe. 'It would be like going to the cinema. Well, if you're right that will be just lovely, won't it? I mean, I love a play or a bit of comedy on the wireless now, but it would be better still if you could see it. And I agree with Kate, it must be interesting work.'

David nodded. 'It's really nice to be in at the beginning of something so exciting.'

Dora nodded. 'He held out for doing that line of work from when he was a young lad,' she said to Kate. 'I thought he would follow his father and brother into the brass industry, but he point-blank refused. His dad wasn't best pleased, I can tell you. There was a terrible to-do at the time and then his teacher at the school came to see me just a couple of months before he was due to leave and told me David had a head on his shoulders and we should get him set on as an apprentice to a trade. He had influence at a firm taking on apprentice electricians, and he said it would suit our David. Course, it weren't as easy as that, because I had to talk the old man round.'

'Yeah,' David said. 'It was the only time I remember you fighting in my corner.'

'But why didn't your husband want David to become an electrician?' Kate asked.

'Well, he'd always worked in the brass,' Dora said. 'Just like his father and uncles, all of them really, and then there was the money side of it, because the brass workers are paid well and David earned a pittance to start with.'

'Yeah, but all that changed when I was out of my apprenticeship, didn't it?' David said. 'With overtime I can earn more than the old man or Lawrence now.'

'I'm glad you got to do what you wanted,' Kate said, putting her hand out to David as she spoke. 'You can tell how much you enjoy it, by the enthusiastic way you talk about it.'

'I do,' David said, 'I don't deny it. The old

man's all right about it now, isn't he, Mom?'

'He is, thank God,' Dora said as she collected up the cups and plates on to the tray. 'And talking of your old man, I wonder where he's got to. I'll wash these up anyway and maybe he will have come home by then.'

David ignored the reference to his father and said, 'It still gets Lawrence's goat, though, that I can earn more than him.'

'I think you imagine that.'

'No, I don't.'

Dora sighed, but she said nothing further to. her son and instead lifted the tray and made her way to the kitchen. Kate thought that if she put her hand out she could almost touch the atmosphere in that room. 'I'll give you a hand,' she said, getting to her feet.

'No,' Dora said. 'Not at all. You go and sit with our David.'

David pulled Kate down to sit beside him as Dora went back to the kitchen, and said, 'I must warn you about Lawrence.'

'What about him?'

'He's a terrible flirt.'

'Surely not with me – his brother's girlfriend?'

'Especially with you.'

'Oh, look, David, some men are like that,' Kate said. 'I can handle Lawrence. Please don't argue with him on my account.'

David smiled at her and kissed her gently on the lips as he said, 'For your sake, I will try really hard not to.'

Suddenly Kate heard the crunch of boots in the entry and she looked at David. 'Here they come

148

now,' he said. 'And you'll soon see what I mean about Lawrence.'

She caught a glimpse of two men walking down the yard as David drew her to her feet and held her close. Dora was still in the kitchen and Kate heard her open the door. Then she came in ahead of her husband and son, saying as she did so, 'David's here already with his young lady.'

Kate had the feeling that Dora had said it as a sort of warning to the two men who followed her into the room, and she could sense the tension running through David. Alf Burton, David's father, was as tall and thin as his wife was little and plump, so that 'Tom Tall and Butter Ball' sprang to Kate's mind. Lawrence was taller still, but he was so like his father that Kate could bet that Alf had looked the same as his son when he had been younger. He had a fine head of dark hair that she imagined Alf had once had, though the sparse hair left on his head now was steel grey. They had the same ruddy complexion and slightly squashed-looking nose, but Lawrence's thin lips were inherited from his mother, because his father's were thick and full.

She did feel uncomfortable as she saw Lawrence's lingering, speculative eyes raking over her with such intensity. Suddenly he stepped in front of his father and strode towards them. He held out his hand and, with a disdainful curl of those thin lips, said, 'And David's young lady is very nice, yes, very nice indeed.'

Kate moved away from David's embrace and took the proffered hand and shook it as she stared into Lawrence's leering brown eyes. He retained her hand longer than was necessary and even gave it a tight squeeze as he said, 'I am very pleased to meet *you*.'

David's hands hung by his sides but were balled into fists. Because he had promised Kate he would try not to fight with Lawrence, he would leave them there, though he longed to lay his brother out on the floor. He contented himself with saying though gritted teeth, 'Leave it out, Lawrence.'

Lawrence, still retaining Kate's hand, turned to David, his face a picture of mock innocence as he said, 'Leave what out, our kid? I'm only giving your young lady a warm welcome.'

Kate had no idea what to do; without jerking her hand from Lawrence's, she could not free herself, but then she saw Dora's head jerk towards her husband and he stepped forward and took Kate's hand from Lawrence.

'Lawrence is right,' he said as he shook her hand. 'You are welcome, my dear, very welcome.' Then he turned to his wife and said, 'A cup of tea would go down well – it's real brass-monkey weather out there.'

'I have some homemade vegetable soup. We can all have a cup of that for now,' Dora said. 'Warm you up better than tea and it won't take me a jiffy to heat it up.' Everyone was agreeable to that and Kate stuck like glue to David and ignored the ogling glances that Lawrence was throwing her way.

He said little to her as they bunched around the fire drinking the wholesome and appetizing soup, but she told Alf, too, of her home and family in the cottage in Ireland, and her reasons for coming to Birmingham. She went on to say that she had met David at the weekly dance she and Susie went to. Lawrence gave his brother's leg a kick as he said, 'Didn't know you could dance, our kid. If I was asked I would have said you had two left feet.'

'Then you would have been wrong,' Kate snapped out, louder than she intended because she was suddenly angered by Lawrence's supercilious tone. Her words and the way she had spoken had surprised everyone; they were all looking at her and she felt herself growing hot with embarrassment as she said, 'Sorry, but I hate people taking the mickey like that.' And she turned to Lawrence and said, 'David is a very good dancer.'

'Good teacher perhaps?'

'Not at all,' Kate said. 'I didn't teach David to dance. I didn't need to.'

'Oh, regular Fred Astaire, our David,' Lawrence sneered, then turned to Dora and said, 'Bet you didn't know that, Mom?'

Alf chuckled but Dora looked at the frown on Kate's face and said, 'That will do now, Lawrence.'

'Only having a bit of a laugh,' Lawrence said.

'Well, you've had it,' Dora snapped. 'Let that be the end of it.' And turning to Kate, she said, 'Tell me, my dear, are you a Catholic?'

'Yes,' Kate said, and added, 'in fact, until I came here I had never met anyone who wasn't a Catholic.'

'Oh, you meet all sorts here,' Dora said. 'Church of England, Baptists, Methodists, Jews and–'

'Then there are people like us,' Lawrence put in. 'Who don't give a damn either way.'

Everything he says, thought Kate, has an extra edge to it, and she decided to ignore him. She finished off the soup and handed the cup back to Dora, saying as she did so, 'That was lovely soup. Thank you.'

'Think nothing of it,' Dora said, though she was obviously pleased. 'I make a lot of soup in the winter. I hope you like the tea as much. And talking of tea,' she said to Alf, 'I lit the fire in there. Well, you check it and put more coal on.'

'Will do that readily enough,' Alf said. 'That room is like an ice box without a fire.'

And so when they went in later, a cheerful fire was crackling in the cold black grate, which was set into a tiled hearth enclosed by a brass fender. A fluffy dark red rug lay in front of that, and the table fair groaned with food.

There were ham sandwiches and others made with salmon, and then Dora brought in a large, piping-hot cheese-and-onion pie and another that she said was bacon-and-egg. There were also mouth-watering pastries, two plates of assorted cakes and a great big Victoria sponge filled with jam and cream and dusted with sugar.

With such lovely food and so much of it, coupled with the general chitchat and banter around the table, Kate would have liked to relax a little, but she was only too aware that Lawrence continued to stare at her. It was unnerving to find his eyes boring into her every time she raised her head, and so to try to deflect attention away from herself, she turned to Alf and said, 'David was telling me that you work in the brass industry?'

'I do,' Alf said proudly. 'Birmingham is famous

for its brass. Did you know that?'

Kate nodded. 'Frank Mason told me. He said the heat in the brass foundries is colossal.'

'Aye,' Alf agreed. 'Has to be, see, because we have to turn copper and zinc into molten metal and to do that you need heat – and lots of it.'

'Yeah,' Lawrence said in agreement. 'The furnaces are white-hot.'

'So that's how brass is made, by mixing copper and zinc,' Kate said in amazement. 'I never knew that.'

'Why would you?' Lawrence said. 'Then, when it's turned to liquid, we pour it into crucibles. Got to be real careful then. It's heavy work and one drop of that stuff on your skin and you would be badly burned.'

'That's right,' Alf said. 'Our overalls would be no good at all. A steady eye and a steady nerve is what's needed.'

'They're filthy dirty when they come home as well,' Dora said. 'And always glad of a wash and a clean dry shirt because the one they've been wearing all day is usually dripping with sweat.'

'It sounds awful.'

Alf shrugged. 'It's a job,' he said. 'And it pays well. I mean, our David is earning good money now, but he didn't for ages, did you, son?'

'Well, no, but that's because I was learning the trade,' David said. 'I didn't really warrant earning a lot of money when I either didn't really know what I was doing, or someone else had to check everything I did to make sure that I was doing it right.'

'Face it, David,' Lawrence said mockingly, 'you

153

hadn't got the bottle to go in the brass foundry anyway.'

David looked across the table to Lawrence and said disparagingly, 'It's nothing to do with not having the bottle.'

Lawrence was angered by David's tone and there was a steely glint in his eyes as he snapped, 'Yeah, that's just what it was.'

'Don't be so daft,' David said. 'I went to be an electrician because I was good with my hands and I liked electrics. The teacher came and talked to Mom about it and he was right. I earn plenty now and I always have loads of work on.'

'And I'd say you'll have more, not less, before you're much older,' Alf said, jumping in quickly before Lawrence could find some other retort to annoy David further. 'The gaffer was only telling me on Friday that they are fitting new dies to some of the lines next week and they will be making war-related stuff. It's bound to affect you as well.'

'Yeah, I suppose so. If we do declare war, I should say that even more people will want wirelesses.'

Kate's eyes when she turned to him were very wide and fear-filled. 'But there isn't going to be a war, is there?' she said. 'I mean, we had that agreement with Hitler in October last year.'

'Well, I'd say not everyone thinks that Hitler will keep his word,' David said. 'Dad's right. Everyone seems to be getting ready for something and the number of people buying wirelesses has gone up. That's why I'm so busy.'

'Yes, but more people might have been buying

wirelesses anyway,' Kate said. 'You said yourself that once electricity was fitted into the houses they would want to change the old ones they had. It doesn't necessarily mean that we are going to war.'

Dora saw Kate's agitation and didn't blame her – she hated all this talk about war as well. Wasn't as if it was going to make any difference, however much they talked about it. She patted Kate's hand comfortingly as she said, 'Course it doesn't, Kate. It's men like all this war talk. Fair turns a body off their meals, it does. Well, there's to be no more of it for today at least,' she said, glaring around the table. 'Let's eat our tea in peace, for pity's sake.'

For a few minutes there was silence. Then David said, 'Tell you what, dear brother, if the balloon does go up we'll see who has the bottle in this family. I will volunteer for the Air Force. It will be interesting to see what you'll do.'

Lawrence leapt to his feet, his face almost purple with rage as he demanded, 'Just what are you insinuating?' As he spoke he made a lunge at his brother and caught hold of his shirt and hauled him from his seat.

Alf, however, had anticipated this, and got between them and broke Lawrence's hold. Meanwhile, Dora, after one cry of dismay, had begun to weep. 'For God's sake, how old are the pair of you?' she cried brokenly.

As for Kate, she had sat in horrified silence. She knew that if it hadn't been for Alf's timely intervention, that comment might have easily led to a full-scale fight between the two brothers. Lawrence still stood like a bull ready to charge at any moment, gasping as he glared at his brother.

Alf looked at David and said, 'Was there any need for that?'

David straightened his clothes but did not sit down as he said, 'Probably not, but there is no need for him to say that I was afraid to go into the brass works. When war comes, it will sort out the men from the boys and we'll see who the brave ones are then.'

'Are you saying I'm a coward?' Lawrence snapped.

David shrugged. 'If the cap fits,' he said.

Lawrence made another lunge, countered again by his father, as Dora said through her tears, 'For God's sake, David, will you shut up and sit down and eat your tea? I have slaved all day to put nice food on the table and you have taken away my appetite with your goings-on. And I don't know what your young lady must be thinking.'

'Sorry, Ma,' David said. 'It's just—'

'Just nothing,' Dora said dismissively. 'If war is declared, there will be time enough to worry about it, and God help us if it does. Then neither of you will have a choice in whether you fight or not, because there will be a call-up and that will be the end of it.'

Kate knew that too, and she hoped and prayed that David was wrong and that war could be averted. However, she said nothing, and an uncomfortable silence settled round the table.

Kate left as soon as she could after tea and, when they were clear of the house, David apologized for his family's behaviour and especially the scene around the table. Inwardly, Kate thought that David hadn't helped the situation, and in fact had inflamed it at times, but she sensed he didn't want criticism from her. Instead, she said, 'Will you stop saying sorry? No one is responsible for their families. That being said, I don't like your brother much and it's more than obvious that you don't either, but why do you let him rile you so much?'

'He started flirting with you the minute he came into the house.'

'He's that kind of man,' Kate said. 'I have met his sort before, and I can deal with him – like most women can. I didn't respond to him, and never would. I really think he does it to make you cross. When you react, he's won, so don't react. Ignore him.'

'That's easier said than done.'

'Look, David, how often do we have to see your family, including Lawrence?'

'Not often, if it's up to me,' David said.

'That suits me as well,' Kate said. 'And now, are we going to spend the rest of the night discussing the failings of your family, or are we going to make arrangements to meet again?'

'I didn't know that you'd want to meet me again.'

'Why wouldn't I?' Kate said. 'Unless you are bringing the family along.'

David laughed. 'I'll say not.'

'Well,' said Kate. *The Thief of Bagdad* is on at the Plaza.'

NINE

Kate told Susie all about what had happened at the Burton's house the next day on the way to work. 'It was bedlam,' she said. 'Honestly, Lawrence and David seem to really hate each other. And anything can start them off.'

'Who's the worst?'

'I'd say they're mainly as bad as each other,' Kate said. 'Though I suppose, apart from that comment David made that they nearly came to blows over, I would say Lawrence has the edge. He seemed to set out to wind David up, flirting with me and so on. You know the sort of stuff.'

'I know. I hate creepy men like that.'

'Me too, but it is a bit difficult to know how to deal with him in front of his family.'

'Oh, yes, I can see that.'

'Anyway, David hardly speaks, and if he does, his brother usually makes some sarcastic comment about it,' Kate said.

Susie smiled. 'Good job you're not marrying the family.'

'I'll say,' Kate said. 'And yet his parents are all right, on the whole, but I haven't the least interest in getting to know Lawrence any better.'

'Don't blame you,' Susie said. 'The lads knew him while they were growing up. Martin always said that he was glad the Burtons didn't go to his school because Lawrence was a year older than

158

him and a big bruiser of a lad. He used to bully Martin mercilessly if he got him out on the street on his own.'

'Why didn't you warn me?'

'Because it was years ago,' Susie said. 'And he could have been a changed person, for all I knew. Anyway, I thought you should make your own mind up.'

'And I did.'

'And what's the verdict?'

'That Lawrence Burton is a nasty piece of work and I will steer well clear of him.'

'Bit difficult if you are going to see much of David's family.'

'Well, I'll see to it that we don't,' Kate said. 'He won't mind that; he said he has always felt an outsider.'

'Why?'

'Well, he overheard his dad talking one day,' Kate told Susie. 'And he said that once Lawrence was born, he and Dora didn't really want any more nippers. And when Dora fell for David, it was a very unpleasant shock for the both of them.'

'Yeah, but people say things like that and get over it.'

'I don't think his dad did totally,' Kate said. 'David said his dad seldom took him for a kick-about in the park, but he went with Lawrence every week, and they went to see the Villa play a fair few times and he was never taken along, and Alf taught Lawrence to swim in the cut. David still can't swim. Then Lawrence followed his dad into the brass foundry. When they go out for a pint at night or Sunday afternoon, David is never asked to go along with them.'

Susie wrinkled her nose. 'Seems a bit mean,' she said.

'I agree,' Kate said. 'But none of us can help the families we are born into, so we will go our own way regardless.'

'So you are seeing him again?'

'You bet I am,' Kate said. 'We're going to the pictures tonight, as a matter of fact.'

'What's on?'

'The Thief of Bagdad.'

'Oh, I'd love to see that,' Susie cried. 'Can me and Nick come too?'

'Course you can,' Kate said, linking Susie's arm as they alighted from the tram and set off down the road. 'The more the merrier, I say.'

The four of them had a great night at the cinema. When they came out, as they were all hungry, they bought fish and chips and walked home eating them out of the newspaper. David and Kate bade goodnight to Susie and Nick at the head of Marsh Lane and walked down the slight incline to Kate's flat; they had finished their supper when they reached the front door. Kate wiped her greasy fingers on the newspaper and said, 'I think a cup of tea is in order. What about you?'

'I think that would be just the job,' David said, and a few moments later they were sitting either side of the fire drinking the very welcome tea. When they had the tea drunk, knowing that they would have the flat to themselves for another hour or so until Sally came home, Kate snuggled into David's arms quite willingly.

The kisses that she had once simply submitted to, now made her body tingle all over and left her gasping for more, but David went no further than that. Kate was both relieved and a little disappointed, because she was certain that what she felt now for David Burton was true love. In her weekly letter home, she told her mother all about David – the first time that she had ever mentioned him, or any other man either. She was so disappointed with the reply she got, because all her mother said about the new love in Kate's life was, 'I hope this man that you seem so fond of is a good, practising Catholic.'

He wasn't. 'Neither is Nick,' Susie said. 'And he has already told me that he has no intention of turning. Why should he have to? And I'll tell you one thing, no priest or Catholic Church will dictate to me who I am going to spend the rest of my life with.'

'What about your parents, though?'

'I told them what Nick had said and they said it was up to me.'

'Oh, God,' Kate said. 'I doubt mine would be that understanding.'

'Mine don't live in a small Irish village,' Susie said. 'And it has to make a difference. Ask David – he might turn, you never know.'

Kate didn't say a word because they had never discussed marriage and she didn't want to appear too forward. Sally, whom she had confided in, agreed with Susie. 'Phil is C of E,' she said. 'But he doesn't care about anything much and said he only goes to church to please his mother. She likes the vicar, who he said was very good to her when his father died. But he said that it wouldn't bother him to change sides if it would make life easier for me.'

Kate was surprised that Phil and her sister had discussed marriage, given they were both still so young. 'I know I can't do anything about it yet,' Sally said when Kate expressed concern. 'I mean, Mammy will hardly give me consent to marry a man she has never met when she is trying to pretend I never existed. I'll be seventeen next week and there's not even a card from Ireland.' She turned bright eyes that glittered with unshed tears as she said that, and Kate felt so sorry for her as she went on: 'And it still hurts.'

'Ah, Sally, I can do nothing about that situation,' Kate said. 'But I will give you a birthday to remember. You see if I don't.'

'Oh, Kate, you have been great,' Sally said. 'But with Mammy not really caring whether I live or die, it won't make a jot of difference whether Phil turns or not, so I said he can do as he pleases. And,' she said, 'I'll tell you something else: I would want to marry Phil if he was a Hindu, Sikh or Jew, because it's the person who counts.'

'I know that,' Kate said. 'But how shall I answer Mammy?'

'I would ignore the comment and just write your normal letter,' Sally said. 'In the end, she will probably get the message. Mammy isn't stupid.'

Kate did as her sister advised, stressing how kind David was and how generous and gentle. She sketched over the visit to his home for Sunday tea and mentioned his brother only briefly. She concentrated instead on the things they had done together and how they often made up a foursome with Susie and her boyfriend, Nick Kassel, because she thought that would reassure her mother that she was not getting up to things she shouldn't be getting up to.

But she didn't forget what her sister had said, and on her birthday Sally had cards from all the Masons as well as Susie and Kate, and Kate had also bought her a rose-coloured blouse in shiny satin, which Sally was ecstatic about. She needn't have worried, though: she wasn't the only one determined to make sure Sally had a good day, for flowers were delivered before Kate left for work, and if there had been any doubt who had sent them there was a card attached:

To Sally with all my love – Phil.

'They are gorgeous,' Kate declared. 'And they will make the room smell lovely.'

Kate was drinking a cup of tea prior to going to bed as Sally burst through the door that night; she had a bag full of cards and presents. 'Look at all these, Kate. Everyone made such a fuss of me because I am the youngest there.'

Kate looked at the boxes of chocolates and toiletries on the chair and all the lovely cards and remarked, 'You have been thoroughly spoiled.'

'I know,' Sally said with a grin. 'Isn't it lovely? And this is what Phil gave me.' She withdrew a beautiful heart-shaped card and a small jewellery box where a silver locket encircled a velvet pad.

'Oh, goodness,' Kate said, lifting it out and playing it between her fingers. 'Isn't it absolutely splendid? I thought the flowers were Phil's present.'

'Just part of it, he said,' Sally told her sister.

'Well, you are a very lucky girl,' Kate said, and Sally grinned mischievously as she said, 'I know.'

With Christmas, the New Year and Sally's birthday out of the way, Kate and Sally began to look for a bigger flat. Sally had had a rise as she had been at the cinema for three months, which was their trial period, so they could afford more rent. Everyone was on the lookout for them. It wasn't easy, and anything suitable had usually been snapped up before they could get to see it; both felt frustrated as the time slipped by.

But in other ways, Kate was happier than she had ever been, for she was so much at ease with David, as if she had known him all her life. They could and did talk about anything and everything. As they grew closer and closer, Kate wondered why she had ever been hesitant with the man she now loved totally.

Her mother, in her letters, still occasionally harped on the one thing that mattered to her, and that was David's religion, or lack of it. In her replies, as Sally had advised, Kate ignored any questions like that, but continued to write in the same vein as she had the first time. She told her mother again of the cinema visits and occasional trips to the music hall and the walks she enjoyed with David on fine Sunday afternoons.

As the winter finally relinquished its icy grip on the city, and blustery winds of early spring began to billow through those dusty streets, Kate found

Sally waiting for her one evening as she alighted from the tram on her way home from work. Sally was hopping agitatedly from one foot to the other. That had never happened before, and Kate was startled. 'What is it?' she asked.

'I've seen a flat and it's much bigger than ours,' Sally burst out. 'One of the other usherettes heard about it and came to tell me and I went round to see it before work. It's really nice, but I said I had to ask you and she said she'd hold it till six and it's nearly that now. I was given leave to come and meet you off the tram.'

'Better get a move on, Kate,' said Susie. 'Best of luck.'

'Yeah, see you tomorrow, Susie,' Kate said with a wave of her hand, and to Sally she said, 'Where is this place?'

'That's the beauty of it,' Sally said. 'It's only a bit further down the Slade.'

And so it was. A converted house like the one they were in and in very good condition too. The landlady lived on the ground floor and she answered the door with a smile on her face when she recognized Sally. 'You've just made it,' she said. 'I've had a number after it but I said I would hold it until six.'

'I couldn't get here any earlier,' Kate said. 'I've come straight from work.'

'Your sister said as much,' the landlady said as she crossed the tiled hall to the stairs. 'Now,' she went on as she climbed the stairs with some difficulty because she was a very large lady. 'My name is Dolly Donovan and the available flat, as your sister knows, is the one at the top of the house.

And climbing all these stairs does me no good at all.'

It certainly didn't appear to, Kate thought, as she listened to the landlady's laboured breathing every step of the way. She was wheezing heavily when the flat was finally reached. 'It's one hefty climb,' she panted, and Kate agreed, particularly after a day at work, but it was well worth it. The front door opened into a small hall with a rug covering most of the lino; a door opened either side of it. The door to the right was a large room that stretched from one end of the house to the other, with a window either end. Like the hall, the whole place had lino on the floor, but a rug lay in front of the gas fireplace. A small brown moquette three-piece suite stood in front of the fire and by the far window was a table and four chairs. 'Oh, it's lovely,' Kate exclaimed, stepping into the room.

'The other room was originally the same size as this,' Dolly said. 'But when the house was converted to flats, a proportion of it was taken off to make a kitchen. Access to that is from the living room.' She led the way down the room as she spoke and opened another door, at the far end by the table and chairs. It was a far cry from the curtained area they had now. There was nothing rickety about these shelves and there were two wall cupboards besides – one housed crockery and glasses and the other was empty and could house foodstuffs. The sink was set by the window and below it was another cupboard. 'Pots and pans and the like are in there,' Dolly said, and Kate had a look in and was impressed by the amount and quality of the cooking utensils. But best of all was the fairly new gas stove with four burners and an oven – Kate knew she would just love cooking on that. The bedroom was sizeable and housed two single beds. 'Oh, single beds!' Kate exclaimed. She said to Dolly, 'That's much better. Sally and I share a bed at the moment.'

'Yeah,' Sally said. 'And every time I turn over in the night I fall out.'

'Oh, you and me both,' Kate said, and Dolly laughed at the pair of them. 'No danger of that here,' she said. 'I'm sure you will be able to sleep the night through.'

'And we have a wardrobe.'

'Yes,' Dolly said. 'When George was fitting this out, I insisted on a wardrobe, and you have a chest of drawers and a dressing table to share too.'

'That's grand,' Kate said.

'Bathroom is on the next floor down, next to the broom cupboard with brushes and mops and all,' Dolly said. 'I expect these places to be kept clean. We don't want to be overrun with mice or rats.'

'And are baths by arrangement, like they are in our place at the moment?' Kate asked.

'Yeah,' said Dolly. 'But you will be well used to that.'

'Oh, yes, we are, that's fine.'

Dolly nodded. 'That's about all then. Oh, there is a basement area to do any washing you may have, with a gas boiler and two big sinks. And there are lines indoors and out.'

'Oh,' Kate said. 'You seem to have thought of

everything. What's the rent?'

'Seven and sixpence,' Dolly said. 'And wouldn't be so cheap if it wasn't right at the top of the house.'

It was still half as much again as they were paying for the one room, but with two wages they could manage it. So, when Dolly asked, 'Would you like a few minutes to talk it over?' Kate's eyes met the shining ones of her sister and she said, 'That won't be necessary, Mrs Donovan, er Dolly. My sister and I will take it and welcome.'

Just over a week after they had first seen it, they were ready to move in. David, Nick and Susie came to help and Sally was given the afternoon off too, and their bits and pieces were moved in no time. 'You really have fallen on your feet this time,' Nick said in approval.

'I'll say,' Kate said. 'I knew straight away it would suit us both down to the ground. Clever girl, Sally, for finding it.'

'Didn't do much,' Sally said. 'That's the good of telling everyone. Someone is bound to come up with something sooner or later. As it is, the mother of Dulcie – who I work with – is quite good friends with Dolly Donovan and she put in a word when she knew she had a flat vacant. Dulcie said that she is real particular who she has in her place. I suppose 'cos she lives there her-self.'

'Particular you say,' David mused with a twinkle in his eye. 'And yet she took you two on.'

'Oh, you,' Kate said, giving him a push as the others laughed. 'Don't do that,' he cautioned. 'I have something hidden beneath my jacket and

I'd hate you to break it.'

'Why, what is it?'

'This,' said David, producing a bottle of champagne.

'Ooh,' said Susie and Kate together.

'I've never tasted champagne,' Sally said. 'I haven't tasted much alcohol really.'

'That's because of your tender age,' David said. 'But today we'll make an exception. Get some glasses, Kate, and we'll drink to the future.'

Despite the rumblings in Europe, which the girls thought too far away for them to worry about, the future looked rosy. They all had jobs, and so they had money in their pockets, plenty of entertainment to encourage them to part with it – and added to that, they were in love.

Kate had never been happier than she was in the spring of 1939. They had been to see David's parents again one cloudy day in late February, though David said he would rather have gone to the pictures if it wasn't a fit day to go out. But Kate, though she had no real desire to go to the Burton's either, didn't want David's parents to think that she was keeping him away. 'Why should they?' David asked. 'I never spent much time at home before I met you anyway.'

'Even so–'

'They don't want to see me either,' David said. 'Since that first time, they have never asked us up, have they?'

'No,' Kate had to agree. 'Maybe it's me they don't like.'

'Shouldn't think so,' David said. 'And anyway,

I'm not going without you.'

'Look,' cajoled Kate. 'All we have to do is call in, have a cup of tea and leave again. That's not so hard.'

'Oh, all right, if you're so determined.'

'And don't argue with your brother, will you?'

David looked at her and smiled. 'Any more demands?' he said, and then, as Kate was about to speak, he lifted his hand and said, 'I will do my level best not to fight with Lawrence. Mainly because of what you said last time, about him winning if I react.'

'And so he will,' Kate said. 'So keep your temper.'

'I'll try.'

Kate sighed. That would have to do, and so they walked to the Burtons' that blustery cold Sunday afternoon. But even Kate acknowledged later that none of them seemed to care whether they were there or not. Dora was in the middle of baking scones for tea and Alf and Lawrence, newly returned from the pub, were half asleep in the chairs either side of the fire. However, Lawrence perked up considerably when he caught sight of Kate, much to her dismay. 'Well hello,' he said, jumping to his feet and catching hold of her hand before she had the chance to snatch it away. To David he said, 'What brings you here then, our kid?'

David stared at him before saying, 'It might have escaped your notice, but I live here.'

'Do you?' Lawrence said with mock incredulity. 'D'you hear that, Ma? David lives here? No one would realize that, with the little time you spend here.'

'And can you wonder at it when this is the sort of welcome I get?'

'Well, what sort of welcome do you want from your own family?' Alf asked.

'That's right,' Lawrence said. 'But you, my dear,' he went on, turning to face Kate and giving the hand he was still holding a squeeze, 'you can have as warm a welcome as you please.'

Beside her, Kate heard David's sharp intake of breath. She decided she would show him how she dealt with men like Lawrence Burton, so she smiled sweetly and said, 'That's very nice of you. I might feel more comfortable if you loosed my hand.'

He gave a hard laugh and she saw the glitter of malice in his eyes, but he did let her go. David put his arm around her and, turning to his mother, he said, 'Are we going to be asked to sit down, and is there a cup of tea in the offing?'

'And we had the tea and scones straight from the oven, and Dora is a good cook and they should have been delicious,' Kate told Susie the next morning as they changed in the cloakroom. 'But, you know, they tasted like sawdust and I found them hard to swallow because the atmosphere was poisonous.'

'What d'you mean?' one of the other girls asked, hearing what Kate said.

'It's mainly down to his brother, Lawrence,' Kate said. She then added, 'No, actually, that's not true. His parents are just as bad not saying a word about it. He's constantly making snide remarks and mocking almost anything David says,' she said in explanation.

'And flirting with you, don't forget.'

'Yeah, openly flirting,' Kate said.

'With his own brother's girl?'

Kate nodded. 'That's the point,' she said, 'it's all done to make David mad. And this isn't banter between brothers, this is real malicious stuff.'

'He's a nasty piece of work,' Susie said. 'One of my brothers had a taste of his bullying tactics when he was younger. Seems he hasn't improved with age.'

'No,' Kate said. 'And you know I talked David into going to see them in the first place.'

'More fool you then,' another of her workmates said. 'Be a while before you'd do that again, I'd say.'

'Yeah,' Kate agreed, 'and you'd say right.'

Neither Kate nor David discussed that awful visit, for there was nothing really to say; instead, they took joy in one another's company on Sundays as they continued their jaunts out. They wandered down to Salford Bridge the following Sunday, where David explained why the locks on the canals were necessary and how they worked, and Kate saw some of the brightly painted, spick-and-span little barges, and noticed with some surprise the lace curtains at the windows. Another day they went on to Aston Park and David took Kate out in a rowing boat. She had never been on a boat and she found getting into one and bobbing about on the swirling grey-blue water a very scary business; she wouldn't have been a bit surprised if she had landed up getting very wet indeed.

However, all was well, and when they both

climbed out, David took her to see Aston Hall. It's well worth a look,' he said. 'And what you have to remember is at one time this park would be owned by one family.'

Aston Hall was enormous. To either side of the main structure were extra wings and, at the back, amongst the many chimneys, were three blue domes, and on the front of the middle one was set a large clock. Kate thought it quite wrong that this large, lavish house and all the land surrounding it should belong to one family.

'It's the way it was then,' David said with a shrug when she said this. 'Lots of this city's parks are the same. At least now they are open for everyone to enjoy.'

'Yes,' said Kate. 'Until I met you I'd never bothered going to any of the parks around. You have opened my eyes.'

In mid-April, Kate was just about to get into bed when she heard Sally's key in the lock. This was normal – usually Sally would make a drink and come to bed herself without disturbing Kate, who often wouldn't see her till the next morning. However, that night she opened the bedroom door and said plaintively, 'Oh, Kate, I'm glad you're not asleep.'

Kate glanced up. The sight of Sally's woebegone face and red-rimmed eyes drove the sleepiness from her and she shot out of bed and put her arms around her sister. 'What is it? What's up?' she asked.

Tears trickled down Sally's cheeks as she said brokenly, 'It's Phil. Oh, Kate, he's been called up.'

'Called up?' Kate repeated. 'Do you mean called up for the Army?'

Sally nodded and Kate said, 'But why?'

'Case there's a war, I suppose,' Sally said. 'He isn't the only one. He met a man he was at school with on the way to work and he had his papers too, and the son of a woman at work as well.' She looked at Kate and said, 'Makes it horribly real somehow, doesn't it?'

'It does,' Kate conceded, wrapping herself in her dressing gown as she spoke.

'What are you doing?'

'What's it look like?' Kate said. 'I might not know much, but what I do know is that there will be no sleep for either of us with all this churning around in our minds. How about me making us a nice mug of cocoa?'

Sally sighed and then nodded. 'I suppose,' she said. 'Sorry to disturb you, Kate. I know you have to get up early in the morning.'

'Don't worry about it,' Kate said. 'Like I said, I wouldn't be able to sleep anyway.'

Nothing more was said, each busy with their own thoughts until the cocoa was made and they were seated either side of the gas fire, relit and glowing comfortingly in front of them. Then Kate said, 'It could still just be getting ready, in case, you know.'

'I'd really like to believe you, Kate,' Sally said. 'You are trying to protect me like you did when I was little and you could always scare the hobgoblins and other night terrors away. But I'm not little any more and this, I think, will be bigger than both of us. I don't want to think of war any more than you do, but if it happens, Phil and others like him will be in the forefront of any fighting, because they will be the only ones trained. That thought terrifies me.'

'It will probably terrify his mother too,' Kate said quietly.

'Yeah, it has,' Sally said. 'Phil said she was really upset. How will either of us bear it if Phil is sent away to fight?'

'You will bear it because you must,' Kate said. 'But don't start worrying until you have to.'

'I'll try not to,' Sally said. 'It will be hard, though, because that isn't all either. One of the girls has a brother in the Territorials, and he was in France on manoeuvres and was suddenly recalled last month, with no explanation and just halfway through the course. I think war now is a foregone conclusion, which will mean our lives will never be the same again. But I hope to God I'm wrong.'

TEN

Phillip Reynard and all young men of a similar age left for the training camp in Cannock Chase in mid-May. Life went on. Sally consoled herself that he wasn't in any danger there. She wrote him long letters and was always making him up nice little parcels, and said she was glad to have her job because it passed the time. Kate felt very sorry for her and even asked her along on their Sunday jaunts if she was off work, but she always refused. 'You don't want me tagging along,' she said. 'Not really. Anyway, it's on Sunday that Phil's mother said time hangs very heavily for her, and so I think I will go and see her on free Sunday afternoons.' Kate couldn't really argue with that.

As spring gave way to a beautiful summer, and one glorious day in mid-July, on a blisteringly hot day, Kate and David walked to the little train station on Gravelly Hill to take the train to Sutton Park. They alighted from the train at Sutton Coldfield and walked down the hill to the park entrance; they had to pay money at the gate to go in because they didn't live in the town itself. 'Isn't it strange to have to pay to go into a park?' Kate asked David.

'I suppose it is,' David said. 'But this is a very special park, and it only costs coppers if you go in on foot. More by car, of course, because you can drive around here – not that there's that

176

many cars around.'

And there weren't, but a few did pass them as they strolled hand in hand through the grass. The trees in the woods were in full bloom, and the light coming through the trees dappled and danced in front of them, shading them from the heat of the day. Kate would have liked to remove her stockings and paddle in the meandering stream to cool her feet, but some of the stones on the riverbed looked sharp and she knew that David wanted to find the five large lakes that he said were there.

In that they were disappointed, because they were stopped from going all over the park when they found that a fair bit of it had been given over to the military. Climbing a nearby hill later, they could see the fields fair peppered with Army-issue tents. 'Isn't it unnerving, all these preparations for war?' Kate said. 'It's almost as if people are willing us into it.'

'There aren't many options left for us, I don't think,' David said. 'I know you don't want to believe it, my darling, but I think now that war is inevitable. Phil's call-up will be just one of hundreds more.'

'That means you too, you and Nick?'

'It means every able man in Britain if we are even to have a chance of beating Germany. They've ridden roughshod over half of Europe already and have spent years preparing for another war. They have had call-up there for some years now, but I shan't wait to be called up. I'm going to enlist and join the Air Force.'

Kate shivered. 'Don't!'

David swung Kate to face him and, holding her shoulders, he looked deep into her eyes. Kate noted the uncertainty in his as he said, 'I need to talk to you and I must do it now before I lose my nerve altogether.'

'What? Why should you be nervous of me?'

'Because I am going to ask you something and I'm not sure what your answer will be,' David said. 'It's been in my mind for ages and often lately on the tip of my tongue, but I have always bitten it back, afraid you might think me presumptuous.'

'You want me to wait for you?' Kate said. 'Is that it, because I'll gladly do that?'

'Kate, I want to marry you,' David said earnestly, and he felt Kate jump beneath his hands in shock, because they had never discussed marriage. David went on quickly: 'I love you dearly and I know you love me. I want to make you totally mine, and love you as I long to, because if I'm right and war is imminent, then we don't know how much time we might have together.'

Kate was silent. She knew exactly what David meant when he said he wanted to love her properly, because they had progressed very far along the line from the chaste kiss Kate had allowed at first. Now, when David kissed and caressed her, she felt strange yearnings course though her body. She often ached for love of David and longed for fulfilment. She couldn't allow it, of course, not before marriage, and yet in her heart of hearts she wasn't sure whether it would have happened regardless if they'd ever had the flat totally to themselves. She could only be grateful that the potential imminent arrival of Sally had helped put the brakes on their love-making more than once, because it was getting harder and harder to pull back.

This wouldn't matter if she was married to David, when they could give full rein to their feelings. Yet marriage was more than tumbling into bed together, however enjoyable. They had to think of where they would live, for a start, and she had to consider Sally's welfare too – she couldn't leave her on her own in the flat they had just moved into, for she would never manage the rent on her salary for one thing, and the other was that she would worry about her left on her own.

But she knew the main reason for her hesitation was that David was not a Catholic and she had no right to ask him to become one. She knew there were those in Ireland who would probably not understand how she could think of marrying such a man. In Donegal there had been a few people in the town who went to a different church from the Catholic one, but she hadn't really known any of them.

In Birmingham the situation was totally differ-ent – there were many people of all different faiths and some, like the Burtons, of no faith at all. Her parents would more than likely feel so ashamed and shocked at her news that they would prob-ably seek the advice of the parish priest, too, who would probably feel he had a perfect right to interfere in her life, having known Kate since she was a young child.

Oh, yes, the letter she would send to her mother about her and David would stir up a right hornet's nest and her parents would never give her their blessing. She asked herself would it matter, but she knew it would – she had always sought their approval. 'Kate,' David said, and she looked at her beloved's bleak eyes, certain her silence meant she would refuse him, but she suddenly knew, despite all the problems, she wanted this man in her life. Surely she had the right to choose who she was to spend the rest of her life with. If David was right and war was a foregone conclusion, they had no time to waste. And so she turned to face him and said in a small voice that was little more than a whisper, 'Yes.'

However, disappointment had so seeped into David's consciousness that he didn't register what Kate had said at first and began to bluster, 'I'm sorry, Kate, springing it on you like that. I shouldn't have spoken.'

'I said yes,' Kate repeated a little louder.

'I mean, it isn't as if we have discussed marriage, except in the very vaguest terms,' David said. 'And then to jump in like that with no lead...' And then his brain registered that she had spoken and he said, 'What did you say?'

Kate had a broad grin on her face as she said, 'I think you are going deaf in your old age. I said yes.'

'You said yes,' David cried in delight. 'Oh, my darling girl,' and he put his arms around Kate and hugged her tight while he planted little kisses all over her face. 'I can hardly believe it.'

'You'd better had,' Kate said. 'I've already said it three times.'

Still with the smile on her face, she pulled

herself out of David's embrace and, holding his hand tightly, said, 'There are a few problems to be sorted out, but they can be gone into later. For now I'd like to explore what we can of this park, if it's all right with you.'

'Perfectly all right, Miss Munroe,' David said in mock formality. 'But I really need a kiss to be going on with.'

'Ah, David,' Kate said, and felt herself enfolded in his arms again.

There were mixed reactions when Kate and David told everyone of their plans, but most people could understand the desire for speed and pronounced themselves all for the young couple. And Sally had a solution to the problem of where they were to live. 'Have you anywhere in mind?' she said.

'Well, no,' Kate said. 'I mean, David sprung it on me rather, but now we will have to think about it – and quickly too. You know the trouble we had getting this place.'

Sally nodded. 'I might be able to help you then,' she said. 'Look, I didn't tell you at the time, not sure you would approve, but when Phil got his call-up papers, we got secretly engaged.'

'Sally!' cried Kate, but she asked herself why she was so shocked. It had been obvious how much Phil and Sally loved each other, and so, despite the fact that Sally was only just seventeen, engagement was a natural progression.

'Don't say I'm too young or anything, will you?'

'No, Sally,' Kate said. 'I have no intention of saying anything like that.' And she hadn't, because she knew that since Sally had come to Birmingham she had grown up and matured a great deal; she was a girl who knew her own mind.

Sally gave a sigh of relief. She pulled at a chain around her neck that she had tucked inside a jumper to reveal a cluster of diamonds set into a golden ring.

'Oh,' Kate breathed. 'Oh, it's beautiful, and there is no need to hide it. I won't judge you.'

'I'm glad,' Sally said. 'I hated hiding it from you. Anyway, Phil's mother asked me if I would consider living with her once Phil left, as company for one another, but I refused because I wouldn't leave you. I could do that now, though, and David could move in here.'

'It's certainly an idea,' Kate said. 'You'd not mind living with Phil's mother?'

'No,' Sally said. 'I like her. We get on fine. I suppose you'd have to clear it with Dolly, but I don't see that as a major problem, and then all you'd need is a new double bed, unless,' she added with a wry smile, 'you'd like to start married life with two singles.'

'Oh, I think David will insist on a double,' Kate said with an answering smile. 'In fact, it will probably be our first purchase. You moving in with Phil's mother would seem to be the best solution all round.'

Phil's mother was delighted too at the turn of events, which is what Kate wrote and told her parents a few days later. She had dreaded writing that letter, though she knew it had to be done. She'd hoped the fact that they had a place to live already organized might sweeten the pill even a little.

In actual fact it made things worse. Philomena had asked many times if David was a Catholic, and the fact that Kate had never even acknowledged the question gave Philomena her answer. But, she had hoped and prayed and offered up a novena that the relationship was not as strong as it appeared and Kate would remember that she was Catholic girl, a member of the One True Church, and end the affair with this David.

When she found that not only had Kate agreed to marry this man, but they had already sorted out somewhere to live, she was furious and also disappointed. Kate had always in the past been a compliant daughter, and one eager to please. So, a week later, when she had calmed down a little, she sent a censorious letter back, asking her if she knew what she was doing. Didn't she mind that she was choosing to deny her faith in this way? The priest himself could hardly credit it, with her being brought up such a good Catholic girl.

Kate knew that, because there was also a letter from the parish priest. This was worse than her mother's, as it spoke of the contempt that she had shown for her parents after the values they had gone to pains to instil in her. She had, he said, shown a complete absence of any sort of filial duty that she owed them. He advised her to think very carefully about what she was intending to do, which he called the height of selfishness. He reminded her that marriage was for life, and he ended his judicious epistle: *What matter, Kate, if you gain your heart's desire and lose your immortal soul in the process? Remember the road to Hell is lined with sinners.*

David was amazed at the fuss made and a little worried by the way the letter from the priest was worded, though Kate seemed to be taking it in her stride. 'It's only what I expected,' she said, when David expressed concern.

'But it's almost threatening,' David said, scanning the letter again.

'I know, it's how they go on,' Kate said.

'It doesn't sort of put you off?' David asked.

'Not a bit of it,' Kate declared emphatically.

'Is there anything I can do to make things better for you?' David asked, who was still a little anxious of the effect the letters might be having on Kate, for all she said they didn't bother her. 'Maybe if I was to write to your parents...?'

Kate shook her head and smiled. 'That wouldn't help,' she said. 'The only way you could cool things down is if you took instruction and became a Catholic.' And added, 'Then the fact that you might have two heads wouldn't matter a dot.'

'It's almost unbelievable,' David said. 'Do you want me to do that, become a Catholic?'

It would solve all Kate's problems and yet she said, 'Do you want to?'

'To be honest, no.'

'Then why should you do something you don't want to do in order to marry me?' Kate said. 'I'm used to pressure like this, and there will be more of the same when I see the priest on Sunday about reading the banns.'

'How long does that take?' David asked.

'Three weeks,' Kate said.

'I don't think we have that much time,' David

said. 'It's the first of August tomorrow and it will be the sixth before you see the priest. Then it will the end of August or beginning of September before we could marry.'

'And that is too late? Is that what you're saying?'

David shook his head. 'I don't know, not anything definite anyway. I just have this feeling of dread on me.'

'So what do you want to do?'

'Well, we could get married in the register office in no time.'

Kate was suddenly very still for she hadn't expected that. She didn't want to get married in any register office; she wanted at least a marriage in church, and she also knew if she was to do as David asked, she would not be married in the eyes of the Catholic Church and they would regard her as living in sin. She fought with the image of what she wanted and the reality of living in a country on the verge of war, which might mean things had to be done in a different way. Surely what mattered at the end of the day was that they would be legally married as far as the law of the land went, and so she nodded her head. 'All right, then. If that's what you want.'

It was a very quiet wedding on Saturday 12 August, and when she woke that morning she was feeling quite dispirited about the whole business, but she kept those feelings to herself lest David feel bad encouraging her to make do with such a shabby performance. Whenever she had visualized her wedding, she had been dressed in a flowing white dress in a church attended by family and friends and possibly her sister and her cousins, Geraldine, Maggie and Bridget, as bridesmaids. However, for this wedding she had bought a navy-and-white costume at C&A Modes, and with it she wore silk stockings, navy court shoes with a higher heel than usual and a navy hat with veil. A smallish posy of flowers was all that the florist could make up at such short notice. She was despondent about the whole thing, she couldn't deny it, but tried to keep her thoughts to herself, especially in front of Susie and Sally, who came round the evening before the wedding. She paraded her outfit in front of them and, though they praised her choice of clothes and said she looked fine, she could sense their disappointment.

Still, they were both round in the morning before the wedding to help Kate dress and fashion her hair in a sort of coronet that looked a treat with the hat she had bought, and Kate was glad to have her friend and sister beside her, given that her stomach was behaving most strangely. She really needed their steadying influence. And she was never more grateful for this than when she stepped out of the taxi and came face to face with Alf and Dora Burton waiting for her at the bottom of the steps of the register office.

Kate hadn't seen either of them since that last awful day she had called round with David a few months before, though David had been on his own since to tell them of his marriage. She was a little nervous to see them there because David hadn't been at all sure that they were going to turn up, and Sally and Susie flanking Kate were well aware of how she was feeling. However, the couple were more pleasant than she had ever known them, even though Dora said, 'I'm glad at any rate you were sensible and got that costume, which is more serviceable altogether and better than a wedding dress you'll never wear again.'

Kate knew she was probably right, but she didn't really want to wear clothes described as serviceable on her wedding day. 'Do I look all right?'

'Oh, you look far better than just all right, girl,' Alf said. 'Our David is a lucky man and I hope he appreciates that.'

'I agree with that,' Susie said, and Sally nodded vigorously. 'You look beautiful, Kate, you really do.'

'There'll be a rush of weddings soon, you wait and see,' Alf said to her. 'Just like it was in the last lot. Soon as war's official, like, there'll be loads of couples want to be married before they are parted.'

'That's why we did it in a rush,' Kate said. 'David said he's not waiting to be called up. He wants to join the RAF. But do you think there is no way now of averting war?'

'Can't see how,' Alf said. 'We promised to go to Poland's aid and Hitler's armies are massing on the border. Only a matter of time, I think.'

'Anyway,' Dora said, 'these aren't the thoughts that you should be having on your wedding day.'

Then suddenly Mary Mason was by her side, squeezing her arm, and Susie – knowing her mother maybe wanted a quiet word with Kate – moved away with Sally and Dora. Alf followed them. Kate was suddenly overcome with emotion for this lovely lady who had mothered her since she had arrived in Birmingham, and who she knew was disappointed at this slightly shoddy wedding, for she had seen that in her eyes. She knew she only wanted better for her because she cared about her, and Kate felt tears pricking her eyes as she hugged Mary tight, taking no heed of her protests that she would crush her clothes.

Mary felt dampness on the shoulder of her outfit, though, and heard the slight sniffly noises Kate was making. 'You're not crying, are you?' she demanded. 'Oh, my dear girl,' she exclaimed, dabbing at Kate's face with a white lacy hanky. 'That husband of yours will have my guts for garters if he thinks I've been upsetting you.'

'You haven't.'

'Good, because you are very dear to us, you know,' Mary said. 'Oh, now don't start again. You mustn't cry at your own wedding. You let others do the crying for you on that day. Now, are you ready? Because they will all be waiting and you look so very beautiful. David will be bowled over by the sight of you.'

Kate was glad to have had those few words with Mary, because when she went into the room where the wedding was to take place, she thought it a most depressing place. It was stark and bare, and chairs were arranged in rows in front of a table at the far end. David and Nick, his best man, were in the front row, and, hearing the door open, David turned. The breath stopped in his throat at Kate's simple beauty as she stood framed in the doorway for a few minutes on the arm of Frank Mason.

Kate's eyes caught David's and she was suddenly filled with love for the man waiting for her, so that she felt as though she might explode with happiness and the room no longer mattered. She concentrated her gaze on the man standing waiting for her, and found it was hard to walk respectably and sensibly at Frank's side. When she reached David, their eyes seemed to fuse together; as their hands touched, she felt tingling all over her body. Suddenly the only important thing to her was that she was being married to this man that she loved so very, very much.

And, after a few words, said and repeated in that bare room, David and Kate were man and wife, and David took Kate in his arms. 'I love you, Mrs Burton,' he said.

Kate was unable to answer because David's lips descended on hers and she gave herself up to the enjoyment of it. The small wedding party went off to a room in a pub nearest the register office and Kate was able at last to thank all those who had come. Sally had brought Ruby Reynard. 'I love a good wedding,' she told Kate, who noticed she had a handkerchief rolled up in her hand. Seeing Kate noticed this, she said, 'I nearly always cry at weddings. Phil used to tease me about it. He said I wouldn't feel I'd enjoyed myself if I hadn't had a good old cry.'

'And how did mine measure up, Ruby?' Kate asked with a smile.

'Oh, I shed tears at yours, my dear,' Ruby admitted. 'But you'll be all right because you have a good man there.'

'I know,' Kate said.

'David was saying that none of your people

were able to make it,' Dora said to Kate as she appeared by her side. 'Terrible shame that.'

'Yes,' Kate said, 'but it's difficult to leave the farm in the summertime.'

'Ah, yes, it must be,' Dora said.

But to Susie, Kate told the truth, and she stared at her as if she couldn't comprehend it. 'You never even told them you were getting married?' she repeated incredulously.

'What was the point?' Kate said. 'What I told Dora was partially true anyway, because this is a busy time on any farm.'

The real reason, though, was because she couldn't think of a way to tell her mother that she was being married in a register office, which to them would mean no marriage at all. But it was a marriage, she told herself, and the only one that she was ever going to have.

Kate loved being married to David. They had had two days in Blackpool, where the sun shone down from a cornflower-blue sky. The first day they strolled along the sands, hand in hand, and paddled their feet at the water's edge. Kate had never owned a bathing costume in her life, and anyway she thought she might feel embarrassed taking her clothes off. She didn't mind slipping her shoes off, though, and paddling along feeling her toes curl over the small pebbles, or sink in the soft sand, David beside her doing the same with his trousers turned up to his knees.

Sometimes they just sat and watched the world go by, the children making endless sandcastles and trying to fill the moat; they smiled at their consternation when their buckets of water seeped through the sand, or they watched them squealing with excitement as they rode the donkeys. 'Isn't this a grand place for children?' Kate remarked.

'Mmm,' David said, lying back on the rug they had brought. 'Someday we'll bring our children here.'

'You want children then?'

David opened his eyes a crack and peered at Kate. 'Course,' he said. 'Don't you?'

'These are the sort of questions that we should have asked before we decided to get married,' Kate said.

'You mean you don't want children?' David said incredulously.

'I mean I'm joking,' Kate said. 'Don't know that there is any way of stopping them anyway, if we continue to get up to the shenanigans that we got up to last night.'

'Didn't hear you complaining.'

'I didn't,' Kate said. 'And I'm not complaining now either, just making a comment.'

'It's just that there are ways of preventing pregnancy,' David said.

'Not for a Catholic,' Kate said. 'Birth control is forbidden.'

'Thank God, I'm not a Catholic then,' David said. 'For much as I want children, I don't want the body pulled out of you with a baby every year, and if I have to wear something then I will. But it's too hot for discussions like this. Let's go and find someone selling ice creams.'

Kate followed behind David, but thoughts were

tumbling in her head. David wasn't a Catholic right enough, but she was, so was it still a sin for her to have sex, knowing that he was using something to prevent pregnancy? She wasn't sure and couldn't really ask. She would be embarrassed talking about sex with anyone, let alone a priest. She would just have to follow her conscience.

'Penny for them,' David said, jerking her back to the present. She turned and took the cornet that he offered her and then said with a coy smile, 'My thoughts are worth more than a mere penny, I'll have you know, David Burton.'

But she didn't offer to share them, because she decided that she wouldn't waste a minute more on a problem that was hers alone, and when David said, 'Shall we make for the fair?' she nodded her head eagerly.

Kate screamed her way round the Big Dipper, nearly had a heart attack in the Ghost Train, was made deliciously dizzy on the Carousel and the Waltzers, bruised to bits on the Bumper Cars and laughed herself silly in the Hall of Mirrors. They had fish and chips with bread and butter and as much tea as they wanted in one of the cafés along the front and then ate candy floss on the way home to the boarding house. And all the way back it was as if bubbles of joy were inside Kate, for she had never felt such happiness before and her only wish was that the future that lay before them was not marred by the rumblings of war.

ELEVEN

By the time Kate and David came back from their honeymoon, preparations for war had gathered momentum, and when they went to Brookvale Park on their usual Sunday-afternoon jaunt, they found great ditches had been dug just along the park's perimeter. Kate looked at them with distaste. 'Why are we so concerned with Poland, with any of them?' she asked. 'I mean, this is all happening miles away. Why should it affect us?'

'Because of the type of man Hitler is, I suppose,' David said. 'I don't for one moment think that a man who has been amassing armaments and training servicemen for years will be satisfied with Poland. He will turn next to Belgium, Holland too maybe, and then France – and we are just a short Channel hop away from France. He has got to be stopped somewhere along the line. Surely you can see that?'

Kate sighed. 'I can, of course, but I don't really want to see it,' she said. 'I want to stick my head in the sand and let life go on without me, and I will resurface again when life is very much more peaceful.'

David laughed. 'Can't do that,' he said. 'It will be all hands to the pump when hostilities do start.'

'And you still intend to enlist?'

David nodded. 'There is no way of getting out of

it. It would only postpone the inevitable because I would be called up anyway. This way, I at least can go into the RAF as I want to.'

'You will be in so much danger then,' Kate said. 'Every paper you open says that this war will be won in the air.'

David nodded. 'I think it will too,' he said. 'You only have to look at what German planes did to Guernica a couple of years ago to see just how powerful the Luftwaffe, his Air Force, are.'

'And what he is capable of,' Kate said, and she remembered the photographs in the papers, of the distressed people in shock and disbelief, looking at the mounds and mounds of rubble that was what their town had been reduced to, the streets littered with bodies. The thought of that happening in the streets of Birmingham, in any part of Great Britain, made her feel sick, and she looked at David and said, 'You think they are going to bomb us like that?'

'I certainly think they will try,' David said. 'And I imagine the RAF will do their damnedest to stop them, but in case any get through, I suppose they have got to try and protect the civilian population as much as they can.'

It seemed that David was right, because the next day on her way to work, Kate passed a brick-built structure that she couldn't remember seeing before. It was like no building she had ever seen because it had no windows at all – at least in what she could see of it, because it was almost completely lagged with sandbags. 'What on earth is that?' she asked Susie as she approached.

'Surface-built shelter,' Susie said. 'The kids

194

were filling up the sandbags all day yesterday.' Kate studied them as she passed. They seemed solid enough and yet she wondered how well they would stand up to bombs hurtling through the air, and she gave a sudden shudder at the thought.

Susie didn't notice because she wanted to hear Kate's news. 'So how's married life? It certainly seems to sit well on you.'

'Married life is great, Susie,' Kate said. 'Why didn't you and Nick make it a double wedding?'

'Mom and Dad wouldn't hear of it,' Susie said. 'I did mention it and I know they can't actually stop me, but they can make life extremely difficult; you know how it is. I didn't want to upset them. Anyway, while you were away they relented enough to let us get engaged.'

'Have you a ring?' Kate asked, because Susie's left hand was unadorned.

'Yeah,' Susie said. 'But not one I wear for work. We'll pop round and see you later and you can have a proper butcher's.'

'I'd love that,' said Kate, 'but what about marriage though?'

'They said no marriage till the end of hostilities,' Susie said disgustedly. 'God alone knows when that will be. Mom said she saw a lot of wartime romances that foundered in peacetime. Marry in haste and repent at leisure sort of thing.'

'Heaven only knows what she thinks of me then.'

'She loves you, Kate, you know that,' Susie said. 'And in a way she feels sorry for you.'

'Sorry for me?' Kate said, bristling. 'There's no

need for anyone to be sorry for me.'

'You couldn't have been pleased with the wedding,' Susie said. 'My parents want me to have a proper wedding in church, even if I am marrying a Protestant.'

'I doubt my parents would ever have been that welcoming to David wherever I married him,' Kate said. 'But you asked me if I was disappointed with my wedding, and I will just say this: I realized that how you get married doesn't matter. It's not the fancy clothes and food and razzmatazz, or even the white dress; it's marrying the man you love in any way that suits you. If war is declared tomorrow, I will still be glad that I had this precious time with David.'

A lump rose in Susie's throat at Kate's words and, after a moment, she said, 'And I will regret not having that same special time with Nick. You're right, Kate. No one should feel sorry for you.'

There was an announcement on the wireless after the seven o'clock news, which they always turned on as they got ready for work, reminding them that the blackout was to come into force on 1 September.

Kate's eyes met David's as she cried, 'Oh God, with the wedding and honeymoon and everything, this sort of slipped my mind – or, if I'm honest, I didn't want to remember it. How stupid is that, because if we haven't got blackout curtains or shutters at the windows in four days' time we will be fined two hundred pounds. I'd better go down the Bull Ring after work and see

196

what I can pick up. Hope they still have stuff I can use. It will cost something to curtain this lot – and how on earth will I get it done in time?'

'I can make shutters for some of the windows and that will save time and material,' David said. 'You get what you can and I will have a hunt round for the bits to make the shutters.'

'Oh, David, thanks,' Kate said. 'That's a real load off my mind.'

She told Susie on the way to work, who was amazed she hadn't even started on the blackout curtains. 'Mom will help,' she said. 'I know she will, because she has done it for other people – she has that sewing machine Dad bought her at Christmas.'

Kate knew all about Mary Burton's sewing machine. She had turned out lots of things using it, starting with curtains and straight things, but going on to make dresses for herself and Susie.

'I don't know,' Kate said. 'I mean, it's a bit of a cheek.'

'Don't see why when she's done it for others,' Susie said.

'Are you sure she won't mind?' Kate asked anxiously.

'Absolutely sure.'

And that is what Kate told David when she arrived home later that night with a bale of black cloth. 'Wasn't that thoughtful of Susie. Her mother is very like that, you know: really helpful to everybody.'

'The Masons are a nice family,' David said. 'Everyone says so. Anyway, I was having a look before you came in. I have got enough wood and fixings to do shutters for the kitchen windows and the bedroom, but there are two sizable windows in the living room and I think curtains would be better there.'

And while Kate was helping David measure up the windows she suddenly said, 'But it's not just the curtains, is it? I mean, how are people to go about in the pitch-black?'

David shrugged. 'Search me,' he said. 'I think that we're going to have to get used to things we never had to do before, because there was another announcement on the wireless before you got in tonight.'

'Oh, what other delights are being planned for us?'

'In a word, gas masks!'

Kate turned an aghast face to David and repeated, 'Gas masks?'

'Yes, gas masks,' David said. 'Every man, woman and child has to have one and carry it with them at all times.'

'Oh God,' Kate said. 'I don't relish wearing one of those.'

'Neither do I, to be honest, but it's probably better than being gassed to death.'

'Yeah, but just how likely is that?'

'I don't know,' David said, 'and probably neither does anyone else, but the Germans used gas in the last war. I suppose they can't take the risk. Anyway, the announcer said there will be various collection points organized, and you can pick your gas masks up from those from the first of September as well.'

'That certainly seems to be a very important

date in the calendar,' Kate said, picking up the parcel and shoving the measurements into her pocket. 'But just for now I'd best take these before it gets too late.' Mary Mason was only too pleased to help Kate, and said as they were only straight seams she could have them done for her the next day. 'I'm ever so grateful, Mrs Mason.'

'That's all right, Kate,' Mary said. 'We all have to pull together, it seems to me, and between the two of us I really love using the machine. So if you call in tomorrow, I will have the curtains ready for you.'

And she did, and Kate went home and hung them straight away. She felt depressed to see such hideous black curtains at the windows; the only consolation was that everybody else would be in the same boat.

On Friday, after work, Kate and Susie went to get their gas masks. They too were hideous, and when the woman showed them how to put them on, Kate thought the smell was obnoxious. Susie felt the same and she ripped hers off again almost immediately. 'God, they smell vile.'

'You might be glad of that mask, smell and all, before you are much older,' the woman chided. Kate tugged her mask off too, as Susie said, 'Well, let me tell you something. They would have to be pretty certain gas was heading our way before I would put this mask near my face. And another thing, I could hardly breathe when I had it on. You can't tell me that that's a healthy way to be.'

'I couldn't breathe either,' agreed Kate. 'The Germans don't really have to send the gas – just threaten to, and we'd all be asphyxiated in our masks.'

The woman obviously didn't appreciate their levity, and this amused the girls still further; they left her frowning in disapproval and went out with the gas masks hung around their necks in the boxes supplied. 'I think humour will be all that we have left,' Kate said as they made their way home. 'When war comes, life will be tougher for all of us. I mean, it's light enough to come home now, but can you imagine what it will be like trying to get to work and back in the pitch-black?'

'Yeah,' Susie said, 'it will be murder. I agree with you – humour and laughter will be all we have to make life worth living.'

'It's true,' said Kate. 'And now let's run for that tram because I have got to cook the tea when I get in and I am as hungry as a hunter now, and I can't see anything funny in that at all.'

When she got home, though, David told her not to bother cooking and said that he would go out for fish and chips. Kate felt her mouth watering at the thought and she said, 'Ooh, David, that will be lovely. What were you doing when I came in?'

'Putting tape across the windows,' David said. 'It was a government recommendation to prevent flying glass in case of an air raid.'

Kate felt an icy thread run down her spine as she said, 'David, war hasn't been declared yet.'

'Might as well be,' David said grimly. 'It came through on the news earlier. Hitler's armies have invaded Poland and the Poles are fighting for their lives. The prime minister is speaking on the wireless on Sunday morning, just after eleven.'

That Sunday, Sally and Ruby Reynard came to the flat to listen to the prime minister's speech as they had no wireless of their own – and anyway, Kate had wanted Sally with her. Never had the time passed so slowly, or the eleven chimes of Big Ben sounded so loud, and eventually the waiting, anxious people heard the voice of Neville Chamberlain:

I am speaking to you from the cabinet room at Ten Downing Street. This morning the British ambassador in Berlin handed the German government a final note, stating that unless we heard from them by eleven o'clock that they were prepared at once to withdraw their troops from Poland, a state of war would exist between us. I have to tell you now that no such undertaking has been received and that consequently this country is at war with Germany...

There was more about how sorry Chamberlain was and how hard he had tried to avoid conflict and that he was sure that all Britons would play their part with calmness and courage. Kate knew that David would do just that, and join the RAF as soon as he could, and she felt him stiffen with resolve beside her. In contrast, Sally's face was chalk white and Ruby Reynard began to sob. Kate felt sorry for both of them, for they knew that Phil would now be in the forefront of the fighting.

David knew it too and he said, 'I often think that it's harder for those waiting at home than the servicemen themselves. Kate will be joining those ranks soon, because I am enlisting as soon as I am able.'

'You want to join the RAF, don't you?' Sally said, and David gave a nod. 'And so does Nick. We will go first thing tomorrow, because you get more choice if you enlist rather than wait to be called up.'

'Won't you be scared up in the air in one of those little planes?' Ruby asked.

However, before David was able to answer her, a horrendous sound rent the air, a sound Birmingham was going to become very familiar with. For a moment no one really knew what to do, and then David said, 'Let's go down to the cellar. It's bound to be safer than here.'

The others were only too glad someone had taken charge, and they pounded down the stairs, as others were coming out of their flats on the second floor and the first, obviously with the same idea as themselves. When they reached the cellar it was to find the Donovan family already there. Apprehension or pure naked fear was written across every face and they waited, listening intently for the sound of bombs. But nothing happened, and after a few minutes more, another siren blasted out. 'All Clear,' George Donovan grumbled. 'Bloody false alarm.'

Kate was glad it was and wondered if the sirens were sounded out intentionally to jolt the country into a realization that this was what war meant. It certainly had that effect on her. For weeks the papers had been running articles on government directives, such as what to do in air raids and the like, and she had avoided them like the plague. One of them, however, David had drawn her attention to – it recommended filling a shelter bag with identity cards, insurance policies, and bank and post office books and treasured photographs. Kate had agreed with David that it was a good idea, but she had done nothing about it. Now she decided to remedy that as soon as possible. 'My days of burying my head in the sand are over,' she told David as they got ready for bed that night. 'We are at war and that will mean challenges for us all, I think. We must be ready to meet them.'

'You don't have to,' David said. 'Birmingham is likely to be a prime target, being such a big city. You could always go back to Ireland if you wanted to.'

'No,' Kate said indignantly. 'David, I am not a hothouse flower and I am going to stay here with everyone else. We can't all run away; if we tried to, who would run the country while all you men are away chasing Germans?'

'All right, you win, you feisty lady,' David said, holding her close. 'And I am proud of you for saying that, but I know that I shall worry about you just as much as you will about me.'

When Kate and Susie got off the tram the next day, Sally was waiting at the stop. 'Anything wrong?' Kate asked her.

'Not exactly.'

'How not exactly?' Kate asked. 'And why are you not at work for starters?'

'Well, that's it,' said Sally. 'I haven't got a job any more – none of us have.'

'What are you on about?'

'I'm trying to tell you,' Sally said. 'The government have closed down all places of entertainment.'

'All places?' Susie asked.

Sally nodded. 'Everything, the boss said: cinemas, theatres, dance halls. Anywhere where large numbers of people gather. I don't think they're opening the schools either, not that that will worry the children, but it means I've lost my job.'

'How long for?'

'Dunno,' Sally said. 'Could be for the duration, for all I know. It's all 'cos of the bombing.'

'What bombing?' Susie said. 'There hasn't been any bombing.'

'I know, but they must think that it might start any minute,' Sally said. 'If it doesn't, they might open again, but I can't wait around to see if that happens. I need another job. Ruby said to see you.'

'There's nothing going at our place that I know of,' Susie said.

'Not at the moment anyway,' Kate agreed. 'There will be when the men are called up, but that hasn't happened yet.'

'But we are at war,' Susie said. 'So jobs should be easy to find.'

'Yes, course they are,' Kate said. 'Look, I'll pick the paper up on the way home and come round later tonight and we'll have a look.'

'I'd rather come now if it's all the same to you,' Sally said. 'I hate coming home in the dark in the blackout.'

'Oh, God, yes,' Kate said. 'I forgot about that. Come on now, then. See you tomorrow, Susie.'

'Yeah, see you tomorrow, Kate,' Susie said with a wave to them both. 'Best of luck, Sally.'

'Thanks.'

'You'll hardly need luck,' Kate said. 'You help me get the dinner on the go when we get in and then we can study the jobs.'

'Will David be there?'

'He might be,' Kate said. 'He intended enlisting today, but he said he had to see his boss as well and see if he wants him to work notice and if so how much, so they might be discussing that after work.'

David wasn't in but came home as they were both poring over the jobs' section. Sally told him why she was looking for another job and he said, 'Ah, what a shame, and you made a first-class usherette.'

Sally coloured slightly as she said, 'Thanks. It was a great job, and though it wasn't that well paid, we did get tips sometimes, and if you threw in the cost of all those cinema tickets, it wasn't that bad really. But I suppose now me and Phil are engaged, I could do with earning more so I could save a bit.'

'Well, all the war-related jobs pay the best,' Kate said. 'And look, there's a new engineering works opened in Witton. That isn't far away – I should say there would be a variety of jobs you could do there.'

'Yeah,' Sally said. 'And I suppose I could be trained as well as anybody else.'

'Course you could,' Kate said, leaping to her feet and dragging her sister with her. 'Come on, that concoction in the pan – that passes for stew with a little imagination – is nearly ready if the smell is anything to go by. If I dish up now you'll be able to eat it and still be home before it's truly dark.'

'I can't blame you for being nervous of the blackout,' David said. 'And as the days shorten you'll be going out in the dark and coming home in the dark.'

'I know,' Sally said. 'Coming home from work on Saturday was bad enough.'

'I can see accidents happening,' Kate said.

'Don't suppose the dark will worry me where I shall be in a fortnight's time,' David said. 'Darkness is often the friend of the pilot.'

'You got in,' Kate said, feigning pleasure because she knew it was what David wanted, but he wasn't fooled and he slipped an arm around her as he said, 'Yeah, 'fraid I did, old girl. At least, subject to a medical, I will be accepted for training at Castle Bromwich Aerodrome, which isn't a million miles away. Whether I will be passed as a pilot is another thing altogether, apparently, although it's the only thing I want to do. Then I would be part of the 605 Squadron. But, as the Commanding Officer said, all the young men want to fly, but there are other important jobs to do in the RAF.'

'None of which you would consider?'

'I don't think anyone has that much choice in the Forces,' David said. 'They say jump and you jump. But I would hate to be behind a desk doing any job, however important, that could be done by one of the WAAFs just as easily.'

'They don't get the chance to fly then?' Sally

asked with a wry smile.

David returned the smile as he said, 'Not to my knowledge, no, but the point is, there will be a job going at our place in a fortnight or so.' And he turned to Kate and said, 'That's the notice I have to work, and I could definitely put a word in for Sally if she's not fixed up by then. There's plenty of work at the moment, because we're building transmitters as well as standard wirelesses.'

Sally wrinkled her nose. 'Sounds awfully complicated.'

'No, it isn't,' David assured her. 'Honest, you'd soon pick it up.'

'Thanks, David,' Sally said. 'But I do need to get a job as soon as possible. Ruby is not well off and misses Phil's money, for all he sends her what he can every week. I need to be paying my share as soon as possible. The engineering works will probably suit me well enough.'

TWELVE

Kate told David that he owed it to his family to tell them what he had done. He wasn't keen, but agreed she had a point and they set off on Sunday afternoon.

'It won't be any surprise to them anyway,' Kate said as they turned down the road. 'You have made no secret of it. I wonder what branch of the services your brother will choose?'

'Huh,' said David. 'All Lawrence cares about most of the time is himself. It wouldn't surprise me in the least if he tried to wriggle out of active service of any description.'

'I don't think it is something that people can choose.'

'No, nor do I, but if there is any kind of loophole you can bet that Lawrence will find it, aided and abetted by Dad, no doubt, because the two of them are like bosom pals.'

Kate saw that for herself just a little later. 'Can't wait to play the conquering hero, can you?' Lawrence said sneeringly when David told them he had enlisted in the RAF.

David decided to let the remark pass and so he said pleasantly enough, 'Well, it was only a matter of time, anyway, like it will be for you eventually.'

'Maybe not.'

'What you on about?' David said. 'You registering yourself as a conscientious objector, or what?'

'Oh, no need for all that unpleasantness,' Lawrence said with a supercilious drawl. 'But there is a medical to pass.'

'What of it?' David demanded. 'You're as fit as I am.'

'No, I'm not. I have problems with my chest.'

'Since when?'

'Since now,' Lawrence said. 'Comes from years working in the intense heat – isn't that right, Dad?'

'Are you party to this fabrication too?' David said, turning to his father.

Kate saw that Alf was embarrassed. 'Well,' he said, 'Lawrence could probably claim exemption anyway because he is in a reserved occupation. Almost all the brassworks are now making war-related goods. If he has a doctor's say-so about his bad chest, too, that will probably clinch it.'

'A doctor will do that?' David asked incredulously.

'Not the one we've used the few times we've needed one,' Alf admitted. 'But there are some who'll do it if the price is right.'

David's mouth dropped open with surprise and shock and Kate too could scarcely believe what she was hearing. She glanced at David to see his face brick-red with anger and his eyes smouldering as he spat out: 'You are despicable, both of you. And you have only got to look at Lawrence to see how fit he is. Women are taking on men's roles now, so there is no need to try and claim exemption.'

'Oh, I disagree with you, dear brother,' Lawrence said in his supercilious tone. 'I think there is every reason.'

'And you, Ma, are you are party to this fantasy?' David demanded, turning to face his mother.

Dora was embarrassed and couldn't meet David's eyes, bending her head as she mumbled, 'Isn't it enough of a sacrifice to risk the life of one son?'

'Don't give me that,' David spat out. 'None of you give a tuppenny damn for the life of this son. This whole plan has been hatched to keep lily-livered Lawrence safe.'

Before any of them could find an answer to this, Lawrence gave a smug smile and said to David, 'Look on the bright side, our kid. This way I'll be able to keep an eye on your pretty young wife.'

David's fists were balled and Kate felt him taut beside her, like a tiger waiting to spring. She felt blisteringly angry as she snapped out, 'No, you will not, Lawrence Burton. You turn up at my door and I will show you that quick enough.'

'Ooh, Miss Hoity-Toity,' Lawrence said.

'Not at all,' Kate said in a voice as cold as steel. 'I'm just particular about the company I keep.'

'Hey,' said Dora. 'There's no need to talk to our Lawrence like that.'

All Kate's life she had been taught respect for her elders, but so incensed was she now that she barked back at Dora, 'There is every need, and if you can't see that then there is something radically wrong with you.'

Dora was stunned, but before she could think up a reply Kate turned to David and said, 'Shall we go? We have done what we came to do.'

David too had been amazed by the way Kate

had handled both Lawrence and his mother and he got to his feet as he said, 'Yes, I'll be glad to go. The air round here stinks.'

Outside in the street, he began to smile ruefully, but it had turned into a chuckle before Kate noticed because she still felt upset. Eventually, she said, 'All right, what's so blinking funny?'

'You are,' David said. 'I don't think anyone has ever spoken to Lawrence like that before.'

'I meant every word,' Kate said. 'If he comes near me I will brain him with the nearest thing to hand, but maybe I shouldn't have spoken to your mother the way I did.'

'You were perfectly right,' David said. 'My parents are as bad condoning Lawrence doing this, and what my dear brother said to you was totally unacceptable. I wanted to smash his face in, if you want the truth.'

'I know,' Kate said. 'I could feel the rage running through you. I told you, I can deal with men like Lawrence.'

'You've convinced me, you very special lady,' David said.

Kate was glad that David was reassured because really the encounter had disturbed her. She told Susie about it the following morning as they made their way to work. Susie felt, like David, that she had been quite justified in what she had said and she was horrified at Lawrence trying to wriggle out of fighting for his country.

'You could report them for that, I should think,' she said.

'Probably,' Kate said. 'That would mean David shopping his own parents though, and this

211

doctor chap as well.'

'A doctor like that needs shopping,' Susie said angrily.

'I feel the same way,' Kate said. 'But doctors are important people, aren't they? People listen to them and take note of what they say. If David was to speak out against one of them, it could cause a heap of trouble for him, and if anything stopped him going into the RAF, he would be destroyed – that's all he's talked about since the possibility of us going to war was spoken about.'

'And Nick too,' Susie said. 'And you're right. Things like that do happen. David could find himself tainted just because he is Lawrence's brother.'

'Exactly, so that's why we are keeping it to ourselves,' Kate said. 'So don't say anything to the others.'

'You know I can keep things close to my chest if I have to,' Susie said. 'But you have nothing to be ashamed about.'

'I know, but I don't even want to be related by marriage to someone so cowardly,' Kate said.

Susie said nothing for minute or two because she knew how Kate felt. She couldn't blame her because she knew she would feel much the same. Finally, she burst out, 'I know what you're saying, Kate, but I think it's not flipping well fair.'

Kate shrugged. 'Don't suppose it is, but no one ever promised us a fair deal and this war might not be fair to many people, I wouldn't have thought. But let's not bother talking about Lawrence Burton any more – he's not worth wasting our breath on.

That last week sped by and Kate often wished she had the power to stop time so that she could enjoy the company of her new husband a little longer. Susie felt the same way about Nick, and what made it worse was that there was little to take their minds off what lay ahead because the cinemas, theatres and dance halls remained closed. Not that these would have been easy to go out to with the blackout as intense as it was. It was no pleasure going anywhere much. Getting home from work was usually enough of an ordeal and people tended to stay put in the evenings.

Never had Kate been more grateful that they had the wireless. She loved cuddling up to David on the sofa, enjoying the plays and comedy programmes and concerts. There was also news on the hour, which they both listened to avidly. Kate began to wonder how she had managed so long without such a source of entertainment and information. She now always brought a paper home and David would devour this each evening and read her out snippets from it as she prepared the evening meal. It wasn't hard to read it all so quickly given that, since war had been declared, in an effort to save paper, the newspapers were only about four sheets of extremely small print, so the more in-depth news on the wireless was even more important.

Many of the women and girls Kate and Susie worked with were also worried about their men folk. The initial call-up of lads aged twenty and twenty-one that had begun in April meant more than a few of the girls had boyfriends in the Forces like Sally had, and others had husbands, sons or brothers, either awaiting their own call-up, or who had enlisted on the declaration of war. It was only a matter of time, everyone knew, until they were all conscripted. Kate thought that Birmingham would be a very strange place when, along with other cities, it would be denuded of all their young, fit men.

'Good job we have a job of work to go to, that's all I can say,' Kate said to Susie as they sat on the tram on their way home through the deepening dusk. It was the Friday before David and Nick had to report to the aerodrome. 'I'd go mad in the flat all day, especially after David leaves tomorrow.'

'Oh, I'll say,' Susie said. 'I'd like to think if they both make it as pilots, they can look out for each other.'

Kate shook her head. 'It would be lovely to imagine that might happen,' she said. 'But I really think that when they are in those planes it's every man for himself.'

'I suppose,' Susie agreed. 'And I do wish that Mom and Dad had let Nick and I get married. I know now why you two did, because before he goes to face God-alone-knows-what, I really want to love Nick properly, you know?'

Oh, Kate knew all right. She and David were both aware of the short time they had together, and so their passion rose quickly and their love-making was even better. And after the rapturous loving was over, she would feel blissfully satiated and utterly, utterly content. Remembering it now she was glad the dark morning hid the crimson flush on her cheeks. 'Last night we nearly... Well, you know what I mean?' Susie went on. 'It isn't always easy to say no, especially when you don't want to.'

'I know that only too well.'

'In the end, I got scared,' Susie said. 'What if I was to get pregnant? I couldn't do that to Mom and Dad, but God it was hard.'

Kate felt sorry for her friend, but she had done the right thing – for an unmarried girl to become pregnant was a terrible disgrace. Maybe people's attitudes in Birmingham were not as bad as those in Ireland, but they were still bad enough, and the shame of it impinged on the whole family. 'If you feel that strongly you ought to stand up to your parents,' she said.

'Bit late now.'

'No, it isn't,' Kate insisted. 'Nick and David will both have leave when their training is finished and you can arrange special licences to get married quick. You can't have the big church wedding though. There won't be time.'

'That will upset my mother,' Susie said. 'And then, as I told you, she is very anti wartime marriages.'

Kate saw her friend biting on her bottom lip as she did when she was disturbed about something or other and she said gently, 'I am very fond of your parents; I wouldn't hurt them for the world and I know you feel the same way. Your mother is only saying this about wartime marriages because she wants to save you from heartache. And most parents, and brides if asked, will say that ideally they would like the big white wedding. But we are adults now, and no one can protect us from sorrow and loss. It isn't ever an ideal world and

215

now we are at war as well, normal rules don't apply.'

'You think we should just do it, don't you?'

'It doesn't matter what I think,' Kate said. 'This doesn't concern me and all I want you to do is follow your heart. And remember that this is your life and to live as an independent person or couple means that sometimes you might have to go against what your parents want and ignore their advice.'

Susie didn't speak for a moment and then she said, 'And when are you going to tell your parents about your marriage, Kate?'

'I dread doing that, to be honest,' Kate said. 'But now David has enlisted I can say that, though we wanted to get married in the normal way, he was called up and we were married by that special licence I told you about, because there was no time to do anything else. And I will promise my mother that we will have the marriage blessed in church when we can.'

'Will she be all right about that?'

Kate shrugged. 'I don't know,' she said. 'Probably not, but it's the best I can do. Maybe then I can start going back to church.'

'Don't you go now then?'

'No,' Kate said. 'I told Sally I went to an earlier Mass, since we always used to go together, but now she knows that's not true because Father Patterson collared her last week and asked her if I was sick.'

'What did she say?'

'She's a quick thinker, Sally,' Kate said. 'And she would never knowingly drop me in it, so she

216

said I had a really bad cold, but then she came round on the way home to find out what was wrong. I promised I would start to go again – that will be easier when David is away. I was enjoying our Sunday morning cuddles too much to get up and scurry along to Mass. I valued our time together because I knew it was limited.'

'Anyone would understand that.'

'Yes, anyone but a Catholic priest.'

'Yeah, they do seem to be a law unto themselves,' Susie said. 'And often have a set of values at variance with everyone else's.'

The tram pulled up at their stop and they had alighted before Kate said, 'There was another reason, too, why I felt awkward going to church after getting married in the register office. I mean, he won't recognize my marriage, will he?'

'Does he have to know?'

'I'd say so,' Kate said. 'You can't keep a secret of a thing like that. I shan't rush to tell him, though, but when David has leave he will be living with me – and what if I was to have a child?'

'Oh. I hadn't thought that far ahead,' Susie said. 'Do you want a child? I mean, when we are at war and everything?'

'It isn't a case of wanting or not wanting, is it?' Kate said. 'Not when you're a Catholic. You know that. I suppose if a baby comes then it comes.'

'But do you want one?'

'Not really,' Kate admitted. 'Not yet, anyway, but in the meantime I'll keep Father Patterson sweet by turning up at church on Sunday mornings.'

'You will take care, won't you?' Kate asked David

anxiously the following morning as she watched him buttoning up his top coat. Then she gave a wry smile as she went on, 'What nonsense we speak at times. You're not joining up to keep safe, are you?'

David gave a shake of his head, 'No, not really.'

'I suppose what I mean is, don't be a hero or anything.'

'I'll do my level best to come back to you safe and sound,' David said. 'Will that do?'

'I suppose it will have to,' Kate said.

'Anyway,' David said, 'you are getting ahead of yourself. Even if I do pass the medical and the other tests to see if I am pilot material, I will only be training for some time yet.'

'I know,' Kate said in a soft voice.

David lifted her head up and felt his heart contract as he saw her eyes full of trepidation, and he wrapped his arms around her as he said gently, 'You know, I love you more than life itself and what I want is to come home to you when this little lot is over.'

Tears were trickling down Kate's cheeks and she was annoyed, for those were the tears that she promised herself she would never shed because it might make things harder for David. She cried brokenly, 'That's what I want too.'

The kiss nearly took her breath away; it was as if a furnace had been lit inside her and she moaned and leaned against David and felt him harden. He pushed her away, saying, 'We have no time for that alas. Now come no further than the door; I want you waiting for me here when I come home again.'

218

'I will be,' Kate said. 'And for me it can't come soon enough.'

'I feel the same,' David said, and he kissed her tenderly on the lips. She watched him clattering down the stairs through a haze of tears.

As soon as he had gone from view, she ran across to the living-room window to see him striding down the street. Then she sat down and scribbled a note to her mother, explaining her rush to get married as she told Susie she would; then, before all courage deserted her, she posted the letter straight away.

The boys had been gone just a few days when cinemas, theatres and dance halls opened up again. No bombs had fallen and the government decided that these places of enjoyment were good for the morale of the nation. Everyone was relieved, though there was still the blackout to contend with. 'Will you try and get your old job back?' Kate asked Sally, who she was visiting the Saturday after the announcement.

Sally shook her head. 'No, I don't think so.'

'Lure of the money too much for you?'

'It isn't only the money,' Sally said. 'Though two pounds five shillings is not to be sneezed at. But there are downsides. Nothing had prepared me for the noise, and at first I was so tired when I came home, but I am getting more used to that now. There's loads of dirt and dust, and the stench of the oil makes our clothes pong something awful, even under the overalls; I can even smell it on my skin when I get undressed. And my hair is permanently lank, however much I wash it.'

'It must have been awful for you at first,' Kate said sympathetically. 'Factories are very dirty, noisy places. I didn't think I would stick it at first and I might not have done if I hadn't known that Susie had spoken up for me and I didn't want to let her down. After all, she had been there since she was fourteen and coped with it. Anyway, it wouldn't have been a very sensible thing to do to leave my job, because Britain was in the middle of a massive slump and jobs were much harder to come by then than they are today.'

'Well, I got to thinking about Phil,' Sally said. 'He didn't choose to go in the Army or get a choice in whether he was to be taught to kill people or not.'

'So, you feel you're doing your bit?'

'Yeah, sort of.'

'I fully understand that,' Kate said. 'And while you make mortar bombs, the radiator grilles that we are finishing off in the polishing shop now are for military vehicles, troop trucks and the like. I am proud of that.'

'That's it,' Sally said. 'I mean, when most of the youngish, fit men are drafted into the Forces, there will only be us left to make the ammo and guns and tanks and so on that the Army can't fight without.'

Ruby came into the room at that moment and, hearing Sally's comments, said, 'And we have to fight and fight to win. Murdering bastards they are, the lot of them. Mark my words, the only good Germans are the dead ones. I'm proud of Phil and all the other young fellows like him. And,' she added to Sally, 'talking of Phil, you have a letter, and if it says the same as mine, which I'm sure it will, then you'll be a very happy girl.'

Sally took the letter from Ruby and ripped the envelope in her haste to read what Phil had to say. She scanned it quickly and then turned to Kate, her bright eyes shining as she said, 'He's coming home, Kate. Phil's coming home on leave.'

Kate made her way home feeling pleased and happy for her sister – and also for Ruby – as Phil had been away many months. But she was also apprehensive because she knew that Phil's leave was probably embarkation leave and he would soon be in the thick of it, fighting an army that had goose-stepped its way almost effortlessly through half of Europe, like some sort of unstoppable monster.

A week later, Phil was home. Any trace of the boy that might have lingered when he left was gone, and in its place was a man with a resolute step and a confident air. But he was as courteous and kindly as ever and had eyes only for Sally. It almost hurt Kate to see such love and she knew that, though they were young, the love they had for one another was the sort that would last a lifetime. She trembled for Sally and Phil and herself and David and all other lovers facing such a fractured future.

Kate said nothing of her fears in the weekly letter she wrote to David, though she mentioned that Phil had come home for a spot of leave, nor did she make any mention of the censorious letter she had received from her mother. It said more or less what Kate was expecting: that Kate was living in mortal sin and didn't she care about her immortal soul, destined for Hell's Flames, or any children of this union that would be bastards? There was more in the same vein, but Kate folded up the letter, pushed it back in the envelope and put it in the box with all her mother's other letters.

Once upon a time, such a letter would have greatly upset her, but she found it hardly mattered what her mother thought of her life. She had more than enough to worry about already without adding more to the list. What she did tell David was about her adventures in the blackout.

She had been part of the army of women that painted a white line down the edge of the road. Dolly and quite a few of the tenants came out to help.

'What good do they think white lines are going to be?' one woman remarked. 'My old man says as how white has to have summat to reflect against to do any good at all.'

'Maybe if there was a full moon?' Dolly ventured, but another woman pooh-poohed that idea. 'D'you think in these smoky, cloudy skies you would see a helpful moon?'

'I'd say not,' said another. 'Nor any twinkling stars either.'

'Well, I don't know,' said the first woman. 'But summat has to be done. I apologized to three pillar boxes, two trees and a telephone box that I bumped into on my way home from work last night.'

The women laughed heartily, but really it was no laughing matter. People had been injured bashing into things or falling off kerbs, or being run over and even killed by motor vehicles, which were allowed no lights either in darkness that was sometimes as thick as pitch. 'This blackout is Hitler's secret weapon,' Kate said. 'He isn't going to bother bombing us at all. Just wait till we all kill ourselves bumbling about in the blackout.'

'You could be right at that,' one woman said.

'Yeah, but in case you're wrong, maybe we should do what we volunteered for,' another remarked.

Grumbling good-naturedly, though realizing the futility of what they were doing, they painted white lines on the kerbs and rings around the odd tree or pillar box. It didn't help and no one really thought it would and, as the nights drew in, everyone had to take extra care getting to and from work.

But though in her letters to David she told this in a comical way, she found the inky blackness very depressing. 'You're not even safe on the buses,' she complained one morning. 'Look at that one yesterday that went straight over an island because he didn't see it.'

'And it's so cold and blustery as well,' Susie said. 'The constantly grey skies don't help anyone's mood and the low clouds mean that it's dark by early afternoon. That lovely hot summer is just a memory now.'

'I know,' Kate said. 'No chance of an Indian summer this year.'

'No, indeed not,' Susie said.

And the girls were right because all through October, every day seemed colder than the one before, with an icy nip in the air. In November, rain-driven gale-force winds began battering the coast, and 100,000 Anderson shelters were delivered to Birmingham. Kate did not find this reassuring, she found it terrifying, but Susie had been perplexed when she had said so.

'If the Germans drop bombs from the air, then isn't it good that people have somewhere to shelter away from them?' she asked.

'Yes, I suppose,' Kate said. 'I mean, yes, of course, but it's just–'

'You don't like the thought of aerial bombing,' Susie said. 'And neither do I, but we can't do anything to stop it if it happens.'

'Burrowing down in the ground like that is awful,' Kate said. 'Like some sort of animal.'

'I'd rather be underground than up top if bombs are going to be flying about,' Susie said. 'Anyway, Dad has applied for one.'

'Has he?'

'Yes, the garden is big enough,' Susie said. 'And people say if you put enough dirt on top you can grow things. Anyway, Mom said better be safe than sorry, and so Dad sent off straight away because he said he wants to build one while the boys are still there to give him a hand digging the trench and before the ground is too hard with frost and that.' Then she looked at Kate and said, 'What will you do?'

'A woman at work said Birmingham will be safe from aerial raids, being two hundred miles from the coast.'

Susie grimaced as she said, 'I doubt that could be true, because I would say that planes can cover a great distance in a short space of time. Anyway, if they thought Birmingham was so safe, they wouldn't be insisting on a blackout here or have all these Anderson shelters delivered. So just say the woman is wrong and a raid starts, where will you go? Is your landlady installing an Anderson?'

'There wouldn't be any point, would there?' Kate said. 'The house is all flats. It would have to be a mighty big shelter to fit us all in. Dolly said that if there are raids we're all to go down the basement. That will do me, anyway.'

'Check it's reinforced then,' Susie advised. 'Because it might have to withstand the weight of the house falling on top of it.'

'Oh, Susie, stop being such a worry-guts,' Kate said.

'Someone has to be.'

'Why?' Kate asked. 'No bombs have fallen yet.'

'Famous last words,' said Susie.

The staggering list of casualty figures on the roads caused the government to have a rethink about the blackout. The result of the rethink meant that shielded headlights on cars were allowed and the also said that people could carry shielded torch-

It was amazing, Kate thought, how comfor^{1g} that thin pencil of light could be – that was ^{jou} could get hold of a torch and batteries, ^{ich} disappeared from the shops faster than th^{eed} of light. But still, if you were the owner^{hese} precious commodities, it was a little ^{and} safer to get about, and yet as Novemb^{into} December, Kate couldn't work up $^{nthu-}$

225

siasm for a wartime Christmas.

Christmas spirit was hard to find, even in the city centre, where there were no lights festooning the city streets, no spluttering gas flares turning the Bull Ring into fairyland, and not even flashing window displays in the shops to tempt a person inside. And it was a depressing sight when you did go in, because there was little to buy. 'They say rationing is being started in January,' Susie said. 'But a lot of what you ask for now in the shops is unavailable.'

'Yeah, and if you complain in any way, they say that there's a war on.'

'That's right,' Susie agreed, and added with a sigh, ''case it might have slipped your mind like.'

The two girls felt very despondent, and Sally was little better. 'I was so looking forward to Phil coming home,' she said. 'It was really terrific and that, but when he went back I had to learn to live without him again, and this time it's worse because I know that he is now "somewhere in France", so how can I get excited about Christmas? I do try to keep my worries to myself for Ruby's sake, but it's flipping hard to do.'

'I know it is,' Kate said. 'Come to my house for Christmas dinner at least and we'll try to cheer each other up.'

'Thanks,' Sally said. 'It would be nice to be together anyway.'

'And then all of you come to mine afterwards,' Susie said. 'And we'll do our level best to enjoy ourselves.'

Having agreed on their plans, she then had a letter from David to say that he and Nick had

226

both been given leave over Christmas, and the world suddenly seemed a much happier place. Kate was determined that she would give David a Christmas to remember. And she would make an effort to make the place look more Christmassy, to try to offset the dreary black curtains at the windows.

She hunted through the trunk in the bedroom and unearthed the tree. It looked a bit battered but she was sure it would look much better with festive things pinned on it and tinsel draped over the balder bits. The garlands that she and Susie had made for her first Christmas in Birmingham had also seen better days, but teased out gently they didn't look too bad. And lastly she hung the cards received from those in Ireland, and a few from the girls at work, on string fastened above the hearth. The effect when she had finished was not bad at all, and it did look as if Christmas was not far away.

THIRTEEN

David arrived around midday on Sunday 24 December. When Kate saw him walk through the door she thought her heart would burst with love for him; it seemed to fill her whole body so that she ached with it. She had stayed in the flat as he had asked her to, and her nerve-ends began to tingle as she watched him surveying the room. She was so glad that she had made the effort when she saw his smile, and then he looked at her with his eyes shining and she felt her knees go weak and he was across the room in two strides and took her in his arms.

And when his lips met hers she could no more have stopped the moan of desire that escaped from her than she could have stopped the sun from shining. When they broke apart they were both breathless, their eyes alive with longing. 'Oh, my darling,' David said with a sigh and held her close.

'Are you hungry?' Kate asked.

'Ah, yes,' David said. 'I'm very hungry for only one thing at the moment.' And then he scooped her up in his arms, kicked open the bedroom door and laid her on the bed and began to pull his clothes off.

'David,' Kate said, slightly shocked. 'It's the middle of the day.'

'What's that got to do with anything?'

'It seems sort of wrong.'

'Why should it be?'

Kate shrugged. 'I don't really know,' she admitted.

'Kate, do you love me?'

'Oh, I'm surprised that you have to ask that,' Kate said. 'I love you more than I thought it was possible to love anyone.'

'Don't you want to show me how much?' David asked as he lay by her side. 'I have thought of this moment for weeks, but I'll not take you against your will.'

Kate felt ashamed that she had even hesitated, and she kissed David's lips gently and began to pull off her clothes as she said, 'It won't be against my will, my darling. It will be instead my heart's desire,' and she pulled David into her arms.

Their coming together that day was euphoric. Kate's passion equalled David's and he smiled when she let out a shout of pure joy when she felt that she could bear it no more. 'It makes me happy that I satisfy you so,' David said.

'Satisfy me?' Kate cried. 'There are many words and phrases that I could use to describe our love-making, and satisfaction would not be top of the list.'

'What would head it, my darling?' David asked.

Kate thought for a minute. 'Warmth and tenderness, I suppose,' she said at last. 'You make me feel so ... so cherished. Yes, that's the word – cherished.'

Kate snuggled against David so that her head was in the crook of his arm and thought suddenly of the war Britain was engaged in that could tear their happiness apart. She gave a sudden shiver.

'No sad thoughts,' David said, feeling the slight trembling of her body. 'I am here for such a short time and I want to take happy memories away with me.'

'I know,' Kate said.

'So relax,' David said, and kissed her eyes gently so that she closed them. 'I'm not tired,' she said. 'Not really, for all I was too excited about you coming home to sleep much last night. I just feel cosy and comfortable and blissfully happy.'

When she awoke it was dark, but suddenly the light went on and she saw David dressed and framed in the doorway holding a tray. She struggled to sit up. 'What time is it?' she cried. 'I must see to the blackouts.'

David pushed her gently back on the pillows. 'I have done the blackouts, as you can see,' he said, and she saw the shutters fitted up at the windows. 'It's only four o'clock, but such a grey and miserable day that I thought tea and some of the biscuits I bought from the NAAFI at the camp might cheer us up.'

'Oh, yes,' said Kate. 'But I should be the one looking after you.'

'Why?'

'Well, you know,' she said. 'You're the one on leave.'

'So what?' David said, plonking the tray on the bed and handing Kate a cup of tea. 'Don't you think we get well enough looked after at the base?'

Kate smiled. 'I wouldn't know what happens at the base,' she said. 'Apart from telling me you played in the odd football match, you don't say much about it, and Nick is no better in the letters he writes to Susie.'

'There is a good reason for that,' David said. 'If we said much more, the censor would only cut it out anyway.'

'We don't even know if you made it to be pilots.'

'Didn't you notice the wings on my jacket?'

'Hardly,' Kate said with a laugh. 'From the moment you came in the door I barely had time to notice anything. You had everything off in no time.'

'Well, you're the cause of that,' David said, unabashed. 'You shouldn't look so lovely and inviting.' He lifted his uniform jacket from the floor as he spoke and Kate saw the wings pinned to his lapel.

She felt dread tighten in her stomach but David had said no sadness and so she forced her stiff lips into a smile and said, 'That's great, David. Well done!'

'This is about the most exciting thing that has ever happened to me.'

'I know that,' Kate said. 'And I am trying to be happy for you.'

'And doing a grand job,' David said approvingly as Kate got out of bed and began to dress.

'They seem such mundane presents,' Kate said the following morning, handing David some packages as they sat having breakfast. 'I couldn't even get festive paper to wrap them in,' she complained, viewing the brown paper with distaste.

'The woman at the paper shop looked at me as if I was asking for the moon when I asked her if she had anything more cheery. "None of that sort of thing now, dearie," she said. And then added as if I was some sort of half-wit, "There is a war on, you know".'

David laughed at Kate's disgruntled face. 'She's right in a way,' he said. 'I mean, you only throw the paper away. Anyway, surely the important thing is what the present is, and not what it's wrapped in?'

'That's just it though, isn't it?' Kate said. 'Hankies, cigarettes, bull's-eyes and socks would not inspire anyone.'

'Stop beating yourself up,' David said. 'First of all, I'm grateful for all these things. I am nearly out of hankies, I love bull's-eyes, cigarettes are often the very devil to get hold of and I'm more than grateful for the socks. Some of the old hands told us to get the boots a bit big so that we could put on two pairs of socks. It can get nippy in the old Spits 'cos they're not fitted with central heating, you know. I mean, when you're up there fighting Jerry, you don't want to be worried about cold tootsies, do you?'

The thought of David up in the air fighting anyone caused Kate's heart to give a flip, but she told herself not to be so stupid. David was a pilot, had wanted to be a pilot, and she had to get used to it. And so she let a wry smile play around her lips as she said, 'In that case I shall take up knitting and send you a steady supply of them. It's not so hard. A few of the women at work do it and they offered to teach me.'

'Well, I would be glad of them, as I said,' David said. 'And while you're complaining about having

232

no festive paper to wrap things in, I couldn't get any paper at all – the shop had run out and so I had to make do with a paper carrier bag.'

When Kate put her hand in the bag she was delighted. 'Ah, David,' she exclaimed, as she pulled out two pairs of silk stockings. 'They are just beautiful. Where on earth did you get them?'

David wagged a finger in front of Kate's face. 'That's as bad as asking me how much they cost.'

'No, it isn't.'

'Well, all the answer you are going to get is, ask no questions and you will be told no lies,' David declared. 'And have another look because there is something else.'

'Evening in Paris is just about my favourite perfume,' Kate said, spinning round with excitement with the bottle in her hand. She stopped pirouetting long enough to kiss David on the lips before saying, 'Did you know that?'

David shook his head. 'All I know about scent is that you always smell nice and the man selling this lot said most of the ladies went a bundle on it.'

Kate knew that probably David had got the things from the black market and normally she would have had no truck with it, but how could she take the light from David's eyes by refusing the presents, especially when she didn't want to? What she did say was, 'Well, I can't tell you how glad I am to have these things, so I am going to be very unpatriotic and say I don't care where you got them from, I'm just thankful you did.' And her eyes met David's and her heart suddenly lurched with love for this fine man and she put her arms around his neck, kissed him gently on the lips and said, 'Happy Christmas, Mr Burton.'

They had a lovely Christmas dinner, tucking into the chicken that Kate had queued for three solid hours to buy in the meat market the day before Christmas Eve, although for Sally and Ruby it was tinged with regret that Phil had been unable to join them. Sally brought some mince pies she had made from a few jars of mincemeat her grocer had got in just a few days before, and Ruby had made a small cake and produced a bottle of whisky that she said had been languishing in the cupboard since Phil had left.

'Won't he mind?' Kate said.

'Why should he?' Ruby said. 'We'll buy another one when he comes back home with this bloody war over.'

Ah, thought Kate. When will that be? Not soon if she was any judge. However, Christmas Day was not the day to share such thoughts and she took the bottle from Ruby with thanks. All in all it was a truly lovely dinner, and not long after it they set off for the Masons' before it got too dark.

Kate had barely got in the door before Susie pounced on her. 'I've got something to tell you.'

Kate looked at her friend and knew only one thing would make her eyes shine so and she burst out, 'You're getting married?'

'That's right,' Susie said, drawing Nick to her side. 'On Nick's next leave, whenever it is. Mom and Dad have agreed, haven't you?'

'We have,' Frank said. 'Though I still have my misgivings, for all we know Nick to be a fine young

234

man, but we went down under the onslaught.'

'He's talking about me,' Susie's elder brother, Derek, said. 'I have got my call-up papers, and as Gillian and I were going to get married anyway, we shuffled it along a bit to get it in before I'm called up. It's obvious that most couples would want to do that.'

'So, we don't know when this great event is going to be?' Kate said.

Nick smiled ruefully and said, 'Unfortunately the powers-that-be do not confide in me, but as soon as there is a sniff of the next spot of leave I will set things in motion.'

'Won't be any time soon though, I wouldn't have thought,' David said, 'now we have got our wings. I do want to get some flying in.'

'Oh, me too,' Nick said. 'I just can't wait to take the kite up and have a go at Jerry.'

'What will you be flying?' Susie's other brother, Martin, asked. 'Spitfires?'

'Yeah,' Nick said. 'Without doubt the best plane in the Air Force, and made just across the road from the base at the Vickers factory.'

'Yeah, they close the road at seven o'clock and push them across,' David said. 'And that's a sight in itself because the road is very busy in the daytime. People come and watch. Then we keep what planes we need and the others are flown down to other bases.'

'God, I bet the Germans would like to know where that factory is.'

'I bet,' David said. 'It must be heavily reinforced because the rumour is that they are going to start making Lancaster bombers there as well.'

'I'd say they'd be pretty redundant because there's been no bombing yet, has there?' Martin said with a slight laugh.

'What about our ships being sunk?' Frank asked him.

'Yeah,' Martin said airily. 'I know there's that, but it don't affect us much. Some of the lads at work are calling this the Bore War and I don't blame them.'

'War is not something to make a joke of,' Frank snapped. His face was creased in annoyance as he went on. 'Those young unarmed sailors who lost their lives trying to bring food in wouldn't call it boring either. Ships, stacked full of essential foodstuffs, are lying on the sea bed now. You'll soon care about that when it affects your belly because there's no food to put on the table.'

It was strange to see Frank so vehement about anything, and Kate noticed that Martin had coloured up in embarrassment. Mary, trying to pour oil on troubled waters, said soothingly, 'I'm sure he meant no harm, Frank. After all, it is Christmas Day, not a day for anger and upset. The truth is this war is making us all edgy and out of sorts. Now come up to the table. Food will, I'm sure, make us all feel a wee bit better tempered.'

After the meal, Derek went off to collect his young lady, Gillian, and Kate helped clear the table and wash up the tea things. It was as she was passing the hall from the kitchen that Derek came in. Kate had met Gillian before and thought her very pretty, with her wavy brown hair that fell to her shoulders held back from her face by a red velvet band. She had a pert little nose and small mouth and dark eyes to match her hair. And Kate saw those eyes were fastened on Derek as he helped her off with her coat, and she knew that Gillian was completely smitten with him. 'I'll put your coat up with all the others,' Derek said. 'The drinks are in the kitchen. There's a very nice punch made by the old man especially for Christmas. Drink that with caution because it sometimes has a kick like a mule. Isn't that right, Kate?'

'In a way,' Kate said with a laugh as she retraced her steps to the kitchen. 'Happy Christmas, by the way. Have you had a good day so far?'

Gillian made a face. 'Not really,' she said. 'I'm hoping the fun starts now.'

'Ah, well, this will most definitely help,' Kate said, pouring Gillian a glass of dark orange-coloured liquid from the glass bowl on the table. 'No one knows what goes into this. It's always made by Susie's father and it's very drinkable.'

Gillian took the glass from Kate and said; 'I think I am going to enjoy this for all my parents would be shocked to the core.'

'Don't they approve?'

Gillian shook her head. 'I was brought up hearing all about the evils of drink. But I like a drink and they hate that, and I certainly couldn't imbibe at home. I wanted to be here earlier. If not for dinner, then at least tea, but my parents wouldn't hear of it. They reminded me that this was my last Christmas as a single girl, not that I would ever be a married woman at all if they had had their way.'

'Oh, really?' Kate asked in surprise.

'Oh, they would criticize Prince Charming if he

took too much notice of me,' Gillian said. 'I am an only one, see.'

'They must love you very much.'

'Yeah, too much,' Gillian said. 'It's more like smothering than mothering.'

'My parents wouldn't have approved of David either because he is the wrong religion,' Kate said, leading the way to the sitting room at the back where the younger ones had congregated. 'Though, actually, he's not religious at all.'

'Best way, if you ask me,' Gillian said. 'My Dad says there are more wars started by religion than anything else.'

Derek, coming towards them, heard Gillian's words and said, 'All talk of war, any war, is banned today. Come on, Susie's waiting, and determined to have us all play charades.'

'Oh,' Gillian cried. 'I haven't played that in ages.'

'Nor me,' said Kate to Derek. 'I'd never even heard of it till I met you all.'

'So, are you up for it or not?'

'You bet I am,' Kate said, catching hold of David's hand. 'If people can't be silly on Christmas Day, there's no hope for any of us.'

David had to report back to base on Wednesday, 27 December, and Kate was pleased that because Christmas Eve had been on a Sunday, she had a couple of days off in lieu and hadn't got to go back to work until the following day, so would be able to see him off at the station. David hadn't wanted her to do that, because the cold was extreme and a thick frost had formed over the couple of inches of snow that had fallen and it was very hazardous underfoot, but she insisted. 'I had to come,' she said as they went into New Street Station. 'Because when you go, this time it's for real.'

'Poor darling,' David said, and put a comforting arm around Kate's shoulder. 'I do know how you feel and I will miss you like crazy, but in a way I am luckier than most because I won't be stationed far away. And I'll stay at Castle Bromwich unless the whole squadron is moved elsewhere. As I told you last night, ideally I will have three weeks of duty and another three on standby and then some free time. Sometimes we might be given leave to come home for a day or two. But that can't be guaranteed, and more especially in wartime.'

Kate didn't say anything, for there was nothing to say, but she wished that she could wrap her love around David like a protective shield, but all she could do was pray for him and she intended to do that often.

The air smelt of damp soot and it was chilly enough for wispy puff-balls to escape from a person's mouth when they spoke. Despite her thick coat, Kate trembled, though she wasn't sure if that was just due to the cold. There were a fair few young men on the platform, almost all in uniforms, returning to their various bases after their Christmas leave, Kate assumed, and their chatter, shouts and laughter rose over the general clamour of the station. The train was waiting with its doors open, dripping water sizzling around the wheels and the engine billowing smoke like some crazed beast that couldn't wait to be off.

David suddenly spotted Nick and waved. He came to meet them, dragging Susie behind him, and Kate was so glad to see her friend. 'I thought it might be more packed than this,' Nick said. 'Thought we'd never find each other.'

'Yeah, it's not too bad,' David said. 'Still, we'd best get aboard soon if we want to nab a seat.'

'Yes,' Nick said. 'Though it's not that far to Castle Bromwich Station if we have to squat on our kit bags.'

'Suppose not,' David said. 'Still, there's no sense in prolonging things.' And at this he opened his arms and on that public platform Kate kissed David more intensely than she had ever done. The porters were urging those wishing to take the train to get on it, and David turned away from her with difficulty and followed Nick on to the train. Susie reached out and held Kate's hand, the train doors slammed and the guard blew his whistle.

Some women saying goodbye to their men folk ran along by the side of the train as it began to chug out of the station, but Kate and Susie just watched until the train disappeared into the tunnel. Kate felt the tears she hadn't let fall in front of David trickle down her cheeks. She brushed them away impatiently, for crying never did anyone any good, and she gave Susie a watery smile.

Neither wanted to return home straight away, though, and so they made their way to a National Milk Bar and in a few minutes were drinking tea out of thick earthenware cups and regarding the tired-looking scones on their plates with slight disgust. 'I didn't think it was possible to ruin scones,' Susie said in a whisper.

'I think it's the flour,' Kate said quietly. 'David was saying our wheat isn't strong enough or some-

240

thing. We have to import from Canada.'

'And the Canadian wheat might be lying on some sea bed as we speak.'

Kate nodded. 'That's about the strength of it, so it's a case of making do with our substandard stuff.'

'That's probably right about our wheat because Mom was only saying the other day that in the last war bread flour was mixed with potatoes,' Susie said. 'She told me it tasted foul, but if it was that or nothing, then you ate it.'

'We'd better follow her example then,' Kate said, splitting her scone in half and beginning to spread it with the greasy lump in the dish that called itself butter. 'Come on,' she urged. 'It won't kill us and it's criminal to waste food. And I'll tell you what,' she added, 'it was more than David got in his parents' house.'

'He did see them over Christmas then?' Susie said. 'In our house on Christmas Day he said he wasn't sure he would go near them at all.'

Kate nodded. 'I know what he said, but I convinced him,' she said. 'You know, Christmas means families and all that, and the fact that he was on leave prior to him taking up active service, I thought they might want to see him, wish him luck or something.'

'And I presume they didn't?'

'No, and I don't know why I bothered. I decided not to go with him because I thought it might be easier, and he went up on Boxing Day. He said afterwards he didn't think it would have made any difference if I had been there, because as it was they barely gave him the time of day, weren't interested in anything he was doing and didn't offer him as much as a cup of tea, never mind a sandwich or a mince pie.'

'God!' Susie breathed. 'Some people! I mean, offering a cup of tea is just basic hospitality, never mind giving one to your own son when you don't know when you'll him see again.'

'You know,' Kate said, 'I don't think that would bother them, as long as they still had Lawrence.'

'Yes, their lily-livered golden boy.'

'I don't know how he lives with himself, a big fit man like that, prepared to sit on his backside and let others fight for him, and gloating about it to David.'

'Proper gets your goat, doesn't it?'

'It doesn't half,' Kate said. 'Anyway, David didn't stay long. He said if he had lingered any longer he might have been forced to send Lawrence's teeth down his throat.'

Susie laughed. 'Isn't that the way he normally feels when he spends any time at all with his brother?'

'Yeah, more or less.'

'No change there then,' Susie said, and Kate laughed too. 'No, they just hate the sight of one another.'

'Good gracious, is that the time?' Susie said, catching sight of the clock on the wall. 'I'd best get off. Mom will wonder where I am.'

'Yes,' Kate said, getting to her feet. 'I'd better make sure that I have everything ready for work tomorrow. I'll be glad to go back, won't you?'

'Oh, yes,' Susie said fervently. 'Now that Nick's leave is over, work is a godsend.'

FOURTEEN

New Year's Eve 1939, the first New Year of the war, was a fairly muted affair, held at the Masons' because they had the biggest house. Kate tried to lift her mood as she watched Frank filling up the glasses as it grew near the witching hour, though it was hard to find anything to look forward to and a lot more to be apprehensive or downright fearful about. She was glad when the chimes of Big Ben rang out over the wireless and they could all chink glasses and pretend that things would be somehow magically improved in 1940.

In fact, the only thing that she could get even marginally excited about was the marriage of Derek Mason and Gillian White, held on Saturday, 20 January. Kate sat in the unfamiliar church and watched Gillian walk down the aisle on the arm of her father, his disapproval of the whole affair clear in his eyes and the lines pulling his face into a frown. Gillian, on the other hand, was radiant. She was wearing a long-sleeved pale pink dress in shimmering silk with a matching fur-trimmed jacket. It set off her dark hair beautifully and her sparkling happy eyes and her lovely smile dimpling her cheeks gladdened many a heart, despite those still sniffing into handkerchiefs.

She relinquished her father's arm and stepped forward eagerly to stand by Derek, who was waiting for her with his best man, his brother,

Martin, by his other side. Beside her she heard Susie give a deep, heartfelt sigh.

'I am so envious,' she said later as they stood outside the church, shivering as they waited for the bride and groom to emerge. 'I mean, if my parents had seen reason, I could have married Nick before he went back. As you said, it's the marriage bit that's important, not the party. I mean a sort of more Spartan wedding worked for you, didn't it?'

'Yeah, it did, 'Kate said. 'I can't tell you how glad I am we went ahead with it, and I was pleased with the little do we had afterwards. It does no good to expect a feast laid out as it might have been in pre-war days.'

When she reached the Masons' house just a short time later, though, she was amazed at Mary's skill in producing the food she had laid out on the table. Pride of place was of course the wedding cake, resplendent in the centre with the figures of the bride and groom on the top. Susie caught up with her there and, seeing her interest in the cake, said, 'Those figures are from the cake my parents had when they were married.'

'They are lovely, aren't they?'

'Yeah,' Susie said. 'Mom thought so too, and that's why she insisted on having them from her cake. None of us had any idea that she'd kept something like this from her own wedding years ago, until she produced them last night. Anyway, enough of that, I have just introduced myself to Gillian's parents, and what miseries they are. It's a wonder Gillian has turned out so normal with parents like those.'

'I guessed they would be difficult,' Kate said. 'How?'

'Oh, from little snippets picked up from your brother, and Gillian herself said quite a few things that pointed that way.'

'Difficult,' Susie said. 'Actually, I could think of another name for people like that. I don't know who they think they are, but they are definitely looking down their noses at us lot.'

Kate glanced across the room to the disgruntled couple. 'They certainly don't look very happy,' she said. 'I think I'll go and introduce myself and maybe try to jolly them up a bit. After all, it is their daughter's big day. You'd think they could make a bit of an effort,' and Kate went striding across to Gillian's parents.

They looked remarkably alike, and sat with pained expressions on their grey, pinched faces, their mouths like thin red slits that turned down gloomily. Her heart sank, as she doubted that she could make any impression on a couple so determined to be miserable. This was compounded when they ignored her outstretched hand. She sighed inwardly and introduced herself and said how she was connected to the family. She waited a moment but there was no reaction to that and so she said, 'You don't seem to have a drink. Can I fetch you one?'

The man looked Kate up and down and, judging by the look on his face and the lift of his chin, wasn't that impressed by her. In a thin, slightly nasal voice, he said, 'I have explained already that we don't indulge in alcohol.'

'Well, I'm not asking you to,' Kate pointed out.

'I asked if you wanted a drink – it doesn't have to be alcoholic.'

The woman gave a very expressive sniff and said in a voice very similar to her husband's but slightly higher and with more of a sneer, 'It isn't just the drink. It's also the place.'

'Place?' Kate repeated. 'What's wrong with the place? It's just the back room of a pub.'

'Exactly!'

'What's that mean? Exactly?'

'Just that we do not frequent places like this,' the man said.

'No,' the woman put in. 'We've never been in a public house – dens of iniquity they are – and our Gillian was brought up the same way. Until she met that Derek Mason, she was a good and dutiful daughter.'

'Now look here a minute,' Kate said, her dander well and truly up. 'Gillian can't always do things your way and it would be odd if she did. She has to make her own decisions about things and live a life of her own.'

'Fiddlesticks,' the man said. 'It is a daughter's duty to obey her parents.'

'Gillian had no need for a man in her life,' the woman said, and her glittering eyes raked over Kate. 'She has a good job. She had ambition once; now all she can think about is him. You know nothing about our Gillian.'

'I don't know her that well,' Kate conceded. 'But I know she loves Derek Mason because it is as clear as a bell.'

'She has no need for him or anyone else,' Gillian's father cried, his voice rising in agitation.

'We have done everything for that girl. She has wanted for nothing.'

'Yes,' put in his wife. 'She owes us some loyalty.'

'No,' Kate said firmly. 'You can't extract payment now for the way you have brought her up. I would say most parents do their best for their children, and Gillian can respect you for that, love you as her parents, but she must follow her own heart and live her own life. Can't you even see her point of view?'

'No, I can't,' the woman yelled, so that people turned to look at the disturbance. Across the room, Gillian had just become aware of her parents having some sort of altercation with Kate, and she started towards them, but Derek caught her by the arm. He gave a jerk of his head to his father who was in charge of the gramophone and stack of records, and as the strains of 'Moonlight Serenade' filled the room, Derek took Gillian in his arms. Others followed his lead and Kate, with a smile playing around her mouth, watched the dancers surround the couple, so cutting off Gillian's view of her malcontent parents. Mary Mason, sensing trouble, approached them just in time to hear Gillian's mother burst out, 'And to make matters worse, to shame us properly, she chose to get friendly with a Roman. She knows what we think of Catholics: hypocrites and idolaters the lot of them. Do what they like and tell the priest and then it's all right again, and that Derek Mason is just like that, as bad as they come.'

Mary Mason did not shout or even raise her voice, but her eyes flashed fire and her voice was as cold as steel as she said, 'You are talking about my son, and I am afraid that I cannot allow you to abuse him in such a way, or destroy the young couple's happiness, particularly on this, their special day. For all told they will have very little time together.'

The woman ignored Mary's reference to Derek and instead said, 'Well, it's madness marrying in wartime.'

'The young people wanted to be together.'

'Stuff and nonsense,' the woman cried, while the man said, 'We forbade Gillian to think of marriage of any sort till after the war. She defied us.'

'And that was your son's doing,' the woman said, a look of repugnance on her face as she faced Mary.

'How on earth do you work that one out?'

'She never would have gone against us on her own,' the woman said. 'Never, if it hadn't been for your son persuading and inveigling her.' And she pointed an accusing finger at Mary as she shrieked out, 'If you'd looked after your son properly and kept on eye on what he was about and put a stop to it, this might never have happened.'

The music had drawn to a close and so everyone heard Gillian's mother's last outburst. Gillian's face flamed in embarrassment and she put her hands over her face, and Derek took her in his arms as she began to weep. A hush had settled over the whole wedding party and Derek looked from his shocked guests to his distraught wife and felt anger course all through him. He suddenly pushed Gillian towards his father. All eyes were on him as he strode across the room until he stood in front of Gillian's mother and glared at her as he ground out, 'All right, you loathsome viper, you have spread poison over my wedding day long enough. I would like you to leave immediately and take your abusive, bad-tempered husband with you.'

'How dare you talk to me like that?' the woman said, affronted. She turned to her husband and said, 'Are you going to let him speak to me like that?'

In the presence of a very angry young man, Gillian's father was silent. 'And have you no control over your son's insolence?' she asked Mary.

'None whatsoever,' Mary answered mildly. 'So, that being the case, I would do as he says.'

'You can't do this,' the woman cried. 'This is my daughter's wedding day.'

'That daughter is also my wife,' Derek said in a voice as cold as ice. 'As such, she is under my protection, and I would ask anyone to leave who was upsetting her, regardless of who they were. So far, the only ones who have done so are you and your husband, and so you either leave peaceably or I may feel obliged to help you.'

Kate felt like giving Derek a big round of applause, because she saw the man, unnerved by Derek's resolute stance and eyes still smouldering in temper, was already on his feet. When he strode out of the room, arm in arm with his wife and with all the dignity he could muster, an audible sigh of relief ran round the room.

The chatter began again, Frank ferreted through the records and soon 'Chattanooga Choo Choo' was belting out from the gramophone and the dancers took to the floor again. Under cover of the music, Kate said, 'Derek, you were magnificent.'

'I agree,' said Mary. 'I wanted to cheer.'

'So did I,' Kate said with a grin. 'Or clap, or something.'

'Thank goodness you didn't,' Derek said. 'That wouldn't have helped matters.'

'That just shows how circumspect we can be,' Mary said. 'And now I will go and have a well-earned drink and check that all our other guests are all right.'

When Mary had gone, Derek said to Kate, 'I didn't feel magnificent, I just felt angry and flabbergasted that anyone would behave that way. You know I'm not at all sure that that pair love Gillian, but they want to control her all right. I went through the mill when we were courting. She had never been out with anyone before and she was frightened of her own shadow. And the limitations they laid on her, ridiculous times for her to be home because they went to bed early, and if she ever disobeyed them, she would find herself locked out. Not that she ever *did* disobey them; she bent over backwards to please them and I sometimes doubted we would ever make it down the aisle. But now,' he said, scanning the room, 'I can't see her. She might be upset because it was her parents I verbally attacked, after all. All I could think of was her so upset and that I had to do something about it. She might be hiding out in the Ladies'. Kate, will you check for me?'

'Course I will,' Kate said, and there she found Gillian with a tear-trailed crimson face and red-rimmed swollen eyes. The tears had stopped now, but she had cried for so long that sobs still shook her frame. Kate took her in her arms as she said, 'I don't know how you can bear to look at me.'

'What are you on about?'

'Everyone will think I'm stupid.'

'They will think nothing of the sort.'

'They'll think Derek a fool to marry me.'

'They won't at all,' Kate said. 'But do you know, it wouldn't matter if they did, because Derek doesn't and he is the one that matters. I told you my parents didn't approve of my marriage, but we are not letting their opinion spoil our lives.'

'You're right,' Gillian said, pulling herself out of Kate's arms. 'This has decided me,' she said, turning to Kate. 'Two of the girls I work with have husbands in the Forces, and they have rented this three-bedroomed house in Witton, not far from work. They offered me a place in it where I would have a double bedroom and shared use of the house and I turned it down.'

'Why?'

'Why d'you think?' Gillian said with a sigh. 'I thought it would be too much of a shock for my parents; my getting married and moving out straight away might be too much for them to cope with, and I thought I would stay at home for a bit. But I see now that that is not going to work and so, if the room is available, I will take it, and if not I will look for something else. After their performance today, I don't want to live with them ever again.'

'No one will blame you for that,' Kate said. 'In fact, someone not so far away would be delighted to hear it, and he is the one so worried about you he sent me into the Ladies' to see if you were here. I imagine he is pacing the floor outside. Why don't you go out to him now and take charge of your new life together?'

'I will, yes, I will, and thank you, Kate.'

'God,' Kate said to Susie later. 'I thought my parents were bad enough.'

'I know, and I can't understand why certain people think they are better than others.'

'Nor me,' said Kate.

'My wedding will be different,' Susie said. 'Tell you that for nothing.'

'Mm,' said Kate. 'Probably have to be a bit of a rush job, won't it?'

'Yes, my parents know this and also know that is partly their fault for putting obstacles in the way when we did have a little bit more time,' Susie said.

'See, it's parents again,' Kate said with a smile. 'They're the very devil, parents.'

'I'll say,' Susie said. 'But I think a lot of weddings will have to be a bit rushed now; the priest said as much and he's put himself on standby.'

'Isn't he bothered that Nick is a non-Catholic?'

'Not really,' Susie said. 'Maybe being at war and Nick in the Air Force makes a difference. He knows how we feel about one another and, like I said, he is on standby.'

'Hmm,' Kate mused. 'I somehow don't think that Father Patterson would see it that way.'

'Has he said anything to you then?'

'No, but he doesn't know, does he?' Kate said. 'I make sure that he sees me at Mass, but me and Sally duck out early before he can notice the wedding ring on my finger and ask awkward questions.'

'Don't you think it mad that we should be so worried about a priest's reaction?' Susie said. 'Nick can't understand it, and I am no good explaining it because I don't fully understand it myself.'

'It's conditioning,' Kate said. 'It was drummed into us for years and we obeyed, even when we didn't know the real reason why, like not being able to attend a service in another church, so you can't go to a Protestant friend's wedding or show your respects at a funeral. Why is that?'

Susie shrugged. 'Maybe they'd think we'd be corrupted. But you're right. It is a crazy rule.'

'And why can't we eat meat on Friday and must fast before we can take communion? There are loads of things I don't understand, but my mother told me that I shouldn't question the Mother Church when I asked for explanations about things.'

'You are so right,' Susie said. 'I'm asked questions about my religion sometimes and I always feel silly for not knowing the answers.'

'Just for now though,' said Kate, 'I am going along with everything because I need the Almighty to be listening and on my side when I am praying for David. He needs support from somewhere. He gets precious little from his family.'

Later that evening, back in her flat, she reflected on how much support she received from her own parents. They were a distance away, but even so. They had two daughters living in a country that was at war, one with her husband in the RAF and

253

the other with her boyfriend in the Army, and her mother hadn't even begun to understand or sympathize with how either of them might be feeling. Far from it; in fact, she seemed only to care about the marriage to David that she refused to recognize, sending letters full of vitriolic rants.

Life limped along wearily. Nothing seemed to be happening in terms of the war, except that meat had been added to the ration and most of the evacuated children had returned home. Then, towards the end of March, Susie received the letter she had been waiting for. Nick and David had leave and would be arriving on 21 March. Kate scanned the letter Susie had given her at the tram stop and said, 'Will you fit a wedding in? They have to be back on the twenty-fourth.'

'I know,' Susie said, 'that's why everything must be in place. Mom's going round to see the priest today and I'm going down the Bull Ring on Saturday to see what I can find to wear. D'you want to come? We'll have to find something for you too because I want you as my matron of honour.'

'Oh, Susie,' Kate cried. 'You couldn't have pleased me more. You just try to stop me going to the Bull Ring with you. Budget wedding or not, you want to look nice for your man and I wouldn't trust you out on your own.'

'Cheek,' Susie said, but she took Kate's hand as she spoke and gave it a squeeze.

Susie's happiness shone out of her that day at work and infected all around. They were all pleased for her. 'Got to snatch at every bit of happiness,' one woman said to her. 'And try and hold on to it tight, because life is too short to do anything else. That matters even more in wartime, so God bless the two of you, I say.'

'Yes,' said another, 'I think that goes for us all.'

'I'll say it does,' said a third. 'I pity you young ones trying to get married and everything with this war hanging over us, and Madge is right: you have to take what happiness you can.'

'My mother's not too happy about it,' Susie said. 'Is she, Kate?'

'Well no,' Kate said. 'But she has more or less accepted it now, hasn't she?'

Susie shrugged. 'Sort of,' she said. 'But I know she is struggling with it.'

'Don't they like the feller?' one of the younger girls asked.

'Oh, no,' Susie said. 'They like Nick well enough.'

'Then I don't see the problem.'

'I think,' said Kate, 'they are trying to save Susie further heartache.'

'Every mother in the land would like to do that for their children,' said an older woman. 'I know I would.'

'And me and all,' another agreed. 'Only you can't, can you? They have to learn from their own mistakes.'

'Anyway,' Kate said, 'Susie won't love Nick any more or less, whether she marries him or not. My sister is engaged to a chap that she would marry tomorrow if she could, and she loves him with a passion. She would be heartbroken if anything happened to him.'

'I can see that,' the first woman said as they

made their way to the factory floor. 'Marriage will make no difference at all.'

'Well, let's hope that it's not put to the test,' another said. 'May God be with the pair of you too, anyway,' she said as she nodded at Susie.

It was as they made their way home that night that Kate asked Susie if she was having any sort of honeymoon. She shook her head. 'Not really, though Dad's trying to get us a couple of nights in a nice hotel,' she said. 'It will have to be somewhere local, with Nick due back on the air base on Friday, but it will be nice just to be together.'

'Yes, of course it will,' Kate said, getting to her feet as their stop was next. 'I am so happy for you both.'

They alighted from the tram and Susie suddenly threw her arms around Kate and said, 'I can't believe I am actually getting married.'

Kate laughed at her friend's exuberance as she disentangled herself, but held on to both her hands as she said, 'And tomorrow we'll buy the clothes for that wedding. Don't worry we'll have you dressed to kill.'

'I'd rather be dressed for love,' Susie said.

'Oh,' said Kate, with a broad smile, 'you get undressed if you want to indulge in that sort of caper. And ideally everything has to come off. Nakedness is the name of the game.'

A lady walking past overheard what Kate had said and both girls saw the outrage in her face in the dusky half-light. 'Girls! Really!' she snapped, and they barely waited until she was out of earshot before they burst into gales of laughter.

Susie found just the thing for her wedding in the Rag Market, which was vibrant and busy, as it was every Saturday, the air filled with the cries of the stallholders shouting their wares and a pervading smell of fish because the Rag Market was also the Fish Market on weekdays. Normally, the girls would wander around having a good look at all the things for sale, but that day they were in too much of a hurry to find suitable clothes for the wedding.

'Oh, look,' cried Susie suddenly as they thumbed through the rails of one stall. She pulled out a cream dress and looked at the label on the back. 'Would you believe it's my size,' she said, and isn't it just gorgeous?'

'Oh, yes,' Kate said, for the dress was cream silk with frills down the fitted bodice and lace at the neck and the skirt embroidered with designs in a deeper lemon. It fell in soft folds to mid-calf; there was a jacket of the same material and similarly embroidered, fitted to the waist, which went down over the hips. 'Oh, I never thought I would find anything like this,' Susie said. 'I thought I would have to settle for something frightful because I am so fat.'

'Susie, you are not fat,' Kate objected.

'I'm fatter than you.'

'That wouldn't be difficult,' the stallholder said, overhearing the conversation. 'Your friend is very slender.'

'Skinny is the word,' Kate said.

'Not at all,' the stallholder insisted. 'A skinny person hasn't got the good figure you have. But your friend with the fuller figure is just as attractive, and this dress shows her bust off perfectly.' She turned to Susie as she spoke and said, 'I presume that this outfit is for a special occasion?'

'Just about the most special ever in my life,' Susie said, and added with a little flush of pride, 'Wednesday will be my wedding day. My husband-to-be is a pilot and he has a seventy-two-hour pass so that we can marry.'

The news rippled around the Market Hall, and when Susie said that her friend, Kate, was already married to a pilot and that she was going to be her matron of honour, the stallholders seemed to be on a mission to dress the girls to the nines. Nothing was too much trouble. They decided to dress the bride first. 'Navy is the thing to wear with that colour cream,' said one.

'Are you sure?' Susie said, looking at the navy court shoes the stallholder was holding that had higher heels than she had ever attempted to wear before. 'You don't think navy a trifle stark?'

'Not a bit of it,' the stallholder said, brushing away her concerns. 'Trust me, my dear, these are the height of fashion, and I have a bag just the same shade.'

'She'll need a hat,' said another.

'Yes,' said the first, surveying Susie as she teetered slightly in the unfamiliar shoes. 'But nothing with a wide brim, I don't think. It would swamp her face.'

Susie had her hair curled up into a bun on the back of her head and another stallholder cried, 'I have just the thing,' and produced a cloche hat with a feather in the side and a veil that she could wear down or up. It fitted beautifully over her hair.

'Go and put it all on, my dear,' the first stall-holder said, and she pushed a packet into Susie's hand. 'Oh, silk stockings!' Susie said.

'Yes, and they are a present from me, and your friend will have the same.'

'Oh, no, really,' Kate said, and the stallholder held up her hand.

'No, you must accept this small gift,' she said. 'You just look after those men of yours, that's all I ask, and I think I speak for us all.'

There was murmur of agreement, and she urged Susie, 'Go and put it all on, my dear.'

Susie disappeared behind the curtain and the stall-holder grinned at Kate. 'Now, your turn, my dear,' she said, and Kate was suddenly touched by the kindness of these rough-and-ready stall-holders.

'A girl with your figure is easy to dress,' the stallholder went on. 'And I have just the thing.' She drew from the rail a black silken dress with swirls of white and grey, again fitted to the waist with quite heavy lace along the neckline and the same on the cuffs. 'It looks better on,' she told Kate. 'It doesn't look much on the rail.'

'Yes,' said Kate, taking it from her. 'I know what you mean. Some dresses you just have to try on. But what accessories, and d'you think black a little severe for a wedding?'

'Um, maybe all black,' the stallholder said. 'But the swirls make all the difference, and if you had grey accessories...'

'Oh, yes, grey would be good,' put in another. 'I have some lovely shoes here that would go a treat.'

However, before the shoes could be produced, Susie stepped from behind the curtain. There was a gasp of admiration from the stallholders and Kate even saw some of them surreptitiously wipe a trickling tear away. Susie looked so lovely. The cream costume could have been made for her and the stallholders were right, Kate thought, the navy accessories made the whole outfit. No one spoke for a second or two and Susie began to feel nervous. 'Will I do?' she asked, and Kate exclaimed, 'Do? I'd say you'll more than just do. Wait until Nick catches sight of you.'

'See for yourself,' the stallholder said, pulling a full-length mirror from behind the stall. 'Oh,' Susie said, for the reflection didn't even look like her. It looked far too glamorous, and she looked around at them all, her face one beam of happiness.

'There you are,' Kate said. 'You look absolutely terrific and I would give you a hug, but I might crush something.'

Susie looked at Kate and her eyes were very bright and her voice a little choked as she said, 'You are just about the best friend a girl could ever have.' Then she looked around the satisfied stallholders and said, 'And thank you all so much. Now can you help find something for Kate?'

'I have the dress already,' Kate said, holding it aloft. 'Just the accessories to choose.'

They were chosen, and soon Kate was in the dress, which showed off her slender shape to perfection. She also wore silk stockings, grey court shoes and she carried a grey handbag and had a cloche hat similar to Susie's, which was black with a grey trim, the colours complementing Susie's outfit perfectly.

They paid for their purchases and made their way to the Masons' house where Mary insisted on seeing both girls in their wedding outfits. When she saw them she suppressed a sigh of relief. At least she thought Susie would look respectable. It wasn't the wedding she planned for her, but Susie was happy and, as Frank had said, they couldn't run Susie's life for her. The world was a scary place, and maybe that was the very time you needed a loved one beside you.

'The outfits are so very pretty,' she told the two girls. 'Don't they look a treat, Frank?'

'They do indeed,' Frank said. 'That man at work who loaned me his Box Brownie for Derek and Gillian's wedding is prepared to do the same again, because I certainly would like a picture of them dressed in their finery.'

'Maybe we should buy a camera of our own?' Mary mused.

'Maybe we should,' Frank said with a smile. 'And if you find a shop selling them, I will buy one quick enough.'

'I bet you won't though, Mom.' Susie said. 'Don't you know there's a war on?' And they all burst out laughing.

Kate was like a cat on hot bricks waiting for David to arrive home. She knew he had arranged a lift and so she was watching through the window when the army truck pulled to a stop just outside and David climbed out, dragging his kit bag after him. He immediately looked up at the window, guessing that Kate would be there, and he waved his hand and smiled. Kate, feeling as if her whole body was on fire, ran out of the flat to see him, leaping down the stairs two at a time. Then she was in his arms with a squeal, wondering if it was possible to die from happiness because she felt as if her heart had stopped beating.

David kicked the flat door shut with his foot. 'Oh, my beautiful darling,' he murmured, kissing Kate's hair and neck and throat and finally her lips. 'How I have longed for this moment. It's thoughts of you keep me going. And yet,' he added, 'this time it nearly didn't happen.'

His words brought Kate's head up sharply. 'Oh, that would have been dreadful.'

'I'll say,' David said.

'But how could they stop you coming home just like that?'

'They can because they are the RAF and so a law unto themselves,' David said. 'But this was the fellows' own fault. See, we had a bit of a bachelor do for Nick last night. Some of the lads set out at the start of the night to get Nick paralytic drunk and they had succeeded, so as best man it was up to me to look after him. I knew I had to keep my wits about me, because as the beer flowed, more and more bizarre things were being suggested that mainly centred on stripping him and leaving him tied up in various places on the air base. Anyway, before this could be attempted, tempers got frayed and a fight broke out – windows were broken and chairs and tables were smashed. The barman took refuge behind the counter as they continued to trash the Mess

Room and then some of the men started helping themselves to booze. Anyway, the alarm was raised and the officers took a very dim view of it and cancelled all leave.'

'I don't blame them, in all fairness,' Kate said. 'So how come you're here?'

'Ah, well, that came about because of deviousness on our part,' David said. 'Nick went in and pleaded to be allowed home because he was going to marry his fiancée and had to marry her because she was pregnant.'

'Goodness!' Kate exclaimed. 'She isn't though, is she? She would have told me if she was.'

'Course she isn't,' David said. 'And if she was, according to Nick, it would be another immaculate conception because he hasn't been able to get near her, not in that way.'

'Well, I didn't let you near me before we got married.'

'Made up for it since, though, my little sex bomb,' David said lustfully, giving Kate a squeeze.

'Less of that,' she said, slapping his hands away playfully. 'Go on with the tale.'

David shrugged. 'Not much more to tell,' he said. 'Nick got a right earful, of course, and he was called a bloody fool and much worse. But then the commanding officer said he didn't want any irate fathers up at the camp causing mayhem because one of his pilots couldn't keep it in his trousers, and he had better do his duty by the girl and I was let go with him as his best man.'

'What a good job he said that.'

'I'll say,' David agreed, 'otherwise Susie would have been left high and dry at the altar. Our CO

263

knew we weren't involved in the fracas anyway, because as soon as I saw it was getting ugly, I got Nick out of there fast, though I had to near carry him. But luckily the officer saw us leaving.'

Kate thought of all that the next morning as she walked behind Susie and her father towards the altar, thinking that she had never seen anyone happier than her friend.

Much later, with the food almost gone and the bride and groom toasted, Kate went up to Susie's room to help her pack. As she put the fancy lace nightie and negligee bought especially for that night into the case, she looked at Kate and said, 'I'm ever so nervous. Were you?'

Kate nodded. 'I think everyone is.'

'Does it hurt?'

'A bit, but honestly you'll hardly notice.'

'I probably will. You know what a baby I am about pain?'

Kate nodded. 'Tell Nick to go easy,' she said. 'There's no good going at it like a bull at a gate. Take your time and you'll be grand.' And then, as Susie still looked doubtful, she gripped her arm and said, 'Honestly. Trust me, I wouldn't tell you a lie – and it can't be too bad, because there are plenty at it.'

Susie laughed. 'There is that,' she said as she heaved the case off the bed. 'Come on, Dad has a taxi ordered to take us to New Street Station and it should be here soon.'

'Do you know where you are going yet?' Kate asked, because she knew Frank had refused to tell them where he had booked.

'Yeah,' Susie said. 'He had to tell us in the end,

didn't he? Anyway, he told me just before I came up to change. It's in the countryside, outside a little market town called Hampton-in-Arden, and the train takes you right into the town.'

'Convenient, anyway.'

'Very,' Susie said, and added determinedly, 'And though we have only two days, we intend to make the most of them.'

And so do I, thought Kate, but she kept the thought to herself. She had taken some of her holidays due and she had no intention of wasting them.

David, she found, was of the same mind. The weather was kind to them and they spent the time together enjoying one another's company. Kate didn't even care where they went, though they did go to Sutton Park on Thursday as it held a special significance for Kate because David had proposed to her there. And they saw *Gone With the Wind*, which Kate had wanted to see for ages because all the girls at work had been on about it. They said she would cry and she did, and David gently teased her about it all the way home. But what she liked best was sitting by their own fireside, where she could snuggle up beside David to her heart's content and look forward to a time when he would never have to leave her again.

FIFTEEN

After Nick and David returned, Kate made a decision to see more of her sister and be more of a support to her, and so after Mass on Sunday, Sally came back to the flat and they ate breakfast together. Kate felt immeasurably sorry for her, being separated from Phil for so long, and she had seen the longing in her eyes when she told her about the few days that she and David had spent together. 'You are so lucky,' Sally said. 'Sometimes it's hard to conjure up Phil's face at all. Course,' she went on, 'I can say none of this in front of Ruby, because it would probably upset her. Honest to God, Kate, everything seems to upset her just now.'

'She's probably worried sick about Phil – bound to be, I'd say.'

'I'm worried sick about Phil too,' Sally said. 'I think about him nearly every minute of the day and I have like a knot of fear that stays inside me all the time.'

'I know,' Kate said. 'I feel like that too.'

'And it does no good going on about it all the time,' Sally said. 'But Ruby...'

Her voice tailed off and Kate felt her heart turn over in sympathy. 'Do you find her hard going?' she said. 'Because you could come back to live with me again if you want to. God knows when David will make it home again. He's warned us it may be ages and you could always bunk on the settee if he does manage to get any leave. It will only be for a day or two at the most.'

'No, thanks all the same,' Sally said. 'I think Ruby might go out of her mind altogether if I left her now, though Phoebe Jenkins is very good, and she and Ruby get on well.'

'Phoebe Jenkins?'

'Yeah, she lives next door,' Sally said. 'She was left with seven children when her husband was killed in the Great War and then she lost two daughters to influenza in 1919, so she can really appreciate what Ruby is going through now. Course she rattles round in the house now, like Ruby did before I moved in. She says that before the war the family were always on about her moving to some smaller place, but she's like Ruby and never wants to move because, as they both say, their memories are all wrapped up in that house.'

'I can see that though, can't you?'

'Oh, yes, I can see that all right,' Sally said. 'And I think when you have lost people dear to you, then maybe you need to hold on to something permanent, like, a house where you were so happy once.'

'So, you and Ruby are staying put?'

'You bet we are,' Sally said. 'Waiting till Phil comes home again.'

Just over a week later, German troops attacked Denmark and invaded Norway. 'Germany's like some sort of creeping monster, devouring all before it,' Susie said as they made their way to work. 'And our Martin was telling me that if

Norway falls, Germany will have a naval base for all military craft, including the U-boats that are doing such a good job of sinking our merchant ships already.'

'Oh, it's bad enough now,' Kate said. 'Your father might be right about having no food to put on the table.'

'He just might be,' Susie commented wryly. 'I mean, Hitler hasn't invaded these countries just for the fun of it.'

'No,' Kate agreed with a sigh. 'Sally will be worried to death at the latest news.'

'I bet,' Susie said. 'Mind you, the man on the wireless last night said that Belgium has this underground fort that is said to be impregnable. And it protects three strategic bridges, and without these bridges the Germans couldn't get men and machines into Belgium, because the other way, the border with France has the Maginot Line, which runs all the way to the Ardennes Forest and that is also impregnable.'

'So even if Norway is defeated, the German armies could be stopped at the borders of Belgium?'

'That's what he seemed to be saying.'

'I really hope he's right.'

'So do I,' Kate said. ''Cos if he's wrong, then we are sunk.'

As the fighting went on, the women coped the best way they could. Derek finished his basic training and came home on embarkation leave, Martin was called up, and Kate arrived home one evening in late April to find Father Patterson waiting for her, sitting on the settee in her living room.

She gazed at him, completely astounded. 'How did you get in here?'

'Your landlady let me in,' he said calmly, as if it was the most natural thing in the world.

Kate could hardly believe her ears. 'She let you into my flat?' she said. 'She had no right to do that and you, Father ... I'm sorry, but you shouldn't have taken advantage of that.'

'What she should have done and I should not have done hardly matters,' said the priest. 'I told her I had come to see you and you weren't home, and Mrs Donovan – being a good God-fearing woman, and also a member of my flock – said that, as I was your parish priest, she was sure that you wouldn't mind my waiting inside the flat.'

'But you see, I do mind,' Kate cried. 'I mind a great deal that you are calmly sitting in my own personal living room that I pay rent for and I shall make that fact clear to my landlady at the earliest opportunity.'

The priest stood up and faced her, his dark grey eyes like steel chips in his heavily lined, mournful-looking face with the beaked nose and thin lips. 'That is a very belligerent way to speak to anyone, Kate, and especially your parish priest.'

Kate supposed it was. She certainly had never spoken to any priest in such a manner before, but then none had inveigled their way into her flat when she wasn't there. Oh, Dolly would hear of this. Meanwhile, however, she had the priest to deal with, and suddenly she was furious. 'Belligerent!' she exploded. 'I am not only belligerent,

Father, I am angry, bloody angry. You had no right to come in uninvited. You knew I would be at work. You did this on purpose and then talked Dolly into letting you in.'

'Maybe she was more concerned about your immortal soul than you appear to be.'

'I don't know what you are on about,' Kate said.

'So, you have no idea why I have come?' the priest snapped out, and Kate heard the peremptory tone in his voice and saw the look in those penetrating eyes and knew full well why the priest had come, but she was not going to make it easy for him. 'No, I don't,' she said.

'I have had a very distressing letter from your parish priest in Donegal,' the priest said, looking with reproach at Kate. 'Apparently, your mother told him that you had entered some sort of marriage with a serviceman and were living with him as his wife.'

White-hot fury coursed through Kate's veins as she spat out, 'I have not entered into "some form of marriage" with anyone. I married David Burton according to the law of the land. And when the RAF allows, I live with him as his legally wedded wife, because that is who I am.'

'You are not married in the eyes of the Church.'

'I am aware of that,' Kate said. 'But we hadn't time. We wanted to get married before David was called up.'

'That is neither here nor there,' the priest snapped out. 'Every time you lie with this man you are committing adultery and any children you bear will be illegitimate, bastards.'

Kate had had enough. She crossed to the door and held it open. 'Get out,' she said, 'you sanctimonious prig, and don't even try coming back. And you won't be seeing me at St Mary and St John's any more, so if I were you I would say daily prayers for my soul, which is surely as black as pitch.'

'Kate–'

'Get out!' Kate screamed. 'Just get out before I kick you out.'

Hugely affronted, the priest swept out. 'Your mother will hear of this appalling behaviour,' he said as he passed her.

'Good!' Kate said, and shut the door with such suddenness and such power that the priest had to jump out of the way.

She leant against the door, temporarily spent, for never had she behaved so or spoken in such a way to a priest. She knew her mother would get to hear of it and be scandalized. But suddenly that ceased to matter when compared to what was happening in Europe. She began to laugh, but there was a touch of hysteria mixed with it, and when the laughter turned to tears she wasn't surprised.

Dolly came up later that evening. 'Oh, Lord, I'm that sorry, Kate,' she said when Kate opened the door. She was puffing like a steam train, but she went on: 'George was that mad with me letting the priest in here before you had got home from work. He said he doesn't know what I was thinking of. Oh, I tell you I've had it in the neck from him right and proper, but see, I've never said no to a priest.'

271

Dolly's eyes looked troubled and Kate watched as tears seeped from them and ran down her rosy cheeks; she felt suddenly sorry for her because she knew just how some priests behaved and this kindly woman would be no match for them. 'Don't get upset,' she said, opening the door wider. 'Come in.'

Dolly gave a sigh of relief and went into the flat and Kate pressed her into a chair in the kitchen as she went on. 'He was that insistent, you see,' Dolly said as Kate busied herself with the kettle. 'I said he could wait for you in my place, but he said that it was imperative he saw you as soon as possible. It was a matter of grave importance. I did think something might have happened to those in Ireland, or even young Sally.'

'No,' Kate said, 'it was nothing like that.'

She knew Dolly was very anxious to find out what the priest had come about, but she wasn't going to ask and Kate was a little nervous of telling her because what if she also thought that she was living in sin with David? She might even ask her to leave. 'Any road,' Dolly said with a sniff, 'George said it don't matter what he wanted and who he was, I had no right to let him in to your private place. I really am sorry about it, Kate, and I promise I will never do anything like that again.'

Kate placed a cup of tea in front of Dolly and said with a wry smile, 'I doubt very much it will happen again, for I sent him away with a flea in his ear. I've never spoken to a priest like that before – I called him a sanctimonious prig.'

Dolly had a hand wrapped around her mouth in shock. 'You never did, Kate?'

'Oh, I did,' Kate said. 'And then I threw him out and told him not to dare try to come back.'

'Oh, Lord, what would I have given to be a fly on the wall then,' Dolly spluttered. She began to laugh and her laughter overtook her whole body so that her three chins began to wobble and then her stomach and she laughed and laughed. It was such an infectious laugh that Kate joined in too, and the tears that ran from Dolly's eyes were tears of hilarity.

When they were quieter and Dolly had wiped her eyes and taken a sip of her tea, Kate said, 'I think Father Patterson wanted to get in here to poke about. It makes me sick to think of him touching any of my things. He told me you just opened the door to him.'

'I never did, Kate,' Dolly said. 'Not like that I didn't. He was so determined though.'

'I know, I believe you,' Kate said.

'But why would he want to go through your things?'

'Possibly to check that what he had been told by my parish priest in Donegal was right. Look, you may as well know he was here mainly to tell me I was living in sin with David.'

'And are you?'

'Only as far as the Church is concerned,' Kate said. 'I am legally married, but we had no time for the big church do before David enlisted.'

'Well,' said Dolly slowly, 'I think these are strange times and you might have to move with them and I am not going to blame you for striking out for a bit of happiness.'

273

Dolly's attitude helped when the expected and censorious letter from Kate's mother arrived the following Friday, castigating her for the way she behaved before the priest and the insulting way she'd spoken to him. She said she was disgusted, surprised and hurt that a daughter of hers should behave in such a dreadful way. Strangely, Kate felt no remorse. She had discussed it briefly with Susie and then she had called in to see Sally after work to tell her of her altercation with the priest and her mother's reaction to it. And although Sally agreed that the priest had been particularly nasty in the things he had said to Kate and the way he had inveigled himself into the flat in the first place, she was startled when Kate said she wouldn't be going to church any more. 'What about your immortal soul?' she asked in slightly awed tones.

'What about it?' Kate said carelessly. 'The bloody priests would have a person afraid of their own shadow.'

'They have power, Kate,' Sally warned.

'Only because we allow them to have it,' Kate retorted. 'They should be more concerned with what's happening in the world. They go about as if the war is no concern of theirs.'

'Mammy is all for the priests, however they behave,' Sally said, scanning the letter. 'Now you're in her bad books as well as me.'

'Looks that way, certainly,' Kate said.

'How will you answer a letter like that?'

Kate shrugged. 'Don't know,' she said. 'But I'll tell you one thing. I will lose no sleep over it. And if you want to go to Mass, that's up to you – come round for your breakfast afterwards as normal.'

'I will,' Sally said. 'It gives us an opportunity for a good chat.'

However, before Kate met up with Sally again, she had a much more welcome letter on Saturday, for it was a note from David, and although it was short she treasured every word.

My darling Kate,
Things are very hectic here and there is little time to write letters. I can tell you nothing, but I'm sure you listen to the wireless and read the paper and so you'll be well aware of what is going on. Every plane and every pilot is needed and I see no light at the end of the tunnel yet. Be strong, my darling, and remember I love you with all my heart and I always will,
Lots of love,
David

Kate showed her sister the letter the following day when she called in after Mass, and they were finishing their breakfast when they heard on the news that the Crown Prince of Norway and his Cabinet had fled to London. There was no official surrender and sporadic fighting still continued, but the writing was on the wall as far as Norway was concerned. It was as if the whole world waited to see what Hitler's next move might be.

They hadn't long to wait, because just days later, Blitzkrieg, or Lightning War, was inflicted on Holland, culminating in a raid on Rotterdam that left over a thousand people dead and countless more injured. The pictures in the paper were heart-breaking, desperate: despairing people fleeing with all that they could carry, while behind them plumes of smoke filled the air as their city burned. Worse news, though, was that German paratroopers had landed on the fort everyone had said was impregnable, and had taken control of the bridges. Men and machines had begun trundling across them and German tanks had also ploughed through Ardennes Forest, another apparently impregnable obstacle. The papers all reported that the French were fighting for their lives.

When Kate called to see Sally the following evening, she saw that Ruby was in a dreadful state. She had deep score marks in her face, which was a muddy grey colour; the frizzy hair that framed her face had not a vestige of brown left. But what upset Kate most were her eyes, reddened like Sally's and ringed with black: they were full of pain and fear. Her humour and feisty nature seemed to have deserted her altogether: 'We're neither of us able to eat anything,' she told Kate.

Kate nodded. 'My appetite seems to have gone too,' she said. 'But please don't think the worst yet.'

'How can we not?' Ruby cried. 'Look at this map – it was in the paper today.' And as she spoke she spread it out on the table. 'See, those bloody swastikas are everywhere.'

They were too, and Kate's eyes opened wider, because seeing it like that really brought it home to her just how alone Britain was. 'The Allies must be surrounded by the German armies,' Sally said. 'And as far as I can see, the only place they can retreat to are the beaches. Then they will have to bloody swim for it. I mean, think about it, how many prisoners can the Germans take? And a nation that can callously kill innocent civilians will not be very kind to the soldiers of an invading army.'

'Yeah,' Ruby agreed. 'And even if they aren't captured, I reckon they will just be picked off on the beaches or bombed to kingdom come because there is nowhere else they can go.' The eyes she turned on Kate were bleak and lacking in all hope as she said, 'I can't even cry. My fear for Phil goes deeper than that, and inside me and Sally are falling to pieces.'

There was a strange message broadcast from the Admiralty that no one fully understood, for it was requesting all owners of self-propelled pleasure craft between thirty and a hundred foot in length to send specifications to the Admiralty within fourteen days. Shortly after this, the Allies were ordered to retreat, making for the beaches of Dunkirk, where they found the big destroyers sent to take them home had to be anchored out in deep water, so the soldiers couldn't reach them, despite the pier heads they built from discarded equipment.

And then the meaning of the message from the Admiralty was made clear as a flotilla of boats of all shapes and sizes, yachts, cruisers, even fishing smacks, manned by a motley crew of civilians, sailed over to the beaches, filled up their vessels with servicemen and ferried them out to the waiting ships. It was called Operation Dynamo and its objective was to lift as many men off the beaches as possible. In the end, 700 boats took part in this, for when the veil of secrecy was lifted and everyone knew what was at stake, many owners of boats set off on their own without Admiralty clearance.

The papers reported on the men's return, and in the accompanying photographs Kate saw them waving from the carriages of trains or being greeted by the WVS. Some had blankets around their shivering bodies as they gulped at the scalding tea in the thick white mugs, and there were harrowing accounts of the conditions on the beaches. A great many had stood waist-high in the freezing water for up to thirty-six hours without food or water before being rescued.

When the operation was brought to a close on 4 June, the papers reported over 300,000 Allies had been saved, and that included 140,000 French.

'It was amazing to get so many men home,' Kate said one day to Susie about a week later. 'But the cost has been colossal in the loss of so much stuff.'

'Yeah, that's why overtime is compulsory,' Susie said. 'They need more Jeeps so they need more radiators for them.'

'They need everything if we are ever to win this damned war,' Kate said. 'And the need to win is even greater now, or those left behind on the beaches of Dunkirk will have died in vain.'

'They might not have died,' Susie said. 'They might have been taken prisoner.'

'The chances of that are very slim,' Kate said. 'Rumour has it that few were taken captive.'

'Yeah, I can believe that of the murdering Krauts,' Susie said bitterly. 'Some of those returning are little more than boys, and I suppose they are the lucky ones. Has Sally had any news about Phil?'

'Not yet, but, as I said to her, no news is usually good news, and with over three hundred thousand rescued, it might take time to sort out where everyone is. She says it's the not knowing that's hard,' Kate said. 'And I know it is, but the only thing she wants to know is that he is alive and well.'

'That's what anyone would want to know, though.'

'Yes,' Kate agreed. 'And I do feel sorry for her. But I am trying to cheer her up. I mean, it could be good news if he was injured, as long as it wasn't that bad and, if he was, he could be anywhere they had space, but I do know that she has scrutinized every picture in every paper.'

'You and I would do the same as well,' Susie said with a smile. 'We didn't even know our men had been involved till they sent that note to say they were safe.'

'Good job I didn't know in advance,' Kate said. 'I'd have been a nervous wreck. I think the Phoney War, or Bore War as some called it, is definitely over.'

'I think so too,' Susie said. 'And now we're being asked to hide maps and disable cars and bikes not in use.'

'I know,' Kate said. 'And just today I saw a man painting out the road signs... I don't mind admitting that I'm scared stiff. Only a small stretch of water separates us from France – if you ask me, Britain is staring a full-scale invasion in the face.'

SIXTEEN

Just a few mornings later, Kate was at work when she was approached by the supervisor, Mrs Higgins. The machine shop was a noisy place, far too noisy for normal conversation, but Mrs Higgins indicated that Kate should follow her. She was surprised because this had never happened before; as she turned off her machine, Susie, who worked beside her, looked up and raised her eyebrows in enquiry. Kate gave a shrug before following behind the supervisor, past the line of girls at machines just like her own, who all looked at her curiously.

Outside the machine shop it was much quieter, though the throb and rumbling could still be heard, and Mrs Higgins said, 'Sorry about that, Kate, but Mr Tanner said to fetch you.'

'He did?' said Kate in astonishment, because Mr Tanner was boss of the whole place and she hadn't been in his office since the day she had been interviewed for the job a few years before. 'D'you know what this is about?' she asked. 'I can't think of anything I have done wrong.'

'Don't worry,' the supervisor said, and her eyes were sympathetic as she went on, 'I don't think it is about anything you have done. I think you should prepare yourself, though. Your sister is here.'

'My sister?' Kate echoed, knowing only a catastrophe of some magnitude would have caused Sally to seek her out.

The supervisor nodded. 'Yes,' she said dolefully. 'She told Mr Tanner that she was your sister – she's very distressed.'

The blood drained from Kate's face. 'Oh God,' she breathed.

They reached the office and Mrs Higgins said, 'You can go straight in. He is expecting you.'

From behind the door came the muffled sound of weeping and Kate mentally straightened her shoulders before opening it. The last time that she'd been in the room, Mr Tanner had sat in a black leather chair behind a large, highly polished wooden desk. There was another black chair facing the desk, and that was where she had sat nervously for her interview.

Now her sister, still in the overalls she wore for work, sat in that chair, rocking backwards and forwards, the tears dripping through the hands she had covering her face. Mr Tanner was beside her, looking decidedly uncomfortable and patting her shoulder gently. He gave an audible sigh of relief when he saw Kate. 'Ah, Mrs Burton,' he said against the backdrop of Sally's sobs, 'I'm afraid your sister has had some distressing news.'

At his words, Sally took her hands away from her face, but the tears still trickled from her puffy eyes and made tear trails through her dirt-smeared face. Kate felt a wave of pity wash over her, for it was like looking at two pools of sadness, and then she noticed the buff telegram crumpled in her sister's begrimed hand. 'Oh, Kate,' Sally cried. 'What am I to do? Phil's dead.' And she waved the telegram as she went on: 'This came this morning. His was one of the bodies left at Dunkirk.'

Although Kate had more or less known what her sister would say, the words were still shocking, and she gasped as she fell to her knees and wrapped her arms around her sorrowful sister, breathing in the stench of oil on her overalls. Mr Tanner had gratefully stepped to one side and he said to Kate, 'I think you should take your sister home, Mrs Burton. You need to be together at this dreadful time.'

'I will,' Kate said. 'Thank you, sir. Maybe you can get word to Susie Kassel? She will be wondering – we always go home together.'

'I will,' Mr Tanner said. 'Don't you worry about a thing. You just get yourselves away.'

'Thank you, Mr Tanner,' Kate said as she stood up. Drawing Sally gently to her feet, she said, 'Come on, my dear. I must get my things from the cloakroom and then we can go.'

'I left everything behind,' Sally said, brokenly. 'I couldn't think of anything except needing to see you.'

Kate's heart lurched as she realized how terribly young she was to deal with this, though she knew Sally wouldn't be the only one mourning a boyfriend, husband, son or brother. She hurriedly shrugged herself into her coat, retrieved her bag from her locker and linked an arm through Sally's. She looked so pale, Kate was afraid she was going to faint on her. As they walked to the tram stop, Kate said, 'We'd best go to your place first. Ruby will–'

'Ruby won't be there,' Sally said. 'She is in hospital. She had a stroke or heart attack or something when the letter came.'

'Ah, dear, poor woman.'

'She was on her own, see, so I don't know what happened. The telegram was delivered after I had left for work. Phoebe had seen the telegraph boy knock on her door, and when he had gone she heard Ruby cry out and went in to see if she was all right. She found her spark out on the floor with the telegram in her hand. She called Dr Butler out and he ordered an ambulance and then she brought the telegram to me.'

'So you don't know how bad Ruby is?'

Sally shook her head. 'Not a clue, though Phoebe said that she didn't look good,' she said. 'Don't even know where she has been taken either, though it's probably the General.'

'More than likely,' Kate said. 'Initially, anyway.'

'I know I should go and find out,' Sally said as the tram pulled up and they clambered aboard. 'It would be what Phil would want, but I can't seem to work up enthusiasm for anything.'

'I'll do all that as soon as I get you settled,' Kate promised. 'You really need to eat something and then sleep if you can.'

Sally shook her head. 'I doubt that I could sleep,' she said. 'My whole body is like jumping about inside and yet I am so weary I ache everywhere.' She looked at Kate with red-rimmed, pain-filled eyes. 'But none of this matters, does it?' she said in a voice little above a whisper as she fought the tears threatening to engulf her again. 'What does matter is that I will never see my darling Phil again, and I am just realizing what that means and I won't have any kind of future without him. And don't say that I will find someone else, because I don't want anyone else.'

Kate didn't say anything. She hadn't any words that would help assuage the intense grief she knew Sally was feeling at that moment. She needed to grieve and it was healthy that she did so; Kate decided she would shield her from those urging her to get over it until she was ready.

When they alighted from the tram, Sally was so weary she was unsteady, and Kate supported much of her weight as they made their way to the flat. The stairs were a great challenge for both of them. However, eventually, they were inside, and Kate lowered Sally into an easy chair and put on the kettle before stripping her of her dirty work clothes. She used some of the water to make a cup of tea, which Sally gulped at gratefully, and with the rest of the warm water she washed her gently as if she was a child.

'Now it's bed for you,' she insisted. 'Pop a nightie of mine on and tuck yourself up while I make some more tea and some toast.'

'Just tea,' Sally said. 'I couldn't eat.'

'I'll make it anyway,' Kate insisted. 'I'm only talking about a couple of slices of toast, and you may feel like it when you see it. If not, there's no harm done.'

Sally just nodded as she pulled one of Kate's nighties over her head, too tired to argue, and when Kate went into the bedroom later with the tea and toast, she found Sally tucked up in her bed. Despite her declaration that she didn't think she'd sleep, she was indeed in a deep slumber.

Kate lost no time, but first she knocked on Dolly's door and told her what had happened and asked her if she would sit with her sister for a while. 'I must find out what has happened to Ruby and then go to Sally's place of work and tell them about Phil but I don't want to leave her alone and her to wake up when I'm gone.'

'I'll sit with her, never fear,' Dolly said. 'Poor little love. You do what you have to do, Kate.'

Ruby was in the General Hospital and a nurse agreed to let Kate see her when she explained who she was. 'But she is extremely ill,' she cautioned. 'You can have a few minutes, no more.'

Kate nodded and opened the curtain. When she saw the shrunken, comatose figure of Ruby on the bed, her face as white as the pillow her head lay on, she knew she was looking at a very sick woman. It didn't look a bit like the feisty person Kate knew her to be. It was as if the spirit of her had gone.

The doctor was waiting for her and was very grave. 'It was a massive stroke that Mrs Reynard sustained,' he said.

'Will she recover?'

'It's too early to say categorically,' the doctor said. 'But early indications point to the fact that, if she was to recover, she would have quite extensive brain damage.'

'I see.'

'Are you a relative?'

'No,' Kate told him. 'My sister lived with Ruby because she was engaged to her son Phillip, who is – I mean was – in the Army.'

'And it was the arrival of the telegram telling her

of the death of her son that brought this on,' the doctor said. 'That much the ambulance drivers were told by the neighbour who found Mrs Reynard unconscious.'

'Yes, my sister was at work, and when the neighbour told her what had happened she came to find me.'

'And has Mrs Reynard other family?'

'She had,' Kate said. 'They were all wiped out with TB, and Phil was the only one spared. I don't know if there were other relations; my sister always said that it had just been Phil and his mother for years.'

The doctor shook his head. 'The human mind is very powerful,' he said. 'Sometimes, people make remarkable recoveries, many of which confound the doctors, usually when the patient has powerful reasons to want to go on living. In Mrs Reynard's case, on the other hand...'

He didn't have to complete the sentence; his meaning was abundantly clear. Kate thanked him for his time and went to get the tram to Sally's place of work. She went to the main office to say who she was and why she had come, but it was lunchtime, and so when she went into the cloakroom to collect up Sally's handbag and normal clothes she was inundated by her work colleagues, eager to find out what had happened. They were all stunned. Some shed tears; many were aware they could receive such news about their loved ones at any time. 'We thought it must have been summat big like,' one of the girls said to Kate. 'You can't talk in the factory, but someone come and took her away like and we never saw her again.'

'I feel ever so sorry for her,' one of the others said, and there was a murmur of agreement, and another went on, 'Ah, it's ever so sad. Sally was always talking about Phil.'

'Yeah, and they really did love each other,' another girl told Kate. 'I worked at the Plaza with Sally before we came here and you only had to see them together... You could almost feel it. I don't know what she will do or how she will recover from this. I knew Phil as well and he was always happy. He was smashing.'

'I know he was,' Kate said. 'It will take Sally some time to get over the loss of him.'

'Yeah, if she ever does.'

'Oh, she must eventually,' Kate said. 'Because that is what Phil would want.'

Sally was up and dressed in Kate's clothes and Dolly had gone back to her own flat when Kate arrived home. When Kate told her how ill Ruby was, she insisted on going up to see her that afternoon. Kate went with her, but let Sally go in to see Ruby alone while she sat on the bench in the corridor. She saw the shock on her sister's face when she approached her later. 'It's like she's already gone,' she said. 'In fact, I said goodbye to her.'

'Ah, Sally.'

'Don't be too sympathetic, or I will start blubbing again,' Sally warned.

'No harm in that.'

'Yes there is if you do too much of it,' Sally said, and she struggled for control as she went on: 'I have to learn to live a life without Phillip in it, and at the moment that realization is very painful; so painful it's as if a shard of glass is piercing my very soul.'

Kate was overcome by the sadness of it herself. She wrapped her arms around her sister and they wept together. Eventually, Sally pulled herself out of Kate's arms and said shakily, 'I warned you what would happen if you did that.'

'Maybe you needed that release,' Kate said.

'Maybe I did,' Sally said. 'But all the tears in the world will not change the fact that my beloved Phil is dead.' And Kate marvelled at her young sister's courage when she went on: 'I think Ruby will not regain consciousness and I hope she doesn't. Life for her without Phil would be too hard.'

'And what about you?'

Sally lifted her chin in the air in a gesture of almost defiance as she said, 'I will do what Phil would expect me to do, and that is to go on and do anything I can to help win this war, so that his death will not be in vain. And now,' she added, 'we had better go home. We can do no good here.' But as they made their way to the tram, Sally said, 'We need to see Reverend Simpson, the vicar of St Mark's, as well, so we may as well do it now.'

Kate guessed that Sally was giving herself no time to think and asked, 'Is it far?'

'No distance at all from the house,' Sally said. 'In fact, you nearly pass it on the way to the house because it's on the corner of Bleak Hill and Hesketh Crescent. If we take the tram as far as the Stockland pub instead of getting off nearer the flat, it's only a step away.'

'The vicar will know who Ruby is, I suppose.'

'Oh, yeah,' Sally said. 'Ruby used to go regularly, and Phil too before he joined up, so he'll want to know what has happened to them.'

'Well then, we can call at the house as well and collect some stuff for you at the same time,' Kate said.

'And I need to see Phoebe next door as well,' Sally said. 'She will be wondering and she was right fond of Ruby.' And then she looked at Kate and asked, 'I suppose it is all right if I move in with you for a bit?'

'Of course it is,' Kate said. 'But let's get a move on because we have a lot to do today.'

Reverend Simpson was upset at the news Sally gave him. His lugubrious grey eyes darkened still further and his slack mouth drooped further downwards as he commiserated with her. And when she cried at the sympathy in his voice, he didn't seem to feel any awkwardness or embarrassment and knew all the right things to say. Kate was impressed, conceding that he couldn't help his long face and mournful expression. In fact, in his job, to look like that could even be considered an added advantage. The man certainly seemed genuine and concerned, and said he would go straight away to see Ruby in the hospital. 'And,' he added to Sally, 'remember, my door is always open should you have need of anything or even if you just want to talk.'

'He looks like the prophet of gloom and doom,' Kate said as they walked away. 'But I think his heart is in the right place.'

'Oh, I think it is,' Sally said. 'Phil used to say...'

She stopped and swallowed deeply before going on in a firmer voice: 'Phil always spoke highly of him and, even though he was only a little boy when his father died, his mother had always said how good he had been then, and Phil could remember how much he helped them until he left school and went to work.'

'I like to hear of clergymen practising what they preach,' Kate said. 'But I had a thought when we were in there.'

'What?'

'Well, if Ruby dies, you shouldn't really go to the funeral.'

'Why not?'

'I never understood why we couldn't,' Kate said. 'But it's forbidden in the Catholic Church.'

'Well,' said Sally with a toss of her head, 'you know what the Catholic Church can do, don't you, because if you think I am not going to Ruby's funeral because of some daft rule we don't even know the reason for, then you can think again.'

'I'm not the enemy here,' Kate said gently. 'As a matter of fact, I think you are right, and I'll go with you. If we are cast into Hell's flames because of it, then at least we will be together.'

A ghost of a smile played around Sally's mouth at Kate's words and a wave of love for her older sister rose up inside her. She grasped hold of her arm as she said, 'Oh, Kate, I do love you and appreciate your support and everything.'

Kate was embarrassed beyond measure and she coloured slightly as she said, 'Course I'll support you, you daft ha'p'orth. That's what big sisters do. Now we'll go and see that neighbour of yours and collect some clothes and anything else we can carry that you might need.'

Phoebe came to the door with an apron tight around her middle and a turban on her head. Kate saw a stout lady about Ruby's age with startling blue eyes, which darkened with sympathy as Sally told her the news. 'I guessed it would be bad,' she said. 'And you and all, Bab. What shocking news for you. That's why I got stuck into the cleaning. Nothing like it to stop you thinking. Have you time for a cup of tea?'

'No, thanks all the same,' Sally said. 'We only came back to fetch some clothes because I am staying with my sister for a bit.'

'Ah, you do right,' Phoebe said, removing her apron as she spoke. 'Better to be with your own at a time like this. And I'll be away to the hospital to see if I can see old Rube. And you know where I am if you should need owt.'

'Yeah, thanks, Phoebe,' Sally said. As they moved away she added to Kate, 'Nosey as anything. Wants to know the ins and outs of everyone's business, but she would do anything for you. Salt of the earth, Ruby used to say she was.' Kate heard the slight sob in Sally's voice as she said Ruby's name, but she didn't comment on it. She knew that any sympathy might cause Sally to break down, and as she sensed she was holding herself together with difficulty, they walked back to the flat in silence.

Ruby died the following day. The hospital made all the arrangements for the funeral and Sally found an insurance policy in Ruby's shelter bag that would pay for the cost of it. She was glad of this because she couldn't have allowed Ruby to lie in a pauper's grave, and yet the cost of even a modest funeral staggered her.

As it was, Ruby went out in grand style in a shiny mahogany coffin with brass handles. Susie was astounded at the number of people at the funeral. Ruby had lived in the same house all her life, and so Phoebe wasn't the only neighbour who came to show their respects. Susie and her mother had broken the Roman Catholic rule too and come along to support Sally.

There were a fair few young people as well, girls who Sally worked with and some young men in uniform who had been friends of Phil's. Phil would have no service and no grave, but as a couple of them explained to Kate later, they felt the least they could do was attend Ruby's, for she had been well known to them when they had been boys together. They were sure, they said, that Phil would have expected them to do that.

Reverend Simpson also took this fact on board and mentioned Phil in the address, saying he was sadly missed as well. He said he had been one of the country's heroes and a fine young man who had paid the ultimate price in the fight for freedom and justice. 'He will live on in the hearts and minds of many,' he said. 'This funeral is for his mother, a dear lady I knew well who loved her son. So this funeral is also dedicated to Phil's memory.'

Even Kate had a lump in her throat when he finished speaking, and from the snuffling and sniffing around her, she knew Sally wasn't the only one in tears. And then they travelled to nearby Witton Cemetery for the burial. No other relations had been traced, and so it was Sally who was asked to throw the first clod of earth and then Kate and Susie. And, as the dirt thudded on to the coffin, Sally felt as if it had been a brief interlude in her life that was now over, almost as though it had never happened.

After the funeral, Sally stopped taking the sleeping tablets that the doctor had prescribed for her just after Phil's death because she thought they were making her feel too lethargic. 'I seem to be exhausted all the time,' she complained to Kate. 'I'm frustrated with myself.'

'Why worry?' Kate said 'There is nothing spoiling, and you have been signed off sick from work for a few days. I will have to go back tomorrow but you haven't to rush.'

'It's the rent on the house,' Sally said. 'I have to make a decision about it soon.'

'Are you going to keep it on?'

'Well, I can't afford the rent on my own,' Sally said. 'And it is far too big for just me anyway, but I was wondering if you and David would like it instead of this flat. It isn't much more to pay than you do now and it has a bathroom upstairs and three bedrooms, so when David came home I wouldn't have to move out.'

Kate thought about it and thought it would be lovely to have her own bathroom and her own front door and little patch of garden back and front; it was a semi-detached and a better and bigger house than the one David's parents had. Houses were like gold dust to obtain – in fact if she passed this one up, they might not have another chance of one for years.

'D'you know, Sally, that's a great idea,' Kate said. 'I really should ask David what he thinks, though I don't imagine he'll object. But trying to get hold of him now is very difficult, and his replies take even longer to reach me, so I'll write and tell him. Meanwhile, I'll give notice here and start moving into Ruby's old house, if you're sure?'

'Course I'm sure.'

'And you won't be haunted by bad memories?'

'Memories are not held in bricks and mortar,' Sally said, 'though I think Ruby thought differently. But my memories – both good and bad – are locked in my heart. I had a lot of happy times in that house, so, yes, I would like to go back to living there again, especially with you.'

A fortnight later, after an almost tearful goodbye to Dolly Donovan, who said they had been model tenants whom she would miss very much, they were ready for the off. Everyone lent a hand to move Kate and Sally and their possessions to their new abode, much to Phoebe's delight. Kate was incredibly grateful to Frank Mason, because with petrol at a premium, finding a lorry or a van was well-nigh impossible unless you were willing to pay the earth for it, but Frank knew a man with a horse and cart. 'We can move most of the stuff on that,' he told the two girls. 'Most of it will have to have a tarpaulin over it so that we can tie it down.'

'What's he charging for it?' Kate asked; and had a broad smile on her face when Frank said, 'He said he'd settle for a couple of bales of hay.'

And eventually it was all done, the beds put up,

the pictures on the walls and the rugs on the floor, the things they didn't want out in the garden for the horse to pull back to the tip. Sally and Kate sat down with a welcome cup of tea. 'Well, that's a good job finished,' Kate said with a sigh. 'I think we will be happy here.'

'Yeah, I suppose.'

'What's up?'

'Nothing.'

'Yes, there is,' Kate insisted. 'I can always tell. What's on your mind?'

'All right then,' Sally said. 'Ever since Phil died, I've been thinking that I should be doing more for the war effort.'

'You're making shell cases now.'

'I know, and I wouldn't stop,' Sally said. 'This will be sort of in the evenings and that, like being an ARP warden. I mean, I know there aren't many bombs falling round here yet, but according to the papers and that man on the BBC, France will not be able to hold out much longer, and, meanwhile, Hitler, they say, is massing all sorts of boats, barges and landing craft on the other side of a very small channel. Before any invasion, they reckon there'll be a heavy bombing campaign to soften us up. The thought of bombs dropping from the sky and then exploding frightens me to death, to be honest.'

'Any sane person would be scared,' Kate said. 'I certainly will be.'

'Yeah, but Phil probably was as well,' Sally said. 'And a good proportion of those men and boys who were called to be soldiers most likely felt the same a lot of the time, but they still had to conquer that fear and go on. I want to prove that I can do the same.' And then she looked Kate full in the face and said, 'I think I will get over Phil's death quicker if I do this. In a funny way I think I will feel closer to him. Anyway, I feel I have languished long enough and I am going back to work next week.'

'D'you think you're well enough?'

'Course I am,' Sally said. 'All a person does at home is think too hard about things and end up feeling sorry for themselves.'

'I agree with that totally,' Kate said.

'Anyway, how can I think about taking up extra work for the war effort if I am not able to do the job I'm paid to do?'

Kate was impressed with her sister and the way she had thought the whole thing through and so she said, 'Sally, every word you said made sense. So much so that I want to help in some way as well. We'll look into this ARP business just as soon as we can.'

SEVENTEEN

Before they were able to find anything out about ARP wardens, Kate had word that David was coming home on a forty-eight-hour pass. Susie had heard that Nick had leave too, but neither girl could be spared from work the first day the men were back, which was on Friday, when Nick and David were arriving about lunchtime.

As the two girls travelled to work that Friday morning, Susie said, 'Thank goodness we will have Saturday off at least.'

'Yeah,' Kate said. 'Hope the weather holds.' It was the last week in June and the weather had been glorious for nearly a week. 'Might cheer me up a bit as well,' she added. 'I mean, I know it was a foregone conclusion that France would fall, but to actually sign an alliance with the country that is going to rule over you, as they did last week, seems all wrong to me.'

'And me,' Susie said. 'And it does mean that now Britain is completely alone.'

Kate nodded. 'Sally wants to do her bit, you know,' she said. 'She wants to become an ARP warden.'

'Well, all they have to do at the moment is patrol the streets in the blackout,' Susie said. 'And I suppose see if anyone is showing a light.'

'Yeah, but she and I think things will hot up very soon. The Germans will be bombing towns and cities before an invasion – like they did Rotter-dam.'

'Yeah, frightening the Dutch government so much they gave up without a fight,' Susie said grimly.

'That won't happen here though, will it?' Kate said. 'Somehow I just can't see Churchill giving in so easy.'

'No, nor me,' Susie agreed, and then went on: 'I read somewhere that these barrage balloons hovering above the city streets are a form of protection against the air raids, though I don't see what earthly use they will be.'

'Nor me,' Kate said. 'And when the bombing does start, that's when the ARPs will be needed... So I've decided to volunteer as well.'

Susie nodded. 'I think you're right,' she said. 'Are you going to talk to your boy in blue and ask what he thinks about it first?'

'Ask his permission?' Kate said. 'The answer is no. David never asked if I minded him joining the Air Force. He told me that was what he intended to do long before he was called up and, if I remember rightly, Nick did the same.'

Susie nodded again. 'He did and you're right,' she said. 'They didn't ask us so there is no earthly reason why you should ask David. You know,' she went on, 'I wouldn't mind coming along too. I imagine that duties will be arranged in the evenings or weekends and I'm doing nothing else. I'd feel I was doing my bit too, and anyway I'm finding life deadly dull just now.'

'Yeah, I'm finding life a bit of a drag as well,' Kate said. 'I mean, I don't really feel right going dancing without the chaps.'

'Nor me,' Susie said. 'Not that there's much dancing to be had. The single girls who do go say that there are so few men, except the odd one home on leave, that they spend the time either sitting at the tables getting bored to death, or dancing with their friends. Lots of the stars of the Music Hall are off entertaining the troops, so there's only the pictures left.'

'All us bored married women,' Kate said with a smile. 'Think what a contribution to the war effort we could make.'

'Yeah, we might be the means of turning this war and planned invasion around completely,' Susie responded in like vein.

'Well, we can give it a bloody good try anyway,' said Kate, getting to her feet as the factory came into view and the two girls ran giggling down the tram stairs.

David spent the first afternoon of his leave with Nick at the Masons' house, but they both went up to meet the girls from work that evening. Kate tingled all over when she emerged from the factory gates and saw David standing there. She flew into his arms. And then she took his face between her hands and examined him critically. 'You are thinner,' she said, 'and there are blue tinges under your eyes.'

'Well,' said David, 'you can put my thinness down to the culinary delights of NAAFI food, and the bags under my eyes to the fact that I don't get much shut-eye.'

'Right,' Kate said. 'I will see what I can do for

both of those problems now you're here at last.'

'Looking forward to that,' David said. 'But how tired are you at the moment?'

'It's Friday night,' Kate said. 'What do you think?'

'Are you too tired to walk home?'

Kate thought a little teasing wouldn't come amiss and, looking at him coyly, she said, 'That would depend on who was asking me.'

'You cheeky monkey,' David said in mock annoyance. 'I hope you would not walk home with any Tom, Dick or Harry. It's me asking you – David Burton, your lawful wedded husband.'

'Is it really?' Kate said. 'Well, as he was the one that I promised to love, honour and obey, I'd better accept.' And with that she stepped on tiptoe so she could reach David's face and, despite the others from the factory streaming past her, she kissed him gently on the lips. 'Welcome home, darling,' she said. 'It is so good to see you.'

'And you,' David said, tucking her arm through his as they began to walk through the balmy evening. 'I think of you a lot through the day and dream of you at night, and I live for your letters. I was real sorry to hear about Phil, by the way, and his mother too. It must have been a lot for Sally to cope with?'

'Oh, it was,' Kate said. 'She took some time coming to terms with it. But she is all right now and working out her own salvation.'

'Oh,' David said. 'What's that?'

Kate told him. 'She says it will help her to get over her own tragedy helping others,' she explained. 'And it will certainly not allow her much time to think and brood.'

'And it's a very worthwhile thing to do.'

Kate decided to bite the bullet, and so, taking a deep breath, she said, 'Would you feel the same if I was to take it on too?'

David looked at her and said, 'You are joking?'

'Why should I be joking?'

There was a steely note to David's voice as he said, 'I would think that obvious. You are a married woman.'

'Right. So my life stops, does it?'

'Of course not,' David said. 'Now you're being silly.'

Kate pulled out of David's embrace and faced him. In the evening sunlight he saw her eyes flashing as she said, 'No, David, I am not being silly – remember, you are a married man.'

'That's different. Surely you can see that?' David said.

'No, I really can't,' Kate said. 'How is it?'

'Look, Kate...' David began. 'No, I can't allow it. As an ARP warden you'll be out in the teeth of the raids.'

'I know that,' Kate said. 'And, as for you not allowing it, you can forget that for a start, because I'm not asking permission anyway. I am telling you what I am going to do, and if you say one word about my promising to love, honour and obey you, I will brain you, because this is something I must do.'

'All right,' David snapped angrily. 'I won't remind you of your vows, but that didn't mean that the marriage didn't happen. You did say those words and now, just months later, you are going to defy me.'

'Yes, if that's the way you want to think of it,' Kate said a little sadly. 'I really thought you might understand. I feel I must do this, in the same way you felt you had to join the RAF.'

'Oh, tit for tat, is that it?'

'Oh, don't be so childish!' Kate snapped. 'Of course it isn't.'

'It's dangerous work,' David said. 'I don't think you understand—'

'Of course I understand,' Kate said testily. 'I am not a fool. I suppose flying a fighter plane is as safe as a vicar's tea party, is it?'

David gave a wry smile. 'Hardly, but Kate, you are a woman. It's not right. I mean, won't you be frightened?'

'Sometimes probably,' Kate said. 'Aren't you ever?'

'We never talk about fear.'

'But not talking about it does not mean you never experience it. You have had to learn to deal with it the same as I will.'

'But I would worry about you so much.'

'Oh, David,' Kate cried. 'Don't you realize I have a sick knot of worry inside me all the time you are away, no doubt taking no end of risks? Again, that is something I have to deal with.'

David still had a mulish face on and so Kate went on: 'It's a different world now, David, because it has to be. Women have had to work in places that formerly were male preserves: brass foundries, drop forges, all sorts of places. Haven't you seen the women car mechanics and those driving lorries and buses and trams? And who do you think is making the machine-guns you fire and the rifles and the pistols and the bullets to go in them; who is making up the bombs and sewing the parachutes and the uniforms you wear? Me, making radiator grilles for Jeeps. I could go on and on. And we have women in the forces, don't we?'

'Yes, but the WAAFs usually only do the clerical work.'

'All of them?'

'Well, we do have women mechanics and fitters and such, but they don't go into combat.'

'But we won't have a choice if the bombs come,' Kate said. 'Someone's got to be out there helping wherever help is needed, and there are only women and old men left – and many of the older men have already been drafted into the Home Guard. And a lot of the women taking on extra duties like these will be married, some of them mothers doing their bit to help win this dreadful war. I want to be part of it.'

David wanted his Kate to be as safe as it was possible to be, if the bombing raids came, but he realized that he had married a woman with her own mind and one who was as stubborn as a mule. Despite the fact he was still a little annoyed with her high-handedness, he had a grudging admiration for her determination.

'Come on, David,' Kate said impatiently. 'Sally said doing work like this will help her feel closer to Phil, and both Susie and I understand what she means.'

'Is Susie involved in this as well?' David said. 'I might have known really.'

'Yes, you should have,' Kate said. 'We'll be like

the three musketeers. And I bet Nick will be fully supportive of her decision, not like the grouch I'm married to!'

David laughed and his irritation melted away, though the misgivings remained. 'All right then,' he said. 'Join the wretched organization if it means so much to you. And while I'm still not totally happy about it, I am very proud of all three of you for even thinking about it.' He took her arm again and they walked on for a while before he said, 'That was our first argument. We have never disagreed about anything before.'

'It wasn't a bad fight,' Kate said. 'Not really. I just had to point out to you that I haven't stopped being a person just because I'm married.'

'I never thought you had, Mrs Burton?' David said, and a jocular tone was back in his voice.

'Well, it didn't sound like that, Mr Burton,' said Kate.

'Is this what married life is all about?' David asked.

'I'm afraid it probably will be a lot of the time,' Kate admitted. 'Can you stand it, do you think?'

'Oh, yes, my darling girl,' said David. 'I think I will be able to stand it very well indeed.'

David was very impressed with the house they would now be living in, though he said Kate had described it well in her letters to him. When he saw Sally was already home, he was quick to offer his condolences to her. She thanked him, but her smile didn't touch her eyes. They had a bleak look to them, and the bloom was gone from her cheeks, and he knew whatever public face she was putting on, she was still grieving. But it was early days yet, he thought as he followed behind Kate, who left Sally putting finishing touches to the meal while she showed David around. 'It's just great,' he said when they arrived back in the kitchen. 'I mean, it's one thing hearing about it in a letter, but quite another seeing it,' he said. He grabbed hold of Kate and kissed her as he added, 'I think that we have been very lucky.'

'Yes, and I had to snap it up while I had the chance.'

'You did absolutely the right thing,' David said. 'But I'm surprised that you have no Anderson shelter – the garden is big enough.'

'Ruby was offered one last November when they were first delivered to Birmingham,' Sally said. 'But she refused to have one.'

'Why?'

'Oh, she said that no Hitler was getting her out of her house into some hole in the ground like an animal, and that she would sit out any raids under the stairs.' And then Sally smiled and went on: 'No one could budge her. She could be a cussed old woman at times.'

'Well, I don't really think that is a very sensible option,' David said. 'And I couldn't rest easy if I thought about you huddled under the stairs. If the house was hit then you could be buried.'

'Bit late now though.'

'No, I shouldn't think so,' David said. 'The council have a sort of duty to try and keep you all safe, so you could enquire about that. I would have to dig the hole out for you, because it has to be four foot deep, and that will have to be done before any shelter can be delivered.'

Kate wasn't sure that she wanted to hide away in a hole in the ground any more than Ruby had, so she said, 'Oh, don't bother with that now. We'll get it all seen to when you've gone.'

'No, Kate, there's no time to waste,' David said. 'Nick will help and maybe Susie's dad, he's a decent fellow. Pity Martin has been called up, because he is another strapping chap, but between us we'll manage it. And it would be better to start first thing tomorrow.'

And that's exactly what happened. Saturday dawned fine and clear and, instead of walking through some leafy park and soaking up the sunshine and enjoying being together, Kate watched David and the other men begin digging up the turf of the scrappy little lawn and then slicing through the dusty earth beneath it. The dryness of the recent weather made light work of it, and so by the time they stopped for a bite to eat there was a sizeable hole just outside the kitchen door, deep enough to semi-bury the Anderson shelter as the government had advised people to do.

Kate, surveying the hole later, said, 'I know it's safer, but in a way it brings the war a little closer.'

'And that's exactly why you needed the shelter,' David said.

A little later, as they sat side by side on the settee, David said, 'I have something to tell you.'

'Is it bad news?'

'No ... well, not really,' David said. 'Some might even consider it good news.'

'Go on then.'

'I've been made up to squadron leader, and so

306

has Nick.'

'Oh, but that's wonderful, isn't it?'

'In a way, I suppose,' David said. He didn't say that they more or less had to be squadron leaders, because they were two of the few that had survived so far, but his face was very expressive and Kate guessed a lot by what he didn't say. She gave a sudden shudder and David held her tight. 'What's going to happen?' she said. 'Surely, as squadron leaders, you are given more information?'

David shook his head. 'We are told nothing, my darling, and I have no wish to alarm you, but I feel we are moving into uncharted waters. Things will get much worse before they get better.'

'Oh, David, I am so frightened about what is to come,' Kate said.

'Only a fool wouldn't be at the very least nervous,' David said. 'Our backs are to the wall, no doubt about it. Civilians – men, women and children – will all be at risk, and you most of all, out in the teeth of raids, but I will not ask you to reconsider, because you are doing what you think is right and I am proud of you for that. But soon I may not be able to write much, so don't worry unduly if letters are few and far between.'

'D'you think I have a little worry button I can turn on and off at will?' Kate said to David. 'Of course I will worry when I don't hear from you, but I will put up with it the best way I can. I suppose your leaves might be severely cut too.'

David nodded. 'I'd say so.'

'Then let's make the most of the limited time we have,' Kate said, getting up and pulling David to stand beside her. Though it was only very early in the evening, she said, 'Let's go to bed.'

David didn't argue. 'Yes,' he said simply, and he took hold of Kate's hand and led the way up the stairs.

Three days after the men left, the Anderson shelter had been delivered, erected and sunk into the hole. Sally and Kate piled the earth on the top; as they worked, Sally said, 'One of the women at work said that if you put enough earth on it you can grow things.'

Kate stared at her. 'What sort of things?'

Sally shrugged. 'Anything, I suppose. I mean, she said they grow potatoes. Everyone's into growing stuff now, aren't they, with the ships being sunk and all? I mean, what if there wasn't enough food for everyone? There's little enough now sometimes, but if there was even less we'd really be in the mire.'

'I suppose we would,' Kate said. 'I never really thought that we might actually run out of food, but as we are an island it is a real possibility, with those bloody German U-boats attacking our shipping. That's why they have dug up the flower-beds in the parks and planted vegetables. All right then,' Kate went on. 'If they can do it, so can we. Let's put our backs into this and put the sandbags around and we can go and see if we can get some seeds. I think Hiron's the flower shop are selling them now.'

'Yeah,' Sally said with some spirit. 'Just let Hitler try and starve us out – he won't win that way either.'

'He won't win it anyway,' Kate said fiercely.

'Otherwise young men like your Phil will have died in vain.'

But though Kate spoke so bravely and bought and planted the seeds that same evening, she thought most of the country seemed to be waiting. Travelling anywhere was very difficult because street names, signposts and railway-station names had been obliterated to confuse German spies or an invading army. Posters were everywhere, proclaiming CARELESS TALK COSTS LIVES and BE LIKE DAD AND KEEP MUM, and many German people – and Italians, too, now that they had joined the fray – were rounded up and put into internment camps.

However, the girls' plans to be ARP wardens continued, and the day they were due to start, Kate and Susie discussed it on the tram on their way to work. 'Was your mother all right about it?'

'Yeah,' Susie said. 'I didn't say anything to my parents until Nick went and I told him not to mention it either. I didn't want to risk spoiling his short leave with a scene. It was bad enough talking him round.'

'I know, David was the same,' Kate said. 'We had a real fight about it in the end.'

'Well, all told, Mom wasn't bad at all,' Susie said. 'I mean, she made the usual noises, you know, but I reminded her about the boys and so then she shut up, especially when Dad came down on my side. Anyway, she's getting a job herself and she dropped that bombshell at the dinner table last night.'

'Golly, that is a surprise,' Kate exclaimed. 'Your mother working, fancy that. Where's the job?'

'You'll never guess,' Susie said, but without giving Kate time to answer, she said, 'It's in the jewellery quarter.'

'Crikey!'

'Apparently, a woman was talking about it after Mass last week and arranged an interview for Mom that she never told anyone about,' Susie said. 'She got it and starts next week and they are not making jewellery any more, she told us, but building radar instead.'

'Are they?' Kate said in surprise. 'But then I suppose it makes sense. They would probably have all the machines for fine work. Mind you, anyone who does work like that would have to be fairly dexterous, I'd say. I'd probably be all fingers and thumbs, but your Mom is so good with her hands I think that sort of work will suit her very well.'

'Well, she's excited enough,' Susie said. 'She says it will be good to have her own money in her pocket that she can spend as she likes. She has never had that; it was expected in those days that the women would stay at home after marriage.'

'And do what exactly?' Kate said. 'Thank goodness the war has knocked such outdated notions on the head.'

'Yeah, I agree,' Susie said. 'Did your Mom have an opinion about this ARP business?'

'She doesn't know what it entails really,' Kate said. 'She just repeated what she has said since war was declared – that if the bombs start falling, I am to go home to Ireland.'

'And will you?'

'Not likely,' Kate said. 'I'm not running away. Birmingham is where I've made my home and I will fight for it if I have to. Anyway, what about Sally? Mammy would never welcome her back home.'

'I really can't understand her being so hard-hearted about Sally,' Susie said. 'She was kindness itself to me when I was a child. Even though I knew that she hated me going on about Birmingham at first, I was always made welcome in your home. Not knowing about this great non-romance with you and Tim Munroe, you could have knocked me down with a feather when she began not only positively encouraging me to talk about the delights of Birmingham, but asking if I could find you a job and place to live over here.'

'I know,' Kate said, smiling at the memory. 'Your face was a picture.'

'Yeah, I bet,' Susie said. 'But I never would have said she was a cold woman.'

'Nor would I,' Kate said. 'It must be because my parents particularly made so much of Sally when she was little and incredibly sweet; maybe because they spoilt her, she had farther to fall.'

'What d'you mean?'

'Well, what did she actually do wrong?' Kate said. 'She ran away from home, but she only did that after she had overheard Mammy telling a neighbour that she would not let Sally come over here, not even on a holiday, and that she wanted her to find a local man to marry when the time came. Sally told me she thought of all the men and boys she knew and none of them inspired her, so the thought of marrying one of them and being buried in the country filled her with gloom.'

'Oh, I can well understand that,' Susie said. 'I

mean, it is a beautiful place, but a bit of a dead-and-alive hole for a young girl.'

'Yeah, well, Sally decided to take matters into her own hands,' Kate said. 'But she had no money of her own, so she took Mammy's egg money. But if she'd been given a wage for the work she did, she would have had no need to do that. I'm not saying that what she did wasn't wrong,' Kate said. 'But I can understand that desperation, that need to flee and no money to do it, and the temptation of the egg money just lying there.'

'Oh, so can I.'

'Anyway, she knows she did wrong and she has apologized for it over and over and paid every penny back, and still she is not forgiven,' Kate said. 'And yet I married a man in a registry office, and sent Father Patterson away with a flea in his ear. Mammy was angry and upset, as I expected she would be, but she didn't actually disown me. I find the whole thing hard to understand.'

'And I would,' Susie said, getting up. 'Come on, this is our stop. What are the arrangements for tonight anyway?'

'All the volunteers have been told to assemble outside the council house at seven o'clock, so try not to hang about after work.'

'Don't worry,' Susie said. 'I will be out of there like a shot as soon as the buzzer goes.'

There was a motley group of them collected together that summer's evening at the foot of the marble steps leading up to the council house in Birmingham, and though most were women of varying ages, there were two older men. As Kate surveyed them, she wondered if any of them would be any good at the tasks that they might soon have to deal with, for they looked a very raggle-taggle group.

Even while she was thinking this, however, a woman came determinedly out of the building and stood on the second step to address them. Just by her stance, it was clear she was obviously a no-nonsense sort of woman, and that was before you looked at her resolute face. She had the sort of eyes that missed nothing and she scanned them all and gave a small nod. Kate knew that if anyone could lick them into any sort of shape, then she could. The woman thanked them for coming and introduced herself as Mrs Camfrey. 'Now, if you would like to follow me,' she said, and led the group up the steps and into the reception hall, where they were told that all the ARP activities – as well as various other organizations helping Birmingham prepare for possible air raids – were supervised by an Emergency Powers Committee.

'Sounds very grand,' Kate whispered to Sally and Susie out of the corner of her mouth.

'They work from a fortified gas-proofed basement,' Mrs Camfrey told them. 'And that is where I'm taking you now.'

Kate followed the others down the steps. Now she was actually here she had butterflies in her stomach, especially when she thought of the piles of concrete over her head. Noises from the city were effectively cut off in the bunker, but she knew that, above her, life was still going on.

The bunker too seemed a hive of activity. Mrs

Camfrey led them along a corridor; in the rooms leading off on either side, people were busy working. Eventually, she stopped at a small room and ushered them inside. The chairs were in rows and they took their places while she stood behind the desk. Kate glanced around and saw most of the others, including Sally and Susie, looked as nervous as she was. 'What sort of hours will we be working, like?' one of the men asked. 'I mean, I want to do my bit and all that, but since Dunkirk I've been working a minimum of fifty hours a week.'

'Haven't we all, granddad?' a young, heavily made-up girl snapped out rudely. 'What you doing here if you're not prepared to do owt?'

'You are impudent, miss,' the man said, outraged. 'I never said I wasn't willing to help. Let me tell you, I was in the last little lot and I should have retired last year but offered to stay on. I am no slacker, I'll have you know.'

The girl shrugged and another older woman said, 'Anyway, it's a reasonable request,' and she glared at the younger woman.

'And I suppose I'm entitled to an opinion, same as anyone else?' the girl snapped back. Kate could see even the girl she was with looked embarrassed. 'Oh, crikey, Sylv,' she cried, 'put a sock in it, do.'

'Yes,' put in another women. 'Makes me wonder who the enemy is. Thought we were fighting Jerry, not each other.'

'And so we are,' Mrs Camfrey said. 'And if you stop arguing amongst yourselves, I will tell you all you will need to know. Before I do, let me

314

remind you that, in the event of a raid, you might easily have to depend on each other. Personal issues have no place here and neither do disrespectful remarks.' She glanced reprovingly at the young girl as she spoke. Kate could see, even under her make-up, that she had coloured up, though she still looked incredibly sulky as Mrs Camfrey continued: 'Account is taken of the fact that a great many of those here will have full- or part-time jobs of one kind or another, and so the hours of duty will be split into day and night shifts, and you will work the hours that you are able to within that shift.'

There was a little sigh of relief and then the other, younger man asked, 'And what will our duties be?'

'At the moment you will have to patrol the streets making sure people are sticking to the blackout restrictions,' Mrs Camfrey said. 'You will also be trained in identifying a gas attack, given a whistle and a rattle to sound the alarm, and taught what to do in the event of a raid, assisting and directing people to shelters, reporting when necessary to emergency services and assisting in rescue afterwards. You will also learn the correct way to douse incendiary bombs and other fires and you will learn basic first aid.'

'My friend has been a warden for a while and said we have to practise all these things,' said another younger woman.

'You certainly do,' Mrs Camfrey said. 'It is really important – maybe to people's survival – that you are proficient at these things. It is no good us just telling you: you must actually do it.'

They fell to talking of the kind of exercises they would be engaged in and the questions came thick and fast. Eventually, Mrs Camfrey said, 'Now, if there are no more questions, is everyone all right about what they must do?'

They all nodded except Sylv, who gave an indifferent shrug, and Mrs Camfrey looked sharply at her but went on: 'Now then, it is organized like this. Groups of six or more will be called a sector and will be headed by a senior sector marshal, and each sector will be in charge of an area housing approximately five hundred people.' Kate looked askance at Sally and Susie – she thought five hundred people were a lot to be responsible for.

'Now, if you make an orderly line in front of this door, you will be told what to do next,' Mrs Camfrey said, and they all obediently queued up and filed into a room where two ATS girls were sitting behind counters. While one marked each one of them off on a register and assigned them to a sector, the other dished out uniforms, tin helmets, a whistle and a rattle.

'Now,' Mrs Camfrey said when they had all been seen to. 'Remember you are going to be the first line of defence in the raids. People will look to you for help or advice, such as where the shelters are and so on. You will be doing a very valuable job, so always remember that. Please report tomorrow night to the sector you were assigned to – you will meet your fellow colleagues and the sector marshal then.'

On the way home, the three girls looked at each other. Even in the half-light, Kate could see the slight shock registering on the faces of the others. 'I thought they'd just sort of tell us all about it and let us go away and have a think whether we want to do it or not,' Susie said.

'Don't think they have the time for niceties like that,' Kate said. 'Anyway, isn't it great that we have been assigned to the same sector and the warden post is only in Marsh Lane?'

'Yeah, that is good,' Susie said. 'And I'll tell you what I'm pleased about as well – that that girl Sylv is not in our sector. She was right behind me in the line and I was scared that she would be.'

'Yeah,' Kate said. 'Don't know what she's doing here anyway. She doesn't seem that bothered.'

'And she bit the head off that old man,' Sally said.

'Yeah, I wouldn't say working with her would be a bundle of laughs,' Kate maintained. 'And, as you once said, Susie, humour is all we have.'

'I stick to it as well,' Susie said. 'At least we three are all together, and someone else will have to deal with Sylv. Now I just hope our sector marshal is nice.'

They were to find out that she was very nice. Kate guessed her to be in her thirties; she had her brown hair cut in a bob. She greeted them all warmly in a very pleasant-sounding voice with only a slight trace of a Brummie accent. 'My name is Jane Goodman,' she said. 'And we don't need to stand on ceremony amongst ourselves.' She shook hands with them all and Kate noticed her kindly grey eyes and just knew she would get on well with her.

After the introductions, Jane said they had to

report to Erdington Baths where St Johns' Ambulance would be conducting classes in first aid. 'See,' Kate said to the other two as they made their way there, 'it's a bit like marriage. We are in now, for better or worse.'

EIGHTEEN

Over the next weeks, as the summer took hold of the city, the German offensive began, with the Luftwaffe attacking coastal towns through July. More shipping convoys were sunk and there were more raids. The three girls were only too aware that the RAF squadrons from airfields through-out Britain were being sent to try to repulse these attacks and also to try to save the ships. The announcements on the wireless and those in the newspapers were reporting on what they called, 'The Battle of Britain'. Dogfights were common and the results were printed in the papers, and were even on notice boards in the city centre, the girls heard. 'It's like some game they are playing, and if the Germans lose twenty-three planes to our eight or nine, it is counted as a victory. Yet each loss is a tragedy,' Kate said.

She knew too that one of those planes lost could have her husband or Susie's inside it, and that thought made her feel sick. And yet she knew it had to be done, because across a very small stretch of water, Hitler had amassed an armada and was ready for invasion. The papers and broadcasters on the wireless assured them that if ever the RAF lost supremacy in the air, there would be nothing to stop German craft carrying men and machines from landing in Britain.

Everyone was talking about the heroism of the

boys in blue, well aware that the survival of Britain rested on the slim shoulders of these young pilots. The need for pilots was so pressing that most of those being sent up into the air to face merciless enemy gunfire had only had time for a very basic training course lasting a scant six weeks. But knowing her husband was doing an essential job did nothing to ease the aching worry that often deprived Kate of sleep and took away her appetite.

And she knew that without her work with her fellow ARP wardens, she would be a lot worse off. This way she had less time to think. As Mrs Camfrey told them, they were being trained for things they might have to do in the event of raids on the city. And so they engaged in realistic exercises in parks and roads, rescued mock casualties from damaged buildings, put out blazes, dealt with incendiaries in specially constructed huts and made trial runs from the depots to check the time it took to cover the area they were responsible for. They also practised decontamination routines.

On top of this they went two nights a week to learn first aid and practised the skills taught on volunteer victims. This, together with working overtime, ensured that Kate at least went to bed exhausted. But once she lay down, the visions would come to haunt her. She wasn't helped by the reports she read in the papers of the long hours the pilots spent flying: quite often they would be on seven sorties a day. Far too many: surely tiredness affected reaction times? And a tired pilot might make mistakes and any mistakes made in the air might be catastrophic.

As David had once said, he lived for her letters, so now she lived for his. They came spasmodically and they were brief missives, but though he could tell her little, the fact that he had written at all showed Kate that he was still alive – and that was the greatest news of all.

And Birmingham continued to wait. No one now believed that being two hundred miles from the coast would protect them.

On 1 August, Hitler issued a directive ordering an intensification of the air war prior to an invasion of Britain. This news was conveyed to Kate and Sally by the sneering voice of Lord Haw-Haw, the traitor who broadcast on a programme called *Germany Calling*. The British were not supposed to listen to it, but many did, because the man seemed to know what was happening, though he delivered it in a hateful way as he revelled in the defeat of the British. 'We will soon be invading your shores and unopposed when we have blown the Air Force out of the sky,' he said with glee one evening. 'You will no longer have the Air Force so prepare yourself for a blood bath.'

Sally looked at the colour draining out of Kate's face and she snapped off the wireless. 'Why do we listen to him anyway?' she said to Kate. 'He is nothing but a scaremonger. What does he know?'

Kate didn't answer. She wished she could believe Sally, but she knew that Lord Haw-Haw was accurate a lot of the time and she felt as if she had a coiled spring wrapped tight inside her, crushing her heart.

And Haw-Haw seemed to be just as accurate this time, for almost immediately the Luftwaffe began to attack the airfields, though they kept up the pressure on the ports and shipping too, and the raids stretched as far as the Thames Estuary and Liverpool. In the middle of this, the first bombs fell in Erdington on 9 August. Few in Birmingham were even aware of the three bombs that were dropped; no sirens were sounded and the first many knew about it was the report in the paper, when they saw the devastation caused to the houses in Lydford Grove, Montague Road and Erdington Hall Road, where the bombs fell. And although the people from the ruined homes were shaken and some had to be pulled from the rubble, the only fatality was a young soldier who had survived Dunkirk and was home on leave.

Birmingham suffered almost daily raids from then on, but these were localized and few came that close to Erdington, although the girls were out at the post in Marsh Lane through many of them, watching the arc lights illuminate the sky in the distance and listening to the tattoo of the anti-aircraft guns. 'Glad to know someone's awake anyway,' Kate said one night. 'Don't know where the spotters are, though – those sirens never sound, do they?'

'No,' Susie agreed. 'According to Dad, the Royal Observer Corps should relay information to us, and we have to send that information to factories and schools where the sirens are.'

'Well, we can't send information on if we don't have it in the first place,' Kate said. 'And I would say that they can't be that good at observing if they can't see a formation of planes heading our way till they're on top of us. A policeman pedalling through the streets blowing a whistle is not good enough. Maybe a more efficient system should be set up?'

Kate gave a yawn and said wearily, 'I wish the "All Clear" would go now, though. I haven't heard explosions for a while and I am dead beat.'

'Not sleeping?' Susie asked, and Kate gave a grimace. 'Is anyone in this godawful war?'

'No,' Susie admitted. 'I'm the same. Mom says this is the fretting she was hoping to avoid for me and that was why she didn't want me to marry, but what difference would that have made?'

'None at all,' Sally told her. 'I wasn't married to Phil, for all I loved him enough to marry him, and when I heard that he had died I wanted to follow him. It still catches me now at times.'

'I'm not surprised at that at all,' Kate said. 'If you love someone then you love them – married or not, makes no odds.'

'I agree totally,' Susie said. And then before anyone could say any more the 'All Clear' sounded and Kate gave a sigh of relief. 'Thank God for that,' she said. 'Well, I'm away home. I might just surprise myself and drop off.'

Even people in the government acknowledged the fine job the RAF was doing, and Winston Churchill made a speech about it in Parliament on 21 August that was broadcast on the wireless. It was a long speech, but a few phrases seemed to sum it up for Kate.

The gratitude of every home in our island, in our Empire, and indeed throughout the world, except in the abodes of the guilty, goes out to the British airmen who, undaunted by odds, unweakened by their constant challenge and mortal danger, are turning the tide of world war by their prowess and their devotion.

Never in the field of human conflict was so much owed by so many to so few.

It was stirring stuff, and just what the exhausted airmen wanted to hear. But the fighting went on, and just a few days after this, on Saturday evening, there was another raid. The main thrust of it seemed to be in Aston. All three girls were on duty, and when they were told that the wardens there were shorthanded and asked for volunteers, it was the words of that speech that encouraged Kate to put up her hand. Sally and then Susie followed her lead.

As no sirens had sounded again, many had slept through the policeman's shrill whistle, and the first they had known about the raid was the sound of the bombs falling. Mothers had struggled to dress themselves and their children and they had more or less tumbled out on to the streets. Frightened toddlers clung to their mothers' skirts, swaddled babies cried and older children rubbed their sleepy eyes and staggered as they looked wide-eyed at the scene before them. There were the crackling fires from incendiary bombs, the weaving arc lights, piles of masonry and debris from the houses already destroyed, and the crump and crash of bombs dropping from the droning planes above them. The air was thick with the smell of brick dust, cordite, heat and smoke.

The girls could see straight away that the most important thing was to get people under cover, but the back-to-back houses did not have gardens to put any kind of shelter in, and the nearest public one was under the tennis courts in Aston Park. Kate and another warden who introduced herself as Trudy led the way there, while Sally and Susie searched the area for people still in their houses.

'It's ever so good of you to come over like this,' said Trudy as they shepherded the people along as quickly as they were able. 'Should be six of us, but Beattie has gone down with a chest infection. I saw her myself and she is in a bad way. And as for Babs, she got a crack on the head from a falling roof beam in an earlier do. Split her head clean open and she is in the hospital herself, and so is Chris because her boy has the whooping cough and he took a turn for the worse this afternoon and she has gone to be with him, poor little bugger. My own mother lost two with the whooping cough, but I don't know what the three of us would have done with so many people.'

'Think nothing of it,' Kate said. 'We all have to pull together.'

'You're right,' Trudy said. 'And the sooner we get this lot inside, the better I will like it, and then we can have a go at fighting them bloody fires. No point in observing the blackout with the fires lighting the whole area for them murdering buggers above.'

'No point at all,' Kate said. And she worked with Trudy all night. Though the raid was not fast and furious, it was relentless, and the 'All Clear' did not go until seven and a half hours later. And so it was the early hours when the weary girls got home, very glad the next day was Sunday.

However, the next night the bombers were back, this time in force, and the scream of the sirens used for the first time sent fear coursing through many a person. Neither Sally nor Kate was on duty that night, but neither could rest, and they went out into the streets. The city centre was attacked in the main, although parts of Aston also caught it, and the bottom of Slade Road was heavily bombed, and so Kate and Sally were kept busy there and, as the raid continued in its intensity, they were joined by Susie.

It was strange, Kate thought, as she helped to douse the fires: she was never afraid, despite the cacophony of noise, the throb of the planes, the boom of bombs, the sliding crashes of the disintegrating buildings, the ack-ack's response, the cries and screams from the people and the bells of the emergency services ringing frantically as they tore through the streets. And the searchlights were constantly combing the sky, illuminating the bombers releasing their instruments of death.

There were some people who didn't want to use any sort of shelter and would hide out in pantries under the stairs, and if the house was hit these people had to be dug out of the rubble. The same thing sometimes happened with those who had used Anderson shelters and thought themselves safe. If the shelter was caught in the blast, it would often collapse, burying people inside. Some people would be dug out virtually unscathed, but other times people were injured and often burnt.

Never was Kate more grateful for her first-aid training, but this was no practice, this was for real. It was the first time Kate realized that blood had a smell all of its own or that the stench of burned human flesh was enough to turn the strongest stomach.

When the 'All Clear' sounded, she hurried home, hoping like the others that she would be able to snatch a few hours' sleep before the alarm would peal out. And surprisingly she did sleep, only her dreams were often lurid and upsetting.

The next day they found out the extent of the damage elsewhere in the city. Much of it was in the Bull Ring. The Market Hall was hit, the roof shattered, and it was completely burned out inside. Fortunately, it being a Sunday, few people were about and no one was in the Market Hall; the night watchman, seeing the bombers heading his way, had managed to release all the animals from their cages before taking cover himself.

'Must have been a brave man to do that,' Sally said to Kate as she read it out in the paper.

'Must have been,' Kate agreed. 'I think there is a lot of bravery in war situations. I mean, you are still so young, and yet you work as hard as any of us, and never show any fear, even when we are in the thick of it.'

'You haven't time to be scared,' Sally said.

Sally was right, but Kate was still filled with respect for her and the way she was coping. The previous evening she had taken great risks in crawling into buildings in danger of collapse, searching for survivors. She was often the only one small enough to wriggle into tiny spaces that people had managed to uncover; many had told Kate they were astounded by her courage.

'Mind you,' Sally said, 'I wouldn't mind a night in my own bed tonight. Do you think Jerry might give us a rest?'

'Don't know,' Kate said, with a shrug, 'but I wish he would.'

Alas, it was not to be, and she had barely closed her eyes when the sirens wailed a short time after midnight. Groaning, they clambered from their beds and dressed hurriedly, but because they weren't on duty and the raid didn't seem that near, they carried blankets and pillows down to the shelter and settled themselves side by side on one of the hard benches Frank had fitted to either side. They tried to get comfortable, but the corrugated iron structure sunk into the earth was cold, and so damp that condensation ran in rivulets down the walls. It was very dark, too, despite the candles Kate had brought down in her pockets, and the only positive thing to say about the shelter was that the raid was a little bit more muffled in there. 'We must make this a little bit more comfy,' Kate said with a sudden shudder. 'If Jerry is going to hit us like this every night, we might be forced to spend more time in here after all.'

'Don't see why,' Sally said, a little disgruntled. 'It isn't half as comfortable as the warden post, and if I'm not on duty, I have a mind to stay in bed and chance it.'

'You saw the state of some of the poor beggars who stayed in their houses the other day?'

'Yeah, I did, but the ones where the shelter had

collapsed on them were nearly as bad.'

'I know that, and I don't say they are foolproof,' Kate said. 'But sunken into the ground the way they are, they have to be a little safer than the house. David certainly thought so anyway.'

'And you have a sort of responsibility to David to keep yourself as safe as you can,' Sally said. 'But I haven't got to do that.'

'What do you mean?'

'Well, I only have you,' Sally said simply, but Kate detected the pain behind the words. 'I have parents who don't care for me, a little brother who will never know me and the two people who loved me, apart from you, were Phil and his mother – and they are both dead and gone.'

'Ah, Sally,' Kate said, putting an arm around her sister.

'Don't, Kate, or I will blub,' Sally said brokenly. In the lights from the candles, Kate could see her eyes were sparkling with unshed tears.

'Blub away,' Kate said. 'To my mind you haven't done near enough of it.'

Sally gave a sudden cry and the tears spilled down her face. She cried out her heartache and anguish on losing her beloved fiancé and the pain of rejection from her parents. Sometime, while she wept, Kate also felt tears welling in her eyes, and their tears mingled together. When the 'All Clear' roused them, they found that they had fallen asleep cuddled against one another with their arms linked. Sally yawned and said with a watery smile to her sister, 'I didn't sleep very well and I have an almighty crick in my neck and yet I feel somewhat lighter in myself.'

'Glad to hear it,' Kate said, and she glanced at her watch as she hauled Sally to her feet and put an arm around her shoulder. 'Come on,' she urged. 'It's just after six. Let's go and have a cuppa.'

The indiscriminate bombings continued every night, and people got used to doing without much sleep, but in a lull in mid-September the three girls went down to the Bull Ring to assess the damage, knowing the city centre had taken the brunt of many of the attacks. Many of the shops leading down from the High Street were just shells, filled with debris and masonry that had also spilled on to the road. Listing walls leant drunkenly against their neighbours.

'We'll find the Market Hall in the same state, according to them at work anyway,' Sally said, and it was. There was slight damage to St Martin's, but the Market Hall was open to the sky. Only the walls stood, and there was a massive hole blasted in one of those. The girls peered in. It was a sea of rubble. Blackened beams lay amongst broken bricks, the buckled iron frames of the stalls, sparkling shards of glass, scorched utensils and the burnt remains of other items for sale. 'What a mess,' Susie said, wrinkling her nose at the smell. 'And that beautiful clock is burnt to a crisp.'

'I know, what a shame that is,' Kate said.

'Someone has stuck Union Jacks in the rubble,' Sally said. 'I still think it's sad though. Look, that trader Albert Pope still has his name plaque here.'

'So has someone called Yates,' Kate said. 'But he

has gone one step further. Look, he has his new address already written down and a note in defiance to Hitler, "Burnt But Not Broke". Maybe that is the right attitude. We can do nothing about the bombing, but do our level best not to let it get us down.'

'Yes, you're right,' Sally said. 'The Bull Ring is the people, not buildings, and life is still going on, isn't it? Traders are still selling things and their banter is the same as ever and the buzz is only slightly muted. Hitler can do his worst, but the Brummie spirit is alive and well.'

It was hard to keep that buoyant mood, though, when a little later, as they made for the tram, they walked up Colmore Row and saw the extensive damage to Snow Hill Station. A little further on, where there had been warehouses, small factories, and shops ringed in the square around St Paul's, the start of Birmingham's Jewellery Quarter was just one massive sea of rubble.

The very next day there was a wireless report of an immensely important battle between the RAF and the Luftwaffe. Everyone knew that for Hitler to invade Britain successfully he had to render the RAF ineffective, and to do it before winter gales in the channel made the crossing more hazardous. That day, however, the RAF emerged victorious. They had maintained their supremacy. According to the man on the wireless, that meant that the planned invasion was most unlikely to take place.

Kate's delight that the invasion plans had been routed was tinged with fear for David. She didn't know whether he had been involved or not, but the paper reported on squadrons from all over the country being drafted in to deliver a crushing defeat to the enemy. She was well aware that, whoever won, there would have been pilots lost on either side, and that her beloved husband could have been one of them.

The bombers returned the following night but, though the girls were all on duty, the planes came nowhere near them. On Tuesday morning, everyone was talking about an accident with a barrage balloon. 'What's that?' Kate asked as she was getting into her overalls.

'Didn't you hear about it?' one of the girls said. 'Apparently, one of the bombers last night collided with the cable of a barrage balloon and crashed. Three of the crew were killed and two were captured.'

'That's the best news I've heard in ages,' Kate said with a smile. 'And wasn't it you, Susie, who said that barrage balloons were no good as a deterrent against bombs?'

'It was,' Susie said with a laugh. 'And I remember you agreeing with me too. I didn't realize they were good for capturing Germans.'

There was a burst of laughter at that, and Susie declared, 'Well, I for one will never moan about them again.'

'Nor me,' Kate said.

'That's all very well,' one of the women said with a laugh. 'But we'll have to take its place with summat. I mean, life's not worth living without a good moan now and then.'

'Are you joking or what?' one of the others said. 'Spoilt for choice, we are.'

'I'll say,' said another. 'We could go on from now until doomsday talking about the bloody rations, for a start.'

There was a collective groan from the others. 'I would say that that's worth a good old moan, and one we would all join in with,' said the first woman. 'I mean with tea, marg, cooking fat and cheese added to the rations, it gets harder and harder to make up a decent meal.'

'And not being able to spend more than one shilling and tuppence each on meat every week?' said another. 'What can you get for that?'

'Not enough to fill my old man, that's for sure,' said the first woman. 'It isn't even as if you can get what you are entitled to every week, 'cos even the rationed goods are sometimes not available.'

There was a murmur of agreement and one put in, 'Yeah, and what's this about one egg a fortnight? You're lucky if you see one egg a month.'

'You're right,' Kate said. 'I can't remember the last time I had an egg.'

'And it's considered bad form to moan too much,' Susie said. 'Affects morale or something.'

'Don't do no good any road,' one of the older women said. 'If you say owt they just tell you that there's a war on.'

There was more laughter then because they had all experienced that. 'Yeah,' said another. 'Like you might have dropped in from another planet or summat.'

Before anyone could make a comment on this, Mrs Higgins the supervisor came into the cloakroom clapping her hands. 'This chatter will have to wait till lunchtime. Remember, if you're late clocking on you'll lose five shillings. Mr Tanner doesn't pay you to stand around blethering, so I suggest you get on to the shop floor and start work, sharpish.'

They went without another word, because five shillings was a lot of money to lose.

After the episode with the barrage balloon, the raids in Birmingham lessened considerably. They became sporadic and light and were more like skirmishes than the full raids the Birmingham people had become used to. 'I suppose it's too much to hope that it's over for us?' Susie said one day as she and Kate travelled home.

'Are you kidding?' Kate said. 'I think Hitler has got something really nasty lined up for us.'

'Ooh, don't,' Susie said. 'Do you have to be so gleeful about it?'

Kate laughed. 'I'm not being gleeful,' she protested. 'I call it being realistic, but we can take advantage of the quieter nights now, whatever is in store for us later.'

'I know,' Susie said. 'It's lovely to think that nights I am not on duty I can stretch in my own bed and be fairly certain that I will wake up in it the following morning. I used to fantasize about a nice long sleep.'

'So did I,' Kate admitted. 'Just shows you what exciting lives we lead.'

After this there were a few daylight raids through September, taking advantage of the cloudy, autumnal Birmingham skies that the German planes could hide behind before suddenly swooping down. These were scary enough for any caught out, for the pilots weren't averse to strafing them with machine-gun fire, but the evenings and nights remained quiet until early October, when they began again with as much intensity as before.

On 14 October, Clementine Churchill, the prime minister's wife, paid a visit to Birmingham. Susie had bought a paper on the way to work because it gave details of the proposed visit. After scanning it that morning on the way to work, she said to Kate, 'Says here she intends visiting two factories and one neighbourhood affected by bombing.'

'Huh,' Kate said. 'I'd say she will have plenty to choose from.'

'Wouldn't mind having a look at her though,' Susie said. ''Cos people say she is really nice.'

'Have to be, I'd say, married to Churchill,' Kate said. 'I wouldn't have said he was an easy man to live with.'

'Are any of them?'

'Well, neither of us would really know that at the moment,' Kate said wistfully.

'No, we wouldn't,' Susie agreed. 'And I don't think we'll get to see our men anytime soon either. Not until things are a lot quieter.'

'Oh, I suppose you are right,' Kate said morosely. 'But, talking of quiet, I hope Jerry is quiet tonight. It would never do to have the prime minister's wife bombed in Birmingham.'

'Oh, no,' Susie said with a broad smile. 'Indeed not.'

There were pictures of Clementine Churchill in all the Birmingham papers. Kate, looking at those

335

in the *Birmingham Mail*, thought she did look a nice lady. She seemed genuinely moved to see the damage and devastation to just one of the many areas of Birmingham attacked by the Luftwaffe.

The paper reported that she had got out of her car and talked to the homeless and dispossessed people. And that the crowd had warmed to her for doing that. She'd been impressed by the fact that many had stuck Union Jacks in the mounds of rubble that had once been their homes, and one woman was reported to have said to her, 'Our houses might be down but our spirits are still up.' Clementine was stunned by what she called the stoicism of the people whom she said had shown unflinching courage.

That stoicism and unflinching courage was tested yet again when there was another fierce raid the following night, and every night from then on, as prolonged and heavy as they had been before. The girls were drafted wherever they were needed. In one raid, the Plaza was hit along with houses down Slade Road, and there were two houses bombed in Marsh Hill, the families in their shelter crushed when it caved in on them with the power of the blast. 'Oh, they are really safe, those underground shelters,' Sally said sarcastically, but Kate said nothing in reply for she was too distressed by the heart-rending scenes she had witnessed that night.

NINETEEN

November was only a few days old when Kate got a letter from David. He was coming home for a few days' leave and, though she longed to see him, she was so weary and worn down she found it hard to work up any enthusiasm. Susie felt the same way as Kate, her excitement at seeing Nick somewhat muted because she was just as tired. The sirens rung out every night and had been doing so for a fortnight; the raids had been fierce and the resultant fires ferocious, and so, whether they were on duty or not, when the sirens sounded, the three girls reported to the warden post and went wherever they were needed.

Jane Goodman, the sector controller, liked all three girls; they had worked night after night and often above and beyond the call of duty. Looking at Kate and Susie as they told her the news of their men coming home, she saw beyond their beaming smiles to the white pallor of their skin and their eyes deadened by extreme fatigue, and knew they needed a break if they were going to continue to be of any use to anyone. And so she said they had both worked so hard they could have time off from their ARP work while their husbands were home.

They really would have liked to have had time off from the factory too, but there was no joy there. 'If you could have given me more notice, something might have been worked out,' Mrs Higgins said. 'But as it is...'

'We told you as soon as we knew.'

'I'm sorry, but this order has to be completed in time,' Mrs Higgins told them. 'The military are waiting.'

'And the annoying thing is, she's right,' Susie said as they headed for home that evening.

'I know,' Kate said with a sigh. 'No point in getting in a snit about it. After all,' she added with a smile, 'don't you know there's a war on?'

Susie gave a wry laugh and said, 'Is there really? Well, would you believe it?'

'But regardless of how tired I am, I can't wait to see David and Nick,' Kate said. 'After what they must have gone through, it will be great to see them home for a while, hale and hearty.'

They were coming into New Street Station on the train on Thursday, 7 November at half past five. Kate and Susie got off early and went to meet them and, as Kate watched David get out of the train, her words came back to her. They were home all right, but she thought they both looked as if it would require some time recuperating at home before they could be said to be hale and hearty.

Once, Kate would have flung her arms around David as soon as she saw him get off the train, and she did move forward to do just that. But he had a sort of invisible barrier around him and she saw him stiffen, so instead, she kissed his cheek gently. 'Welcome home, darling,' she said.

The smile didn't reach his eyes, and when she

linked her arm through his, it seemed awkward and unnatural. Nick seemed in as bad a state, she noticed, and she was very glad of Susie, because between them they kept the conversation going as they walked to the tram stop. She saw the men's eyes looking round them, but with their only light being their shielded torches, she knew they wouldn't have any idea of the full horror of the bombing they had endured. They were mostly silent on the tram, too, and again it was the two girls that kept up a running commentary about everything and nothing, because it was better than uncomfortable bouts of silence. Kate was sorry to part with her friend at the top of Bleak Hill.

Sally had already fixed the blackout curtains in place, so as they stepped into the hall, Kate turned on the light. Because of the dimness of the station and the shaded lights on the tram, Kate hadn't had a proper look at David. Sally had come through to welcome him, but she just stopped in the doorway and stared. Kate did the same.

David wasn't just thin, he was gaunt – so gaunt that his cheeks had sunk inwards and his nose looked very prominent; but it was his eyes that brought a lump to Kate's throat. Though they were bloodshot and puffy, with huge black bags beneath them, it was the expression in them that mattered most. Kate had never seen David's eyes so full of heartache and wretchedness. Even his posture was wrong. He had always held himself erect, with his shoulders back, but now he stood with them slightly stooped, as if he carried the weight of the world between them.

David looked at the two girls staring at him in shock and said, 'What?'

His words galvanized Kate into action, and she thought the best thing to do was say nothing about the way he looked. And so she said with a tight smile, 'Take your coat off, David. You look as if you're not stopping. And come in the room to the fire. You must be cold – it's a damp and perishing day.'

She helped David off with his coat as she spoke, and Sally, following her lead, said, 'I'll put the kettle on,' and escaped to the kitchen. Kate led the way into the living room, where she stood looking at her husband warming his hands at the fire. The uniform that had once fitted him hung on his sparse frame, and eventually she could bear it no longer and she said, 'David, have you been ill?'

David raised his pain-filled eyes and said, 'Depends what you mean by ill. I've been raving a lot of the time.'

Kate's eyes opened wider and David said, 'Oh, yes, raving. It was the deaths that got to me in the end. I had boys in my squadron, not long out of school, and they had six weeks learning to fly a kite before they were thrown into the melee, facing the brutal German Air Force. They were shot down in their droves.'

He closed his eyes for a minute and Kate knew he was remembering, and when he opened them again he fastened them on Kate and went on: 'By the time we had fought in that aerial battle in mid-September, heralded as a big success, not just in that battle but in the many sorties we had flown before that, we had lost half the pilots we started with.' He stared at her and then, as if to emphasize the point, he said again, 'Half our Air Force gone, just like that. You feel worse when you are a squadron leader, because you feel responsible for the lads in your squadron. You watch helpless as the planes and the men in them are shot to pieces. Some explode in mid-air, some go down in a plume of smoke, or even well alight, until they land in the drink or crash to the ground and burst into flames. And if any pilots manage to get out and are floating down on their parachutes, the murdering German bastards go after them and shoot them as they hang there.'

Kate felt as if her heart was breaking at the bereft and hopeless look on David's face. 'Oh, God, David,' she breathed as she put her hand on his arm. 'I am so very sorry.'

'I know you are,' David said as he sank with a sigh into her embrace. 'But you will understand that I thought our marvellous victory was a hollow one.'

And then David began to cry – great, gulping sobs – and even though he was in such distress, he kept apologizing for unloading himself on her, and for the tears he seemed unable to stop. Sally came in with the tea as Kate was helping David across the room to the settee; she left it on a table and withdrew as Kate pulled David down beside her and wrapped her arms tightly around him. She didn't urge him not to upset himself because she thought he really needed to shed those tears.

Much later, when the only sound in the room were the coals settling in the fire, Sally came in quietly. 'Is he asleep?' she mouthed. Kate nodded her head as she settled David's head on a cushion, slid herself from underneath him and lifted his legs on to the sofa. He lay like one dead and Kate said, 'I'll go and fetch a blanket.'

'I thought he would be hungry,' Sally said.

'He probably is, but the tiredness overtook him,' Kate said. 'I really hope Jerry gives us a break tonight and he can have his sleep out.'

'You have a chance,' Sally said. 'I looked out of the kitchen window just a minute ago and there is thick fog.'

'Well, thank God for that,' Kate said fervently.

The Germans did give Birmingham a break that night. Sally was on duty, but if she hadn't been she would have volunteered, because she thought David and Kate deserved time together. Kate was glad she would have something nourishing for David to eat when he woke for she'd had a scrag end of mutton to put in the stew with the vegetables and then the butcher slipped her in a couple of kidneys when she told him David was coming home on leave. People were kind and very grateful to the men in the RAF, and mindful of the ultimate sacrifice so many of them had already made. The woman in the newsagent's had said that to her when she gave Kate a bag of bull's-eyes. 'Your man used to like these, I re-member,' she said. 'Before this awful war. So you give him them with my love.'

She wondered what these people would make of poor, damaged David now, and could only hope she could help him recover before he had to return to it again. She had a meagre amount of the stew herself, and filled up with bread, so that she could leave a couple of bowlfuls for David. He needed more meat on those bones. She sat on after Sally left, reading one of her library books – she wouldn't put the wireless on lest it would disturb David's sleep – and when he did stir it was after ten. He struggled to sit up. 'I can't believe I've slept so long or so deeply,' he said. 'I feel more rested than I have felt in ages.'

'I'm glad,' Kate said. 'It was what you needed, and I hope you are hungry now as I have a nice stew for you.'

'Lead me to it, Kate,' David said, 'I'm ravenous.'

Kate watched with delight as David polished off two bowls of stew, which he declared delicious, and she had just finished the washing up when Sally came in, pleased and relieved to see David looking so much better. He was still tired, though, despite his earlier snooze. 'When the fighting was at its height, none of us slept really,' he told Kate. 'This could go on for days at a time. Even when you weren't actually flying, you were sitting about in all your flying gear, knowing that at any minute you might be told to scramble, and that meant running across the tarmac, often buttoning up your tunic as you went, and then into the air as quickly as possible to meet with the incoming Messerschmitts or Heinkels.'

'And you have the nerve to say that you would worry about me being an ARP warden?' Kate said incredulously.

David shrugged. 'It's how it is when you love a person as much as I love you,' he said. 'And I still wish that you weren't putting yourself in danger; that you were safe, or at least safer, in the shelter.'

Kate thought about the people killed in their shelters just yards away from their houses. But David knew nothing about that and she certainly wasn't going to tell him. Instead, she said, 'And now, if you're tired, let's go to bed. I have to get up for work early anyway and I am dead beat.'

And Kate was dead beat and yet she lay for hours after David's even breathing told her he was asleep, and then she was woken in the early hours by him in the throes of a nightmare when he told her he'd thought he was in the cockpit of his plane, shooting all before him.

Nick was in a similar state to David, Susie told Kate the following morning as they made their way to work. 'He's totally and completely exhausted,' she said.

'Oh, so is David,' Kate said. 'And very upset by the death of all those young pilots. But he wouldn't be the man I thought he was if he was able to shrug his shoulders as if he really didn't care. And yet they had to go on day after day and watch it happen again and again.'

'I know,' Susie said. 'That's why Nick and David have got leave now. They are suffering from what they call battle fatigue and are to be stood down for a few weeks when they go back, providing of course there are no emergencies.'

'David didn't say.'

'Well, I'm sure he'd have got round to telling you sometime,' Susie said. 'Nick only mentioned it this morning. He woke up as I was getting ready for work and was going to get up with me. But I stopped him and said he had to have a good lie-in.'

'I left David in bed too,' Kate said. 'I carried my clothes out and dressed in the bathroom and left him sleeping peacefully. I was glad to see that because he had a nightmare in the night.'

'Small wonder,' Susie said.

'Indeed,' Kate agreed. 'I hope he will have a good sleep because I doubt Jerry will leave us alone again tonight. Last night was just a bonus.'

'Yes, but you are right, and it was just lovely to be able to cuddle up together,' Susie said, with a smile of satisfaction playing around her lips. Then she added with a sigh, 'But there is no fog today, so far at least.'

'No, it's a fine day, though a cold one,' Kate said. 'So at least the men will be able to get out if they want to, and isn't it good that they have each other for company while we are at work?'

David and Nick were waiting for the girls, and as they walked to the tram stop they said they had been into town to survey the bomb damage that the girls had not been able to tell them anything about. 'Well, you know why we could say nothing,' Kate said. 'Didn't you hear reports of the raids on the wireless?'

'Yeah,' Nick said. 'But they hardly ever mentioned Birmingham. They just said a Midlands town, and that could have been anywhere.'

'I know they did,' Kate said. 'It was really annoying because other places were mentioned.'

'Dad said he thought it was because Birmingham makes so much for the war effort that they didn't want the Germans to know they had hit the target, but it was maddening not to have a mention. But couldn't you see the damage from the air?'

'Yes,' David said. 'But not in any detail. Our job was to repulse the Luftwaffe, so our main battles were maybe over the Channel or Kent, or somewhere on the south coast. After they bombed the capital, the main thrust was there too, because those bombers were protected by fighter planes like ours are. Going out on a mission, our attention was targeted on that, and coming back we were usually absolutely shattered, and in the dark with the blackout in place, of course we couldn't see much. We did see fires sometimes after a raid but not much more than that.'

'We experienced a couple of raids,' Nick said. 'The camp was bombed and they destroyed a fair number of planes and buggered up a couple of airstrips, and they bombed the factory across the road that makes many of the planes, but in a way that was understandable.'

'Yeah,' David said in agreement, 'it was the extent of the bombing here that got me.'

'Marshall and Snelgrove's has gone, hasn't it?' Susie said. 'That only happened about a week ago and we haven't been in to see that yet.'

'It's not just the store, it's the whole corner,' David said. 'There were lots of shops there, and all that's left is a great charred mound with twisted iron girders sticking up through it.'

'Some of our wardens were drafted in to help fight the fires that night,' Kate said. 'And Sally volunteered as well but the store was past saving, and she said so hot that much of the tar was alight and had slid into the gutters. There were dirty great craters in the middle of the road, and this of course had buckled the tram lines to kingdom come.'

'Well, the holes have been filled in and tram lines straightened, or new ones laid or whatever,' Nick said. 'But the whole thing shook us up, and that was before we went to the Bull Ring and saw the roofless Market Hall and the damage to St Martin's.'

'Snow Street Station is unusable as well,' David said.

'And did you see the Jewellery Quarter where Mum works?' Susie asked them.

'Yeah,' Nick said. 'I was surprised that she had taken a job there in the first place, and more surprised that she has still got one when I saw the vast sea of rubble it had been reduced to.'

'She had to move to a different workshop, but she is still there. The radars are needed, and of course lots of the delicate equipment they use was lost in the raids.'

Nick looked at David's slightly shocked face, and though he too was unnerved by the scale of destruction, he said, 'You can bet our Bomber Command probably do the same thing. War is bloody, whichever way you look at it.'

It was, and it did no good going on and on about it, so, as they settled themselves in the tram, David said, 'Well, we both think you need a bit of spoiling, so how about going for a nice meal tonight?'

'Nice thought, but a nice meal seems to be a

thing of the past as well,' Kate said wryly.

'Yeah,' said Susie with a laugh. 'You'll probably get something with spam.'

'Anyway,' Kate said, 'there will in all likelihood be a raid tonight. We probably only got away with it last night because of the fog.'

'But you said you haven't got to be on duty while I'm here.'

'No, I haven't,' Kate said. 'But these raids are severe. You'd not want to be caught out in one.' And then she caught sight of David's disappointed face and said, 'Look, when we get off the tram let's see if the fish shop has any fish in? That's as near as we get to a feast these days.'

David was quiet as they alighted from the tram a little later, and Kate slipped her arm through his. 'Stop sulking,' she admonished. 'This is just the way life is at the moment, and if we have to put up with it, then I'm afraid you do too. And look, judging by the queue outside, at least they have got some fish in.'

Their wait was rewarded with fish and chips for three, and they hurried home to eat them while they were hot. They had all finished, and Kate was clearing up the plates, when Sally said, 'Fish and chips was the first meal I had in Birmingham. Remember Kate? I was so scared of what your reaction might be to seeing me, and cold and miserable and so hungry, and I thought the fish and chips you brought in that day was the nicest food I had ever tasted.'

The siren wailed out before Kate was able to reply to this, and Sally jumped up from the table. 'Better get my uniform on.'

'You were on duty yesterday,' Kate said.

'I know, and this isn't official or anything,' Sally said. 'But I would rather be out there being of some use and that.'

Kate wondered if it was that, or if she felt awkward and maybe envious seeing her and David together. 'What do we do?' David said as the drone of planes could be heard in the distance.

'We take blankets and pillows from the bedroom and make ourselves as comfortable as possible in the shelter,' Kate said.

But David was to find there was little comfort to be had in the cold, sunken corrugated shack, with potatoes growing in the roof, a muddy puddle on the floor, condensation down the walls and the only light from the candles that Kate had brought from the kitchen. And no end of pillows and blankets could make rigid benches anything other than basic so, even though he was still incredibly tired, he didn't think he would get much sleep in that place. He hoped the raid would not be a long one.

The planes were flying above their heads, and from the numbers of them Kate guessed the raid would be fast and furious and could last some hours. She didn't share this with David, but noticing him shivering she did say, 'Are you very cold?'

'Yeah, it's the damp that makes it worse.'

'I know,' Kate said as the first crump of explosions could be heard. 'Some of the women at work have paraffin lamps or even heaters in their shelters, though of course the paraffin is sometimes hard to get hold of. Another woman was telling me today to light a candle and put a flowerpot with holes in the bottom over it, and that supposedly takes the chill off the place a bit. But Sally and I hardly ever use the shelter, so it hardly seems worth it.'

There was silence for a moment or two and then Kate, her head cocked on one side listening, said, 'It doesn't seem to be our turn tonight, not yet anyway. I would close your eyes and try and rest while you can. Would it help if you put your head on my knee?'

'I'm sure that will make all the difference,' David said with a leering look at Kate.

'Take that look off your face, or you won't get within a hundred yards of me,' Kate said sharply, sitting down on the bench. 'I am offering you a cushion for your head and that is all.'

'I know,' David said with a grin. 'And I will be good, at least until I get you inside and into bed properly.'

The following day the rain was teeming down, bouncing off the pavements. David, bored, was twiddling with the wireless trying to find something to listen to, and got a news programme announcing that Neville Chamberlain had died that day. 'Ah, that's a shame,' said Kate. 'He only resigned as prime minister in May. He must have been ill then.'

'Mm,' said David. 'I couldn't ever work out whether he really believed that Hitler would stick to that agreement they drew up in Munich in 1938, or whether it was a ploy to give us time to prepare for war because we just weren't ready then.'

'We'll probably never know for sure,' Kate said, looking through the window at the depressing weather. 'Will you just look at that rain?'

'Yes,' David said, joining her. 'What d'you fancy doing this afternoon?'

'Let's cheer ourselves up and go to the pictures,' Kate said. '*The Maltese Falcon* is showing at the Plaza.'

'The Plaza is still operational then? You said it was bombed.'

'It was,' Kate said. 'But it was only closed for a few days.'

When they arrived at the Plaza they found that Susie and Nick had had the same idea. 'Sally not with you?' Susie asked.

'No,' Kate said. 'The offer was there but she didn't want to be a gooseberry.'

'I think we're a bit past cooing and canoodling in the back row,' Nick said.

'You speak for yourself,' David said. 'That's all I'm coming for.'

'Then you best go with someone else,' Kate said. 'Because I want to watch the film.'

'Spoilsport!' David muttered and, ignoring him, Kate said, 'It's not that we're past it, it's just that we don't have to do that any more.'

'Are you kidding?' David said. 'If you ask me, the biggest passion killers are Hitler and his bloody Air Force.'

'That's true,' said Kate. 'But I think that despite the rain they will pay us a visit tonight, so let's go to the cinema and forget the war for a bit.'

There was a raid that night, and the planes returned on Sunday evening as well.

The raid was in full swing as David kissed Kate goodbye and she watched him swing himself into the truck that would take him and Nick back to the airfield. Kate was surprised at the relief that flowed through her, because she had the feeling that David hadn't enjoyed his leave that much. The wet, cold weather hadn't helped, and the raids curtailed anything else and ensured that he didn't sleep very well either, and so he only looked marginally better than when he had arrived home.

TWENTY

Four days after David and Nick went back, German bombers, taking advantage of a fine night and a full moon, had launched a raid of some magnitude on Birmingham. The girls had been on duty throughout. After a scant few hours' sleep, Sally and Kate rose the next morning, still tired, and Sally put on the wireless as they ate breakfast to hear the details of the memorial service being held in St Martin's in the Bull Ring that day for Neville Chamberlain.

Suddenly a voice cut across the eulogies for the ex-prime minister. 'Reports are coming in of a massive attack on Coventry.'

The girls looked in alarm at each other. Coventry was only about fifteen miles from Birmingham; it also made lots of things for the war. It had been bombed before, but the newscaster announced that the raid on 14 November was the most severe that it had suffered. Over five hundred German bombers had dropped high-explosive bombs, parachute mines, incendiary petrol mines and thousands of incendiary bombs all through the night. It was estimated that six hundred people had been killed, a thousand more seriously injured and sixty thousand buildings either destroyed, or so badly damaged as to be unusable. The *Birmingham Gazette* called it 'Our Guernica'; meanwhile, a new word entered the German language: *Koven-*

trieren or *Coventration,* which described the razing to the ground of a place.

Sally and Kate looked at each other with wide eyes and Kate felt a shudder run all down her back as she said, 'So now we know what a man like that is capable of.'

'Was there any doubt then?' Sally asked.

'No, I suppose not,' Kate said. 'I feel all of atremble inside, and yet I need to leave now or I'll be late for work.'

'Me too,' Sally said. 'It will be on everyone's lips today, I expect, but there are no words written that will bring any sort of ease to those poor people.'

Sally was right, of course, though Kate discussed it over and over with Susie in the tram going to work. When they got to the factory, the whole place was buzzing because they all knew that what had been done in Coventry could just as easily happen in Birmingham.

The majority of the residents of Birmingham were nervous when the siren screamed out the following evening, but it was a light skirmish in comparison to some of those suffered in the past. And so it went on all over the weekend. On Monday, at the warden post, Sally said, 'D'you think maybe Herr Hitler isn't going to give us a pasting like he did Coventry?'

'It would be nice to think you were right,' Susie said. 'But I honestly think that Birmingham is never going to be sidelined.'

'Yeah, but does he know what we make?'

'Course he knows,' another woman put in. 'It's

his job to know. And Lord Haw-Haw knows too, 'cos he was blowing on about it a couple of days ago. More or less said we had it coming.'

'Did he really?' Kate said. 'We hardly listen to him now. Think it's a bit disloyal.'

'Only if you believe the claptrap that comes out of his mouth,' the other woman said. 'He does sometimes give an indication of where the bombs are going to fall.'

'He don't always get it right though, does he?' another piped up. 'Look how he went on about the invasion and what the Germans were going to do when they got here, and they never even tried invading us in the end.'

'Well,' the other woman said, 'I think this time he isn't talking through the top of his head.'

'He says things like that to put the fear of God into us.'

'Does he?' Susie said. 'Well, if that's his intention, then it has worked, because I am terrified of having a Coventration in this city.'

'Here, here,' said Kate in agreement.

The massive raid that Birmingham had been bracing itself for began at seventeen minutes past seven the following day: Tuesday, 19 November. Kate and Sally were already dressed in their uniforms, as they were officially on duty that night, and they only stopped to hang their gas masks around their necks and don their tin hats before they slipped out of the door. They had reached the warden post, with Susie following just behind them as the strains of the siren ceased, and they were aware of a rumbling drumming in the sky.

Kate looked up to see the black waves of planes approaching and she gasped because she had never seen so many at any one time before.

People without their own shelters were streaming out of their homes, carrying all manner of possessions, or sleepy babies or toddlers, small children holding the hands of older ones. In the light of Kate's torch, they all seemed white-faced with terror and began giving little yelps of fear as the incendiaries began falling from the planes like rain, setting up fires all around them. Kate no longer needed her torch, for the night was lit up like daylight with the many flares, illuminating the planes above them. The scream of descending bombs and the resultant explosions seemed to lend wings to people's feet and set up a wail among the children – and a fair few of the adults too.

Kate, like Sally and Susie, was an experienced warden, having been involved in many raids, but none of them had experienced anything like that night before. With the roads empty of civilians, they were set to work to try to douse the crackling fires burning fiercely all around them, licking orange and yellow flames against the night sky. The wave of menacing black planes were filling the sky, releasing bombs that plummeted down with a piercing whistle. The crash of explosions mixed with the clatter of more incendiaries tumbling down to hit the ground in a burst of flame, and the arc lights held the German bombers in silhouette, pinpointing more planes approaching as the ack-ack guns began their response.

Hour after hour it went on. Some time that

night, Kate volunteered to be taken to Aston, where the situation was worse, and where so many wardens had already been injured that additional help was needed. Here the bombs were plunging down in clusters and building after building would sway, topple and fall, leaving not one or two gaps, but a whole sea of devastation awash with fire. People's screams added to the general cacophony.

It was so hot that the tar again had been set alight and had slid into the gutters, mangling up the tram lines. It was difficult to breathe in such intense heat, and the fierce fires were making it almost impossible to reach some of the people trapped and crushed in the collapsed buildings; there was not enough water to douse them, even though the canals had been drained. Many mounds that had once been buildings had to be left to burn, while redundant hosepipes dribbled uselessly in the gutters, and burst and soaking sand bags bled into the pavements. Some of the gas pipes had been fractured too; many people were in danger of being gassed to death, and that was a risk to the victims and rescuers alike.

But along with the smell of gas was the acrid stink of cordite, singed brick dust, the fetid smell of blood, the nauseous stench of scorched human flesh and the black smoke that billowed out from the fires and enveloped everyone. They expected very few survivors and, looking at the seas of rubble, Kate thought it was no surprise. They had to be sure, however, and – dead or alive – they had to get as many bodies out as possible. And through it all the bombs, landmines, parachute mines and incendiaries continued to fall from the sky, and the bells of the emergency services rang frantically as they tried to negotiate their way around war-torn streets.

Time and again, Kate crawled into collapsed buildings, her torch playing before her to try to locate and reach any trapped inside. The buildings were often still smoking and smouldering and she was given a scarf to semi-cover her face to protect it from the heat and the burning ash dropping on her. She would feel and smell the material of her overalls singe as she crawled over broken bricks, assorted mangled debris and shattered glass that cut into her hands and knees. The airless, intense heat made her lungs feel as if they were bursting. The bodies of the children affected her greatly, some so badly burnt they were unrecognizable. The first time she carried out a child's body like that, bile rose in her throat, but she hadn't allowed herself to be sick: far too many people needed her help, and worse by far were the people she would reach who'd crumble away at her touch.

Some people were held fast by mounds of bricks, fractured roof beams or broken, buckled machinery; they would need lifting gear and specialist help. Most of these were already dead and some knocked clean out – Kate thought them the lucky ones. She knew those few still alive and conscious would in all likelihood be burned to death before they could be released; hearing their screams was very hard to bear. She was no stranger to death, but death on such a massive scale was totally mind-numbing and she knew that that night she had seen, heard and done things she thought no human being should ever have to endure.

When it was discovered that Kate had done a first-aid course, though, she was redirected to the makeshift shelter and used her skills to help the Red Cross nurses tend any minor injuries. The poor dispossessed people seemed shocked and bemused; many were covered with a layer of brick dust and only had the clothes they stood up in, and most of those were ripped or stained. A small fleet of ambulances had battled their way through falling masonry and were waiting to ferry the badly injured to any hospital that had room to take them. Kate felt a wave of despair wash over her and she had the urge to sob for those people who had lost everything.

However, tears were another indulgence that she couldn't allow herself, and she sighed and bent to the task in hand as newly injured were being brought in all the time.

Much much later, when the 'All Clear' had sounded, Kate made for home. She needed no torch, though, because so many of the fires still blazed that the whole sky was lit up with a reddy-orange glow as Birmingham burned. This made it easier for Kate as she trudged her weary way home to avoid the sodden sandbags lying everywhere, the bomb craters, the twisted tram lines and the piles of masonry that had spilled on to pavements and roads.

It seemed to take for ever, though, and Kate wondered if any areas of Birmingham had escaped being bombed that night. Slade Road hadn't, she realized, as she passed Salford Bridge and turned into it; she was further upset to see the house where she and Sally had had the flat was just one of many houses that had been extensively damaged. She had a fleeting worry about her own house and wondered for the first time if it was still standing.

She had reached Stockland Green and she turned gratefully into Marsh Lane, but was stopped from going down Bleak Hill and home by a burly policeman holding a stout torch, which he turned on her as he said, 'You live up there, missis?'

'Yes, what's wrong?' Kate said in a voice make husky from the smoke inhaled and slurred with tiredness.

The policeman looked at her with sympathy. She was still in her torn uniform, which was filthy from the smoke and burnt through in places. He couldn't really see much of her face but it was obvious what she had been doing that night and he spoke gently. 'An unexploded petrol bomb is lodged in Hesketh Crescent and the whole area has had to be evacuated until it can be dealt with.'

'Unexploded bomb?' Kate repeated. 'But my young sister is in there. She's only seventeen.'

'No one is in there,' the policeman assured her. 'As I said, this whole area has been evacuated. Every house was checked.'

Kate's eyes opened wider and her mouth was drier than ever as she looked back at the policeman and said fearfully, 'Then... Oh, God, then where is she?'

'That I can't say,' the policemen said. 'I wasn't here when that was done. Just sent now to stand guard like, but try not to worry, I'm sure she'll be all right. You'll be able to locate her tomorrow. And just for now, have you anyone you can stay with? If not I'll have someone take you to a rest centre, because if you don't mind me saying, missis, you look all in.'

'I am,' Kate admitted. 'I've been helping down Aston tonight.' She shook her head sadly. 'It was bad,' she went on. 'So many dead!'

'I know, lass, we see it all the time too,' the policeman said, moved by the bleak look in Kate's eyes. 'Never fails to get to you, though. The minute I am not upset by such things is the day I hang my hat up. Now, my dear, you must think about yourself. Have you anyone to stay with for now?'

Kate thought of the Masons straight away. She knew that she would be made welcome there. 'Yes,' she said, and she heard the policeman sigh with relief. 'I have friends further down Marsh Hill. They will put me up.'

'Then, my dear, I would get yourself down there as soon as possible.'

'I will, yes. Thank you,' Kate said as she walked away.

The Masons' house was quiet and still, but she hammered on the door anyway. It was opened in minutes and she heard Susie gasp with shock as she pulled her inside and threw her arms around her. 'Oh, thank God. I thought you were... Oh, God, you are all right.'

Susie's words brought her parents down the stairs. They were dressed in their nightclothes, Kate noticed, but Susie was still in her warden's uniform, and Kate saw them all looking at her with concern mixed with relief. There was so much she needed to say; she needed to tell them why she was there, about the unexploded bomb and – more importantly – that she didn't know where her sister was, but then, as she opened her mouth to speak, the emotion of that evening proved too much and she sank to the floor in floods of tears.

Mary took charge, lifting Kate gently to her feet. Instructing Frank to put the kettle on and Susie to bring another set of pyjamas down, she put her arm about Kate's heaving shoulders and said, 'I'm going to give you a little wash and dress you in something more comfortable. You are in a state.'

Was she? Kate hadn't given a thought to how she might look, but she caught sight of herself as she passed the mirror in the hall and couldn't believe that the reflection staring back – with the blackened face and large bloodshot and red-rimmed eyes – could be her. She had no idea where her tin hat was and her soot-streaked hair was in tangles around her face. She looked down at her hands and they too were blackened and bloody, the nails torn, her palms calloused and blistered and suddenly very sore. In fact, now she was able to think about it, everywhere was sore; it seemed her whole body throbbed with pain, while specific areas stung like mad. She groaned aloud and Mary's heart was wrung with pity as she half carried Kate into the kitchen.

'Soon have you comfy,' she said, lowering Kate into a kitchen chair. She shooed her husband out of the kitchen as she began to strip the ragged, singed uniform from Kate's body, gasping as she saw the extent of the lacerations, bruising and blistering there was under it. She began to bathe her gently with the warm water from the kettle that she poured into a bowl. Susie came into the kitchen then with clean underclothes and pyjamas and her thick woollen dressing gown and slippers and Kate said to her, 'I can't find Sally. I don't know where she is.'

'Sally is fine,' Susie said. 'We both saw the bomb and the copper told us what had happened and she went home with one of the other wardens. Mind you, she didn't want to go because she was so worried about you. In the end I said that I would wait for first light and start searching for you and check around the hospitals if necessary. That's why I hadn't even bothered getting undressed. Where did you get to?'

'Aston,' Kate said, wincing as Mary began applying salve to her many cuts and scorch marks. 'They were asking for volunteers because it was horrendous down there, and so I said I'd go. I'm surprised Jane didn't tell you and Sally where I'd gone. She said she would – I knew that you would be worried.'

'She probably would have done,' Sally said. 'But she was caught in a blast herself.'

Kate gasped. 'Poor woman. Is she dead?'

'The ambulance men said she was breathing,' Susie said. 'Looked in a bad way to me, though, and she was unconscious when they carried her away.'

'Come and get dressed in these things before you get a chill,' Mary said, and she helped Kate on with the vest and nightdress and tied the dressing gown tight around her as if she was a child. Kate was tired enough to let her do just that. Mary wrapped bandages expertly around Kate's damaged hands and then said, 'Now, I'm going to make you a sandwich. That will be the easiest thing to eat, I would think, and then you are going to be tucked up in Martin's old room.'

'Just now I think I could sleep on a clothesline,' Kate said.

'Well, you can sleep in the morning anyway,' Mary said firmly. 'For there will be no work for you tomorrow with those hands. There might not be work for any of us, because few parts of Birmingham were left unscathed last night, and if the Jewellery Quarter has been hit again, I might be out of a job permanently. Anyway, Kate, I want the doctor to take a look at you.'

'I'm sure I don't need a doctor, Mary,' Kate said. 'I will be fine in a day or so.'

'I'm afraid I must insist,' Mary said, and though her voice was gentle, Kate saw the steely glint in her eye. 'Some of those cuts are deep and the burns extensive and there is always the risk of infection, and so I will ask the doctor to call and I will take the day off myself to look after you.'

Dr Butler was a plump, bluff man with very red cheeks and kind brown eyes. Kate had met him before when she had been concerned about Sally when she'd had news of Phil's death. So he greeted Kate before examining her all over and saying she was a very brave girl, but she had done her bit for a while and she was not to go either to work or

364

warden post until he said it was all right for her to do so.

He unwrapped all the bandages and said that Mary had done a first-rate job, but he applied new salve and fresh gauze and said the dressings had to be changed daily so he would be back in the morning. 'Mary Mason is right to be careful,' he said. 'The risk of infection with injuries like these is very real. And I am concerned about your lungs too,' he went on. 'I know that husky voice is not your natural way of speaking.'

Kate smiled as she shook her head. 'No.'

'There you are, do you see,' the doctor said. 'Could be all sorts of damage there. Mary Mason is more than willing for you to stay here until you are better.'

'She is very kind,' Kate said. 'And yet I will be glad to get back home. That is, of course, if we have a home to go back to.'

'Where do you live now then?' Dr Butler asked, for when he had attended Sally they had been living at the flat.

'Bleak Hill,' Kate said.

'Oh, yes,' the doctor said. 'There's that un-exploded petrol bomb in Hesketh Crescent.'

'That's right.'

'Oh, well, I'm sure they will get back to defusing it or whatever in time,' Dr Butler said and added, 'And I wouldn't be in too much of a rush to leave here if I were you. Haven't you the life of Riley?'

And she had of course. She dozed after the doctor's visit, and when she woke it was to find that Sally and Susie were both at home because both factories had been damaged. Sally's had been destroyed totally, and they would have to look for new premises, but there wasn't much damage to the actual factory Susie and Kate worked in. 'Bit of a mess, like, and all the windows had been blown out, because it had been caught in the blast that destroyed the places across the road,' Susie told her. 'And when they have the place tidied up, they will have to check that it's stable and won't fall in on top of us. And they were saying some of the machines might have to be repaired or replaced as well

'So until then we're ladies of leisure,' Sally said.

'And we can come and look after you so that Mom can go back to work,' Susie put in. 'She's heard that her place is still operational, but the fires just ripped through most of the wooden warehouses and they were burnt to the ground.'

'Susie, your mother can go back to work any time she likes,' Kate said. 'She is a lovely, kind lady, but I don't need looking after by her or anyone else either.'

'Yes, you do, Miss Independent,' Susie said. 'The doctor said he thinks you are suffering from shock as well as everything else, and he said it would be better if you can stay still and preferably in bed for a few days until the blisters and burns begin to heal a little.'

'Anyway,' Sally said, 'what have you got to do that's so pressing? We can't go home yet and you can't go to work, so why can't you stay in bed and recover?'

'I'm just not used to lying in bed.'

'Then get used to it,' Susie said unsympathetically.

'Yeah,' Sally said. 'You just lie there and pray Jerry doesn't pay us another visit tonight, that's all. Give us a chance to recover.'

'If he does then he does,' Susie said. 'Just maybe he will give us a break after last night.'

There was a raid, but it was light in comparison to the previous night's. However, there was a particularly ferocious landmine dropped on Queen's Road in Aston, which wiped out the entire street. Kate was really sorry to hear that because she knew that that area had already suffered so much.

The following night there was no raid and it was the 22 November when the bombers returned in force in a raid that began at just after seven o'clock. Kate lay restless in her bed, listening to the mayhem going on all around her, with bombs falling so close they rattled the windows.

Mary would not allow Kate down to the shelter because she said she really wasn't well enough, and she insisted on sitting it out with her, though Kate could see that she was as nervous as a kitten hearing the raid progressing so clearly. And even Kate was concerned, hearing some of the bombs falling so closely that they might easily set off the bomb that was still lodged in Hesketh Crescent. 'I know I wouldn't be the first in this war to lose my home,' she said to Mary. 'But I would just hate it. I mean, it's far more than just bricks and mortar, don't you think?'

'Oh, I do,' Mary agreed. 'All our memories are tied up in this house. It would take me some time to get over the loss of it.'

'Me too,' Kate said. 'For all we haven't been in it that long, David really liked it. I mean, it is the sort of house we can settle down in together after the war and plan our future, raise any children we might have. I'd hate to have that swiped away from me like so many others have.'

'Let's not think about it any more now,' Mary suggested. 'I think I will make us a cup of tea. It's great for steadying the nerves and maybe the raid won't go on so long. Maybe it'll be more fast and furious.'

However, the raid lasted eleven hours. Kate had been unable to sleep, but Mary had managed an uncomfortable doze in the chair beside her bed and was roused by the 'All Clear'. And when a bedraggled, black-faced and exhausted Susie returned that night, Kate thought she needed something stronger than tea to steady her nerves.

'God, Kate, you should have seen it: vast areas laid waste, streets and streets of houses and factories and all that's left is gigantic mounds of rubbish. The city centre got hit again. New Street Station too, someone said. Grey's and C and A department stores have just been wiped off the map. That makes you angry, but it's the suffering of the people that really tugs on your heart strings.'

'I know.'

'I was sent to the General today,' Susie said. 'We had some seriously injured people in the ambulance and they could only spare the one nurse to travel with them, so when they learnt I had done a first-aid course I was sent to help her. In all my life I will never forget what we saw when we got to that hospital.'

Susie swallowed deeply and went on: 'The place was packed and there were injured still coming in.

Men, women and children. They lay about on trolleys, or the floor, or sat on chairs; others shambled about, looking dazed and confused. Most of them were covered in a reddy-grey dust and it was everywhere, ingrained in the folds of skin and their hair and even gilding their eyelashes and eyebrows. And their clothes were all tattered and torn and were covered with that same dust. But the thing that really got to me was the look in their eyes. Everyone was filled with such deep despair. Even the children, and I know as long as I live I will never forget the look in those eyes.'

'I know, it breaks your heart,' Kate said. 'I've seen it too. In the raid we had on Tuesday, I was pulling crushed, broken or burnt little bodies from the rubble when I knew very few of them had any sort of chance. I felt helpless that I could do so little for them.'

'There's so little the doctors and nurses can do, too, even if they reach the hospital,' Susie said. 'They seem to know that, and you could almost touch their fear and misery. You could certainly smell it; it was all mixed up with the smell of that swirling dust that lodged in my throat, and blood and vomit and charred flesh that overrode even the antiseptic that most hospitals smell of.

'And the noise too was unbelievable. The raid was ongoing outside, but inside there were heart-rending sobs and moans and groans. Some screamed or shrieked and others wept wretchedly; the babies and some of the children whimpered weakly, as if they had no energy for anything more; others bellowed and keened. More than once my eyes filled with tears—'

'So did mine.'

'Bet you didn't let them fall though,' Susie said.

Kate shook her head and Susie said, 'Neither did I. I couldn't allow myself to go to pieces and be of no use to anyone. The nurses were rushed off their feet and they didn't even try and keep order – there was no point. There were just too many patients, and every few minutes more would arrive. They just walked among the poor people, stopping here and there to try to soothe and reassure, especially the children, but sometimes they would have to cover the face of one who had died without even getting the offer of treatment.

'And when I set off to come home, the night was as light as daylight, with all the fires that had to be left burning.' She looked at Kate and said, 'They'll still be raging now. They drained the canals again, just like they did on Tuesday, but it just wasn't enough, and now there is no water in the taps.'

'What do you mean, no water?'

'What I say,' Susie said. 'I walked home with this man who was a volunteer fireman, and he said the planes hit three trunk water mains in Bristol Road, so there is no water in vast parts of the city.'

'Golly!'

'Yes, but for us it's just an inconvenience,' Susie said. 'But if Jerry comes back tonight, Birmingham will be burnt to the ground. It will cease to exist.'

The girls' eyes met; they both knew that that was a distinct possibility.

'Well,' said Kate, throwing back the bedcovers.

'This has decided me.'

'About what?'

'This lying abed all the time has to stop,' Kate said, padding to the window. She lifted the black-out curtain away carefully with her bandaged hand and peered out. The sky was blood-red and a bright orange glow was everywhere. Other fires still raged, spitting orange sparks into the air; curls of smoke rose from other smouldering heaps.

There she had been, worrying about if her house was all right, yet for many poor devils, the unthinkable had happened, and the houses and maybe the places they had worked too had been annihilated. She let the curtain fall back and turned to face Susie. 'Many have suffered worse than me and have carried on,' she said. 'Doctor or no doctor, I am getting up and getting dressed, and I am going to see what is happening with the house and if possible make arrangements to move back as soon as possible. And I will be at the warden post if the sirens go off, because if there is a raid tonight, Birmingham will need all the help it can get.'

'The factory is opening again on Monday,' Susie said, and added with a wry grin, 'that's if it wasn't hammered again last night, of course.'

'That suits me perfectly, if it does open,' Kate said. 'I will be as fit as a fiddle by then.'

'Well, you do what you want, Kate,' Susie said. 'I won't even try to stop you, but I just know I am bushed and need to go to bed.'

'I'm going up to see about the house anyway,' Kate said. 'So I'll leave you to it.' She went out of the room and down the stairs, aware that her legs were slightly wobbly and the unaccustomed clothes were rubbing on areas where she had been burnt or where the lacerations had begun to heal but the skin was still very tender. Her hands were still quite painful when she tried to use them, but she didn't say a word about any of that because she wanted no more mollycoddling.

TWENTY-ONE

The citizens of Birmingham were not told of the fracturing of the water pipes, which had left their city so vulnerable to fire, but if there is no water in the taps, and later there is a member of the Labour Party touring the area in a van with a loud-hailer telling people where to get their water from, it didn't take much working out that something serious was amiss. And so most Brummies were more nervous than usual as night fell. However, there was no attack that night, nor the next. By that time, too, Sally and Kate were back in the house, but the huge crater left in the garden of Hesketh Crescent was a reminder of how close they had come to disaster.

Kate was more than glad that the spate of bombing had eased slightly, allowing her to get fully fit once more, for although there were a few skirmishes, there wasn't a more sustained attack until 3 December, when bombers again attacked the city centre and areas around it; but the water pipes, which had taken five days to repair, were by then fully operational once more.

On 11 December the sirens rang out again at just after six o'clock in the evening. Kate, Susie and Sally reported for duty and it was soon obvious this was another full-blown attack. It was bitterly cold, the sort of cold that ate into a person, and Kate, like all the others, was on the streets helping the people to the shelters. Many of the children were in siren suits, the warm all-in-ones designed to fit over a person's clothes, and yet many shivered with the intense cold. Flares lit up the night like day and Kate urged the tired people to hurry as the bombs could be heard falling in the distance but coming closer every minute.

Then the menacing planes were above them, so close that in the light from the flares she saw the bomb doors open and release their arrows of death. She heard the boom and bang of them exploding not that far away and buildings collapsing with a crash of falling masonry. She thought of her house and whether it could withstand this latest attack and knew that many more would lose their homes that night. The ack-ack guns were again barking into the sky and soon the ringing of the ambulance bells could be heard.

Kate was first directed to deal with any with minor injuries in the public shelter off Marsh Hill; she had finished there and was helping fight the fires when the 'All Clear' sounded after about three hours. Twenty minutes later the attack began again, and people who had not long reached home were encouraged out on to the streets once again when another wave of bombers was seen approaching. Three hours later the whole thing was repeated. 'Playing bloody cat and mouse,' Susie said angrily. 'These poor people don't know whether they are coming or going.'

'I know,' Kate said. 'It's done to play on people's nerves.'

'Yeah, and guess what,' Susie said. 'It's bloody well working.'

The game of cat and mouse went on for thirteen hours, and when they realized that it was finally over and the last people had been released and bodies brought out and the fires reduced to smoky heaps, Kate barely had the energy to make her way home. Sally was in no better shape. Kate returned to the house, and though she would have loved to have thrown herself on the bed and slept the sleep of the totally justified, she had a job of work to go to. She knew she wouldn't be the only one in the factory that would feel like a bit of chewed string. Sally's face was white with exhaustion and she had black bags beneath her eyes. She said to her sister, 'Do I look as bad as I feel?'

'Probably,' Kate said. 'You look absolutely exhausted and I'm probably no better.'

Sally nodded. 'Wouldn't it be wonderful to get our heads down and sleep till lunchtime? And instead of that we must struggle into work?'

''Fraid so.'

'Oh, I know,' Sally said. 'To do anything else is terribly unpatriotic. So I am off to wash my face to wake myself up a little and then will have a bite to eat and be on my way.'

'And I'll do the same,' Kate said.

As she scurried up the road later, she realized that everyone seemed tired; they even walked in a ponderous way, as if it was almost too much trouble to put one foot in front of the other. So many of the faces of the people on the streets, or those who stood silently at the tram stop, were pale and strained, their eyes quite expressionless. 'Can you wonder that they look that way?' Susie said when Kate mentioned this as they took their seats in the tram on their way to work. 'I think everyone's feeling a bit battered, don't you?'

'Well, I am, for one,' Kate stated flatly. 'Battered exactly describes how I feel.'

'Everyone must feel it,' Susie said. 'I feel like death warmed up myself. I mean, I know we were out in the raid, but I would much rather do that and feel I was doing something useful than hide away somewhere listening to every blast.'

'Yes, and that's exactly what you would do, because unless you were in some soundproof bunker fifty foot underground, you couldn't sleep anyway, I wouldn't have thought,' Kate said. 'Isn't King George supposed to be visiting Birmingham today?'

'So people say,' Susie said. 'He's coming to see the extent of the bombing.'

'Well, he's got more to look at after last night,' Kate said. Then, lowering her voice, she went on: 'But, judging by the people I've seen this morning and in the tram with us now, he could easily think that Birmingham is peopled by zombies.'

Susie took a surreptitious look around and gave a wry smile. 'I see what you mean,' she said to Kate.

'We're not likely to get even a sniff of him anyway,' Kate said.

'And our lives will not be the poorer in the slightest because of that,' Susie said, and of course she was right. The King's visiting that ravaged city would make not a ha'p'orth's difference to anyone's lives.

And yet, according to the *Evening Mail* that Kate

bought on the way home, most people thought it admirable of the King of England to come and see what Birmingham had gone through. The reporter said that he was touched and also amazed by the courage and resilience of the people against such tremendous odds, and Kate warmed to him when she read those words.

He visited the Vickers factory where they made the Spitfires and Lancasters, and Kynoch's where they made the bombs and bullets, and he insisted on getting out of the car as they drove through Aston. There were hordes of cheering people standing waiting for him, and when the crowd saw what he was doing they cheered all the louder. Spontaneously, people began singing the National Anthem, and George VI stood to attention throughout. Then he thanked them all and began to walk through the crowds and talk to the people.

Even through the grainy newsprint of the *Evening Mail* that night the excitement his visit generated was obvious and, thought Kate, not a zombie in sight. However tired they were, the visit from the King seemed to lift everyone's spirits. 'Look, they are holding babies and young children up to see him,' Kate said to Sally in amazement as they both examined the paper.

Sally said, 'I wish I'd seen him in real life, and it would have been great to have actually spoken to him. Look what the reporter said about his kind, brown eyes, and how they clouded over when he saw the damage inflicted and listened to the tales the people told him; and because of it he made an unscheduled visit to a rest centre, like he really seemed to care.'

'He maybe does,' Kate said. 'He's as helpless as the rest of us to do anything about it, though, and can you imagine the unholy flap when he visited a rest centre almost on the spur of the moment?'

'Yeah,' Sally said with a grin. 'Royals aren't supposed to do that, and it probably was a headache for the detectives and that, but at least he saw things as they really are.'

There were no further raids after the one on 11 December and yet Kate looked forward to a second wartime Christmas with little enthusiasm. There was even less in the shops to buy, and trying to find anything even the slightest bit festive was fraught with problems.

She didn't bother with any decorations or fetch in the battered tree she had put in the shed outside, because there seemed little point. She and Sally would be having their Christmas dinner at the Masons' house anyway. Gillian, Derek's wife, had been asked too, and Martin got a spot of leave as well. Kate guessed it was embarkation leave, but she was unable to ask him because Mary had declared that there should be no war talk for that day at least and she respected that.

Frank had contacts and had been able to get hold of a large chicken. Kate thought it the most succulent she had tasted in a long time. She might have felt guilty about it, until Frank told her he had grown all the vegetables they were eating in the garden he had dug over.

The food, and the wine that Martin produced, certainly helped the mood around the table that day and it was Martin who proposed the toast to absent friends. There were so many – David and Nick and Derek – and Kate felt a lump in her throat as she raised her glass and thought in particular of Phil. But she pushed her sadness away because that day wasn't the time for sorrow.

In fact, Martin was in the mood for tale-telling; Kate liked him and certainly admired his ready wit. She hadn't realized what a natural storyteller he'd become, and she listened as he regaled the family with one tale after the other and kept them all laughing.

The dinner things were cleared away and washed up in good time so they could all listen to the King's Speech on the wireless. It seemed more pertinent than usual as he had visited their city less than a fortnight before. And after it, everyone braved the cold to go for a bracing walk, returning as darkness was falling to hot toddies and mince pies.

Much, much later, Sally and Kate walked home and Kate felt warmed by the good wishes of her friends. They had made the day she had been dreading extra-special and she knew she would hold on to the memory of it for a long, long time.

Apart from a few raids between January and March 1941, it really did seem as if their ordeal was over. On the other hand, merchant ships continued to be sunk and people were encouraged to 'Dig for Victory'.

More and more parkland and ornamental gardens were dug up and tilled for vegetables, and Kate brought home more seeds for potatoes and carrots, which she and Sally planted to grow on the top of their Anderson shelter as they had the previous year. Despite being farmer's daughters, neither had ever grown anything by themselves, and it had given them great satisfaction to eat the vegetables from their own garden, which they claimed tasted a hundred per cent better than anything you could buy in the greengrocer's.

People were also encouraged to 'Make Do and Mend' their clothes, and to be a 'Squander Bug' was to be the worst in the world. 'And that is all very well if you had plenty to start with,' Kate said. 'But clothes have been hard to get for ages anyway – and what about the poor bombed-out people? They usually only have the clothes they are standing up in.'

'I know, it's awful,' Sally said. 'And it's like the government and Birmingham council have been taken by surprise with these aerial attacks – and yet they must have expected them, else why did we have the blackout, and why were we told to put tape across our windows and have sand-bagged shelters erected and cellars reinforced. What did they expect the people to do?'

'God knows.'

'Good job a lot of the churches have under-stood that and have set up clothes banks and the like.'

'Yeah, that's great,' Kate said. 'I'm sure that everyone is very grateful, but it shouldn't have been left up to them. Mind you, rationing of clothes will start in June anyway and they say that a person will have so many points to buy clothes and when those points are gone that will be it.'

'I hope they give us enough to buy all that we'll

need,' Sally said. She sighed as she went on: 'I know that there are no raids at the moment and that's good, but I think everything is ever so depressing. A few of the girls I work with who live over this way are thinking of going to dancing lessons at this place called Bromford Club in Church Road in Erdington and they wanted me to go with them.'

'Are you going to go?'

Sally shook her head. 'I don't think so.'

'Why not?' Kate said. 'It will do you good, and it's something you never had time to do before with working so many evenings.'

'You know why I can't go.'

'No, I don't,' Kate said. 'I know that you loved Phil and still must miss him like mad, but you are only young, and locking yourself away in the house night after night is no way to go on. From what I knew of the man, he wouldn't expect you to do that.'

'You think so?' Susie asked doubtfully.

Kate gave an emphatic nod. 'I don't think, I *know*. Look, the last time David was home he actually said to me that if anything happened to him he didn't want me to waste my life mourning him, but to live. I didn't like him talking that way and it isn't a thought I like to keep in my head, but it is the way he felt. Phil gave his life fighting for freedom, and if you mourn him all your days and never go beyond the door except to work or to the warden post, what was the point of his sacrifice?'

'Oh, Kate, you make me feel so much better,' Sally said. 'And you are right. From odd things he let slip, he felt the same as David.'

'It's time to start taking up the threads of your life again,' Kate said encouragingly. 'And dancing lessons are a grand way to start. Tell your friends you will go.'

'Right,' said Sally. 'I will.'

However, the type of dancing that Sally learnt – which she often demonstrated at home – surprised Kate. 'It's not like when we learnt dancing,' Kate said to Susie in the tram on the way home one evening in late March. 'Though they have touched on the basics of the waltz and foxtrot, she said dances like those don't go with the modern music.'

'Good job we don't go to the dances any more then,' Susie said. 'We might be right out of our depth.'

'We'd probably pick it up,' Kate said. 'The music she is talking about is only the kind of big band stuff that we used to love and, as I remember, you could do an energetic quickstep to a lot of that. Now, they do things called the swing, and kangaroo hop – and her favourite of all, the jitterbug, is fairly wild apparently.'

'Maybe we'll coerce the boys into taking us to a dance the next leave they have,' Susie said. 'And we will see for ourselves.'

'Um, maybe,' Kate said. 'I just don't feel right going without the men.'

'Not to a dance, no,' Susie said. 'But there is no need for us to go into decline either. Now the raids have stopped and we have some sort of rota in place for ARP duties, what's to stop us going to the cinema once a week?'

'Nothing, I suppose,' Kate said. 'In fact, I would really like that.'

'How about tonight then?' Susie said. '*The Philadelphia Story* is on at the Plaza.'

'Yes, that will be great,' Kate said. 'And we must start going down the Bull Ring as well.'

'We could do that tomorrow if you like,' Susie said. 'There's always a special buzz to it of a Saturday. Tell you what, after Easter we will take stock of our lives again.'

'Yeah,' Kate said, for Easter was only a fortnight away. 'Most people have New Year's resolutions, but we will have Easter resolutions. It's a much better time of year, with the nights drawing out and some warmth in the sun and that makes everything more hopeful.'

When the sirens screamed out on 9 April at just after half past nine at night, Kate and Sally, and in fact, most Brummies, were a bit blasé about it, but when the strains of the sirens died away, there was the rumble of many planes in the air and Kate sighed as her eyes met Sally's. 'Oh, God! Seems like here we go again,' Sally said.

'Yeah,' Kate said, digging out their uniforms, which were hung up in the cupboard under the stairs. 'I really thought he would leave us alone now. We'd sort of had our turn.'

'Huh, he's done this before,' Sally said as she struggled into her uniform. 'Easing off on the raids and then hitting you with a big one.'

'I know,' Kate said as she fastened up her steel-capped boots. 'And I know what a bloody nuisance it is.' She plucked their tin hats from the hook behind the door. The planes were right above them now and they heard the sticks of incendiaries plummeting down and the whistle of the first bomb.

'Ready?' Kate said.

Sally gave a grimace as she said, 'I suppose as ready as I ever will be. Let's go.'

It was soon apparent that this was no light skirmish, but an attack reminiscent of the raids in October and November. Most of the bombs flew over their heads, but they heard them explode not that far away. 'Aston seems to be getting it again,' Sally remarked, and Kate felt her stomach contract in sympathy for the people who had already suffered grievously.

A little later a call came in for help in the city centre, where the firemen were almost over-whelmed with the fires, many of which were out of control. The three girls volunteered immediately because they had been shocked by how much of the city had already been destroyed and they were willing to help save the rest of it. They weren't the only ones to feel this way and a truck took the cluster of girls in, but the driver explained that he could only take them as far as the fire station on the outskirts of the city centre because of the state of the roads.

Outside, though it was after midnight, the crackling fires made it more than light enough to see the planes, droning with their unmistakable intermittent engine noise and flying in formation, like menacing black beetles. Kate looked up and saw two planes caught in the beam of the arc lights raking the sky. Immediately the ack-ack guns spat into the air, but the plane had released the bombs and the girls threw themselves to the floor as one landed with a stupendous crash and then another and then another.

The bomber made off for the city centre as they struggled to their feet, coughing as the dust hit their throats, and the air reeked with the stink of cordite and the smoke that swirled in front of them. They heard the unmistakable sound of falling masonry, and as they reached Steelhouse Lane only moments later, they saw where the bombs had made their mark, for there were big craters in the road. 'They've hit the police station,' Sally said. 'All the windows are gone.'

'And they have got the hospital too,' Kate said. 'Look, a whole corner of it has collapsed.'

They all gazed in horror for a moment, for part of the Casualty department at the hospital where Susie had been just a few short months ago was now just a mound of rubble. Doctors, nurses and waiting patients had already begun moving it brick by brick and the girls joined in to help, while ringing bells announced the arrival of ambulances bringing injured people who probably needed fairly urgent treatment.

It was depressing work, for there were very few survivors pulled from that wreckage; most were either already dead or very badly injured, and that included doctors and nurses as well as patients.

It was very much later when the girls saw what was left of the city centre. By that time most of the rubble had been cleared and Lewis's, a large department store not far from the hospital, had opened its basement to be used. Patients were being referred there, and so the three friends made their way towards the city centre, turning up Colmore Row, trying to avoid the bombs still tumbling down relentlessly, the barking guns seeming to make little impression on them.

They hurried on as fast as they could, aware that Colmore Row had taken another pounding, for rows of shops and offices were just not there any more, and when they tried to cross St Philip's church yard and cut down along Temple Street, they couldn't because the buildings on both sides of the road were in flames. It was the same in Bennett's Hill and so they walked to the end of the road where the town hall and the council house were and looked to both sides. There was a collective gasp. Kate had seen a painting in the art gallery called *Dante's Inferno*, and that came nowhere near what she was seeing that night. To the right of her she could see Broad Street was ablaze, but New Street to the left was a sea of flame. She felt fluttering fear assail her, and then this was overridden by blistering anger. 'Who the bloody hell do the Germans think they are?' she demanded. 'How dare they do this?'

'I dunno who they are or what they think,' Susie said. 'I really have no desire to try and understand a German but, unless we do what we can, there will be no city left after tonight.'

Kate nodded, but she didn't want Sally in that hell on earth. It would be incredibly dangerous for all of them and she said, 'Why don't you go back to the hospital, Sally? You were really good at first aid and you might be a godsend there.'

'Maybe,' Sally said. 'But I didn't come here to

dig people out of buildings. I'm not saying that it was the wrong thing to do, but it was the firemen that asked for help and it looks as if they'll need every bit we can give them.'

'Sally, you're only just turned eighteen.'

'So,' Sally said. 'I can't help that and it doesn't make me bloody helpless. Just now we are wasting time.'

'Aren't you the tiniest bit scared?' Susie said. 'Because I am shaking in my boots.'

'Yeah,' Sally said. 'If you want the truth I'm bloody terrified, but that isn't going to stop me.'

And at that Sally moved forwards towards the blazing New Street and the others had no option but to follow her. The intense heat made it feel as if they were walking into a furnace and the noise was unbelievable as the flames roared and crackled all around and in front of them, mixed with the sound of exploding bombs and the barking ack-ack guns.

Kate took over from an exhausted fireman who smelt of smoke and had a red, glistening face and singed eyebrows and fringes. But it took every ounce of Kate's strength to hold his hose with the water powering through it. Her whole body shook as the strain was so great; within a few minutes her hot red face was bathed in perspiration, her eyes dried out so much that they smarted. She felt dribbles of sweat run down her face and her back and between her breasts.

And the terrible thing was it seemed to make no difference: however many gallons of water they sent shooting into the blazing buildings, those flames could not be vanquished. Beside them and

around, the bombs fell relentlessly, as the un-
quenchable fire ate up building after building and
street after street. Kate was filled with helpless-
ness.

It was after eight o'clock in the morning when
the 'All Clear' went. The girls were almost surprised that they were in one piece, for many
firemen and people working for the auxiliary
service had been injured and even killed that
night. Many fires still burned, but they could do
no more because there was no more water. They
were incredibly weary as they made their way
home, immensely glad that it was Good Friday
and they were on holiday from work.

TWENTY-TWO

The German planes returned the next night but in far fewer numbers than the previous one. The raid didn't last as long and the girls were more than thankful for the respite. After that there were no further raids until a short one on 17 May, and then sporadic short clashes until July. Kate did wonder if Hitler was softening them up for another massive onslaught, but after July there was nothing at all.

With no raids to fight, the ARP wardens were detailed to work with the homeless and dispossessed; there were so many of them in that damaged city. Kate felt so sorry for them, and trying to make life even a little better for them was the sort of work she loved.

Birmingham Council had eventually got their act together in dealing with the people who had lost everything in the raids and so, initially, the people who were homeless but uninjured were cared for by volunteers in rest centres, where they were supplied with clothes and food. From there, many went to one of the city's hostels.

Because Kate had done so much work in Aston, one of the areas so badly hit by the bombing, she was pleased to be drafted in there where she met up with Trudy again. Trudy was just as pleased to see her, and she gave a big grin as she said, 'God, I suppose it says something that we both survived and my house is still standing. How about yours?'

'It's fine,' Kate said. 'It was a near thing, though. An unexploded bomb landed in the road I back on to. If it had gone off, I would have been one of these poor souls bedding down in a church hall or something.'

'I know,' Trudy said. 'It must be awful really to lose everything. Mind, the hostels are really good. The one for this area is in Bevington Road – you know, the road that runs by the side of Aston Park. That's where I am going at the moment so come along with me and I'll introduce you to Rita and John Taylor who run the place, because you'll probably be working quite closely with them anyway.'

'Yeah,' Kate said, falling into step beside Trudy. 'One of my jobs at the moment is helping people move into the hostel from the church halls, or wherever they've been put on a temporary basis, and try and sort out any problems they might have.'

'And some have terrible problems,' Trudy said. 'Especially those coping with a loss of a loved one, and though all deaths are a tragedy of course, if they have lost a child, somehow it is heartbreaking and you just want to do your level best for them.'

'Oh, I do agree,' Kate said. 'I think seeing the little bodies of children killed in the raids is very upsetting. I just can't imagine how a mother copes with that, especially when she has other children to care for and her house is gone too.'

'Yeah and her husband is overseas, or maybe injured or dead as well.' Trudy said. 'We have a fair number of people in that position. I am often stunned by the way they manage to pick up their lives again. They show real courage.'

'I'll say.' Kate agreed wholeheartedly.

'Well, here we are,' Trudy said, stopping outside a very large brick-built building on four floors. Once inside, the introductions were made speedily. Kate liked what she saw of the two no-nonsense stewards and knew that they could work well together. 'It seems a big place,' she said.

'Needs to be,' Rita said. 'These places are built to accommodate two and a half thousand people.'

'Golly!'

'Well, look at all the houses destroyed,' Rita said. 'Whole areas laid waste, and every house knocked down had people in them, some quite big families. Even though two thousand five hundred sounds a lot, that won't be all of them.'

'So what happens to the others?'

'Well, those with families with undamaged houses are usually lodged with them,' John said. 'And the others are billeted in ordinary houses with people willing to take them in.' He gave a nod in Kate's direction and added with a wry smile, 'That will probably be something you have got to sort out as well.'

And it was, of course, but helping the families got her involved with the WVS – the Women's Voluntary Service – because they ran clothes banks and places to obtain extra bedding and so on. Kate had always greatly admired that stalwart band of women who had shown such courage in the Blitz and also provided canteen facilities for the Home Guard and for wounded soldiers at railway stations and control centres. It was one of those women who got the three girls knitting at last.

With the raids well and truly over, they began to knit in earnest. The people's need was great and it was the sight of the poor bemused children with barely enough adequate clothes that tore at Kate's heart, especially as the weather got colder. At first, though, she did as the others did, knitting squares to sew together for blankets. The WVS were very good at getting hold of wool, and on the nights they had no plans to go out, Susie might come round and the three of them would sit listening to a play or music or chatting and the only other sound was the clicking of the needles. They were very industrious, turning out jumpers and cardigans and later balaclavas for boys and knitted bonnets for girls, and Kate and Susie also knitted socks for their men.

'For the first time, I was able to tell Mammy what I've been doing, as long as I don't mention specific places or anything,' Kate said one night as they sat before the fire. 'She said it sounds good and valuable work.'

'Does she know that I am doing the same thing?' Sally asked.

'Well, I tell her,' Kate said.

'And did she comment?'

Kate shook her head slowly and Sally said, 'I wonder if I am really dead to her. I know she said that I was, that I wasn't her daughter and all that, but I wonder if she ever thinks of me, even without meaning to...'

'Well, I've never had kids,' Susie said. 'But I'm sure if I had, then I couldn't just throw them over.'

'I think Mammy is able to put things out of her mind if they are not straight in front of her,' Kate said. 'I mean, she knows I'm married to David and she knows he is in the RAF and I tell her what he has been doing, I mean as far as I can, and when he has leave I tell her all about it and what we've done, you know, films we've seen and things like that. But she never adds as much as the odd comment. In fact, she never mentions him at all, just as if he doesn't exist.'

'And you think that's what she thinks of me?' Sally said, her voice thick with unshed tears and her eyes very bright. 'In her mind, I just don't exist?'

'I don't know,' Kate said gently. 'It's just that I got to thinking about it after the way she ignores any reference to David. But,' she went on to Sally, 'Mammy wouldn't know you from the wee girl who came over here first. You are a grand girl now, and a very mature one, and all the experiences you've had to deal with, even the loss of Phil, has shaped you into the person you are now. I would be proud to have you as my daughter, and it's Mammy's loss that she is not willing to see this herself.'

'It often doesn't feel like Mammy's loss,' Sally said in a small voice. 'It feels like mine.'

'Ah, Sally,' Susie said. 'It is very sad, but I agree with every word that Kate said about you. Would it be any good you trying to contact your father?'

It was Kate who answered: 'There would be no way that Daddy could get a letter that Mammy didn't know about – and he'd hardly go against her, not in something like this. Anyway, I doubt he has ever written a letter in all his life. I mean, he can write, but he doesn't. He leaves all of that kind of thing to Mammy.'

'Yeah,' Susie said, 'I suppose Dad does the same. I mean, it's Mom who writes to Martin and Derek, and from what I know of men, they seem to agree to a lot of things for a quiet life.'

'So there you have it,' Kate said. 'Now, would anyone say no to a cup of tea?'

Kate was upset that Sally was still so distressed by her mother's rejection.

'Well, I don't think that it's something you ever really get over,' Susie said when Kate said this on the tram on the way to work the next morning. 'It probably rankles inside all the time and then comes to the fore every so often.'

'Yeah,' Kate said, 'I think you're right, and I think I will really have to go over and plead her case in person. Point is, though, this is not a good time to cross the Irish Sea. I think I may wait for a while.'

'Anyway, the men will be home again before we know it,' Susie reminded her.

'I know,' Kate said. 'They'll be here in just over a fortnight.'

'Pity they couldn't come for Christmas again,' Susie said. 'And this year there's no Martin either. God knows where he is, but in his last letter he said that he is sweating like a pig most of the time.'

'Lucky devil,' Kate said, wiping the tram window with her gloved hand. There was little to see, as it was almost as black as night, but Kate knew it was cold. It was the sort of damp, clammy cold that set fingers and toes tingling after a few minutes, and if she should try to speak, the cold would catch in her throat and whispery trails would seep from her mouth.

'Dad said Martin should watch what he's writing down.'

'What about Derek?'

'He gives no hint,' Susie said. 'Course, he writes more to Gillian, but he can't tell her much either. She hasn't seen him in absolutely ages. I do feel sorry for her. We are lucky to see ours so often.'

'I know,' Kate said. 'They'll be here on Friday evening and we'll have two full days because they haven't got to report back until midday on Monday, 8 December. Hey, come on,' she said, leaping to her feet, 'this is our stop and we'll go sailing past the factory if we're not careful.'

It was truly lovely having David home, though the weather was filthy. Saturday morning there was a light drizzle falling, and that turned to a downpour by the afternoon. Kate watched the drops of rain bouncing on the pavement and said, 'I think we will have to postpone our trip to the Bull Ring. There's no pleasure going on a day like this. Are you very disappointed?'

David was sitting on the settee and didn't speak, but he smiled the smile that made Kate feel weak at the knees and, stretching out one arm, he pulled her on to the seat beside him. As they snuggled together, he said, 'This is what I enjoy. Letters are not the same – though don't you ever stop writing them because they often make me laugh and they make being away from you just about bearable – but there is no substitute for the real thing; and at the moment my happiness is nearly complete.'

'Nearly complete.'

David drew Kate closer and, when their lips met, Kate felt as if there was liquid gold running through her veins. 'Let's go to bed,' David whispered in her ear.

'Sally might be back at any time,' Kate said. 'You know she's only gone to see her friend.'

'So what if she does come back?' David said. 'She's no longer a child. She will know better than to disturb us if we are in bed with the door shut.'

'She might guess what we are doing.'

David gave a chuckle. 'I should imagine that she will have a very good idea.'

'Yes, well...'

'Well what?' David said, and for a second he watched Kate as she bit her lip in consternation. Then he got to his feet and pulled her up beside him. 'I need my wife beside me in bed now,' he said with a grin. 'And,' he added, 'I will stand no nonsense.'

Kate's eyes met David's. She knew that she could deny him no longer, especially when her own body was trembling in delicious anticipation, and she gave a nod and took David's hand in hers.

Sunday was as bad as Saturday, but Kate and David had been asked up to Sunday dinner with the Masons. Mary seemed to be able to work magic with the rations, and after a mouth-watering rabbit casserole, they had something she called Norfolk pudding, which was like a rice pudding with currants, sultanas and candied peel, and nutmeg sprinkled on the top. It was delicious.

After the meal had been cleared away, they decided to play cards and Susie put the wireless on low because there was dance music on. They played pontoon and then whist and, were just starting on rummy when David suddenly said, 'Ssh,' and turned the volume up on the wireless. The programme had been interrupted with a newsflash, and so they learnt of the Japanese attack on the American fleet anchored in Pearl Harbor.

'God!' Frank said. 'America will have to be pulled in now.'

'What's Japan done that for anyway?' Nick said. 'I thought they were at war with China.'

'Maybe they are,' Frank said. 'But, whichever way you look at it, that was a bloody aggressive, unprovoked act. Just think how many poor servicemen will have lost their lives. America must answer that, and really the only answer is war.'

'Good job we are going back tomorrow,' David said. 'If we weren't, we might have been recalled anyway.'

'Why?' Kate cried. 'This isn't our war. It's America's.'

'The Japanese will be making for Singapore.'

'Well, if they do, they won't find that easy to take,' Frank said confidently. 'Singapore is impregnable.'

'It could just be that it will be our job to see that Singapore stays that way,' David said and then, seeing the look on Kate's face, he went on: 'Course, our squadron might not be involved at all, but they are going to need air cover from somewhere. That really goes without saying.'

The words hung in the air and suddenly Kate wanted to be at home, within her own four walls, and have her husband to herself for the few hours he had left, but of course they couldn't just leave like that and anyway David didn't seem to feel the same urgency as she did. Susie knew how she felt, though, and Kate saw from her eyes that she was apprehensive and unnerved too, but she gave an almost imperceptible shrug as David dealt out the cards for rummy.

The wireless remained on and their card game was punctuated by newsflashes, each one worse than the one before. Then came a report that shocked them to the core: of an aerial attack on Singapore that had begun just a little while after the assault on Pearl Harbor had started. The cards were left on the table as they all listened avidly to the reports of the continual bombardment that in the end took out nearly all Singapore's frontline planes. 'The armies will have no aerial support,' Nick said, aghast.

'Yes, and that could be a bloody disaster,' David said. Kate saw the shock on his face.

Kate and David left soon after that, snuggling together for the cold had intensified as the dusk deepened and the rain fell like sleet. They were glad to get in. Sally was sitting in front of a very welcoming fire, reading a book, and had no idea about any of the new developments. They soon told her what had happened. 'And this place

Singapore is very important then?' Sally said. 'To me it sounds sort of exotic and far too far away for us to worry much about it.'

'Oh, it's important all right,' David said. 'Far too important to fall into Japanese hands. But they have a large army there, and according to the papers a squadron of warships are stationed there too, so they should be able to repulse the Japanese.'

Everyone at the factory was talking about the attack on Pearl Harbor, but most viewed it in a different light to Kate. 'America won't be able to wriggle out of this one,' one of the women declared.

'Yeah,' said another. 'They'll be in now, and about bloody time.'

'Mind you, I haven't much time for Germans,' the first woman said. 'But I'd rather have one any day than a bloody Nip.'

There was a murmur of agreement. 'No,' said the same woman, 'I don't trust those slit-eyed buggers.'

'No, nor me.'

The supervisor came in then, clapping her hands. 'Come along, girls,' she said. 'I know that you're discussing the events of yesterday, but nothing you say will change the outcome one iota. I am quite sure if Churchill says Singapore is too well defended to fall, then we must believe him. Meanwhile, time is money.'

The girls, grumbling a little, followed her on to the factory floor and Kate hoped the supervisor was right. What Sally had said to David the previous day had been true; if anyone had mentioned Singapore to her before yesterday she would have thought it was some tropical island that couldn't possibly have anything to do with the war they were fighting with Germany.

However, the Battle for Singapore went on and a letter came from David just before that dismal, anxiety-ridden Christmas. It was short and to the point.

Darling Kate,
It is as I feared. It is hell here but I am safe so far.
With all my love as always – David.

Susie got a similar brief missive and Kate said, 'You know what David means when he wrote that it was as he feared – those two are in the thick of all this.'

'I know,' Susie cried. 'And we can do nothing.'

'No,' Kate said, 'nothing but wait, and that is the hardest thing in the world to do.'

It was really difficult to engender any Christmas cheer that year and everyone was tuned in to the news as the Allies fought for their lives. In a way, Kate was glad when the festivities were over and she could get back to work. It didn't help that tales were seeping out about the shocking brutality of the Japanese, who were reported to be taking no prisoners, but killing all before them as they pushed forward with a speed that was breathtaking.

The Allies fought long and hard all through January and into February, but in the end they were forced to surrender unconditionally on 15

February. The papers estimated that one hundred thousand Allied soldiers were captured there in Singapore.

The news was as bad as it could be and there was still no word from the men. It wasn't just David and Nick who were silent: Gillian hadn't heard from Derek for three weeks, and it had been longer than that since Mary and Frank had heard from Martin. It was hard for all of them without letters to sustain them and, during this time, Kate found Sally a tower of strength. It wasn't anything she did specially, it was just that she was there; Kate was so glad during that time that she wasn't returning to an empty house.

Eventually, in early March, Susie received a letter from Nick. She was so glad that she ripped it open and scanned it before she left the house because he wrote that he was in a military hospital in a place called Poona, in Ceylon. He had been injured but he was on the mend and awaiting a military hospital ship to take him home. But then he went on to say that David had not been so lucky.

The fighting was fierce and these Japanese Zeros were all around us – above us, below us, to the sides of us – and we were dodging and diving and turning and using our machine-guns at the same time and suddenly I saw David hit and hit again and again. His Spit went into a spin and flames were coming from the cockpit and he bailed out and then this Jap fighter shot him to bits as he dropped through the air.

I got the bastard, but in doing so I left myself open and that's how I was injured, but I managed to reach

Jakarta where I was picked up later. There has been such mayhem that it has taken the authorities some time to ascertain who has survived, who is missing and who has been killed, but whatever the official lines they use for David's telegram, he doesn't stand a chance of still being alive, for even if he was alive when he landed, they would have hunted him down and picked him off. He was the best mate a man could have and there will never be another like him and I'm not ashamed to say I have cried like a baby. But I know I must go on and live my life without him and so must Kate. Be strong for her, my darling, Susie.

All my love – Nick

There were tears in Susie's eyes when she finished the letter: tears for Nick who had lost a dear friend and tears for Kate who had lost her husband. But she had to brush her tears away, glad that the mornings were still dark at that hour because Kate could be eagle-eyed at times. And though she longed to share the good news that Nick was alive she decided she would not mention a word of it to Kate.

It was the following morning when the supervisor indicated that Kate was wanted in the office. Susie bit her lip in consternation as she watched her friend walk across the factory and then she hesitated for just a moment before turning off her own machine and following her. She was aware of all the girls' eyes on her, because no one left their machine unless asked to do so, but she took no notice of their stares. Outside the office door, again she hesitated for just a moment before opening it and sliding inside. The boss glanced across at her and he frowned a little but his attention was on Kate, who stood in front of the desk as he lifted something from it and held it out to her, saying, 'I'm so very sorry, my dear, but this telegram was delivered here by a neighbour of yours this morning.'

Kate took it from the boss with fingers that trembled and ripped it open. Then Susie heard her dear friend give such an anguished cry that she felt a pain pierce her own heart and leapt forward as she saw Kate sway, catching her body before it reached the floor.

Kate had no recollection of getting home, or sending for Sally, but somehow she had reached her own sitting room; her sister and friend looking at her with concerned eyes. She was aware that they were speaking to her, but their voices were muted and muffled, as if they came from a long way off, and they made no impact on Kate, who just had one thought hammering in her head: the one that said David was dead. Never again would she see the smile that used to spread all over his face and light up his eyes, or hear the timbre of his voice, or his infectious hearty chuckle. She would never again feel his arms around her either, or his lips on hers, his hands caressing her body as they made love together, and she felt the pang of loss pierce her heart so that she cried out against it. Susie put her arms around her. 'Let it out, Kate,' she advised. 'You'll feel better.'

Kate shook her head, for nothing would make her feel better. How could it, because everything was over for her? Such a brief marriage she had

had with a wonderful man. She groaned aloud. Sally, the other side of her on the settee, caught hold of her hands and there were tears in her own eyes at the sight of the anguish on her sister's. Sally remembered the deep sorrow she had felt when she'd learned that Phil had died; it was a sorrow that was so intense she had wanted to follow him to the grave, and she said, 'I do know what you are going through. I fully understand.'

Kate's empty eyes sought her sister's. What was she talking about? No one could possibly understand this intense pain that was spreading all through her body, and the stabbing ache in her heart that was shattered into a million pieces. She cried out against it, a primeval howl of deep distress. Eventually, the sobs came, the first tears that Kate had shed.

At first, Sally and Susie were pleased, for the lack of tears had worried them, and they put their arms around Kate on each side of her and tried to hold her close. But Kate's threshing arms fought them off and they sat helpless beside her as sobs racked her whole body and tears cascaded down her face.

The heart-rending sobs went on and on and eventually Susie could stand it no longer. She tried again to put her arms around Kate, and this time it was as if Kate had lost the strength to resist and she sagged against Susie with a sigh. She continued to sob, however, and the sobs were from deep within her. 'Doctor,' Susie mouthed at Sally, who nodded and slipped out of the door.

Dr Butler was very distressed to hear of Kate's collapse and the reason for it and he was glad that he was able to go straight and see her. Meanwhile, Susie, knowing nothing she said would have made any difference, didn't even try to speak to her, but just rocked her gently as if she was a small child.

By the time the doctor came, Kate was calm, but she had cried for so long that now and again a sob escaped from her. She didn't seem the least bit pleased to see him either. 'Hallo, Kate,' he said gently. 'I am so sorry about your husband.'

Kate's dull, pain-filled eyes narrowed slightly as she looked at the doctor. 'Are you?' she said, her voice rasping in her sore and swollen throat. 'Why have you come?'

'Your sister asked me to,' the doctor said. 'She was concerned about you.'

Her eyes slid across to Sally but it was the doctor she spoke to. 'Can you bring David back to stand before me this minute because that is the only medicine I want.'

The doctor shook his head sadly. 'You know I cannot do that, my dear.'

'Then you may as well go.'

'No, I don't think so,' Dr Butler said. He had dealt with more grieving widows than he cared to think about since the war had begun, and the world for them was often a cold and worrying place. But they had to go on with it as best they could, and he had found a no-nonsense approach was best. 'You have had the worst news that anyone can receive,' he said. 'And you must deal with it. While everyone else may be sad that David is dead and desperately sorry for you, no one can share the pain in your heart. Isn't that

405

the case?'

Kate nodded dumbly.

'So sometimes it is all too much to bear and a sedative might–'

'I need no sedative.'

'It really would help you, Kate,' the doctor said.

Sally knelt on the floor in front of her sister and, holding her hands tight, she looked deeply into her eyes and said, 'I know the pain and sense of loss is almost unbearable, so let the doctor try and help you, Kate; if only for my sake, because I am heartbroken to see you like this.'

Kate saw the tears brimming behind Sally's eyes and the huskiness in her voice as she tried to prevent them falling and she nodded briefly. Even that movement hurt her. Everything hurt her as if all her nerve endings were exposed. Sally was right: the intense heartache was unbearable and she needed to get away from it even for a short time. Sally hid her sigh of relief as she watched Kate take the tablets.

And then, when the doctor had left, Sally and Susie helped Kate into bed. She didn't protest because she was feeling pleasantly muzzy and more tired than she'd realized and the two girls watched as Kate sank into blessed oblivion. 'Thank God,' Sally said as they tiptoed from the room. 'For a little time, anyway, she will have some rest.'

'I just don't know how I would be if I lost Nick,' Susie said with a shiver. 'I don't think I could bear it.'

'You could, you know, in time,' Sally said. 'Because there is nothing else to do.'

406

'I suppose but–'

'It feels like the end of the world,' Sally said candidly. 'And at first you can't see any way of going on, even any reason you want to. But then you realize that you can do nothing to change the situation and make things better and you just have to come to terms with it.'

'You are incredibly mature for your age,' Susie said in admiration.

'Well, I have suffered loss, haven't I?' Sally said. 'I have been in that loathsome black place that Kate's in now. But I'll tell you something: before David left this last time, he told her that if anything happened to him then he didn't want her to go into decline. I'm not saying he had a premonition or anything, but I'd say, with the news about Singapore, he would be fairly certain that he would soon be on active service and so he sort of prepared her.'

'Can you ever be prepared for news like that?'

'No,' Sally said. 'Course you can't, not really. It's the news that no one wants to hear. And yet maybe when she is getting over the shock of this a bit, it might help if I remind her what David said. But I will have to see how she is coping with everything first. I just think it's so terribly sad. I suppose I didn't know David all that long, but I really liked him and he and Kate were so happy. Phil thought him a great man, too, and they got on well together. David was upset to hear Phil had died and upset for me too.' She sighed and went on: 'Makes you wonder if there will be any young men left when this war finally grinds to a halt.'

'Yeah,' Susie said. 'I know Mom and Dad are

constantly worried about Derek and Martin, and Nick now as well, and they will be devastated to hear about David, because they thought a lot of him.'

'What about his parents?'

'I know, I've been thinking about them,' Sally said. 'Kate didn't like them and they certainly had little time for David when he was alive.'

'Might be different now he's dead,' Susie said. 'Because people are like that. But still, whatever kind of parents they are, or were, they have a right to know.'

'I know,' Sally said, 'and I don't relish telling them.'

'Oh, no,' Susie said. 'I don't think that we have to do that.'

'Well, someone has to.'

'What if I ask Father Trelawney from St Margaret Mary's to go?' Susie said. 'I know David's family are not Catholics, but Kate was, though she is a bit of a wooden one at the moment – and anyway, priests are trained in that sort of thing.'

Sally nodded. She knew that. 'It would be great if he would,' she said. 'And for all Kate hasn't been going to Mass and that, I bet she'll want a Memorial Mass said for David.'

'Yes, I think she will as well,' Susie said. 'It's all that she will have to mark his passing because, like with your Phil, there will be no grave.'

'I know,' Sally said. 'A funeral sort of closes everything and you can visit and tend a grave – and to some anyway it does bring comfort.' She paused and then went on: 'I visit Ruby's sometimes. I always feel closer to Phil there.'

'I never knew that.'

'No reason why you should,' Sally said, shortly. 'But don't you start feeling sorry for me 'cos it's Kate we have got to be concerned with now. And there is another needs to be told too, and that's Mammy.'

'Yes, of course.'

'And I don't think that Kate will be up to writing for some time,' Sally said. 'So I will write and tell her, but you will have to address the envelope, because if I do she will recognize the handwriting and might throw the letter away unread.'

'Do you think she would after all this time?'

Sally shrugged. 'How do I know?' she said. 'But I imagine that she has done that with the others. She has never answered them, anyway, and I can't risk her not reading the letter telling her of David's death.'

'Yeah, I do see what you mean,' Susie said. 'And I should get that done as soon as you can, certainly before the sedative wears off. I'll go round and see if I can catch Father Trelawney now, if you like?'

'Good idea,' Sally said. 'And David's mother might be able to go round straight away; I don't think she has a job. And I suppose that it is important they are told before the news filters through to them in some other way. And,' she added, 'I must go in and have a word with Phoebe Jenkins next door. She would be the one that took the telegram to the factory. She'll know what news a telegram brings these days, so she'll like to know it all. The thing is, though, the telegram just said "missing presumed dead", so is there a chance that David might have survived?'

Susie shook her head. 'Not a snowball's chance in Hell,' she said. 'I had a letter from Nick the other day that I never told Kate about. Here,' she said, withdrawing it from her bag. 'Read it for yourself.'

Sally took it and, as she returned it to Susie, she said, 'I hope David's wounds were too severe and he died of them.'

'So do I,' Susie said. 'When you are dealing with such a barbaric nation, in a situation like this I think being dead is the best outcome all round.'

TWENTY-THREE

Kate awoke from her drugged sleep some hours later. Her head still felt as if it was filled with cotton wool, but the memories began pushing through the muzziness into her brain and she groaned and closed her eyes again. But then she became aware of voices downstairs. She was still feeling decidedly odd, but thought she should at least get up and see who it was; but when she got out of bed, she had to hold on to the bedpost until the room stopped spinning. Then she cautiously crossed the room and opened the door as Dora Burton's strident voice floated up the stairs. 'I'd never have known where they were living if that girl hadn't told the priest. Fine kettle of fish I call that. Your own son just lives a couple of miles away and you have no idea where.'

But she wouldn't, Kate thought, because David hadn't been near them since they had moved into the house, and when she'd suggested it, he said he wasn't wasting his precious leave visiting people who had shown him plainly they didn't give a tuppenny damn about him. She reached the bottom of the stairs and through the open door saw Dora's eyes raking the room and her mouth turned down in discontent as she went on, 'Mind you, they've done all right for themselves, haven't they? Fine house like this and everything. They were living in a flat.'

411

'I had the house first,' Sally said. 'It was my fiancé's mother's and I lived with her as company when my fiancé was called up. When she died I asked Kate to share with me, because she is my sister, you see.'

'Oh, yes, the first time Kate came to our house she told us about you coming to join her in Birmingham,' Dora told her, and her eyes roved over the room again before saying: 'Still, you got to admit, however it was done, they proper fell on their feet with this place, didn't they?' Dora didn't look a bit pleased about it.

'Yes,' said Sally, a bit irritated that the woman seemed more interested in the house Kate lived in than in any details about the death of her son, and neither of them seemed exactly grief-stricken. But then, she reminded herself, people sometimes act strangely when they are told bad news. It is often the only way they know to deal with it, and so she said gently, 'I'm sure that you were very upset to hear of your son's death?'

'Well, course I was,' Dora answered in quite an aggressive manner. 'What d'you think? We both were. We're here, ain't we? They got Alf out of work, d'aint they?' she demanded of her husband.

'Yeah, they was very nice about it when they heard, like.'

'Any road, we've come to see Kate, our David's wife.'

'The doctor sedated her,' Sally said. 'Shall we have a cup of tea and then I'll see if Kate wants to get up?'

'Well, I don't know,' Dora said. 'We ain't got all

412

day, you know.'

'It's all right,' Kate said from the doorway, pushing the door wide. 'I'm still a bit woozy, but I am up.'

Sally helped her to an armchair where she faced Dora and Alf sitting on the settee then went to make tea. Alf said, 'We were right sorry to hear about our David.'

Were you? was on the tip of Kate's tongue but she knew no purpose would be gained by annoying David's parents – and anyway, Dora was already saying, 'Singapore, that girl told the priest: that's where he copped it. Don't know why we had to bother with those foreign parts anyway. I thought we was fighting Germany and I would have thought that was enough to be going on with just now without taking on a load of Nips as well.'

Sally couldn't blame Dora for feeling that way because she had thought that way herself initially, but talk like this was hardly helpful to Kate who looked so anguished and upset. David's parents, though, seemed intent on discussing anything but David's death. 'We ain't taking on a load of Nips,' Alf said.

'We are,' Dora contradicted. 'That's what lives in Singapore, ain't it?'

'Dora, I explained all this to you.'

Kate looked from one to the other as if she couldn't believe her ears. She felt a roaring in her head and a sense of despair filling her whole body.

'Does any of this matter?' she burst in roughly, her voice husky in her distress. 'It doesn't matter whether he was killed over Germany, Singapore or bloody Timbuktu, the fact is he is dead and none of us will ever see him again, and I am finding that extremely hard to cope with.'

She tried to prevent the tears falling, but they seeped from beneath her lashes and trickled down her cheeks. Alf coughed nervously and said, 'Here, don't take on, old girl.'

'It isn't something I have that much control over,' Kate said through gritted teeth, grateful to Sally who came in then with tea for them all. Dora took a sip of the tea and said patronizingly to Sally, 'You make a good cup of tea, I will say. You will probably make someone a fine wife one day.'

'I doubt it,' Sally said. 'My fiancé never left the beaches of Dunkirk.'

There was silence for a few minutes and then Dora gave a nervous little laugh and said to Sally, 'Yes, but you're still young and–'

'Don't even say that I will find somebody else,' Sally snapped. 'Because I don't want anyone else, and anyway, you are not here to discuss me, but the death of your son.'

'Sally!'

'I'm sorry, Kate,' Sally said. 'It's just how I feel at the moment.'

'Sally is right in a way,' Kate said. 'There are things to talk about. I know there will be no funeral for David, but I want him to have a Commemorative Mass and it doesn't matter a jot that he isn't a Catholic. Have you any objection to that?'

'Well, we ain't churchgoers, as you know,' Alf

said. 'So it don't matter one way or the other.'

'Have we got to come, like?' Dora asked.

'That's entirely up to you,' Kate said. 'I want to do this to say a ... say a...' She swallowed the painful lump in her throat and went on: 'To say a sort of proper goodbye to David.'

'Right,' Alf said. 'Well, we'll see how we are fixed when we know the date and all.'

Kate sighed. 'And Lawrence,' she said. 'Would he like to pay his last respects, d'you think?'

'Oh, he might well,' Dora said angrily. 'But the decisions aren't his to make any more.'

'Why?'

'Because he's been bloody conscripted,' Dora spat out. 'Some bloody busybody made it their business to report him, saying that women are doing his job all over the factory so why was he sitting pretty here when others were risking their lives. And apparently she went on to say that she'd never known him to have a bad chest before. Next thing we know, he had another medical, and then is sent to some training camp somewhere and he's still there.'

'I would have said that that busybody was right,' Sally said with spirit. 'Every man is needed and the fact that I have lost my fiancé and Kate her husband means they need more men, not fewer.'

'You have a lot to say for yourself,' Dora said, getting to her feet. 'And none of it welcome. Come along, Alf.'

Kate had no intention of apologizing for her sister or even trying to smooth down ruffled feathers, so she just said, 'I'll be in touch about

415

the Mass.'

'Yeah,' Dora snapped, still affronted by Sally's words. 'Like Alf said, we'll have to see how we are fixed.'

Sally led the way down the corridor to the front door and when she returned to the room it was to see Kate still sitting in the chair. She said to Sally, 'Did you see the outrage on that woman's face?' Then she began to smile and then laugh as she said, 'Doubt we will see either of them again.'

'That will be no loss then.'

'No,' said Kate, and her laughter rose higher and higher. Sally wasn't at all surprised when that hysteria turned to tears and she clung to Kate and they both cried out their deep sorrow and unhappiness.

The Masons called that evening, shocked by the news but so supportive of Kate. She found it was not a bit stressful like it had been with David's parents. She knew how much they thought of David and they spoke about the things he had done and said and Susie recalled the places they had gone to and the fun they'd had, and if they shed tears it didn't matter. Once, Mary put her hand over Kate's and said, 'We're not distressing you, my dear, are we, talking this way?'

'You could never distress me,' Kate said. 'I like talking about David. I would never like him forgotten. Anyway,' she went on, kissing Mary on the cheek, 'you're like family to me, and I know David thought of you that way too, for he greatly admired you.'

'Admired us?' Mary repeated. 'Oh, no, my dear,

the admiration is all the other way. That young man was a hero, as Sally's Phil was. We owe them all a debt and I am so sorry that David's life was cut so short.'

'And I,' Kate said. 'And I wish I had his child so I would have something of his now.'

'It might be very difficult to bring up a child by yourself.'

'That wouldn't matter,' Kate said. 'Anyway, do you think I would be on my own? Any child I had would have a doting Aunt Sally, not to mention Susie and you two and two honorary uncles in Martin and Derek.'

She had used these arguments with David when she had pleaded with him to make her pregnant. 'I just long to carry your child,' she'd told him.

'And so you shall, you darling girl, when this war is fought and won and I am at home again. We will bring our child up in a world of peace.'

'But I'm not allowed to practise birth control. So how are you stopping...'

David had put a finger over her lips. 'You needn't concern yourself with how,' he said. 'If you know nothing about it, then it can't be a sin for you. Let me deal with that side of things.'

And he had, very effectively. She sighed. Susie heard the sigh and said, 'Are we tiring you?'

'No,' Kate said, and then added more honestly, 'I am tired but I don't want you to go.'

'I'm really glad you have Sally,' Susie said, but as she went to put her arm around Kate, she moved away. 'Sorry, Susie,' she said. 'I can only hold it together if I'm not given too much sympathy. Then I start blubbing.'

'That's all right.'

'Not for me, it isn't,' Kate said. 'Anyway, I intend to return to work on Monday and the warden post the following week.'

'Oh, come on, Kate. Give yourself more time than that.'

'To do what?' Kate said. 'Look at the four walls?' She shook her head and said, 'No, I am better off at work – and anyway, this is what David would have wanted me to do. He even spoke about it on his last leave.'

Susie remembered the conversation she had had with Sally on that very subject, but still she said, 'You don't think you might be doing a bit too much too soon?'

'No,' Kate said. 'It won't make me miss David any less, but I will feel that I am doing something useful – and that's important to me, because I don't ever want to feel that David died in vain. We have got to win.'

The following day, Kate went to arrange the special Mass for David. Sally offered to go with her but it was something Kate wanted to do, needed to do. She was surprised as she walked how many neighbours spoke to her and offered their condolences. She wondered how they had all got to know so quickly, but then she remembered Phoebe Jenkins who had been round the previous evening. She'd already been a great help and possessed a good deal of common sense; she commiserated with Kate, knowing what she was going through, and assured her that if she needed any help she just lived next door. She must have spread the word, and, with a small smile, Kate remembered her father once saying there were three ways of passing messages quickly: 'Telephone, telegraph and tell a woman.'

She didn't mind Phoebe telling their neighbours, and in fact their good wishes helped dispel some of the apprehension she felt in talking to a priest, because the last time she had spoken to one she had been very angry. But she needn't have worried, and was pleasantly surprised at Father Trelawney's attitude. She had never spoken to him before, although he had officiated at Derek's wedding and later at Susie's, but that Friday morning she found him such a nice, understanding man. She told him everything, just as it was, and he patted her agitated hands and said that in wartime things like that happened and never once made her feel as though she had been living in sin with the man she was arranging a Commemorative Mass for. He did ask her if she wanted to make a good confession, and suddenly Kate did, because it meant that she could take communion at the Mass and that was important to her. Father Trelawney didn't even appear to get embarrassed when she cried in the recounting of things she had done.

She returned to work on Monday and even Mrs Higgins the supervisor and Mr Tanner expressed their regret. Susie had told them all what had happened on the factory floor and they were all supportive of Kate and noticed that while she did her work well enough she often seemed miles away, and was thinner and paler than ever. They all understood this because she wasn't the only one there that had lost a loved one and they knew it was just time that could help. Many at the warden post were surprised how composed Kate appeared and how she had returned to her work in the hostel almost eagerly.

Sally knew that was because she was concerned for the often destitute families she dealt with, and knew the help she often gave to them was invaluable. She felt needed, but that was her public face. Privately, she wasn't always as composed as she appeared. Since David's death, Kate ate less than a bird and cried more easily, though Sally sensed she was embarrassed by this and tried to wait until she was alone. Sally would hear her, though, crying in her bed most nights, for all she tried to muffle her tears in the pillow. She never went in, though she often longed to, for she knew Kate wouldn't want that.

On Saturday, 20 March, David's Commemorative Mass was held in St Margaret Mary's Church, which was packed. The Masons came, some RAF chaps who had been friends of David's, work colleagues of Kate's, and neighbours, including Phoebe Jenkins and even John and Rita Taylor, as Sally and Susie had gone to tell them what had happened. The priest was astounded at the turnout. 'He must have been a very popular man,' he said to Susie in the porch. 'One that will be sadly missed.'

'Oh, he will be missed all right,' Susie said. 'It's hard for me to think I will never see him again. Kate is bearing up very well, but inside she is still suffering. You can see it in her eyes. As for being popular, a person would be hard to please all right if they didn't like David, yet his own parents didn't seem to have any time for him. They have not come today, though Kate told them the date and the time. They love only David's elder brother Lawrence.'

'Do they attend any other church?' Father Trelawney asked. 'Kate told me David didn't.'

'No,' Susie said. 'That's not it, Father. Most of these filling the pews today don't go to church on any sort of a regular basis. They are here today to support Kate. David's parents obviously could not be bothered.'

'Families,' the priest said. 'A long time ago I decided I wasn't even going to try and understand them. Shall we go in now?'

Father Trelawney stopped on the way down the aisle and asked Kate if she was all right. She answered him with a tremulous smile and said that she was fine, but thanked him for asking. Sally knew that Kate liked the priest. She was glad, for it might mean that she would go back to church. She would be relieved if she did for Sally was still worried about her sister's immortal soul.

But thinking of immortal souls brought her mother to mind, and the reply she had received from her just the other day. She had been so excited when she had seen a letter in her mother's hand addressed to her on the mat as she came down ready for work. She was, however, apprehensive about what her mother might say and she knew that she needed to open it when she was alone, so she had slipped it into her pocket without a word to Kate about it.

At dinner time that day, Sally escaped to the washroom, and in one of the cubicles she opened the letter from her mother. Philomena thanked Sally for writing and letting her know about the tragedy of David's death and said she hoped that she was being a support to her sister. She said she would write to Kate and it would do them both good to go home to Ireland for a good rest. Sally's heart leapt at that because she said *both of them:* that must mean that she was partly forgiven. She clutched the pages to her chest and closed her eyes. 'Oh, thank you, God,' she whispered, for she had prayed for her mother to forgive her over and over.

However, her mother's next sentence shocked her to the core and ensured that Kate would never be able to read this letter, for she said that though Kate was probably upset about this man she called her husband, when she was over it and more herself, she would probably see it as a blessing in disguise, since the man was a Protestant and mixed marriages never worked.

Sally held the letter in her hand a moment longer. She had waited many years for her mother to say she could go home again, and she would have liked to have kept that important letter and maybe read it again.

But then with a sigh she ripped it into little pieces and threw it down the toilet and flushed it away, in case Kate might see it and be upset.

TWENTY-FOUR

'Mammy asks me in every letter when I am going home,' Kate said to Susie a few months later as they climbed on the tram to go to work.

'Well, why don't you go?' Susie said. 'It would do you good. The bombing is over and done and you always said that you wouldn't go before because Sally wasn't invited, but you say she is now.'

'Yes,' Kate said. 'It happened after David died. She wrote to Mammy, you know.'

'Yes,' Susie said. 'I addressed the envelope.'

'Oh, so that's how she got Mammy to open it,' Kate said. 'I did wonder.'

'And she started the letter pleading with your mother to read it because it was about you.'

'Well, whatever she said, it worked,' Kate said. 'Mind, I don't think Sally would want to go home just now. She has her head turned with all these Americans flooding into the dance halls these days. She says she's glad she went to those dance classes. Mind you, the Americans have their own way of dancing.'

'Haven't they their own way of doing most things?'

'Yeah they have,' said Kate with a smile. 'But even Sally was a bit shocked. She says the boys shoot you through their legs and send you into a spin sometimes, held above their head so that your knickers are on show.'

'I say,' Susie said, and added with a laugh: 'Wouldn't do to forget to put them on one night.'

'Oh, I would say definitely not,' Kate said. 'I did ask her about it, but she said they are just having fun.'

'And let's face it, they've had little enough of that, these youngsters,' Susie said. 'And until the Americans landed, they were very badly off for partners.'

'Yeah, they were,' Kate agreed. 'Course, Sally wouldn't even have gone to dance classes, never mind proper dances, had I not nearly pushed her out of the house.'

'Because of Phil?'

'Yes, showing lack of respect or something,' Kate said. 'And then when we had news of David's death, she stopped going out again. She said that back in Ireland some have a year of mourning – and I remember that myself. I wonder if the one who died wanted people to do that. Neither Phil, nor David certainly, would have wanted Sally to stay in for weeks on end, and I told her that straight.'

'What about you and our weekly trips to the cinema? Is it too early for you?'

Kate shook her head. 'No, not really,' she said, though there was little enthusiasm in her voice. 'I would quite like to see *Dumbo* by Walt Disney if it is on anywhere. I know it's a bit daft wanting to see the story of an elephant at our age, but it's been out a while now and it seems everyone has seen it but us.'

Susie would have much preferred *Casablanca,* but she didn't say that because this was about getting Kate to start going out again and living without David, and so she said, 'Who says we're daft wanting to see a cartoon at our age? Maybe that's what we want in life, a bit of lightness and fun. I'll scour the paper tonight. I'm sure it will be on somewhere.' She scrutinized her friend's face then and said, 'You're sure now that this isn't going to be too hard for you. That it's a bit too soon?'

Kate shook her head. What she could have said was that the hardest thing for her was seeing Nick, who had come home to convalesce, when the hospital had finished with him, after David had been dead a month or so. He had come to see Kate straight away, as she had expected him to, and she was glad he'd come alone. He'd expressed his deep distress at the death of his oldest and dearest friend. 'Your loss must be a grievous one,' he'd said. 'For David was the best friend a man could have and there is not a day goes by when I don't miss him. For you it must be harder still.'

'I still miss him as much as I ever did,' Kate had admitted. 'I have it down to a bearable ache a lot of the time, but it is always there.' She had raised her face to Nick's and said plaintively, 'Sometimes the memories leap into my head and catch me unawares and I feel the emptiness that surrounds me now that he is gone.'

Nick had held her tight and they had cried together and she'd found it a relief to talk about David and mourn his passing with someone who didn't think that she should have got over his death. She knew there was no time limit on such things. Despite this, though, she had avoided the

Masons' until Nick had gone. She didn't resent the happiness and closeness between Nick and her good friend, but it was too painful to witness, so though they urged her to go out with them, or to come to the house for a meal, she always refused and they never pressed her.

'It's great to think that Nick won't be part of any more sorties, isn't it?' Susie said, jerking Kate back into the present.

She nodded dumbly, knowing that had David survived it would have been his last sortie too. Susie had told her that. When Nick's one week of convalescence was over, he didn't return to the Castle Bromwich airfield, but to one down south. That's all he could tell her because that was all he knew. As seasoned veterans, both he and David were due to be transferred to train other fighter pilots. 'D'you think David knew that?' Kate asked Susie.

'I very much doubt it,' Susie said. 'They didn't tell them anything in advance, did they? I suppose they were working on the assumption that, if they are captured, they can't tell what they don't know. Nick wasn't told until he was recovering in the hospital. I couldn't have been more pleased. He won't get home as often, of course, but he is slightly safer – though the southern airfields do get quite a pounding at times.'

'He can't tell you that surely?'

'No, course not, and I don't even know where he's stationed, anyway, but they write about the raids in the paper and it is on the wireless too.'

Kate so wished that David had returned in one piece and was now working alongside Nick in

426

some airfield somewhere, training others to take the risks they had taken often, but it would not help to share those thoughts. David's troubles were now over. He was at peace and she must concentrate on that, and so what she said was, 'Well, thank God, the raids are over for us at last.'

'Oh, yes, I can echo that,' Susie said. 'And it means we can go out and about without a worry. And there is summer to look forward to. Look at today – the sun shining from a blue sky and you could forget that there was a war on at all.'

'Until you start shopping,' Kate said, though she had to admit that the government introducing dried milk in the winter was a boon, because milk was rationed. Dried milk was nothing like the real thing, but meant that you could always get a cup of tea before you set out in the morning, particularly important if the weather was exceptionally cold or wet.

'And we have got dried egg in the shops now, courtesy of the Americans.'

'We have lots of things courtesy of the Americans,' Kate said a little gloomily. 'Namely, GIs with their silver tongues, reminiscent of people you only see on the cinema screen. Their uniforms are much smarter than our boys', they have more money, and gifts of nylons, chocolate and chewing gum are given to the chosen few. Do you know how they were described to me the other day by the grocer's wife?' And at Susie's shake of her head she went on: 'Overpaid, oversexed and over here – and I don't think she was far wrong.'

'Oh, cranky Kate,' Susie mocked gently. 'You are in the dumps and I definitely think that watching the antics of a flying elephant with overlarge ears is just what you need at this moment.' Kate knew Susie had a point: she was being a grump and it wasn't Susie's fault that David was dead and that she was feeling life was quite meaningless, and she knew she had to snap out of it.

They found out that the only cinema showing *Dumbo* was the Odeon in Sutton Coldfield, which meant a small tram ride to Erdington Village and then a Midland Red bus from there into the Royal Town. 'I've never been anywhere in Sutton, but the park,' Kate said to Susie.

'I went a few times to the cinema when I was younger,' Susie said. 'And one thing I do remember is that the bus stops just outside it and before the town itself, so we haven't a chance of getting lost or anything.'

It was just as Susie said, and the film was good, and Kate laughed as loudly as the rest; and though she got a bit weepy when Dumbo and his mother were separated, she had cheered up by the end. She got on the bus going home with a sigh of contentment. Even Susie, who had gone to see *Dumbo* under sufferance to please Kate, had been impressed by the film, which she had enjoyed very much, though even if she hadn't, it had been worth the trek to see a smile on Kate's face for once.

'Are you going out?' Kate said a few days later, seeing Sally getting dolled up. 'You don't usually go out on a Monday.'

'I know, but this girl at work is twenty-one, and she wants us all to go to the Palace with her.'

'The Palace?'

'You know the cinema in Erdington's High Street? Well, there's a ballroom above that.'

'Is there?' Kate said. 'I never knew that.'

'Ah, well, that shows you don't know everything,' Sally said with a grave shake of her head.

'Cheeky young whippersnapper,' Kate said, giving her younger sister a push. 'Let's have some respect for your elders for a change before you go off gallivanting.'

'You don't mind, do you?' Sally said.

'No, I don't mind,' Kate said. 'Why should I?'

'Thought you might be lonely or something.'

'Of course not,' Kate said. 'Go on, for goodness' sake. You can't let the poor girl down.'

'Huh,' said Sally, 'I'd say she's hoping a load of American soldiers will come. If they do, she won't care whether we're there or not.'

'Do many Americans go there then?'

'So people say. That's why she chose it,' Sally said. 'Apparently, they come down on the Midland Red bus. The same one you got to go to the pictures the other night. It runs from St George's Barracks in Sutton Coldfield into Erdington.'

'Well, have a good time then.'

'Oh, Kate, why don't you come with me?' Sally said, suddenly feeling a little guilty for leaving her sister on her own.

'Oh, no,' Kate said. 'I wouldn't feel right. Anyway, you young things don't want the likes of me there.'

'God, Kate,' Sally said with a laugh. 'Anyone would think that you are as old as Methuselah.'

Kate smiled. 'I feel a bit like it sometimes,' she

said. 'Don't forget, last month I was twenty-five.'

'Oh, shock horror,' Sally cried. 'What a great age.'

'It's a quarter of a century.'

'That's nothing. Come on? Shake a leg?'

'No, thanks love,' Kate said. 'I might pop over to Aston and have a look in at the rest centre and see if everyone is okay.'

'You're not on duty tonight,' Sally reminded her. 'You are like a mother hen with that place.'

'Maybe I am,' Kate conceded. 'But you know how I like to keep busy. Anyway, a lot of these Americans are too flashy and brash for me. You watch what you're doing with them too, Sally.'

'No need to worry about me, Kate,' Sally said. 'I like to have fun but I'm not an utter fool. I know what they want in return for presents of nylons and chocolate. They are here to fight a war and one day they will disappear. Some girls don't seem to realize that and some believe everything they say and everything they promise.'

'And you don't?'

'Not likely I don't.'

'And what if one of them catches your heart.'

'No chance of that.' Sally and her bantering tone was gone when she said, 'I once gave my heart to Phillip Reynard, and to part with it again it would have to be someone pretty special. There is no one that I will allow myself to have even a passing fancy for until this bloody war is over.'

'Oh, that is so sensible,' Kate said, and gave her a kiss. 'Now go on and enjoy yourself.'

'Are you sure you won't come?'

'Positive.'

When Sally had gone, though, suddenly Kate felt lonely. She had made no plans to go to Aston; she had just said that off the top of her head. She had no plans at all really. She knew she could go to the Masons', she'd always be welcome there. Then again, she didn't have to go out at all because she had a good book from the library and the wireless might have an entertaining play or concert. But she knew she was too restless to stay in and the night was a fine one. How pleasant to walk the streets when the air was not filled with smoke and cordite and gas and the summer night not ablaze with fires. She put on her short jacket, picked up her handbag and closed the door behind her.

She walked down Slade Road to Salford Bridge over the network of canals. She stopped for a while there and watched the brightly coloured canal boats wend their way through the water. The late summer sun even lent the torpid, oil-slicked water a sheen, so that the scene was pleasant looking and peaceful, but she knew that she was looking at it through rose-tinted glasses and with a sigh she left the canals. Then, thinking that as she was so close she would look in on the hostel anyway, she walked on towards Aston Park. There was a light on in the office in the hostel that was just off the entrance hall, and Kate popped her head around the door. 'Hallo, Kate,' Rita said, as she sat at the desk surrounded by papers. 'This is a nice surprise.'

'You're working late,' Kate said.

'Paperwork,' Rita said. 'You know what it's like with this flipping war, forms for this and forms

431

for that and not enough hours in the day and no peace at all. An hour in here in the evening is like four spent in the day when I am up and down and at everyone's beck and call.'

'Where's John?'

'Fixing a leaking bath,' Rita said. 'But he's no good with the paperwork anyway, and the times he has attempted it, I've had to do it again. Much more the practical type is John. Didn't know it was quite so late though,' she said, glancing at the clock. 'Nearly half nine look.'

'Didn't know it would take me so long to walk.'

'You walked,' Rita exclaimed. 'It's one hefty step from where you live.'

'I know. I'll probably take the tram back.'

'Did you come for anything special?'

'No,' Kate said. 'I was at a loose end and I thought I would pop in and see if you wanted anything.'

'Oh, I do,' Rita said. 'I am gasping for a cup of tea. Could you make one while I finish this sheet?'

'Yeah, course,' Kate said, and she went into the little kitchenette off the office and filled the kettle as John came in the door. She put the kettle on the gas ring, but the water hadn't boiled when the sounds of sirens were heard. They all stopped dead still for a moment, not sure what to do. 'Surely not,' John said. 'It's been a bloody year, for God's sake.'

'Maybe it's a false alarm,' said Kate, but the words weren't quite out of her mouth when the distinct drone of planes could be heard. 'God Almighty, this is no false alarm,' Rita cried. 'Turn that gas off, Kate, and help me and John get everyone into the cellars – and quick.'

There were over two thousand people in the hostel, counting the babies and children, and most were frightened and bemused. They poured from their rooms into the corridors, asking questions and needing answers, but there were no reassuring answers to give. 'They had already lost all before them, all they possessed,' they said. 'And now was it to start again?'

Rita, John and Kate shook their heads helplessly and urged speed. Easier said than done. Many of the elderly stumbled around crying and disorientated in bewilderment and dismay. Babies and young children were already asleep, and often wailing and fractious when woken, too sleepy to be helpful. The older children were little better and the mothers impatient, trying to help them with fingers made clumsy with fear.

The droning planes drew ever nearer and the first explosions could be heard, causing some to let out the odd shriek or yelp to rise above the general noise of the distressed and frightened people. Kate carried many babies and children down into the basement that night, and helped the elderly and the frail, trying to soothe the terribly anxious. She felt no fear for herself, just a smouldering anger.

The raid had been going on for about an hour when John went for a look around after a particularly loud explosion had shook the building. When he came back in he said to Kate, 'Freer Road has had it. Fair few casualties. Can you come?'

'Course I can come,' Kate said. 'I might be able

to treat some of the walking wounded.' And so saying she followed John up the cellar steps as the ack-ack guns began to bark into the dusky summer sky. 'Where were the bloody gunners till now?' John grumbled as they scurried along. 'Fast asleep?'

Kate, once more breathing in the smoke and the dust and feeling the acrid stink of explosives lodge in the back of her throat, said, 'You can hardly blame them. As you said, it has been a full year since there has been anything at all.'

'Yeah, well, let this be a lesson to us all,' John said grimly. 'We can't rest easy in our beds until this blasted war is over and done.'

Freer Road was in disarray. Piles of rubbish and masonry lay in heaps and mounds where there were once people's homes. Two ambulances were loading stretchers when she arrived, but other injured people were milling round, their stunned faces grey with brick dust. And to deal with all these people was one valiant Red Cross worker. 'I'm an ARP warden,' Kate said, 'but I was off duty tonight. I'm fully trained in first aid.' She saw relief pass over the nurse's face as she shrugged her arms helplessly and said, 'Do what you can.'

And Kate did what she could, which was mainly cleaning, dressing and bandaging wounds. It was some time later when she was directed to a specific mound. People pulled out of a collapsed cellar had been seated on the ground, next to a mound of masonry, all that was left of a terrace of houses, when the unstable stack suddenly began to cave in, burying the people who had been near to it.

She set to work immediately, as did many more, moving the debris to reach the trapped people beneath. She didn't notice the fractured roof beam balanced precariously on top of a pile of broken bricks, until it became dislodged as the rescuers toiled on. 'Watch out!' someone called to Kate, and she glanced up to see the beam heading straight for her. She tried to move but it was too late. It cracked on to the side of her head and she knew no more.

When Kate opened her heavy eyes she shut them again quickly because the brightness caused a pain to throb behind them. But the movement had been noted, and when she heard a voice call her name she forced open her eyelids again, squinting to see who it was. 'Where am I?'

'The General Hospital,' the owner of the voice said. 'You had an argument with a roof beam, according to the ambulance driver, and you came off worse.'

Kate remembered the raid and then helping the Red Cross nurse and then the buildings that had collapsed on the people and toiling to free them, but she couldn't remember being hit herself and she told the nurse this. 'Best not remembering that,' the nurse said as she tucked her in. 'Doctor said you must have a skull like an elephant. Have you a headache?'

Kate nodded and then wished she hadn't.

'Daren't give you anything till Doctor says so,' the nurse said. 'But I can get you a drink of water, if you'd like one. Then, if I were you, I'd try to sleep again, because he won't be around for some hours but he will be very pleased that you are conscious at last.'

'Why, how long have I been here?'

'You were brought in about half eleven Monday night,' the nurse said. 'And now it's half past three on Wednesday morning.'

'Wednesday morning!' Kate exclaimed, throwing back the bedclothes. 'I can't stay here. People will be worried about me.'

'It's all right,' the nurse said, settling her back down on the pillows. 'People from a hostel in Aston came to see what had happened to you. Said they were friends.'

'John and Rita Taylor.'

'That's the ones,' the nurse said. 'And they were going to tell everyone how you are and that, and all you have got to do is get better. And now I'll get that water.'

Surprisingly, after a long drink of water, Kate was quite happy to close her eyes again. When she next opened them, bowls of porridge were being distributed.

The doctor, when he came some time after breakfast, seemed very pleased with Kate. 'You are one lucky girl,' he said. 'You have such a gash on your forehead that I was sure you had fractured your skull, but you haven't.'

Kate gingerly fingered the wound she could feel. 'It's been stitched.'

'Oh, yes,' the doctor said. 'It was too deep not to stitch it. That's what I say. That beam must have given you one hell of a crack. As I said before, you are lucky. Your mother didn't get off so lightly, but the indications are that she will make a full recovery in time.'

Kate was staring at him open-mouthed. 'My mother?'

The doctor thought Kate must be suffering lapses of memory because of the bang on the head. He said patiently, 'Yes, she was with you when the building collapsed. She was buried while you–'

'Doctor, you are making a big mistake,' Kate said. 'My mother is alive and well on a farm in Northern Ireland. I don't live in the area I was found in, but in Stockland Green. I am an ARP warden, though not in uniform because I was not officially on duty. I was just visiting friends in a nearby hostel when the bombs hit. As I have first-aid skills and experience in getting people out of buildings, I was asked to help. I'm not related to anyone there.'

'I am very sorry, Mrs Burton,' the doctor said. 'You look so very alike, and pulled in from the same area, I just assumed...'

'It's all right,' Kate said. 'I can understand you thinking that, particularly if there was a strong resemblance.'

'There is. It was almost uncanny.'

'What was her name, as a matter of interest?'

'Ah, let me see,' said the doctor, closing his eyes to try to picture the woman who'd been brought in. 'You must realize that I saw a lot of people that night.'

'Yes, of course.'

'They will have it in the records.'

'Oh, it's not that important.'

'Oh, no, wait,' the doctor cried. 'I have it. The

name on her identity card was Helen something. Helen ... Helen ... Helen ... Logue. That was it! I know it wasn't the same name as yours, but you have a wedding ring, so I didn't expect it would be.'

'No,' Kate said. 'Oh, well, no harm done.'

'None whatsoever,' the doctor said. 'And there's even better news because, if you are a good girl today, rest plenty and do as you are told, you can go home on Friday. You will have to have the injury on your forehead seen to, but that can be done through the clinic in Outpatients.'

'Oh, that's the best news yet,' Kate said happily.

Kate was sitting in a chair by her bed when Susie and Sally went in to see her that evening and were delighted at the news that she would soon be out. 'I bet you were worried,' Kate said to Sally.

'I would have been if I could have got home,' Sally said. 'But we were in the cellar underneath the cinema till the early hours and the "All Clear" went. I would have chanced it and tried to get home but my friends wouldn't come with me and the American boys seemed scared stiff and it wasn't even that bad a raid. Anyway, they talked me into staying, and so when I did reach home I just thought you'd gone to bed. I would have been frantic by the next morning, but that steward you know, John Taylor is it?'

'That's right.'

'Well, he came up and told me,' Sally said. 'Had to knock good and loud 'cos I had gone out like a light when I got in. It didn't half shake me up when he told me what had happened to you and then I sent him to Susie's so she could tell them at work and that.'

'How good of John,' Kate said. 'Is he here? I would love to thank him.'

'No,' Susie said. 'No good them coming; they knew they wouldn't get to see you.'

'Yeah, they were sniffy enough about us,' Sally said. 'In the end I said I had to see you because you were coming home soon and we had to make arrangements.'

'And I said I was your sister too, otherwise I would have had to sit in the corridor,' Susie said. 'And even then they said we could only have a few minutes. The point is above anything else we both wanted to see you. It's all right people saying that you are all right and it is quite another seeing it for ourselves.'

'Are they letting you home soon?' Sally asked.

'Mm, Friday the doctor said.'

'How are you getting home?' Sally asked. 'Are they sending you in an ambulance?'

'Don't be daft, I'll be well enough to go by tram,' Kate said. 'They won't waste ambulances on people like me.'

'Are you sure you will be all right to do that?'

'Yes, perfectly,' Kate said. 'You are not to fuss me, Sally. You know I don't like it.'

'All right, all right,' Sally said. 'Have it your way, as usual, but one thing we are going to do when you are out of here and that is go to Mammy for a while – and as soon as possible. I have already written to ask her.'

'All right,' Kate said. 'But the cut on my forehead had to be stitched and I have to have the stitches taken out in a week or so. I would like to have that done before I go anywhere.'

The nurse put her head around the door to say it was time for Sally and Susie to leave. Sally said as she stood up, 'I'll be up to see you tomorrow evening and then on Friday I will come in on the tram and we can go home together,' Sally said.

'There's no need for you to do that.'

'I know that, you dope, but I'm going to do it anyway,' Sally said decisively.

After they had both gone, Kate wondered why she'd not mentioned Helen Logue to them. Of course they hadn't been allowed to stay long, but Kate somehow knew that however long they'd stayed she would never have told them, and she couldn't explain why that was. She somehow wanted to keep it to herself, and yet she was very curious as to what the woman looked like.

And so, when the night staff came on, she asked the nurse that had attended her when she'd first woken up if she could see her. 'You shouldn't really,' the night nurse said. 'But I understand you wanting a look. I would myself. Honestly, the only difference between you is that you have a plaster on your forehead covering stitches. The likeness between you is unbelievable. We'll have to wait until Matron is out of the way, or we will at the very least have our ears scalded, and you can't stay long because she's heavily sedated and in a room of her own, but I'll give you the nod.'

And so later that night, Kate followed the nurse out of the ward and down the corridor and a few moments later she was looking at a mirror image of herself lying in a hospital bed. The woman was older than Kate, though her face was remarkably unlined, but she looked more mature. Apart from that, the likeness was quite startling.

'Sort of creepy, isn't it?' said the nurse as they stole back to the ward and Kate got back into bed.

'I suppose so,' Kate said. 'But don't they say everyone has got a double?'

'Yeah, I have heard that said all right.'

'Then I'm not going to give it another thought,' Kate said. 'I'm going to concentrate on getting better so that I can go home on Friday.'

'Only thing you can do,' the nurse said, and she turned the light down low and Kate settled herself to sleep.

TWENTY-FIVE

Kate was unable to go to work until her stitches were removed because of the risk of infection. 'Why worry?' Sally said when she told her this on Friday morning. 'You really need to take time off anyway, Kate. You had a real shock to your system. You have done the first-aid course same as me and you know the sort of things shock can do.'

'I'm not the least bit shocked.'

'Course you're not,' Sally said sarcastically. 'Not you, super-woman Kate. Anyway, aren't we decided to go and see Mammy? I wrote to her as I said and had her reply by return saying that she will be delighted to see us both so don't try and wriggle out of that. Susie has arranged holidays from work for you and, as you've never had any proper holidays, she said there was no problem there. And you can make all the arrangements about the boat and train now you'll have the time.'

Kate knew the days would yawn emptily in front of her as she wasn't one to laze about, and she also knew that if the Blitz was going to start again she needed a breathing space. And there was a chance that it might, because there had been another raid the previous night. The hospital had been on the alert to evacuate patients to the basement, but in the end, there had been no need as the raid had been a fairly light one and confined to the south of the city and was over in three hours. 'But Hitler used tactics like that before,' Sally reminded Kate as they travelled home on the tram together. 'You know, softly-softly and then wallop.'

'I know,' Kate said with a sigh. 'I do hope it isn't starting again, though. I mean, the place has taken such a battering already. Birmingham might be wiped off the map altogether if we have another Blitz.'

Sally shivered. 'Ooh, don't let's think about it, Kate,' she advised. 'Let's just concentrate on getting away from it for a while anyway.'

Kate nodded. She knew it didn't do to worry about what might happen. What did happen was quite enough to be going on with. Sally stayed at home with Kate that day and Susie came round that night and they went to see *Masquerade*, which was showing at the Plaza, and they laughed together as if they hadn't got a care in the world.

The following Monday, Kate went in to New Street Station to make the travel arrangements. They would be travelling the following Saturday, 8 August, which fitted in well with the hospital because the nurse at the Outpatient Clinic wanted to remove the stitches in Kate's forehead on the day before. And so that Friday morning, Kate returned to the hospital. 'It's healed up beautifully,' the nurse said as she pulled the last stitch through.

'Will there be a scar?'

The nurse nodded. 'A slight one,' she said. 'Though it will fade in time. Meanwhile, cosmetics will mask it a bit; that is of course if you can find any.'

Kate smiled ruefully because make-up, obviously not considered essential for the nation's survival, had virtually disappeared from the shops. 'It's like looking for a crock of gold at the end of the rainbow trying to get hold of just one lipstick,' she said. 'I might do better to grow a fringe.'

'You might at that,' the nurse agreed with a smile. 'But for now I am going to put a dressing on to protect it a little.'

It was as Kate was walking back through the hospital on her way home that she bumped into the nurse who had dealt with her previously, and greeted her. 'Hallo,' the nurse responded. 'How are you feeling now?'

'Fine.'

'No headaches or anything?'

'Not a thing.'

'Lucky you.'

'That's what you said before,' Kate reminded her. 'So, how's life treating you?'

'Oh, better now I am over the night shift,' the nurse said. 'Oh, I'll tell you a funny thing. You know the woman that looked so like you?'

'Yes, I remember,' Kate said. 'Did she recover all right?'

'Well, I suppose she did,' the nurse said. 'The fact is, she disappeared.'

'Disappeared?'

'Yeah, just a few days after you left, and it was just after one of the nurses had mentioned you – you know, how alike the two of you were – and the next minute she had gone,' the nurse told her. 'I mean, they didn't know she had gone at first. They thought she was in the washroom, and it was only after she had been there some time that they went to look there. It was empty, and when they checked her locker, her clothes and her bag were missing too. She must have smuggled the whole lot into the washroom under her nightie.'

'How odd,' said Kate. 'But it couldn't have been what you said to the woman about me that caused her to take flight, because as I said I had never seen her before in my life.'

'No,' the nurse agreed. 'Must have been a coincidence.'

'Was she well enough to leave hospital?'

'Not really,' the nurse said. 'Especially when she hadn't anywhere to go. You said she was bombed out.'

'Yeah, the whole street was down.'

'Well, there's nothing to stop a person signing themselves out of hospital,' the nurse said. 'Not that she did that, she just walked out.'

'Maybe she had family that took her in?'

The nurse shook her head. 'Don't know that she had any family. No one came to visit her and she told the nurses that she lived alone.'

Kate felt a wave of pity for this woman but didn't understand why she cared about someone she didn't know. She couldn't understand either that once she had left the hospital, and had unaccustomed time on her hands, thoughts of Helen Logue would keep niggling at her. A number of times she almost discussed it with Sally, but she always stopped herself and she didn't know why that was either. She had never considered herself a secretive person.

However, the woman had disappeared into thin air and so she thanked the nurse and left the

445

hospital. Once outside, though, she was loath to go straight home, as the early August day was fine and sunny. She decided to walk over to the Taylors' hostel, show them she was still in the land of the living and thank them, particularly John, for what he had done the night she had been injured. But first she went to Freer Road to see that the whole area had been laid waste by the bombs and resultant fires.

The Taylors were delighted to see her looking so well and they reminisced about that night over a cup of tea. 'They made a right mess of Freer Road,' Kate said. 'Where have all the people been taken that lived there?'

'Oh, them as weren't injured and haven't got folks to move in with were taken to the Sacred Heart school hall, just off Trinity Road there,' John said. 'It was the nearest, and the school is empty now, of course, with the kids all on holiday.'

'Yeah, but they can't stay there for ever.'

'I know,' Rita said, 'and we can't take many more. We have almost reached our quota and I think most hostels are the same.'

'Near enough, I'd say,' John said in agreement. 'Have to twist people's arms to get them to take some of the bombed-out people into their homes.'

'Huh, I've done a bit of arm-twisting too in my time,' Kate said, but she suddenly felt incredibly guilty because she had a spare bedroom in her house. Surely it was wrong to have a bedroom doing nothing with so many in need. And this is what she said now to John and Rita. And they agreed that if people could help then they should, and without delay, so she thanked them for the tea

446

and left.

She soon found the school and, as she approached it, she wondered if she should talk it over
with Sally first before taking a perfect stranger to
live in their house, but really there was nothing to
talk about. The only stipulation she would make
was that she wouldn't have a man, not with two
young women in the house, but most of those
bombed out were women anyway.

When she went into the entrance hall, she
thought that if Helen Logue had returned to the
area where her house had been – and where else
would she have gone? – she could easily be there,
camping out in the main school hall with all the
rest, because she could hardly live on the streets.

So when the volunteer assistant approached
Kate and asked if she could help her, Kate said
she was looking for a lady who had been in
hospital with her as they had both been injured
in the bombing and her name was Helen Logue.
The volunteer consulted a register and told Kate
she was there, and Kate's stomach suddenly tied
into knots. She wondered if she really wanted to
meet this woman who had run away when a
nurse had mentioned their likeness, though as
she had said to the nurse her flight couldn't have
anything to do with that and yet...

'Would you like to see the lady?' the volunteer
asked.

Kate knew that if she refused she would always
wonder. 'Yes,' she said. 'Yes, please.'

Moments later, Kate was facing Helen Logue,
who was looking at Kate with a face drained of all
colour, a trembling bottom lip and beautiful eyes

full of pain and brimming with tears. She gave a sudden sigh and said, 'Hallo, Kate.'

Kate felt apprehension tighten in the pit of her stomach as she demanded, 'How do you know my name?'

'I asked at the hospital,' Helen said. 'Your name is Kate Burton and you were born Katherine Munroe, am I right?'

Kate nodded, more confused than ever. 'And you lived on a farm near Donegal Town in Ireland.'

Unease flowed all through Kate. Who was this woman, this stranger, who seemed to know all about her? 'Just who are you?' she demanded.

The woman didn't answer. Instead, she said, 'I guessed you might try to find me and hoped that you wouldn't succeed. But with no money, possessions or home, I couldn't hide very effectively.'

'Why did you need to hide?'

'I have much to tell you,' Helen said. 'But not here.'

Kate nodded, as the hall was filled with people: noise, chattering, laughing, even arguing people. Giggling children ran away from their mothers' restraining arms and crying babies demanded attention. 'Where then?'

'I don't know,' Helen said helplessly. 'I have very little money for a café or anything.'

'We don't need a café,' Kate said. 'And there would be people there too. I have a funny feeling that I'm not going to like what you are going to say and I would prefer it if we were alone.'

'So would I.'

'Well, then,' Kate said. 'Apart from here, the

rest of the school is empty. Surely there's a classroom we can use if we say that we have some private business to discuss.'

Kate was right; the volunteers opened one of the classrooms for them. It smelt of chalk dust and the chairs stored up on the tables were far too small but, apart from the teacher's big leather one, that was all there was. Helen lifted two down, sat on one herself and indicated for Kate to use the other. Kate did so, squeezing herself into the small, hard, uncomfortable chair. 'Go on then,' she urged, although part of her wondered if she wanted to hear what this stranger was going to say.

And Helen seemed reluctant to start. She twisted her hands on her lap and licked her lips and Kate noticed her eyes were so very bright as she suddenly shot up from the small chair and paced around the room. 'I don't really know where to start.'

'Well, do you know why we look so alike for a start?' Kate asked, and Helen nodded and faced Kate. 'Yes, I know why.'

'I mean, they thought you were my mother.'

'I know,' Helen said, and her voice was little more than a whisper. Then she cried, 'And, oh God, Kate, they were right. I *am* your mother.'

Kate jumped from the chair and stared at Helen, her eyes wide with puzzlement and disbelief. 'What are you on about? What rubbish is this?'

'It's true, Kate,' Helen said. 'Philomena is your aunt and my sister.'

'What?' Kate cried in distress. She didn't want what this woman had said to her to be true and yet she knew by the look in her eyes that it was.

449

She felt as if her world, her secure and safe world, had slid from under her and left her without any base. She said in a voice brittle with the pain of rejection, 'So you gave birth to me and then just gave me away?'

'No, it wasn't like that.'

'What way was it?' Kate demanded. 'So, you're telling me that all of my life so far has been based on lies?'

Helen took hold of one of the hands that Kate was wringing together. She resisted at first, but Helen held tight. She gave Kate's hands a little shake and said, 'Look at me, Kate.'

Kate lifted her head and stared at the woman claiming to be her mother, her mouth an angry and mutinous line. 'I will tell you all,' Helen said. 'And you can ask me any questions you like. And when I am done, if you want nothing more to do with me, I will understand and I will bow out of your life again.'

'Who was my father?' Kate demanded.

'Your father was a man known as Peter Donahue and he was a fine, brave man and one who had enlisted as a soldier to fight in the Great War.'

Memories stirred in Kate's brain and she said, 'You are the one called Ellie, Mammy's younger sister. I suppose I should call the woman who brought me up Aunt Philomena, but that doesn't sit well on me.'

'And why would it after all this time?' Helen said. 'Call her Mammy. I won't mind, I have no right to mind. So she talked about me then?'

'Sometimes,' Kate said. 'Not that much.'

'What else did she say?'

'That you travelled to England with the family you were in service with.'

'That's right," Helen said. 'Our parents and two brothers and a sister had died with cholera in the spring of 1912 and we had to vacate the cottage so the landlord could put another family in it. Philomena had been walking out with Jim and it was decided to push their marriage forward. After it she went to live in the farmhouse with his parents and his brothers, Padraic and Michael.

'There was no space for me and, as I had left school, the priest found me a job in service with the Mountford family. They were devout Catholics but, as their house was just outside Derry, I couldn't come home on my time off because it was too far.'

'How old were you?'

'Twelve,' Helen said. 'That was the age you left school in those days. I'd been with the Mountford's three years when the family moved to England in 1915 and I went with them – there was nothing to keep me in Ireland and I knew that I would have to make my own way in the world. By that time, Jim's parents had died, Michael had enlisted, and Padraic, the next eldest, split the farm three ways and had a house built for Jim and Philomena on his share of the land.'

'I knew about that,' Kate said. 'But Mammy said nothing about any soldier.'

'She didn't know about Peter,' Helen said. 'But let me tell you the story from the beginning.'

'Oh, please do,' said Kate sarcastically.

Helen ignored Kate's tone and began to pace again as she said, 'I met your father one day in

451

the Bull Ring when I was doing some shopping for my mistress and he was recovering from injuries inflicted at the Battle of Ypres. We got talking and he saw me home and, to cut a long story short, we began walking out together. It was a very secretive romance. Philomena wasn't told because I knew that she wouldn't approve, and she might have written to the mistress. We weren't allowed what they called "followers".

'We forgot ourselves just the once, in October 1916. Far too many young men had died at the Somme and amongst the dead were many from Peter's battalion. He would have been there with them if he hadn't been injured earlier, and he felt so sad about their deaths, and almost guilty that he was alive and they were not. In a way, I could understand what he meant, and I tried to comfort him. One thing led to another and we went too far.'

Helen's eyes suddenly looked far away and Kate knew she was remembering their brief and illicit passion. She remembered her own courtship with David and how often they had come very close to that themselves. She felt the first stirring of sympathy for Helen as she said, 'Peter was very worried, especially because his medical was coming up and he was pretty sure he would be pronounced fit to return to active duty and he said that we must get married. But I was only seventeen and couldn't marry without permission and he said I had to go home to Ireland and ask Philomena. Using the excuse of an illness in the family to the Mountford's, I left as soon as I could for speed was essential.

'Philomena was so pleased to see me that I felt ashamed at what I must tell her. I knew to secure her permission I would have to confess what Peter and I had done that might result in a child. I knew that I would find this more especially difficult as that very day Philomena had told me that she was concerned that she had seen no sign of a baby even though she'd been married over four years.

'She said she found this harder to bear because Jim's brother, Padraic, had married a woman called Bridget Murphy in the summer of 1914 and had a son, Timothy, just over a year later, and now she was pregnant again. I knew I was going to hurt her again and I had no wish to do that – she had more than enough on her plate, anyway, as Jim's brother, Michael, had been invalided out of the army with shell shock. Philomena told me he was very odd at times; his nerves had been shot to pieces and he talked to himself and laughed and he was very jumpy and sometimes would shake uncontrollably. They were worried about him, though Philomena said he was a poor, lost wee soul and they certainly didn't consider that he was a danger to anyone.

'The following evening I was walking in the woods, going over in my head how I was going to broach the subject about Peter to Philomena, and so intent was I that I failed to notice Michael, who suddenly stepped from behind a tree directly in front of me. I had tended to keep out of his way since I had arrived because he unnerved me, and that night he bothered me more than ever – even in the dusky half-light I could see his unkempt hair standing on end, the light shining almost yellow in his eyes, his lips moving constantly as he mumbled to himself.'

'That's another lie I've been told,' Kate said. 'Mammy told me that Michael died in the war.'

'In a way she was right,' Helen said. 'Because the war took the essence of him. The person who returned had a broken mind, and I don't think he would ever have totally recovered. I didn't know that then, of course. I didn't know much except that I was so scared my legs were knocking together. I told myself not to be so stupid, that the man was sick, and so I gave a little laugh and said, "Oh, Michael, you scared me half to death."

'Suddenly his hand shot out and he grabbed my arm tight and asked me to go for a walk with him. I said I couldn't, that I had to go back to the house, but he wouldn't let me turn around. He dragged me deeper into the woods. I stumbled often on the uneven forest floor, but his grip was like a steel band and he kept me from falling.

'The trees were closer together the further in Michael went, so that less light penetrated through them. I felt the mud and mulched leaves beneath my feet, branches tugged at my hair, scratched my face and snagged at the shawl I had around my shoulders. I'll tell you, Kate, I have never been so scared in all my life.'

'I'm not surprised,' Kate said. 'Did he rape you?'

'No,' Helen admitted. 'But he tried to. He wanted me to lie down and, in his words, "be nice to him", and when I wouldn't lie down, he gave me a punch between the eyes that knocked me down. I think I must have blacked out for a moment or two, because the next thing I remembered was lying on the ground and feeling the twigs and tree roots sticking into my back and Michael's heavy weight pinning me down. The bodice of my dress had been ripped to the waist and Michael was kneading my breasts roughly.'

Helen stopped and dropped her eyes; Kate noticed her cheeks had gone rather pink and she said, 'I feel awfully embarrassed to be telling you all this.'

'I can understand that,' Kate said. 'But all this had been hidden from me all my life and so now I really need to know. I am a grown woman and an ARP warden, so I have seen some sights – I promise you I won't swoon in shock.'

'Maybe not,' Helen said with a tremulous smile. 'But I might.'

'No, you won't,' said Kate confidently. 'You are tougher than that. Go on.'

'Kneading my breasts and me lying exposed like that was bad enough, but when I felt him pull off my bloomers and ram his fingers inside me, I felt I would die with shame and the agonizing pain of it,' Helen went on. 'And all the time I was writhing and squirming beneath him, but that achieved nothing, except to possibly excite him further. I was also pleading with him to let me go, but when I felt his fingers unbuttoning his trousers, I screamed for all I was worth.

'He clapped a hand over my mouth so tightly that I was unable to breathe, but my mouth was still open and I bit down hard. He leapt away from me with blood dripping down his arm just as Jim and Padraic burst through the trees. While I was being pulled along by Michael, full darkness had fallen, and as I had told Philomena that I was going to walk in the woods, the men had been looking for me. That one scream alerted them to where I was. They took in the scene straight away: my battered face, my body lying exposed, bloomers on the ground and Michael, his hand dripping blood and his manhood dangling from his trousers. And now I knew rescue was at hand and I was safe from any further violation, shock had rendered me speechless.

'Padraic took Michael away and Jim had to help me to my feet, where I staggered and would have fallen if he hadn't got his arms around me. There was not one part of me that didn't ache, my breasts throbbed and I could barely see out of my swollen eyes. But far, far worse was the pain between my legs because that was truly agonizing. As we made our slow and painful walk back to the farmhouse, Jim told me over and over how sorry he was and how ashamed that I should be so abused by his own brother.

'Philomena had been very alarmed when Jim brought me in for I was in a terrible state. She was marvellous, though. She bathed all my cuts and bruises and put salve on and tucked me into bed with a hot-water bottle and slept in a chair by my bed all night in case I should want something.'

'Mammy was always very good like that if ever we were ill,' Kate said. 'Did you ever tell Philomena what had really happened?'

Helen shook her head. 'Jim assumed that Michael had had his way with me and that's what he told Philomena and I couldn't really tell them otherwise then anyway because I could still barely speak.'

'The next morning, Jim came to tell us that sometime in the night Michael had climbed out of the window of the bedroom where he'd been locked overnight; when this was discovered they set out to find him and found his body hanging from a tree in the woods. I felt only relief and so, I think, did Philomena. I saw it in her face, though we never spoke of it.'

'That sort of made him look even more guilty,' Kate said.

'Well, yes, it did,' Helen said. 'And even if I had had the ability to speak, I doubt I would have tried to absolve Michael of anything anyway.'

'No, and I don't blame you,' Kate said. 'I mean, if Daddy and Uncle Padraic hadn't come then, this Michael might have done anything to you. I know you had bitten him, but in a way that might have made things worse for you when he had got over the shock of it.'

Helen nodded. 'I thought that too, because not only was I no match for him, but I was also still dizzy and disorientated and in great pain. But, in any case, I couldn't have found words to tell other people what he had done to me and I didn't want to relive it. I wanted to forget it. After all, it's been hard enough talking about it twenty-five years later, and then I was only seventeen.

'I left the following day. None of them wanted me to go, but all I wanted was to come back to Birmingham and my Peter, though the events of that night had effectively driven from my mind

457

the reason I had gone over to Ireland in the first place. I only remembered that as I watched the boat pulling away from the Irish Coast.

'In the end it was a good job I came back when I did,' Helen said. 'Because Peter had his medical brought forward and he left two days afterwards. He was full of concern for me, especially when he saw my battered face and heard what had happened with Michael, and he fully understood my urgent need to get home. He wasn't surprised that I had forgotten the original need for the visit. He said he hoped that everything would be all right and that we would get married on his next leave if at all possible.'

'And then you found you were pregnant anyway?' Kate said.

'Yes, I was carrying you, Kate, Peter Donahue's child,' Helen said. 'And that realization came just a few days before I heard news of Peter's death at a place called Arras. I was heartbroken, for I had truly loved him so much, but I was also worried to death about having a baby and how I was going to be able to provide for you. You know what it is like to be an unmarried mother, Kate, the stigma attached to it – shame that drags whole families down.'

Kate nodded. She knew that well enough.

'Well, it was even worse then,' Helen said. 'There were few options apart from throwing myself into the canal, and I wondered if I had the courage. Apart from that, there was the workhouse. In there you would be taken from me at birth and reared until you were of an age to go out to work. You would probably never know a kind word or deed and you would be known as a workhouse bastard all the days of your life.

'I worried and fretted and shed many tears, and in the end the only viable option that I could see was to go back to Ireland and pass my baby off as Michael's child, for I knew then they would feel responsible and look after you and your future would be secure. It was a terrible thing to do, but the man was dead and couldn't be hurt further. So, for your sake, Kate, this is what I did.'

Kate looked back to her happy, carefree childhood in rural Ireland with her parents, and surrounded by her cousins, and she contrasted that with the dreadful tales she had heard about workhouses; she knew her life there would probably have been an unhappy and even brutal one. She thought of Helen, alone, frantic and panicking and quite desperate to do the best for her baby, and tears trickled down her cheeks.

Helen put her arms around her, tentatively at first, and then with more confidence as Kate didn't push her away, and tears poured from her eyes as she embraced her daughter for the first time in twenty-five years. The poignancy wasn't lost on Kate, and when they eventually drew apart, Helen said, 'What now? I have told you all and I will understand if you do not want to see me any more.'

'I have a better idea,' said Kate. 'Why don't we go back into that church hall. You can collect your things and come home with me.'

'I can't do that.'

'Why not?' Kate demanded. 'Have you somewhere else to go?'

'No, but...'

'No buts,' Kate said. 'Come on.'

'Kate, I can't,' Helen said. 'Your husband might object.'

'My husband was a pilot,' Kate said. 'And he was shot down earlier in the year, but if he had still been alive, I'm sure he would have been pleased to meet you.'

'I am so sorry, my dear.'

'I am sorry too,' Kate said. 'For I loved him dearly. But I live in a three-bedroomed semi-detached house, and the only one that shares it with me is my sister.'

'A sister,' Helen cried. 'You have a sister?'

'Yes, and a wee brother who is still at home as he is only nine years old.'

'Praise be that Philomena had children of her own.'

'Yes, though she had a long wait for James,' Kate said. 'So, will you come then?'

'You don't know me, Kate.'

'What dark secrets are you hiding?' Kate asked with a smile. 'Are you going to murder us all in our beds with an axe or what?'

'No, of course not,' Helen said. 'But I am a stranger.'

'Yes, and isn't that just tragic that my mother is a stranger to me?' Kate said. She reached for Helen's hand and said, 'Let's put the past behind us and get to know one another.'

Helen gave a brief nod; she was unable to speak because her throat was so full.

As they travelled home on the tram, Kate acknowledged to herself that she wanted to get to know her mother better and had a perfect right to do that, but she could also use her mother's arrival in her life to stave off the visit to Ireland, which she felt she had been coerced into when she wasn't really herself after that crack on the head.

Even before she had found Helen and heard her remarkable story, she had been less than keen about visiting Ireland, although she knew she would value the peace and quiet of Donegal and she did want to see her parents, as she still thought of them, and her little brother. Her apprehension stemmed from the fact that she didn't know how she really felt about Tim Munroe, though the fleeting times she thought of him now, prompted usually because of something her mother put in a letter, she felt nothing. Her heart didn't race, nor did her mouth became unaccountably dry, and her limbs didn't quiver, but she didn't know how she would react if they came face to face, and she had no desire to cause any sort of trouble or upset, for not only was Tim a married man now, he also had a wee son.

And how she had envied Tim for that, because she would have loved a child of her own, a part of David. Oh, yes, she would go to Ireland some-time, but not now, when she was still grieving for her husband whom her Mammy had never met and wouldn't approve of, and when she was coming to terms with finding her real mother after all these years, and the way that would change so many things in her life. She knew Sally and her mother/aunt Philomena would be disappointed, but they would have to get over it.

TWENTY-SIX

The short tram journey home was taken in virtual silence, which Helen was loath to break as she saw that Kate was deep in thought. She was, however, impressed with the house, which she thought very grand. 'I had a couple of rooms, that was all,' she said as they walked down the path. 'Well, I can claim no credit for living here,' Kate said as she opened the front door, and she explained how it had come about.

'You girls have suffered so much,' Helen said. 'Your men both taken by this dreadful war.'

Kate nodded as she took off her coat and indicated that Helen do the same. 'And my father taken by the one before,' she said, leading the way to the kitchen. She filled the kettle and put it on the gas as Helen asked, 'Do you resent me, Kate, for giving you up?'

'How could I?' Kate said. 'Until today, I had no idea you existed. As far as I was concerned, I had a mother and father who I love and who love me and, though I was intrigued about you for some reason that I haven't even got straight in my own head, that didn't go as far as thinking you were my mother. When you told me, my initial feeling was that I didn't want you to be, that my life was fine the way it was. If there was any resentment at all, it was because you were shaking the foundations of everything I had previously believed to

462

be true. D'you see that?'

'I see it very well and I am sorry in a way that this has happened,' Helen said. 'And I can say that it gladdens my heart to have met you; you don't know what it means to me.' She had a blissful look on her face as she spoke, and then she gave a sigh and went on in a quiet voice, 'And yet, because it makes things harder for you, I would say I wish it had never happened.'

'Did you know who I was?'

'When they spoke of our remarkable likeness to one another in the hospital, yes, I knew and I was afraid.'

'Why afraid?' Kate said. 'And how were you so sure? Even if you knew my first name was Katherine, my second name is Burton now, not Munroe.'

'But you were married,' Helen said. 'The nurses who remarked on the resemblance between us called you Mrs Burton.' She sighed and went on: 'I don't know how I knew who you were even without seeing you, I just did. My past was catching up with me and I didn't mind for me, but I did for you.'

'And so you ran away?'

'Yes,' Helen said. 'I wasn't sure you would go on looking for me. I thought if I wasn't at the hospital, you would probably shrug your shoulders and get on with your life. At least that was what I hoped you'd do.'

'Well, I didn't really go looking for you,' Kate said. 'The point is, I had to go to the hospital today anyway to have the stitches taken out of my forehead and the nurse spoke about you. She said that you left just after they commented on how similar we were, but even then I wasn't sure that that was the real reason for you just taking off like that.'

'It was,' Helen said. 'Out of the hospital I felt safer.'

'Well, I certainly wasn't going to chase you all over the city,' Kate said. 'But I was going to call on some friends who run the hostel in Bevington Road anyway. The steward there, John Taylor, went up to the house when I was injured to tell Sally what had happened and my friend Susie too, so I wanted to thank them. But on the way to the hostel, I went for a look at Freer Road, or what's left of it, which isn't much.'

Helen nodded. 'I went for a look myself, and mooched about a bit to see if I could salvage something from the mound of rubble and debris that had once been my home, but there was nothing. I was just standing there coming to terms with it all and with no idea what to do with myself or where to go, and a copper came up and asked if he could help and he told me that all the homeless were taken to the school hall of the Sacred Heart because it was the nearest, and so that's where I ended up.'

'That's what my friend the Taylors said when I asked where the homeless people had been taken,' Kate said. She made tea as she spoke and pushed a cup across the kitchen table to Helen and sat down opposite her and went on: 'I had got to thinking that it was wrong to keep this whole house with just me and Sally in it when we could take at least one homeless person in because we had a spare bedroom. When I reached the hall I nearly didn't ask about you, but then I thought if I didn't I would always wonder – who you were and that – and of course I didn't know if you would even be there. But you were and the rest you know.'

'And I'm very grateful to you,' Helen said. 'Never think I don't appreciate this, but I really think I cannot stay here.'

'Why not?'

Helen shook her head. 'It's just... It's not right.' Her voice was thick with unshed tears and she turned her brimming eyes to Kate and said, 'You must see, Kate. It could throw up all kinds of problems.'

Kate reached out and took hold of one of Helen's hands. 'Drink your tea,' she said, 'and stop shaking.'

Helen obediently picked up the cup and sipped at the amber liquid. Kate did not say another word until Helen had drained the cup and put it down on the table; then she said, 'Please listen to me. I have been denied access to you for twenty-five years. We will never get those years back, and it matters more than I have words to say that I get to know you better and that you find out the kind of person I am. I want you to stay here, Helen, very, very much. It will be a voyage of discovery for both of us. What do you say?'

'Are you sure?'

'Absolutely sure.'

Helen nodded her head. 'All right then.'

Kate was on her feet and dragging Helen up too. 'Come on,' she said, 'you'll want to see your room. I must warn you that it's nothing special,' she added as she led the way upstairs. 'Sally and I have been using it as a bit of a glory hole, chucking all sorts of stuff in there, most of it junk that can easily be thrown out.' She swung the door open as she spoke and Helen gazed in at all the things piled haphazardly on the floor. But she also noted that what she could see of the lino was clean and so were the distempered walls. The window looked out on the modest garden that the shelter virtually filled.

'Got to get you a blackout curtain or something for that window,' Kate said. 'We didn't bother as it wasn't used. I just took the bulb out instead. And we'll have to get a bed and chest of drawers or something.'

'Don't worry about a thing,' Helen said. 'I'll soon get it sorted out.'

'Well, until we get it fixed up, you can have Sally's room and she will share with me.'

'I don't want to put anyone out.'

'And you won't,' Kate assured Helen. 'Sally loves sharing a room with me. What d'you think of our inside toilet and bathroom?'

'It's absolutely wonderful and I know a lot of people are far worse off,' Helen said. 'And don't think you have to buy things for me either,' she went on as she followed Kate back down the stairs. 'I have money of my own because over the years I've not had that much to spend it on. I mean, I have little ready cash right now, but my shelter bag was recovered and they traced me by the bank book that was zipped in the side pocket, and I have that with me. They said everything else, including the ration books and identity card was ruined. So I will have to go to the council house and tell them and get replacements, I suppose. I haven't felt up to it yet.'

'That's because you left hospital before you were fully better,' Kate said. 'And I really think–'

However, whatever Kate was going to say was stopped by Sally letting herself in the front door; she had left work at dinner time as they were going on holiday the following day. She glanced from Kate to Helen and back to Kate as they reached the bottom of the stairs. 'Golly,' she cried. 'You two don't half–'

'Don't say how alike we look,' Kate said. 'Because we know, and there is a reason for it. Sally, meet our new lodger, Helen Logue, who also happens to be my mother.'

'What?' Sally cried. Her mouth dropped open with astonishment and her eyes seemed to stand out as if they were on stalks. 'Don't be daft, Kate.'

'I'm not, I assure you,' Kate said. 'Look, I've heard the tale, so let's go into the kitchen and Helen can tell you while I make us a bite to eat.'

That was agreed on, and so Kate opened a tin of Spam and sliced it to make sandwiches from the dreaded grey national loaf, spread with a minute amount of margarine, and watched Sally's eyes widen and her face take on a look of astonishment and some distress as the story unfolded. Kate put the plate of sandwiches down and brewed tea for them all as Helen finished speaking. Sally stared at Helen. She had asked few questions, and Kate thought looked near to tears. But when she did speak there was no trace of that in her voice, though there was anger. 'I just don't get it,' she said. 'Mammy agreed to look after your baby, right?'

'Yes,' Helen said. 'Thinking it to be Michael's child, they couldn't do enough for me. We all had a big family conference to decide what was to be done and it was agreed that Philomena should have the child and bring her up as her own. She was desperate for a child, anyway, and I knew she would love her dearly.'

'That's the bit I don't get,' Sally said. 'People in Donegal know everything about you. If you had a baby and gave it to Mammy, everyone would get to know about it and we'd get to hear and everyone would know what Kate was and they would call her a fly-blow, a bastard, and she would be known and maybe ostracized because she had no father. And they never forget anything either. It would be passed from one generation to another like a story.'

'Don't you think that we didn't know that too?' Helen said. 'Oh, we knew exactly how cute we had to be. I went back to Birmingham and gave in my notice. I knew that the Mountford's would dismiss me anyway when my pregnancy became obvious. As I said, they were friends of the parish priest and I couldn't risk them contacting him to tell him I was expecting. Then I went to a hardware shop and bought a curtain ring to do as a wedding ring and got a job in the munitions works where I said I had a husband at the Front.

'Meanwhile, Philomena tells everyone that at long last she is having a baby, and everyone is delighted for her and she pads herself accordingly as the months pass. In May, a month before the child is due, she comes to stay with me, telling any who ask that I am going to look after her. And, once we were together in this teeming city, where people didn't know who we were and cared even less, we temporarily swapped identities.' She looked at Kate and said, 'You were the most gorgeous baby and I was unprepared for the powerful surge of love I felt for you. And yet I insisted that Philomena hold you first, because it was important that you two bonded so that Philomena would love you as I wanted you loved. Later, she registered you as Katherine Helen Munroe and we went back to Ireland.

'I hadn't any plans after the birth, but I had assumed I would have some input, however small, in your growing up, but Philomena vetoed that. I know she wanted you to be all hers, because she thought she would never have a natural child of her own. I think that she was worried that if I was part of your life, you might grow to love me more than her – and she couldn't have borne that. She never said this, and in fact the arguments she used were powerful ones. She said if I stayed in contact, it might all come out one day that you were the product of violent rape and a bastard into the bargain. How, she asked, could I risk ruining your life in that way?'

'What of my father? Jim?' Kate asked. 'Did he have no say in any of this?'

'Not really,' Helen said. 'He just went along with it. He knew how much Philomena had yearned for a child and I think he felt a little less likc a man himself. You were like a heaven-sent opportunity, to have a child he considered of his blood to rear as his own, and that would raise his standing in the community. He would be able to walk with his head held high.'

Kate nodded. 'He was a lovely father,' she said. 'Always kind and scrupulously fair and almost too easy-going.'

'I can see him doing just as Helen said, can't you?' Sally asked Kate. 'He always gave in to what Mammy wanted.'

'Well, she wanted you all right,' Helen said. 'And she wanted you to herself. To have told the truth about your true father would not have helped either of us, and so I had to agree with Philomena and get out of your life completely. I stayed until the christening, for it would have seemed odd if I hadn't, and it was a lavish affair. Everyone was so happy, I remember, and I felt as if my heart had been split apart. I left the next day when you were just over two and a half weeks old, and I never cast eyes on you again until I saw you in the school hall today.'

The eyes that Helen fastened on Kate were suddenly very bright, and she began weeping as if her heart was indeed broken. 'It's a terribly sad story, isn't it?' Sally said in a wobbly voice as Kate put her arms around the weeping Helen, her mother who didn't feel in the least like her mother, and she felt sorrow and regret close over her. Helen had given up everything for her and she had never been given the opportunity to get to know this woman at all, and neither had Sally or James, and yet she was their auntie. Then Kate

470

realized that they were no longer her brother and sister but her cousins, and that Tim Munroe was not her first cousin, either and if the truth had been told their love need not have been denied all those years ago. But how could Helen have told the truth later? What would it have achieved and how many lives would it have blown apart if she had?

But things were different now. She was grown up and so was Sally. In fact, they were all older and wiser, and while she knew secrets had to be kept from the townsfolk, as to tell all would hurt too many people, she thought it time the family were told the truth. The subterfuge had gone on long enough, she decided, and she must put her own misgivings about going to Ireland aside. It was time for Helen to go back to Donegal and make her peace with her sister, because she was still so desperately sad and unhappy. 'We were going to Ireland tomorrow,' she said. 'Having met you today, I was going to cancel my holiday.'

'Kate, how can you think of doing that?' Sally cried. 'You know that I couldn't go on my own.'

'I know, Sally,' Kate said. 'But don't you see? I'm still reeling from the things that have come to light.'

'But Mammy asked me to go,' Sally said as tears ran down her cheeks. 'It's something I waited years for, and yet I would be afraid to go on my own. Mammy might not let me in the door.'

Helen looked totally perplexed. 'Why wouldn't she?'

Sally glanced at Kate as she continued to sob and so Kate told Helen about Sally's flight to

England and the reason for it, and that she had taken the egg money because she had never been given money of her own. 'And I was so sorry afterwards,' Sally cried, choking back the tears. 'I paid the money back, every penny, and begged her forgiveness, but she disowned me.'

'When was this?'

'Nineteen thirty-eight,' Kate said.

'And Philomena kept to that all this time?'

Both girls nodded and Sally went on: 'I wrote letters over and over and sent presents and everything. When David died and Kate was so upset, I wrote and told Mammy and got someone else to address the envelope so that she would open the letter.'

Helen was shaking her head. 'I wouldn't have thought that Philomena would ever behave that way. I have never thought her harsh.'

'I think she was pretty harsh with you too,' Kate said. 'And ultimately us too, because as well as being my mother, you are Sally and James's aunt, and yet you don't know them either. I think it's time to set the record straight. I will go to Ireland tomorrow as planned, but I would really like it if you could come with us.'

'I couldn't possibly,' Helen said.

'Yes, you could, Helen,' Kate said. 'And I think you should stop apologizing. You have nothing to be so ashamed of that you have to do penance all the days of your life.'

'What do you mean?' Helen said. 'I had a baby out of wedlock.'

'Oh, yes, and haven't you paid handsomely for that one slip?' Kate said. 'It's one that could easily happen to any of us when we are in love, especially when in your case you were comforting your young lover, who was upset hearing of the death of so many comrades and friends. But your soldier didn't desert you; he urged you to go to Ireland to see your sister and get permission to marry. And that is what you would have done if you hadn't been attacked and near raped by Michael. And I know Mammy would have given her permission if you'd told her that your lovemaking might result in pregnancy. She'd not have wanted that disgrace tainting her family,' Kate reasoned. 'I don't blame you for what you did, and though I had a happy childhood, with loving parents, though Mammy could be strict at times, you should never have been banished totally from my life – it wasn't fair for either of us.'

'Kate's right,' Sally said. 'You should go home and hold your head high. In my opinion, you have suffered more than enough.'

'Come on,' Kate said suddenly, leaping to her feet.

'Why?'

'We're going to the bank before it closes, so bring your book, and then to the council house to get a new ration book, identity card and clothing coupons, and then to the Bull Ring to get you some clothes for your holiday.'

'I'm coming too,' Sally said.

'What about your packing?'

'It's nearly done,' Sally said. 'I did most of it yesterday, and it'll take no time at all to throw the last few things in.'

'Come on then,' Kate said, throwing Sally and Helen their coats from the hooks on the wall. 'We have a lot to do. No time for dawdling.'

TWENTY-SEVEN

As they travelled to Ireland the following day, Helen wondered how in God's name she had allowed herself to be persuaded to go back to Donegal. Then, with a grimace, she remembered that there wasn't much persuasion to it: it was more like being bulldozered. And all she could see was that she would make the situation between her and Philomena ten times worse rather than better.

Kate knew that Helen was in a state of great agitation and hoped and prayed she had done the right thing. She had given it no thought; the idea had come into her head and she had just run with it and yet she knew her mother, Philomena, was a woman of extremes. The way she had behaved with Sally proved that she could bear a grudge. She knew with a sinking heart that she was quite capable of showing Helen the door if she took the notion. If she did that, then Kate would have to leave as well, and that would break something between her and the aunt who had reared her – maybe for ever – and that thought saddened her.

Kate castigated herself – as Helen's anxiety increased as they drew nearer to the home she had left twenty-five years before – and bitterly regretted not going back home on her own to explain gently to Philomena how she had made contact with Helen, and to plead her case, rather than confront her in this way.

Sally, too, was busy with her own thoughts. And very, very nervous, because for years her mother had refused to let her come home, and whatever she had done to make amends had never been enough. Philomena had even said that she was no longer her daughter, and at the time that had cut her to the quick. In this visit she had to make sure that she had been truly forgiven, welcomed back into the fold of the family.

And so it was a fraught group, each with their own concerns, that made the journey in the mail boat over the turbulent waters of the Irish Sea. When they were released from the boat at last, feeling less nauseous and on board the train that would take them across Ireland, Helen said, 'How did you two girls happen to be in Birmingham anyway? So strange that we were in the same city for so long.'

'Oh, I came here because of my friend, Susie,' Kate said, and went on to tell Helen about the little girl sent to her granny with her mother so ill, and about how the friendship developed between them. 'Mammy was lovely with her and always made her welcome.'

'She probably remembered that we both lost our parents young,' Helen said. 'I was not quite twelve and Philomena was eighteen.'

'She probably did,' Kate said. 'But she never spoke of anything like that, did she, Sally?'

Sally shook her head. 'She always said the past should be let lie and that she hates the Irish way of dragging everything up from the year dot.'

'Ah, but now we know that that was because if we had started meddling around asking questions, we might have opened a can of worms,' Kate said. 'I mean, now I remember that Logue was Mammy's maiden name, and though in the hospital I said I knew no one of the name, perhaps I did remember subconsciously.'

'Maybe,' Helen said.

'I would have remembered that about Mammy's maiden name,' Sally said. 'She didn't go on about the past, but we got the odd snippet now and again, and I remember that, but that wouldn't necessarily have pointed to Helen being your mother.'

'No, it wouldn't,' Kate agreed.

'Didn't Philomena mind you coming to such a big city all on your own, Kate?'

'Mammy encouraged her, I remember,' Sally said. 'I wanted her to stop doing that because I didn't want Kate to go anywhere.'

'There was a reason for that too,' Kate said. She looked from Helen to Sally and said, 'As this seems to be the time to bare all, I will tell you the real reason Mammy was anxious for me to leave Donegal. Even you don't know this, Sally.'

'Go on, then,' Sally urged. 'What was it?'

'I was sent away because I loved Tim and was almost certain he loved me too.'

Sally was astounded at this news. 'Tim?' she exclaimed. 'Tim Munroe? Our cousin?'

'Yes, Tim Munroe,' Kate said.

'Golly, how will you feel about him when you see him again?'

Kate shrugged. 'How would I know?'

'Are you nervous?' Sally said. 'I think I would be.'

'A little,' Kate admitted. 'And now I know that he isn't my cousin, or at least not my first cousin, and if we had known the truth we might have been allowed to marry, but at what cost? We still couldn't have done it, because it would have wrecked so many lives.'

'It would,' Helen said. 'Because you are registered as the daughter of Philomena and Jim. I am sorry, Kate.'

'Is that why you never went out with any men at first in Birmingham?' Sally asked. 'Because you still loved him.'

'Yes,' Kate said. 'I only agreed to go out with David because Mammy wrote that Tim was walking out with someone else, but the love I later developed for David was deeper than anything I had ever felt for Tim.' And she looked at Helen and said, 'So you needn't be sorry. I loved David so much that I'm glad I experienced it, even for such a short time.'

'I feel that way about Phil too,' Sally said.

'And my reception here today might have been different if David was still alive,' Kate said, and added, in explanation to Helen, 'because he was a non-Catholic, you see, and it was just before war was declared. So we married in a register office because it was all we had time for. To Mammy that was no marriage at all.'

'Oh God!' Helen exclaimed. 'There are clouds over all of us.'

'Yes, and they might burst very soon,' Kate said. 'Because this is where we change for the rail bus.'

This was the last leg of their journey, as Jim was

meeting them at the station in the town with the horse and cart to drive them home. And when Kate saw him waiting there, her heart swelled with love for him. He might not be her biological father, but he was her father in all that mattered. She watched the slow smile of genuine welcome spread over his face as he spotted them. She hoped that what she had done bringing Helen home wouldn't fracture something between them, because that would really upset her, for he was the gentlest man she knew and she had seldom heard him even raise his voice.

And he didn't now. In fact, the only thing that were raised were his eyebrows as he spied Helen standing behind his daughters, though he must have been astounded to see her there. The rail bus had barely stopped before Kate and Sally had burst out of it and had both thrown their arms around him. Helen had followed more cautiously and he nodded to her as he hauled the cases out of the carriage. 'Helen?' he said carefully, and he shook her hand, a tentative smile on his face, but inwardly he was wondering what had brought her back after all these years and how she had become acquainted with Kate and Sally.

However, this was not the time or place to go into it, and not least because he had young James with him. The boy had been on tenterhooks all day to meet the sisters that his mother said were coming; he could not recall them, though when he caught sight of Sally, slight and vague memories of her tugged at him. But they were more like strangers to him, and he was suddenly shy, half hiding behind his father.

'Come away out of that and greet your sisters,' Jim chided his son as he stacked the cases on the waiting cart. James stepped away from his father, but kept his head lowered as he muttered, 'Hallo.'

'That's no way to make a body feel welcome,' his father told him.

'Leave him, Daddy,' Kate said. 'We are near strangers to him, isn't that right, James?'

James looked up at her, his large blue eyes so like Sally's, and he nodded his head. 'Well, you get up beside us on the cart and tell us all about yourself while Daddy takes us home, and we will be best of friends by the time we get there. What d'you say?'

James said nothing but his smile was answer enough and the way he leapt gladly into the cart. The three women got on more cautiously – Kate remembered leaping up with the same agility as her young brother once, but now to them a horse and cart was a strange way to travel.

'You're a rum one, all right, boy,' Jim said to the child as he climbed in the driving seat and took up the reins. James said nothing, but after another surreptitious wink from Kate he sat down beside her so he was between her and Sally. Helen got into the other side and sat opposite them, as still as a statue. 'You've talked of nothing else but them coming for nearly a week,' Jim went on to his young son. 'And now it's like the cat has got your tongue.'

The cart crossed the river and went past the ruins of the castle and then the Church of Ireland to reach the Diamond in the centre of the town.

Despite the doubts in her mind, Kate felt excitement in the pit of her stomach. Being driven home in a horse and cart through that small town was tugging at her memories, and she wondered what Helen was making of it all, twenty-five years after she had been almost forced to leave. The clip-clop of the horse's hooves and the rumble of the cart on the cobbles was another memory as Jim turned into Main Street with shops on either side.

They passed Magee's, which had been the poshest shop Kate had ever seen until she had seen those in Birmingham – though that was in the pre-war days, before the Luftwaffe had done its level best to wipe Birmingham off the map. Not that she had ever gone inside Magee's, for it was too expensive for the Munroe's. 'Not for the likes of you and me,' Philomena had stated flatly, and that had been that.

'There's St Patrick's Church,' James said suddenly, pointing to the building, its spire pointing skywards and built on a slight incline on the edge of town.

'And the Fever Hospital on the other side,' Sally remarked, and then they were through the town and on to the open road and Kate breathed in the fresh, pure air. She saw the cattle in the fields they passed, placidly chewing the cud, and sheep tugging at the grass relentlessly, some mere dots on the hillsides all around them. Here and there stood squat little whitewashed cottages very like the one she'd been reared in. They almost all had curls of smoke emitting from the chimneys and wafting into the summer air and

481

she looked across to Helen, wondering what emotions rural Ireland had stirred in her. Helen, however, was looking as if she would rather be anywhere other than where she was, and again Kate felt that little nub of anxiety that she had done the wrong thing.

Helen actually felt as if she had a coiled spring inside her and for two pins she would jump back on the rail bus and go somewhere else. She wouldn't care where, as long as it was away from here, where soon, unless she was very much mistaken, she would cause upset and distress to a great many people.

The horse needed no direction to go home, and Sally and Kate were noting things they remembered, aided by comments from Jim. As they neared home, James began talking to them too. He had a ready grin and a pleasant manner, and Kate regretted the years he'd had growing up without knowing her at all.

He almost flung himself from the cart as it turned into the yard and was running towards the farmhouse, his boots ringing on the cobbles as he yelled, 'They're here, Mammy. They're here and there's three of them.'

Jim clicked his tongue with annoyance. 'That boy will be under the cartwheels one of these days. I'm worn out telling him to go easy.'

But the girls weren't listening to him. Their attention was fastened on the woman framed in the doorway. Philomena hadn't needed her son to alert her of the girls' arrival, for she had been watching out for them for the last twenty minutes, but, when the cart turned into the yard and she saw her sister sitting in the cart too, it took all her determination to cross the room and open the door.

She had wanted to run and embrace Kate and Sally, had imagined that that was what she would do, but Helen's presence constrained her. And then she saw the look in her sister's eyes and her conscience smote her and she felt the tears seeping from her eyes. Kate and Sally were appalled; their mother didn't cry, she wasn't that sort, and they ran across the yard and put their arms around her. 'Mammy, what is it?'

'Don't cry. Please don't upset yourself,' they cried.

Helen took one distraught look at them and leapt from the cart. Her whole body was trembling. She couldn't do this. She had upset her sister, as in her heart of hearts she had known she would, and with an anguished cry she ran back up the lane, though she had no idea where she was going. Her only thought was of getting away. Jim wasn't sure what to do at first, but he glanced at his wife being comforted by Kate and Sally, and took off after Helen.

She had run like the wind, and Jim puffed after her, catching up with her on the road. When he put a hand on her arm, she shook him off. 'Leave me, Jim. I should never have come.'

For a moment, Jim was too breathless to speak, but he held tight to Helen and eventually said, 'Yes, you should have. Philomena wants to see you. She has wanted it this long while.'

'No, Jim,' Helen said. 'You must be mistaken.'

Jim shook his head decisively. 'I'm not

mistaken,' he said. 'She has told me so herself. Please come back, Helen.'

He put his arm about her shoulder comfortingly, and, scarcely daring to believe him, Helen nevertheless allowed herself to be led back down the lane and into the room where she saw Philomena sitting on the settee with Kate and Sally either side of her. No one noticed James standing in the corner, anxiously biting his thumbnail because he had never seen his mother cry either and it disturbed him.

Philomena had no eyes for her son, only for her sister standing before her, hanging her head, and she stood to face her. 'Look at me, please, Helen,' Philomena said, and when Helen raised her head, their eyes locked, and Philomena said the words she had wanted to say for years: 'I owe you an apology, Helen, and I am so sorry. Please forgive me.'

It was the last thing Helen expected Philomena to say, and for a moment she was nonplussed, and then she said, 'There is nothing to forgive, and surely the boot's on the other foot?'

'Ah, Helen,' Philomena said, 'what years we have wasted,' and she took Helen in her arms and wept on her sister's shoulder. Kate and Sally both had tears stinging their eyes but, as the sobs filled the air, James had had enough. 'What's everyone crying for?' he demanded in exasperation. 'People said it would be fun when my sisters came.'

Kate could see that neither Philomena nor Helen were capable of answering James, and so she brushed the tears from her own eyes impatiently before turning to her younger brother.

'It will be, James, I promise,' she said. Then added, 'Grown-ups are funny, and they often cry when they are happy.'

'That's plain daft, that is,' James said dogmatically. He waited, staring at them for a few minutes more and they, seeing the confusion on his face, tried to get a grip on themselves. When James saw that the crying had ceased and that his mother was wiping her eyes, he said, 'Is the crying all over now you have stopped being so happy?'

Philomena gathered herself together and said with a watery smile, 'Yes, you cheeky monkey, we've stopped. Now, if you will lay the table for me, we can get on with the meal I have spent hours preparing that is now threatening to spoil in the range oven.'

The meal – succulent slices of ham, and plenty of them, and colcannon with the top crisped and the well dripping with butter, served with creamed carrots and gravy and followed by apple pie and custard – was the finest meal that Helen, Kate or Sally had had in a long, long time. And because of that they did it justice. The conversation around the table though, was a little random, for nothing of any importance, certainly the questions teeming in Philomena and Jim's minds, could be discussed until James went to bed. Such things were not for his ears.

As a result the conversation could have become constrained but for James himself, because he wanted to know what it was like living in a city at war and the three women gladly described the shortages of food and the rationing of almost all products, the terrors and funny instances of a city completely blacked out after dark. Urged on by him, they told him of the terror struck into their hearts when the sirens blasted out and of the heart-stopping bombings themselves. And of the incendiaries that set up pockets of fire and lit the way for the bombers to release their evil loads; when they killed and maimed and toppled buildings and flattened houses and shops and tuned the sky blood red with the numbers of fires burning. Kate did wonder at some of the things they were telling him but he listened almost spellbound.

'Golly,' he said when they had finished, 'it sounds exciting. Scary but exciting. Were you scared?'

Kate glanced at Sally and Helen and said, 'I was sometimes. But,' she added, 'it's not a bad thing to be scared; the really courageous thing is to recognise that and yet go on regardless.'

'Yeah, not let it control you,' Sally said. 'Sometimes we were too busy helping others to be scared ourselves.'

'It gets to be a way of life in the end,' Kate said. 'It showed me that a person can get used to anything in time.'

James gave a sudden yawn and Philomena said, 'Time for bed, young man.'

'Oh, Mammy.'

'Don't "oh, Mammy" me,' Philomena said. 'You were up at the crack of dawn helping your daddy now that it's a holiday from school and you were like a cat on hot bricks all day about your sisters coming. Now they are not going to disappear and will be here when you wake up, but if you don't go to bed now you'll be in no fit state to enjoy their company.'

Grumbling and disgruntled, James bade them all goodnight and the three women hid their smiles at the look on his face. He was tired, that was plain to see and they knew he would be asleep in no time. As soon as he left, they quickly set about clearing away from the meal and they were settled around the table ready to talk when Jim said, 'Padraic needs to hear this. It concerns him too.'

Philomena nodded, for it did of course, and while Jim went to fetch him, she got up to make tea. As she was bringing it to the table on the tray, Padraic came in the door with his wife, Bridget, carrying a bottle of Irish whiskey.

'You two know each other?' Padraic asked in surprise, looking from Helen to Kate and back again.

'We have just met, by chance,' Helen answered.

'Yes, and I have done Helen a grave disservice by denying her access to her daughter all her life,' Philomena said.

'That wasn't how it was,' Helen protested. 'Let me tell the whole thing.' And Helen told it, holding nothing back, and there wasn't one person around that table who wasn't moved by the end of it.

Then Padraic said, 'I still say that we are responsible because it was only chance that Michael didn't rape you, and he certainly did attack you violently.'

'But I was with child and unmarried, and I

purposely misled you all.'

Bridget leaned forward and said earnestly, 'There is not one woman around this table tonight, or indeed in the whole of Ireland, who would not do the same in a similar position.'

'Hear, hear,' said Kate. 'You were not the great sinner here.'

'No, you weren't,' Philomena said with a sigh. 'And I made you feel you were. I was judge and jury and it was wrong.'

'You did what you thought best.'

'No,' Philomena said. 'You have been so honest, and so must I be. I failed you from the beginning. After our parents and siblings died, there was just us two, and I was many years older than you, and yet I allowed the priest to send you away into service, knowing that I would never be able to see you again, even before you went to Birmingham. You must have felt so lost and alone at times.'

'This is years ago; it doesn't matter now.'

'It does to me,' Philomena said. 'It shows a flaw in my nature. When you came because you were pregnant, all I could think about was getting my hands on that baby, and so I did you a disservice as well, Kate.'

'No, I can't have that,' Kate said. 'Whatever reason you did it for, you were good parents to me. None could have been better.'

'You should have got to know your natural mother as well.'

'That would have been nice,' Kate conceded, smiling across at Helen. 'Yes, I would have liked that, but to all intents and purposes I've had a damned good upbringing.'

'I agree with that,' Helen said. 'Kate is a daughter to be proud of.'

'You don't think I was too harsh on you?' Philomena asked Kate anxiously.

'No, not really,' Kate said.

'If I was, it was because I was aware that I had to bring you up well for Helen too,' Philomena said. 'That's why I reacted so when you told me about the marriage you had with the Protestant pilot, one that wasn't recognized in the Church. I wouldn't have wanted your mother to feel ashamed of you.'

'There is nothing Kate could do that would make me ashamed of her,' Helen said. 'For a person to have love in their life is a great gift and, as far as I'm concerned, religion doesn't come into it. All I would ever have wanted is Kate's happiness.'

'Oh, Helen,' Philomena cried, 'I truly didn't realize how I had broken your heart until I gave birth to Sally. Something happens to you when you give birth to a child, and the thought of giving Sally away ... well, if that had happened, I couldn't have gone on.'

'I didn't know that Philomena had sort of banished you,' Jim said. 'I thought it odd that you never came to see the child, and then, when Sally was born, Philomena told me what she had laid on you. She was so upset and filled with guilt and regret, and I too felt it keenly. Padraic and Bridget were told, and Padraic and I tried to find you, but it was hard without letting other people into the know, and we dared not do that. In the meantime, you had stuck rigidly to the agreement and vanished into thin air.'

'And yet Kate found her after all,' Padraic said. 'How did that come about?'

'That was a complete fluke,' Kate said. 'I didn't go looking for Helen because I didn't even know that she existed.'

'Yes, that's right,' Helen said. 'The dressing on Kate's forehead is there to cover the scar from the stitches she had removed yesterday, and she got that injury when she was knocked clean out by a falling roof beam while trying to rescue me and others from buildings that had collapsed due to the bombing. Both her and Sally are very brave girls.' Helen went on: 'During the most ferocious bombing raids, they were out on the street, helping people find shelter, fighting fires, rescuing people from burning buildings, digging people out who'd been buried under masonry rubble and treating the injured.'

'Oh, my goodness,' Philomena said, looking at her two daughters. 'I had no idea of the dangerous work you were engaged in.'

'We couldn't tell you, Mammy,' Kate said. 'The censor would have cut every reference out. We weren't the only ones: Susie is doing it too.'

'Good heavens, Philomena, you wouldn't know the place,' Helen said. 'Women drive buses and lorries and trams, and work in the most dangerous industries, too. In fact, there isn't anything they don't seem to be able to turn their hands to, and then in the evenings they volunteer as ARP wardens or do fire-watching, or work as part of the WVS. Every person seems to be doing something to help Britain win this war.'

'Well, I'm as proud as punch of both of you,' Jim said, beaming approval at both girls.

'Hear hear,' said Padraic heartily.

'I am proud too,' Philomena said. 'Astounded and proud. But go on with your tale, Helen.'

'Oh, yes,' Helen said, and told her sister how the staff at the hospital they were both taken to remarked on their likeness, and that led to a chain of events culminating in Kate eventually making contact with her mother.

'And all the time I wished you would get in touch,' Philomena said. 'But I had been so rigid, just as I was with Sally when she ran away from home. I was hurt and upset, I don't deny that, but people get over these things, and I didn't, not even when she wrote letter after letter saying how sorry she was.'

'Mammy,' Sally said, catching up her mother's hand.

'We can't reclaim lost years. We need to put them to one side and look forward.'

'Well said, Sally,' Jim said. 'And I think there has been enough confessing for one night. The morning comes soon enough, especially for a farmer. So I think I must seek my bed.'

TWENTY-EIGHT

Only two hours after the three women had left the house in Birmingham, a telegraph boy pulled up outside the gate on his little motorbike, walked up the path and pounded on the door. Phoebe Jenkins – her heart in her mouth, for telegrams seldom convey good news – came out of her door and said, 'No good you knocking there because there's nobody in. I mean, they won't be in for a week or more because they've gone on holiday.'

'Oh,' the telegraph boy said. 'The man said it was real important they get this.'

Phoebe thought for a minute and then said, 'Well, they have gone to visit their people in a place called Donegal and that's in Ireland. I don't have the address, but Susie Mason probably has and she only lives on Marsh Hill, number sixty. If you get it from her, they can probably redirect the telegram.'

'Oh, yeah,' the boy said. 'That's a good idea. If I get the address they can do what they want then.'

Phoebe watched him go down the path, mount his bike and roar off. She bit her lip as she went into the house and prayed the two young women she had grown so fond of were not going to get more bad news, because in her opinion they had coped with more than enough already.

The next morning, very early, Jim was in the byre going over in his mind the revelations of the night before, when a car drove down the lane and into the yard. Jim knew who it belonged to, a Shaun Dempsey, and his car doubled as a taxi if anyone needed one, but it had never come down their lane before. Curiosity drew him to the door of the byre and he saw a respectably dressed man get out of the taxi, pay the fare and stride up to the door. Kate was passing the door when the rap came on it; she was surprised because it was strange for someone to knock and she'd not noticed the taxi, but when she opened the door, she staggered for the shock was so great.

'David,' she cried. 'Oh, dear God, David.' She felt blackness overwhelm her and, before David could catch hold of her, she had sunk to the floor in a dead faint.

When she came to, she was in the bedroom, and David, a real, live, living and breathing David, was sitting beside her. 'I can't believe it,' she said. 'Let me touch your face, your eyes. I keep thinking that this is some dream and I'll wake up in a minute.'

David gave a chuckle, the sort of laugh that caused Kate's stomach to go into spasms. 'Maybe this will convince you,' he said, and their lips met in the sweetest kiss imaginable.

'Oh, my, darling love,' David said, holding her close.

'David,' Kate said, savouring the name on her tongue. 'For months I thought you dead and gone.'

'I know you did,' David said. 'And I couldn't let you know otherwise.'

'But...? How...?'

David put his finger to Kate's lips. 'Ssh,' he said. 'I can tell you nothing yet. Your family are waiting downstairs and though I have introduced myself I would not tell them anything else until you were up to hearing it too.'

'My family,' Kate repeated blankly.

'Yes, they are waiting for you downstairs.'

'Do you know...'

'I know that the cut on your head was caused by you trying to rescue people trapped under masonry and one of those was a very beautiful lady by the name of Helen, and she says she is your biological mother.'

'Yes,' Kate said. 'I have only recently found this out myself. But I don't know my father, so do you know what it makes me?'

'Yeah, I know,' David said. 'You are Kate Burton, the same as you were before you uttered that last sentence, and I don't give a tuppenny damn that you don't know your father.'

'You don't?'

'Not one jot,' David assured her. 'Does it bother you?'

'Not much,' Kate admitted. 'And I can't really mourn a man I never knew. Anyway, Jim was just about the best father anyone could have.'

'Stick with that then,' David said, 'For I have a natural father who is bugger-all use to me, and he has been the same since as long as I can remember.'

'But there's more,' Kate protested.

'I'm sure there is, but it can be gone into another time,' David said. 'Because what really matters is you and me.' And so saying, David stripped back the bedclothes, and scooped Kate up in his arms.

'Hey,' Kate protested. 'I am not an invalid.'

'Let me be the judge of that,' David said. 'Anyway, didn't you promise to obey me in a special ceremony a little while ago?'

'Oh, you.'

They were all assembled around the table downstairs and, though everyone was concerned for her, Kate saw the naked envy on Sally's face and fully understood it. 'I haven't really come to terms with this yet,' she said to them all. 'My head isn't really taking it in, but this is my husband, David, and for months I have thought him dead.'

'We got that far,' Padraic said. 'But he would tell us no more until you were here too.'

'Well, I'd like to say that it was all due to my heroism,' David said. 'But really it was all down to the bravery of the people of Sumatra.'

'Sit down and take the weight off your feet,' Jim said.

'Aye, and put that lassie down,' Padraic said with a wink at David. 'For she's a dead weight.'

'You cheeky devil!' Kate cried, but she didn't object when David sat her down on the settee and then sat beside her, with an arm draped over her shoulder. Philomena pushed tea into both their hands and Padraic said, 'Now go on, David; the people of Sumatra, you said.'

'Well, it was a boy saved me really,' David said. 'I would say just a little older than you, James.'

'Golly, what did he do?'

'Well, we retreated after the fall of Singapore,' David said, glancing round at them all. 'And we were pursued by Jap Zero planes and heavily outnumbered. My Spit was hit a number of times and eventually caught fire. I bailed out and was shot to pieces on the way down and lost consciousness as I landed. I was bleeding heavily, so I was told later. This boy took off his shirt and ripped it into strips to bind my wounds, cut through the ropes tying me to the parachute, rolled me into this ditch, covered me over with leaves and left me. I was drifting in and out of consciousness and semi-delirious, but I knew when the Japanese came searching. They stuck bayonets in the ditches and missed my face by tenths of an inch, but they weren't searching as diligently as they might, thank God, because they didn't know where exactly I had landed. I thank God too that they had no dogs, for they would have found me in no time.'

'What about the boy?' James asked.

'Oh, I didn't see him till much later, and then I thanked him for saving my life.'

'Did he understand you?'

'Well, no, he didn't,' David said. 'But some time later that night I was taken to this woman's house in the middle of the jungle on a sort of litter they had got together. It was so painful that I was jerked awake and bit my lip till it bled to try and stop myself yelling out. I wasn't aware of much for about twenty-four hours, or that's what she said, anyway, and when I came round a bit I was surprised to find she was so young – early twenties, I'd say, and she was British.'

'What in God's name was she doing there?' Jim asked.

'Her parents were missionaries,' David explained. 'They'd been expelled from China and had fled to Malaya, but the Japs arrived before they could be rescued and they had kept going to Sumatra. The Japs caught up with them there and bayoneted this woman's parents and her two sisters, and would have done the same to her, but she was behind the others and able to hide. Her name was Julia Greenwood.'

'Terrible thing for anyone, but maybe especially a young girl, to see her parents and sisters killed that way.'

'I agree,' David said. 'They are butchering bastards, because Julia said her sisters were only youngsters. She was the eldest, and the youngest hadn't even reached her teens. She said she didn't have time to grieve much, though, because it was all about survival – and not just her survival but that of the villagers, who would suffer if she was found. So they made her this shelter in the centre of the jungle and they bring her whatever food they have to spare – no one has much – and she tries to cure them when they are sick because she knows a great deal about natural remedies.'

'And she told you about the boy?'

'Yeah, but not straightaway because I was very ill when I arrived. She said I often hovered between life and death and she hadn't been sure I would make it.'

'Oh, I am so glad you did,' Kate said, giving his arm a squeeze.

'And me, darling,' David said. 'Your face used to float before me and I would often wonder if I would ever see you again. Julia got me right in the end, though, and told me how I had managed to survive, and then she summoned the boy and conveyed my thanks to him. She also asked him on my behalf what he had done with the parachute, because if any trace of it had been found in the village, everyone would have been killed and many tortured before they died. They took an immense risk in hiding me.'

'So what did he do with it?'

'He tied a big boulder inside it and tipped it into the sea. It sank without trace.'

'So, did the Japs give up looking for you in the end?' Jim asked.

'More or less,' David said. 'Though there were regular patrols, and then Julia and I would be hidden in the fields. From those who understood a smattering of Japanese, apparently they thought I had landed in the sea and drowned, because no trace of the parachute was ever found.'

'Golly, that's a real exciting story,' James said, greatly impressed. 'And it's even better than that because it's true.'

'Well, I agree with James,' Padraic said. 'That's a truly amazing story, and I would be pleased to welcome you into the family.'

'And I would,' James said decidedly. 'Oh, boy, that would be grand.'

They all laughed and James said, 'Is there any more?'

'Not enough drama for you, is that it?' David said with a grin. 'Well, that's about the end of it now, James, except to say it was a few months before I was well enough to be moved, and then weeks before they could arrange to get me off as safely as possible for all concerned. Julia wouldn't come with me. She said there is nothing for her in England now and the people of Sumatra need her. Now that's what I call real courage.'

'Oh, I'll say,' Kate said. 'Poor girl, though I can see what she means, with all her family wiped out. At least she feels needed there. But if the Japanese ever found her... Oh, it doesn't bear thinking about. Just the thought of them terrifies me.'

'And any other sensible person,' Jim said. 'So how come you're here now, David?'

'Well, they flew me in to Castle Bromwich and I wanted to go straight home, but they said I wasn't well enough and slammed me in the sick bay. I made such a stink, though, that they sent you a telegram telling you I was safe and inviting you up to the airfield, but you were already on your way to Ireland. The telegraph boy told me that some neighbour, probably Phoebe, told the boy to get the address of where you would be from the Masons. I suppose in case the telegram was important. But I was the only one there when he came back, and as soon as I got the address I set off, and caught the night boat. I haven't even got a change of clothes because I wouldn't risk going back to the house, because that's the first place that they would make for.'

'You've gone AWOL,' Kate said. 'Won't you get into trouble?'

'Maybe, but I won't get shot or anything,' David

said. 'They said I had to go for convalescence anyway, and then I will be joining Nick at Biggin Hill Airfield, training other pilots, but first I had to see you.'

'Well, I think you are a fine young man,' Helen said. 'And I'm delighted you are Kate's husband.'

There was a chorus of 'Hear, hear', and then Philomena was chivvying them all to get ready for Mass. 'Aw, Mammy, do we have to go today?' James complained. 'I want to stay and talk to David.'

'Well, that will have to be later,' Philomena said firmly. 'David has travelled all night and needs to sleep, and Kate is staying here to look after him.'

There were times when it was not worth arguing with Philomena, and Kate saw by her brother's doleful face as he trailed after the others that he had found that out for himself.

David was more tired than he realized, for though he had been somewhat animated when he had been telling them all how he had survived, when the tale drew to a close he had felt the tiredness fold over him, and he was glad to snuggle down in the double bed that had originally been earmarked for her to share with Sally. And as Kate came down the stairs after showing David where he was to sleep, her mother called her into the scullery. 'Is there something the matter with Sally?' she asked.

'What sort of something?'

'I don't know,' Philomena said. 'It's just that she was fine when she arrived; I mean a bit nervous and that was natural, but it was when David came really. And she had a really funny look on her face when he carried you downstairs.'

Kate was surprised that her mother had been that perceptive, and Philomena went on: 'Does she not like David? Is that it?'

Kate shook her head with a smile. 'No,' she said. 'She likes David well enough, but Sally also met someone in Birmingham that she was more than fond of. His name was Phil Reynard and he was drafted into the Army like all boys the same age – and that's all most of them were, just boys. Phil and Sally loved each other and they became engaged just before Phil was sent overseas.'

'You told me none of this.'

'So you did read the bits in the letters I wrote telling you about Sally?'

'I did, of course, though I could never bring myself to reply,' Philomena said. 'I regret that now.'

'So do I,' Kate said sadly. 'Because Phil died at Dunkirk. There was just him and his mother, Ruby, who had lost her husband and all her family with TB years before. She had a stroke when the telegram came and she never regained consciousness. As I had never mentioned Phil, because I didn't want you to feel that Sally was doing anything wrong, I couldn't tell you of his death and the terrible heartache she suffered.'

'I feel so ashamed,' Philomena said. 'And yet Sally herself said that lost years couldn't be reclaimed and that we had to put them to one side and look forward.'

'And she's right,' Kate said. 'For Sally to look back is painful. That time is gone and will never come again. But all the things she had gone through have made her the young woman she is today, for there is no sign of the immature girl not long out of childhood that was waiting for me that autumn day in 1938.'

'I know that, through my own pigheadedness, I have lost those years.'

'But you haven't lost her,' Kate said. 'Because she has long wanted your forgiveness, and she needs you more than ever, because that look you saw in her face as she watched me being carried down the stairs was envy, pure and simple. David was alive and Phil dead and gone.'

'God, Kate, but you're a grand girl,' Philomena said, touching her arm lightly as tears sparkled behind her eyes. 'And I will take to heart everything you have said. Sally will never find me lacking again, and when I go to Mass today I shall get down on my knees and thank the Lord, because we have a lot to be thankful for.'

When they had all gone and the cottage had grown silent once more, Kate crept up the stairs and peeped into the bedroom. David lay in the abandonment of total exhaustion, his arms flung to each side of him as he lay on his back, the only sound his even breathing. Kate tiptoed forward and gently kissed his cheek, flushed in sleep, and felt such a rush of love for him. That he had returned to her in such a way was like some sort of miracle.

She suddenly felt restless. She needed to be doing something and decided to climb the hill behind the house, which had always been a favourite haunt of hers. It was steeper than she remembered, and as she toiled up through the springy grass, she remembered the way she would almost run up when she had been younger. She kept going, though, and had gone some way when she heard a voice behind her. The voice was a familiar one, for all she hadn't heard it in seven years. 'Hallo, Kate.'

Kate was not at all sure that she wanted to meet Tim so soon. And yet she knew that she'd have to see him some time, and it was better she meet him now, with David out of the way, and so she turned with a smile on her face towards him, breathing heavily because of the climb.

Tim was not the slightest bit out of breath and devastatingly handsome. The sun was shining directly on them both, turning Tim's light brown hair almost blond, like a halo framing his face. He was smiling a welcome, a smile that lit up his face as if he had turned a light on inside him and set his eyes dancing in his head. It always used to make Kate's legs go weak at the knees. Now she noticed with relief that it had no effect on her as she said, 'Hallo, Tim. Not at Mass with the others?'

'Checking up on me, Kate?' Tim said lightly. 'I went to early Mass, and that's why I missed the high jinks at your house.'

'What high jinks?'

'I don't know,' Tim said. 'You tell me, but my father wouldn't leave Liam and Danny in the middle of milking to go round to your house, just because Mammy came and said so.'

'Ah, well, you will know soon enough,' Kate said. 'My husband, David, whom I believed had been shot down and killed in February trying to defend Singapore, has turned up alive. He arrived here very early this morning after being nursed back from the dead by a missionary lady.'

Tim's mouth had dropped agape. 'You're joking?'

'Course I'm not,' Kate said.

'Sorry.' Tim smiled. 'It's just such an incredible story.'

'I know,' Kate said, 'isn't it? And it has all happened so quickly, I keep thinking he might disappear again, or I may wake up and find that it's some dreadful dream.'

'I bet. Where is he now?'

'Sleeping,' Kate said. 'I obviously knew nothing of his months in the jungle in Sumatra and the efforts to rescue him, and as soon as he reached the airfield he sent me a telegram, but I had left for Ireland. When he found out that was where I'd gone, he followed me on the night boat.'

'God!' breathed Tim. 'Must have been a shock.'

Kate smiled and gave a nod. 'Yeah, when I opened the door to him this morning, I just couldn't believe my eyes. I mean, I've had a memorial service for him and everything. Anyway, when I saw him I went out like a light. Now I'm fine again. Never felt better, in fact.'

'And you're happy?'

'Blissfully.'

Tim gave a chuckle and Kate waited for the butterflies to begin in her stomach, but there was nothing, and she felt herself smiling back, a genuine smile this time. 'Ah, now that's the Kate I remember,' Tim said. 'I missed you a great deal when you went to England. I thought you might write. We had been incredibly close.'

Whoever her mother was, Kate knew that they could never have taken their relationship any further, and that needed to be dealt with, so she faced Tim and said, 'We were too close, and you know it as well as I. I had to leave, it was the only way. Writing to you would only have prolonged things and maybe stopped us going on as we had to.'

Tim sighed. 'You're right. I am still most incredibly fond of you, though, and because of that I'm pleased that you are happy.'

'I'm fond of you, Tim, and always will be, I hope,' Kate said. 'However, I'm a very different person to the naïve eighteen-year-old who left these shores in 1935.'

'I see that,' Tim said. 'I'm different too, even though I have stayed here. I have married, and am father to a wee boy we have called Michael, after his uncle who died in the Great War.'

Kate suppressed a shudder, but Tim didn't need to know the truth about his uncle Michael, and she just said, 'I know all the news because Mammy writes every week. But now I must go down, or David might be awake and wondering where I am.'

'A hug for old time's sake,' Tim said as he took Kate in his arms for the first time. Initially, Kate stiffened slightly, but the hug was a friendly one, as one cousin to another, and she was able to relax. She knew now that any romance with Tim was dead and gone, and she now saw that heady romance for what it had been. They could remain friends, anyway. They descended the hill side by side and had nearly reached the bottom when Tim said, 'Will I get to meet this husband of yours?'

'Of course,' Kate said, but inwardly she wondered how David would feel about Tim. She had opened her heart to him about her feelings for her cousin; now she had to convince him that that was in the past.

David woke up, wondering where he was for a moment or two, and then it all came back to him. Through the window he watched Kate climb the hill. He swung his legs out of bed, intending to dress and join her, but then he spotted the man going up behind her. He had never met Tim Munroe, but he knew who he was and he watched the encounter between them. He remembered the jealousy that he had felt for this man when Kate had told him about her feelings for him first, and that increased tenfold now as he saw them both meet.

He was afraid. Why had Kate suddenly returned home when she had refused to go when he suggested it? She said it was for Helen's sake and Sally's, but was that true, or was it because Kate wanted to rekindle a past love, believing him dead? He felt slightly sick at the thought. He reminded himself that this Tim was married and Kate was not a home-breaker, but even that thought didn't ease his pain. He didn't want to watch them together, and yet he couldn't seem to be able to tear his eyes away from the scene. As they chatted easily, his heart ached with love for Kate. It was the thought of her waiting there for him that had sustained him during those terrifying months waiting for rescue, and she had seemed overwhelmed with happiness when he had appeared at the door. At least he had thought it was happiness; maybe it had been shock, and this little tryst had been planned between her and Tim. Then he knew he was right, and gave a gasp when he saw Tim pull *his* Kate into his arms. He felt as if he had been punched in the stomach.

He got to his feet, unable to watch any more, and hurried out of the room. He didn't know where to go, he just knew he had to go, be by himself for a while and work out what he should do now. For without Kate, his life would have no meaning.

Kate was surprised a few moments later to find that David was not only not in the bedroom, but nowhere else in the house either. She went off to look for him, checking the barns first and causing the dogs to bark, but there was no sign of David and so she set off up the lane.

She saw him standing by the gate that led to the top field where her father had moved most of the cows. He was leaning on the gate just staring into the field. He heard her approach and turned to look at her, but his face held an almost blank expression that she had never seen before. She gave a tentative smile and a little wave. But as he didn't respond in any way, she approached rather cautiously, telling herself what he had gone through was bound to have taken it out of him and she should have patience. He couldn't have had much sleep either, and so that's what she said when she got nearer to him.

'I slept long enough,' David snapped. 'I saw you

through the window with *him*.'

Kate knew who 'him' was, and wished David hadn't seen them together so soon. She heard the misery behind the aggressiveness and she saw jealousy flickering in David's eyes and she told herself to take care. 'Yes,' she said as nonchalantly as she could. 'Tim came to meet me.'

'Meet you,' David said. 'Is that all he did?'

'Yes,' Kate said. 'He was getting ready for early Mass when you arrived but he'd heard something had happened so came to ask me what.'

'He went to early Mass so he could see you when the others had left, is that it?' David demanded.

Kate shook her head. 'No. David, what is this?' she demanded.

'Look, Kate,' David said. 'When you told me all about Tim and how you felt, I said that I was prepared to settle for second best. Well, I'm not any longer. I couldn't bear the thought that, though you lived with me, you wished it was him; longed for his arms rather than mine around you, him making love to you. He would be there all the time, like a spectre in the travesty of the marriage that we would have.'

Kate stared at him, this man that she loved more than life. 'David, you dope. This is nonsense.'

She reached for him, but he pulled away. 'I may be a dope, but I'm not blind, and I saw you in that man's arms.'

'He's my cousin,' Kate said. 'And one I haven't seen for seven years. Did you see him kiss me?'

'No, it would have been like a knife stabbing my heart to see that.'

508

'Well, you should have stayed watching, because it didn't happen,' Kate said. 'You'd have seen it for what it was, just a friendly hug.'

She caught hold of David's arm, and this time he didn't throw her off, and she turned him to face her. She saw the doubt flood over his face and she knew that David wanted to believe her, and she took his face between her hands, looked deep into his eyes and said, 'Tim Munroe is no threat to us and our happiness. He is married with a child, but even if he was free it would make no difference, because I know now I don't love him. Susie was right when she said I never did, and whether I once did or not, that part of my life is over. I certainly have no romantic feelings for him now. Tim is part of my history. There is only one man I love, and that is you, David Burton, my beloved husband.'

'Oh,' David said, scarcely able to believe it. 'Do you mean it?'

'With all my heart and soul,' Kate said sincerely, and David felt as if his own heart had given a leap of joy, and he felt filled with happiness as Kate said, 'There's only one thing I envy Tim for.'

'And what's that?'

'His child,' Kate said, catching up David's hand and leading the way back to the cottage. 'That's what I long for, your child.'

David heard the yearning in Kate's voice and he was silent. He had said they must wait for peace, but it was one hell of a long time coming. When he went back he would be off active duties, and as safe as anyone else was in this godawful war.

'Say something, David, for God's sake?' Kate cried in the end, and David realized the silence had stretched out between them.

'Sorry.'

'Well, what do you think of what I've said?'

'Well,' said David slowly, 'the war might go on for some time yet, but I'm no longer on active service, and so I don't see any reason now why we should delay having a child.'

Kate squealed with delight and threw her arms about David's neck. 'Oh, David,' she said. 'Do you mean it? It's all I really want. When I thought I had lost you, I regretted that I didn't have even a part of you, however hard it might have been.'

David was moved by the emotion in Kate's voice and he held her tight as she changed the mood by saying impishly, 'Anyway, haven't you reminded me earlier that I have already promised to obey you.'

'Is that so?' David said.

'Yes. That's what you said, anyway.'

'Oh, right,' David said with an answering smile. 'If that's the way it is, then I demand a kiss, woman.'

'Pleased to oblige,' Kate said, and she went into David's arms with a sigh of contentment.

The publishers hope that this book has given you enjoyable reading. Large Print Books are especially designed to be as easy to see and hold as possible. If you wish a complete list of our books please ask at your local library or write directly to:

Magna Large Print Books
Magna House, Long Preston,
Skipton, North Yorkshire.
BD23 4ND

This Large Print Book for the partially sighted, who cannot read normal print, is published under the auspices of

THE ULVERSCROFT FOUNDATION

1	21	41	61	81	101	121	141	161	181
2	22	42	62	82	102	122	142	162	182
3	23	43	63	83	103	123	143	163	183
4	24	44	64	84	104	124	144	164	(184)
5	25	45	65	85	105	125	145	165	185
6	26	46	66	86	106	126	146	166	186
7	27	47	67	87	107	127	147	167	187
8	28	48	68	88	108	128	148	168	188
9	29	49	69	89	109	129	149	169	189
10	30	50	70	90	110	(130)	150	170	190
11	31	51	71	91	111	131	151	171	191
12	32	52	72	92	112	132	152	172	192
13	33	53	73	93	113	133	153	173	193
14	34	54	74	94	114	134	154	174	194
15	35	55	75	95	115	135	155	175	195
16	36	56	76	96	116	136	156	176	196
17	37	57	77	97	117	137	157	177	197
18	38	58	78	98	118	138	158	178	198
19	39	59	79	99	119	139	159	179	199
20	40	60	80	100	120	140	160	180	200

201	216	231	246	261	276	291	306	321	336
202	217	232	247	262	277	(292)	307	322	337
203	218	233	248	263	278	293	308	323	338
204	219	234	249	264	279	294	309	324	339
205	220	235	250	265	280	295	310	325	340
206	221	236	251	266	281	296	311	326	341
207	222	237	252	267	282	297	312	327	342
208	223	238	253	268	283	298	313	328	343
209	224	239	254	269	284	299	314	329	344
210	225	240	255	270	285	300	315	330	345
211	226	241	256	271	286	301	316	331	346
212	227	242	257	272	287	302	317	332	347
213	228	243	(258)	273	288	303	318	333	348
214	229	244	259	274	289	304	319	334	349
215	230	245	260	275	290	305	320	335	350